# Diary of a Victorian Colonial and other tales

## About the author

M. G. Sanchez was born and bred in Gibraltar. He is the author of *Rock Black: Ten Gibraltarian Stories* and the book of essays *The Prostitutes of Serruya's Lane.* He is also the editor of *Writing the Rock of Gibraltar: An Anthology of Literary Texts, 1720-1890.* He studied at the University of Leeds, where he obtained three academic degrees, including a PhD in English Literature in 2004.

For more information, please email info@rockscorpion.com or visit www.mgsanchez.net.

# Diary of a Victorian Colonial and other tales

M. G. Sanchez

Rock Scorpion Books
Dewsbury, West Yorks
2008

Published by Rock Scorpion Books, Dewsbury, United Kingdom.



ISBN-10: 0-9552465-4-7
ISBN-13: 978-0-9552465-4-8

For B. D., a true Rock Scorpion

“We all carry within us our places of exile, our crimes, and our ravages. But our task is not to unleash them on the world; it is to fight them in ourselves and in others.”

Albert Camus, *The Rebel*

1

# Diary of a Victorian Colonial

**The seventh day of November, 1888**

I caught my first glimpse of Gibraltar just after the stroke of eight this morning. 'And the ransomed of the Lord shall return,' I solemnly whispered the words of the Prophet Isaiah as the Rock appeared behind the low-lying clouds, 'and come to Zion with songs and everlasting joy upon their heads: they shall obtain joy and gladness, and sorrow and sighing shall flee away.' I found myself whispering these words and yet, if I am to be honest, I could not entirely associate with their redemptive message, finding myself thinking solely about getting off the S.S. *Zadane* and alighting on *terra firma* again. The truth was that it had been a tedious and highly wearisome journey. Our ship had set off on a cold and blustery morning from Southampton five days earlier. Like most steamers of the *Peninsular & Oriental* line, it had been bound for the Ottoman megalopolis of Constantinople, stopping at Lisbon, Gibraltar, Mahon and Malta *en route* to its final destination. From my enquiries I learned that there were approximately two hundred souls on board – a number divided between ten crew members, twenty first-class passengers, fifty second-class ticket holders and the one hundred and twenty luckless individuals with whom I travelled in steerage.

The steerage compartment of the *Zadane,* incidentally, was a hot and intolerably low-ceilinged chamber. Around one hundred sleeping berths had been squeezed into this hellish space, all but four or five of them found in three-tiered bunks within a foot from each other. The claustrophobic smallness of these sleeping conditions was made even worse by the large metal pipes which jutted out of the walls and ceiling, sometimes directly over the bunks themselves. Every time the ship lurched or rode on a swell, the pipes would rattle and make the most awful gurgling sounds, thereby destroying the possibility of sleep for those directly under them. In addition to this, the area of steerage nearest to the exit ladder was cluttered with a series of large wooden barrels. It was impossible to divine what these barrels contained; suffice to say that they had been crafted out of sturdy oak and that they had been fastened down by means of a series of hemp lines tied to the protruding pipework on the walls. One evening, during a particularly rough stretch of our sea voyage, one of the barrels broke free and almost crushed a hapless adolescent who happened to be playing dice in its way. It took seven men to overpower the rolling barrel and bring it to a total stop, an endeavour that elicited much screaming and swooning among the lady passengers in steerage.

To reach steerage from the foredeck one had to climb down a series of dark and slippery metal ladders. I was not carrying much with me apart from an old suitcase filled with a few shirts and some bedding – a state of affairs which made it relatively easy for me to climb down those ladders. Nevertheless, some of the poorer Scottish and Irish families in steerage had to negotiate these treacherous rungs with what seemed like all their earthly possessions strapped on their backs. It was indeed a sorry sight – seeing them struggle down the ladder in this way. Rather unsurprisingly, many of those who entered steerage did so in the certainty that they would remain there until the journey was over – there being nothing more vexatious than to climb up and down those metal rungs on a daily basis. A few of the travelling bachelors, it is true, would sometimes ascend the ladder with the intention of spotting some of the upper-class ladies twirling their parasols on one of the higher decks (an endeavour, it might as well be said, which left the majority of these love-sick gentlemen bitterly disappointed), but most of us remained steadfastly rooted to the place that had been originally apportioned to us, guarding our sleeping space and our meagre possessions with the tenacity of wolves.

This brings me to the subject of my fellow passengers. About half of them were Levantine merchants – little gnarled men with narrow eyes and pointed chins and splendidly embroidered skull-caps. From my enquiries, I learned that most of them were merchants of the lower order, that is to say 'middle-men' who had been sent by their masters in Constantinople or Alexandria to collect monies owed to them in London and the great industrial towns of the north. Contrary to what is generally believed, I found these gentlemen to be perfectly well-mannered and respectable, although I did take some exception to the chanting of their prayers, a practice which I found excessively zealous and something of an irritation. Alongside them, there were the Scottish and Irish immigrant families that I have already mentioned. I will not say much about them here, seeing that it is possible to encounter thousands like them in and around the London docks and the marshlands adjacent to the Thames. The men, in general, all seemed to be big, red-faced fellows, with defiantly twirled moustaches and tempers to match, as ready to slap their wives as to let off thunderous volleys of 'f___s' and 'b______s.' By contrast, the women all looked toothless and consumptive and would sit there giving suckle to their progeny in spite of the quietly staring Mohammedans. From the markings on their cases it was evident that most of these European people were supposed to disembark at Gibraltar and then re-embark on the *S.S. Derbyshire,* a passenger steamer heading towards Australia. Another thing that I noticed was that the immigrant families and the Levantines had no form of transaction with each other, conducting their everyday business as two totally different species of animal would conduct themselves on a savannah plain. This did pain and perplex me somewhat, for are we not all, as the Book of Genesis says, descended from the three tribes formed by Noah's children — Shem, Ham and Japeth — and does this not make us all brothers of a sort?

This lack of international communication was in direct contrast to the lay-out of our sleeping quarters. In principle, the steerage compartment was supposed to be divided into three separate areas: an area towards the front reserved for bachelors of a marriageable age, one across the aft for unmarried ladies, and a space for married couples and children acting as a buffer zone in between. I use the phrase *in principle* because after a few days all these distinctions eroded and everyone spilled out everywhere in a disorderly mess of soiled bedding and intertwined humanity. It is impossible, for that matter, to describe the foul and fetid stench that began to build up in steerage from our second day onwards. In great part, this was because the hall was fitted with a single latrine, a thoroughly despicable measure on the part of the shipowners which shows how much those materialised devils care about their fellow men. After three days, this single latrine, serviceable as it had been in the beginning, became clogged up and unusable and had to be abandoned as a form of filth-evacuation. Consequently, men, women and children were forced to perform their necessaries into a series of buckets lying under the metal ladder – the only reasonably private space in the whole of the compartment. Once these buckets filled up, they would have to be taken across to the other side of the chamber, where they would then be emptied into a recessed hatch which led all the way down to the sea. It was this constant transportation of buckets backwards and forwards – together with the spillages that sea-swells would sometimes bring with them – which overburdened the air and made it less than respirable.

But our problems, alas, went beyond mere olfactory inconveniences. On the third day, an elderly Mohammedan – a rug merchant from Mogadore, we were told by one of his acquaintances – died under somewhat mysterious circumstances. By this I simply mean that he was in perfect health one moment and that he was dead the next, shifting from the world of the living to the world of the dead with all the alacrity of a drunken tightrope walker. Such an expedited passing from one world to the other, you will understand, necessarily makes us reflect on our own mortality. But when it happens in mid-ocean, and within the narrow confines of a steerage compartment to boot, it tends to depress people more than normal. In fact, the following night a second passenger, a tall, gaunt-faced Bristolman known by the name of Skitters, also died – although from the agitated and wheezy nature of his demise it was generally believed that he had died from a simple case of apoplexy and nothing of a contagious nature. This, not surprisingly, quelled the passengers' apprehensions somewhat. Even so, it was a very disturbing matter seeing these two lifeless gentlemen being hauled up the metal ladder by a series of ropes and pulleys – rather like a pair of oversized marionettes that refused to cooperate with their master's bidding. I was reminded of an old painting by one of the Venetian masters that I had once come across in one of my old school books, the name and title of which presently escapes me, which shows our Lord being hauled down from the blessed rood by his Roman tormentors – although, to be perfectly true to what I saw, the Bristolman and our Mogadorian friend were being *hauled up rather than down.*

What more can I write here about those five days and nights travelling from Southampton to Gibraltar? Twice a day we were served the usual sea-faring comestibles — hard bread, salted meat, plus one or two dried vegetables. On two occasions we had warm wheat cakes at breakfast. As far as our consumption of liquid was concerned, I was glad to have brought with me a small quantity of soda powders — the water, as in most transoceanic vessels, having a disturbingly pungent quality to it which made it exceedingly troublesome to swallow. Indeed, it was so bad that the first thing I did after disembarking at Gibraltar was to proceed to the nearest street-fountain and help myself to several cupfuls. 'Blessed be the LORD, who daily loadeth us with benefits. . . .' (Psalms 68:19)

**The eighth day of November, 1888**

I did not mention it yesterday, but I have found some lodgings in Angelo's Gully, a narrow, foul-smelling alley not far from the old mediaeval building popularly known as the *Tower of Homage.* The whole district is a veritable rabbit warren of passages and crooked little steps, twisting one way and then turning the other, the narrowness of which diminishes the circulation of air and seriously depresses the spirit. All the buildings in the vicinity are divided into small habitations, which in turn are subdivided and contracted out by the poor tenants to those even poorer souls they have invited to live with them. A foul smell continuously hangs in the air, the origin of which I have not been able to ascertain, but which probably stems from the overflowing cesspools and the badly-choked latrines which most of these buildings share. I have not seen many people around, but the few that have come my way seem a curiously undersized breed, their faces sallow and scrofulous, bearing the sad, lustreless look of those whose lives are constantly blighted by disease and bereavement. Before stumbling upon my present lodgings, I must have walked through the streets for six or seven hours. In my search for a suitable room, I tried all the streets and places that I was once familiar with — Waterport Street, Governor's Street, the Line-Wall — but the asking prices were so high that I was forced to move to the upper parts of town and all those areas that I never frequented much during my youth. Here my fortunes underwent something of an upturn. After asking one of the natives about the possibility of renting a room, I was directed to a small flour warehouse which doubled-up as a property-renting office. There I came across a wizened old Jew by the name of Esadras,[1] a crooked little man with a gold-rimmed monocle and an exceedingly carbuncular countenance who thought that I was an Englishman and consequently treated me with all the deference that Rock Scorpions,[2] particularly those of Jewish extraction, cannot help exhibiting to their colonial masters. After the introductory pleasantries were over, he led me to a small garret not far from his office and said that I could move into it that very moment — there being nothing better, in his estimation, than an English tenant such as myself. 'Nothing would please me more than to be your English lodger,' I replied, signing myself as 'Charles Blackdoor, Esq.' in the leasing contract and describing myself in the accompanying page as a printer's assistant from Drury Lane, London. I committed this falsehood both to maintain Esadras' good opinion of me and also to cover up the sad and controversial circumstances attached to my real name (which Esadras, being a wily Jewish landlord, I am certain, would have been able to sniff out sooner or later) — although I am not sure that this was such a wise move, seeing that they took down my real name at the pratique and customs formalities yesterday and that they have such stringent residency laws in this place. The room Esadras showed me, by the way, was small and filled with the most intense odour of damp; there were no visible chattels of any sort except a round table with rickety legs, a padded board which had been converted into a *chaise longue* and a heavy, lugubrious, iron-framed bed, very Spanish in

---

[1] Esadras is probably a misspelling of the more common Jewish name Esdras.

[2] In John S. Farmer's *Dictionary of Slang and Colloquial English and its Analogues* (1903), a 'Rock Scorpion' is defined as 'a mongrel Gibraltarine (sic): Spanish, Portuguese, French, Genoese, Barbary Hebrew, Moorish negro — a mixture of all mettles.' Although the phrase originally had derogatory implications, it eventually came to reappropriated and turned into an emblem of self-definition by the local population — very much in the same way that the word 'nigger' has been reappropriated by modern black people.

style and character, which coordinated most appositely with the metal and wood crucifix hanging on the wall above it.

'I thought you were a Jew,' I said to Esadras with a half-smile upon beholding the idolatrous abomination above the bed.

'That, *mi buen señor,* belonged to the *inquilino* who was here before you,' the Jew Esadras speechified in the bastardized form of English used among the natives of the colony. 'I think it adds . . . *como le digo?* . . . something to the room, *no crees,* my good English *señor?*'

'You mean to say he didn't take it with him?'

'No, sir. To the place where he went no one can take anything with them, *entiendes,* my good sir *ingles?*'

I looked at the crucifix more closely and noticed that the body of our Saviour was hanging on the cross from only two points, his left hand having detached itself from the iron nail hammered into the wood. On any other occasion I would have taken this as an augury of ill-omen, but after having spent the last few hours traipsing through the streets of town I was in no condition to indulge in any idle superstitious conjecturing.

'What about water?' I asked, turning once again towards Esadras.

'What about it, sir?'

'What arrangements are in place regarding its supply?'

Esadras smiled obsequiously. 'There is a rainwater tank in the patio downstairs, Mr. Blackdoor. You will need to sort out with the *casero* at what time of the day you will be allowed to queue at the pump. . . . Don't worry,' he said, reassuring me with one of his ingratiatory Jewish smiles. 'He is most friendly with gentlemen of the English persuasion such as yourself.'

'And is the water fit for human consumption?'

Esadras coughed and looked a little embarrassed. 'From what I have been told the water is hard,' he said, 'and somewhat ferruginous in quality, but quite fit for ordinary consumption *de todo los modos.*'

'You mean it tastes like metal?'

'I mean it refreshes most capably and can be used for all ordinary culinary and washing applications *con toda maxima garantia.*'

After the old Jew left, I was able to unpack my suitcase and inspect my new abode in greater detail. The room is rectangular in shape and rather low-ceilinged. On the floor there is a metal chamberpot with a large handle. Next to the pot stands an empty paraffin lamp — unusable, as the glass bulb is cracked in several places. There is a stone fireplace at one end and a recessed alcove at the other. There are also two windows: one overlooking the alley outside and one facing an interior courtyard. Both of them have broken and missing panes, the gaps filled out with crushed balls of paper which have been weighed down with nail-bags. I tried to open the window overlooking the street, but found that it had been screwed down tightly into place. As I took a step back, I noticed a thick layer of dust on the sill, upon which could be seen a series of dried-up little pellets, their form and texture clearly suggestive of mice droppings. I then moved to the other window and found that, yes, I could partially push this one open. Through the small gap in front of me, I saw a typical Gibraltarian patio, crisscrossed with washing lines at all levels. An incredibly overpowering smell, the combination of bleach and mould and stagnant water, rose from the void below and almost made me choke. As I lifted my hand to cover my mouth and nose, I saw a large grey rat stealthily making its way down a piece of external guttering. It looked as well-fed a rat, I have to say, as any that I had ever seen at the 'Pent'. Somewhere down below I could hear a mother and child conversing by means of shouted exchanges:

'*Antonio, ven para arriba que esta la comida lista!*'

'*Qué?*'

*'Que venga parriba, niño, que esta la comida lista!'*

*'Pero estoy jugando, mama!'*

*'Pero que me dice, niño? Ven parriba ante que la comida se enfrie, coño!'*[1]

I continued listening to this curious dialogue for a while, my thoughts repeatedly shifting between my long-lost Gibraltar childhood and the harsh predicament which I now find myself in. Then I shut the window and decided to go to bed.

**The ninth day of November, 1888**
*Thank you, O Lord, for bringing me back to the land of my birth. Thank you for protecting me during the long and desolate years that I spent in prison. Thank you for Deacon Gowan and the books and philosophical tracts that he used to bring to my cell. Thank you for Reverend Rennie and for Pastor Michaels and for the Bible Society missionaries and for everybody else at Pentonville who helped me turn my back on Lucifer and find redemption in the sanctity of Christ Jesus our Redeemer.*

**The tenth day of November, 1888**
I woke up this morning to find an encrustation of blood on my pillow. I thought that my old problem had disappeared many months ago, but the extremely humid conditions in the *Zadane* must have evidently triggered some kind of relapse. After getting dressed and partaking of a crust of bread which the Jew Esadras had been good enough to leave me several days ago, I decided to walk down into town with the intention of seeking employment. It was a fine and largely cloudless day, yesterday's *Levantery*[2] miasmata having dispersed through the course of the night. Near the bottom of Angelo's Gully, I came across a windowless little tavern by the name of the 'Cow Shed.' I had not noticed this establishment either

[1] 'Antonio, come up; the food's ready!' – 'What?' –'I said come upstairs, child; the food's ready' – 'But I'm playing, mummy!' – 'But what are you saying, child. Come upstairs before the food grows cold, for fuck's sake!'

[2] *Levantery* — a made-up adjective linked to the 'Levanter cloud', a thick, low-lying banner cloud which sometimes forms on top of the rock.

yesterday or the day before and I was very much grieved to see a few carters and coalmen and other natives of the lower sort indulging in drink at such an early hour of the day. 'Wretched is the man who seeks refuge in intemperance,' I quietly whispered the words with which the Prophet attacked the slothful Ammonites, 'and wretched the man who succumbs to the demons of indolence within.' A short while later, I found myself walking past my old childhood home at the junction between Governor's Street and Colonial Hospital Ramp. It was truly strange, I must confess — walking under those high, stucco-decorated windows and knowing that all those who had once lived inside the building had either died or moved on to a new existence elsewhere. It was strange and, dare I say it, a little sad — there being nothing more *melancholizing* than for a man to revisit the haunts of his childhood when the dust of oblivion has long since settled upon his memories. From a Musulman shopkeeper I learned that the building had been taken over by a local merchant by the name of Cooper, a most fine and lordly gentleman, as my new acquaintance described him, who was thinking of knocking it down and building a hotel in its place — it always having been the gentleman's dream to own a hotel bearing the name of 'Mr. Cooper's Grand Hotel and Tea Parlour'. Shortly after hearing this, I bade the Islamic gentleman farewell and continued on my way down into the centre of town. Not more than five or six minutes later, I found myself in Waterport Street, the colony's commercial hub and the scene of many a loud-talking transaction. The view before me was just as I remembered it from all those years ago — a dense and fast-moving agglomeration of Talmudic Jews, babbling Musulmans, indolent Spaniards, huffing and puffing Scorpion merchants, and evil-eyed redjackets strutting around with that air of insouciance which is peculiar to the English military classes. It was strange to think that nothing had changed while I had been away. Somehow or the other we imagine that great changes are being wrought in a place while we are not there — but when we revisit these same places we almost always realise that time has stood still and that it is only ourselves who have changed. *The ironies of mutability*, I think a poet would have called it.

My first port of call was the Coaling Station just off the Line-Wall, a rocky manmade pier where they sometimes hire daymen (or as they are known in these parts '*diarios*') to fill up the steamers with coal. I knew that it would be difficult to get a job there in my present debilitated condition, but I was also attracted by the easy informality with which men are supposedly inducted into the coal-heavers' profession (i.e. without too many questions about who you are or where you come from). They were taking people on this morning too, which was quite auspicious. Unfortunately, the foreman in charge of the hiring, a thickly-moustachioed, pipe-smoking Irishman by the name of Sanders, did not appear much interested in my solicitations.

'Show me thee palms of yar hands,' the old teague said when he came to my position in the line of scruffy, ill-fed ragamuffins before him.

I extended my hands out with the palms facing upwards.

'Those are not thee hands of ah stevedore orrah coal-lugger,' the redoubtable Sanders then said with a look of the utmost indifference. 'Go yarself home, will yar?'

'But you're wrong, sir,' I protested by his side. 'I have done my share of manual work before. . . . Look at the scars across my forearms and legs. These are not the arms and legs of some home-staying idler, these are.'

'Just go home, son,' Sanders once again repeated, this time biting the stem of his pipe as he spoke. 'Look arr yar. Yar about as weedy ah wight as ever ee clapped me fecking whoreson's eyes upon. Do yar think thar yar could carry ah hundred pound weight o'coal on yar back for ten hours ah day? Christ and his ministrating angels, who art thou trying to kid now?'

'But, sir, I-'

'Just go home, me boy,' he grunted back angrily, 'and stop wasting me fecking time. I've got ah station to run here, me, in case yar haven't fecking noticed.'

I nodded reluctantly and then stepped out of line. I subsequently made my way to Town Range and then to Irish Town – first to ask if any English officers were looking for major-domos and secondly to enquire about vacancies in the tobacco-rolling manufactories – but I was told on both occasions that there was no present need for any new *mano de obra*. Along the way, I passed near the site of my father's old tobacco manufactory business in Irish Town. It was the first time that I had come near the place since my arrival a few days ago. I could not help feeling a little sad when I saw the name of 'Ezequiel and Bergel' splattered across its walls, particularly as some of the old 'Bestman' lettering could still be discerned under the thin coating of paint used to cover the previous emblems of ownership. By the retail entrance, there was a line of ten or twenty Linenses,[1] all of them ready to buy their cigars and bags of '*picadura*'[2] to smuggle back into Spain and in this way make a few *duros* – just like they used to do twenty-five years ago. Through an open factory door, I was able to catch a glimpse of the women sitting at their little stations – picking up the loose flakes and then packaging them in their tobacco-leaf wraps, rolling and re-rolling with almost pianistic dexterity. Seeing them sitting like that made me reflect on the sad and monotonous plight facing most of these girls. In general *cigarreras* are not very well thought of. They tend to come from poor backgrounds – their fathers and husbands, in most cases, being labourers and goat-herds from La Linea, for whom the three or four *duros* which their women bring in at the end of the week can mean the difference between subsistence and outright destitution. There is not much education among them – most, if not all, of the *cigarreras* being blighted with a vacancy of mind which makes them spend all day giggling and talking about inconsequential things. For a while I was tempted to go inside the warehouse and ask if there

---

[1] Inhabitants of La Linea de la Concepción, the first Spanish town across the border.

[2] A form of finely chopped tobacco.

was some kind of job that I could do within the factory – in some kind of overseering capacity, perchance, or as a handler of accounts – but in the end I resolved that working in my father's old premises would be tempting fate somewhat and decided against the idea.

From Irish Town I made my way to the naval victuallers' office on Ragged Staff. Here I had to endure the maddening indignity of being forced to stand in a queue for two and a half hours only to be told when I reached the front that there were no jobs for someone 'without any employable skills to speak of'. Following this, I returned again to Waterport Street (or Main Street as it is now regularly called) and started a door-to-door sweep of all the commercial establishments that I came across. I tried all the hallowed, well-established names that I remembered from my youth: R. W. Rich, tailors; Beanland, Malin and Co., Printers and Lithographers; Francis Hernandez and Sons, Ironmongers and Decorators; Levy and Co., Sawmillers and General Merchants; Thomas Gamble and Son, General Drapers and Hosiers. Every time I entered the shop of an English merchant I would strive to sound as English as possible, whereas every time I walked into a Rock Scorpion's lair I would try my best to resurrect the little Gib Spanish which (despite my bourgeois father's finest anglicising efforts) still lingered at the back of my mind. Not, alas, that any of this helped my job-procuring efforts. In fact, quite the opposite happened. The English merchants, while pleasant and cordial enough at the beginning of our tête-à-têtes, would gradually realise that they were in the presence of a non-Englishman by the tonal heaviness which still weighs down many of my words (something which is not exactly surprising, given that I spent the first thirteen years of my life in a household populated almost entirely by those who spoke English as a second language). Once cognizant of this fact, they would ask me where it was that I came from originally and I would be forced to admit that I was a son of Gibraltar. This, alas, did not seem to do me any favours – judging from the sudden and rather abrupt manner in which I would subsequently be informed that there were no service opportunities on offer:

'Sorry, my good man, but we are currently fully loaded with staff.'

'All posts are currently occupied, my dear sir.'

'Sorry, chappie. We've no new positions coming up in the foreseeable future. Why don't you try Vargas down the road?'

Initially, I must admit, I was a little confused by this – particularly as most of these English merchants seemed to have sons of Gibraltar in their employ (albeit in menial jobs like attending tills or sweeping shop fronts). Why are they all suddenly giving me the cold shoulder, I wondered? What is it that I have done? After thinking about it for some moments, however, I came to the conclusion that they would rather employ a Scorpion born and bred than one who, having lived in England and realised that fair Albion is not the place of perfection which it is made out to be, might perhaps not treat them with the deference which they feel they deserve. That, at least, is my personal theory on the matter, although I am also conscious that I may be imbuing my thoughts with an *unreasonable degree of subjectivity*.

My dealings with the local merchants were scarcely less problematical. Once again it was language that came between us, this time in the form of my imperfectly remembered Rock Spanish, which, rather than break down barriers and be conducive to some kind of rapprochement as I had imagined it would be, seemed to have an altogether negative effect on the worthies in question.

'But you, sir, really, sir, you say you are a Rock man, sir?' they would ask me in their strongly-accented English, as if unwilling to continue exchanging *frases* with this malingering impostor before them.

'*Si, si . . . desde luego que si,*'[1] I would reply in my stilted Spanish and with a pained expression across my face. 'I am . . . how can I say? . . . *de* Gibraltar. *Mi padre ees* from Gibraltar, *igual* my *abuelo*.'

What made my performances even less credible, if anything, was the fact that every time they asked me from which family I came (a

[1] 'Yes, yes . . . most certainly I am.'

typical Rock Scorpion trait, for those unacquainted with the scrutinous mentality here) I was forced to lie and come up with some invented Gibraltar-sounding name — something like Peter Mañasco or Robert Laguea. This I did, of course, not because I am enamoured of falsehoods — God knows that I abhor liars and despise their base regurgitations! — but because I could not abide the thought of anyone discovering the infamous criminal stain that follows my family name. Such duplicity, you have to understand, may well have been swallowed in a densely populated town like London or Manchester. But in a small Catholic Mediterranean town, where appearances are sacrosanct and where everyone is unnaturally conscious of each other's lineage, it could only be recognised for the egregious breach of faith that it was:

'Mañasco say you?'

'Yes, yes. Mañasco.'

'You mean like Geraldo Mañasco down at the Casemates. The old *caleche* driver and friend of Mr. Sanguinetti the carter?'

'No, no. He's no relation of mine. My father was Joseph Mañasco. A police constable. *Un policia constabulario.*'

'*Que extraño*, sir. Never heard of any *policias* called Mañasco before — and I should know, being four and thirty years supplying uniforms to our officers of the law. . . . Are you sure you are . . . *como se lo digo* . . . getting your particulars right?. . . Perhaps you could try Mr. Beanland, the Lithographer, just up the street. He would be more partial to a Britisher like yourself, *sabes lo que le digo*?'

After five or six of these rebuffs, I decided to abandon my search and return to my abode. It was only then, as I walked one last time through Main Street unencumbered, as it were, of any pretensions to employment, that I realised just how strange it felt to be back within my homeland again. How utterly and totally strange. Many times during the years of my incarceration, I have to admit, I had visualised myself walking on these same cobbles. I had held onto this image no matter what, secured it as my own, turned it into the long-lost grail which would one day be raised to my lips and cure me of my afflictions. The beatings and the intimidations, the bodily woundings and the institutionalised degradations: everything receded when I thought of myself ambling down my hometown's main avenue. Now, however, walking through the street in question, surrounded by so many eyes and faces that meant nothing to me, I felt strangely detached and out of sorts. Perhaps it was because I did not feel that sense of belonging which I had somehow convinced myself I would feel the moment I stepped back on Gibraltarian soil. Perhaps it was because I could not recognise anyone and no one, in turn, seemed to recognise me. That, on reflection, could have well accounted for some of my discomfort. Although as a child, let me explain, I was forever pining to venture beyond our mansion walls, I also recall that strolling through Waterport Street with my nannies was always something of a chore – *so many times were we stopped on our perambulations by relatives and friends of the family wanting to enquire about my mother or my father or anything else that could be enquired about*. That, you have to understand, is the way that things have always been here. Gibraltar, if I may use a classical comparison, is like some gigantic Gordian knot of social and familial relationships: everyone knows you and you in turn know everyone around you (with the possible exception, of course, of the members of the military garrison, who, following the dictates of tradition, generally hold themselves aloof and have no traffic with the civilians under them). For me, alas, all that is gone now. I have been away for so long – and have been so cruelly ravaged by age and illness during my enforced absence – that no one recognises me for the person that I once was. This, of course, is not necessarily a bad thing – what with the infamous past that I am forced to drag like a prisoner's chain behind me – but it does fill me with a strange melancholy of *unbelonging* which makes me wonder if returning here was such a good idea in the first place.

**The eleventh day of November, 1888**

I was woken at three o'clock this morning by the sound of loud shouting. For more than a minute, I lay completely motionless in bed, unable to decide whether I was still dreaming or whether I had in fact died and woken up in some dark and formless chamber in hell. When I finally calmed down, I was able to make the following deductions: (1) the screams were coming from the room next to mine. (2) they were regularly interspersed with insults and angry recriminations in Spanish. (3) the voices taking part in all this belonged to a man and a woman.

'So my neighbours have decided to quarrel at three in the morning,' I sighed to myself at this point.

I subsequently re-laid my head on my pillow and tried to go back to sleep — but quickly discovered that my sensory faculties had been too disturbed to slide back into their previous state of dormancy. Consequently, I got up and lit a candle. I then heated up some tea. While sipping the drink, I continued listening to what the man and the woman were saying, trying to see if I could grasp more than just the odd Spanish swearword. In the room next door to mine, I should perhaps explain, there lives a family of ten or eleven individuals. The father is a sallow little man of indeterminate age – he could very well be anywhere between thirty and sixty, such is the air of general vagueness and non-descriptness which marks out the poorest classes in this part of the world — whose craggy features and permanently blackened hands and arms reveal him as one of the hundreds of coalmen or '*carboneros*' who swarm the garrison. He never smiles and always seems to stink of liquor, although when he is drunk he at least doffs his cap to those around him. He is almost certainly of Genoese or Maltese extraction. Apart from a slouchy adolescent of fifteen or sixteen, the children all range between the ages of two and nine — and are the most unrepresentative specimens of infancy one could possibly hope to behold! They do not cry or play like normal children are wont to do; they merely sit by the doorway, waving away musquitoes or picking out each other's head lice with an almost Oriental sense of languor. At least three of them bear frightful, pus-filled scabs across their faces, most probably impetiginous in origin, the rough and unpleasant appearance of which makes them look like fiendish little dwarves. Their mother, for her part, is no less of a ragged and unkempt creature. Though we are presently in the middle of November, she persists in wearing this pitifully thin dress, cut low around the neck and made 'large' at the waist by several layers of filth-encrusted crinoline, giving her the appearance of an East End charnel-house attendant or some other low-born working woman. Around her neck hangs some kind of beaded religious token; it is made of cheap wood and from it dangles a crucifix which is almost permanently sunk in the cleft between her notoriously overexposed breasts. Perhaps I am judging her unfairly when I say this, but there is a certain freeness about the way she conducts herself in the presence of male company which makes me suspect that she may be a part-time '*femme de la nuit*'. Also, she has a habit of wearing her hemline one or two inches higher than most colonial women — always a useful indicator in the often tricky matter of determining who is a prostitute and who is not around here.

**The twelfth day of November, 1888**

I went to see my father's grave today. It is a large and ostentatious piece, complete with violin-playing *putti* and a sword-wielding granite angel towering above the headstone. The marble must have been imported, there being no other monuments cut out of the same shiny black stone in the vicinity. Across the headstone I was able to discern the following words:

*John Charles Bestman,*
*Servant of Christ*
*& Devoted Family Man*
*Who passed from this Life to the Next*
*On the 2nd day of November, 1874*
*Leaving behind him a Void that no other man can fill*
*And a Memory of Immortality*
*Aged 58 years*

What was that last line supposed to mean — a Memory of Immortality? Did it perhaps signify that my father had left behind an immortal memory? That he was now immortal by virtue of this gigantic memorial? Or had the engraver made one of those infelicitous linguistic errors which one frequently comes across in this strange Anglo-Spanish mishmash of a cemetery? That seemed more likely than anything else, I have to admit. All around North Front Cemetery there are similarly unfortunate inscriptions which, either because of the stonemason's illiteracy or the monument purchaser's instructions, immortalise those whose 'mammary we cherish' or who are 'now resting for ever in the piss of our Lord'. I suppose that's the price us Rock Scorpions have to pay for being second-rate Britons: our clumsy attempts to ape the English follow us all the way to the grave. In a sense, I have to say, it is quite funny – although it is one thing to find the inscriptions amusing and another to laugh openly at them. Even as I walked among the gravestones today, let me explain, I came across an English officer and his parasoled lady companion, who, strolling through our cemetery as one would do through a park, could not stop themselves from pointing at some of the tombstones and laughing at the examples of linguistic incompetence before them. Such lack of respect I find most unbecoming.

But I am digressing. I was elaborating on my father's tomb and the fact that it looked just like the kind of memorial you'd have expected to have been commissioned by a Jewish tobacco supplier who only converted to the Anglican faith in order to further his social and mercantile aspirations. It was hard to imagine, all the same, that my father's remains lay under such a marble monstrosity, quietly putrefying into the rich Gibraltar soil that he once trod with so much lordly self-assurance. Once upon a time, let us not forget, there was a merchant who psychotically believed that each and every word coming out of his mouth had the value of a royal proclamation. Now what is left of him lies rotting under some ridiculously gothic marble monstrosity that looks as if it has been lifted straight from the pages of a Monk Lewis novel. If there isn't some kind of poetical irony mixed among all this, I am not sure that I'll ever comprehend what the term means. Of course, if I had somehow been able to come here just after he died, in the days before Christ Jesus came into my heart, I am sure that I would not have been so phlegmatic about the whole thing. For a start, I would have probably been overwhelmed by very strong feelings of resentment. That I am most certain of. I would have hated my father's memory, I would have spat upon his tombstone, I would have cursed the self-possession that made him thrust his increasingly wayward eccentricities upon me — in short, I would have been filled with all the anger and bitterness that ten years of parental abandonment had inculcated within my breast. But now, nearly fifteen years after I received the note under my cell door saying that my father had passed away, I feel nothing but a calm and steady indifference, a quiet and resigned stillness that is only ruffled slightly by the thought that we were never able to reconcile ourselves with each other in the end. Yes, I forgive you John Charles (or Jamiel Chaviv, as you were known before your moment of apostasy). I forgive you for trying to mould me into everything that I most despised, for pushing me into directions that I never wanted to take, for cutting me out of your will when you realised that I would never live up to your expectations and, worse than any of that, for abandoning me in my hour of greatest need.

After leaving the cemetery, I made my way to the offices of Mr. Aurelius Bettino, Esq., Shipchandler and Commission Agent at number 71, Main Street. I went there on the basis of some information which I received a few days ago and which suggested that the said company was in need of a shipping clerk. But when I arrived at their offices I was told that the vacancy had already been taken and that, in any case, I would have been too old to occupy what in effect was a junior position. Next I made my way to the thin strip of sea-facing land behind the old Club-house Hotel, an area popularly referred to as '*el jardin de Cardoso*' on account of a few potted trees and one or two benches that have been standing in this location since time immemorial. It was very quiet there; all the stone benches were unoccupied and nothing could be heard except the distant rumble of the crowds to-ing and fro-ing through Main Street and its side-alleys. I only meant to tarry here for a while, but such was my lassitude of spirit by this stage that in the end I remained on my bench for over an hour. During this time I slipped into something of a meditative mood and mentally revisited many of the scenes of my distant youth, an involuntary act of remembering which, in no small degree, must have been triggered by the experience of having visited my father's grave. Once again, I was not held captive by feelings of a melancholic or resentful nature; but, rather, sitting there quietly on my own, found myself thinking upon the events of the past in a perplexed and near-mystified manner, unable to believe that such things could have ever happened at all. In particular I remembered my father and his peculiarly anglophilic obsessions. Like most rich colonials, he had been involved in a lifelong battle of appearances — that is to say, he had spent his whole life trying, by all ways and means at his disposal, to *appear as English as possible.* This, if we are to be honest, is a particularity of the Rock Scorpions — nearly all of whom are brought up to associate progress and industry with Britannia's rule, and slothfulness and backwardness with the Bourbon rabble across the border. The poorer classes, for example, continually lord it over the luckless devils on the other side, who they consider damned *desgraciados* and *malditos españoles* — quite unlike themselves, of course, who are Gibraltar-born Britons and Her Majesty's true and proud subjects. The richer classes, for their part, resort to even less edifying tactics: forbidding their children to speak anything but English and trying in this way to eradicate all trace of Hispanic influence from their lives. They do this for two distinct reasons. First, because they associate England with progress and enlightenment, as I have already said. Secondly, because they believe that, by anglicising their names and their manner of speech, they will distance themselves from the poverty and ignorance which most of them, being self-made men, have at some stage or the other suffered — either in their own flesh or vicariously through their own ancestors.

My good father was a case in point. The son of a low-born Tetouanese Jew who made his way over to Gibraltar after the infamous pogrom of 1822, Jamiel Chaviv had spent all his youthful energies trying to get rich, and then, having reached this last objective, trying to disassociate himself from his humble origins. In this respect, I suppose, Jamiel was no different from any other penniless immigrant wanting to better his lot: he was desperate to hide the indigent shabbiness of the life he was fleeing from. The only difference was that, unlike most newly-arrived immigrants, Jamiel did not remain penniless for long. Starting off as a humble *cigarrero* at one of the tobacco manufactories which sprung up after the last great yellow fever epidemic, he was able, through a combination of hard work and Sephardic guile, to undergo the type of meteoric rise which, had the dictates of Protestant tradition not constrained him, my father's stonemason would almost certainly have been forced to chisel upon his patron's gravestone:

*1836. Appointed 'rolling room' supervisor.*

*1839. Marries Lydia Boselli, the manufactory owner's daughter.*

*1840. Appointed member of the board of directors.*

*1845. Aligns himself with two other directors to buy out the company after the creation of the border-protecting agencies El Cuerpo del Resguardo and La Guardia Civil temporarily slowed down the sale of 'contrabandable' tobacco.*

*1847. Buys out the other members of the consortium to become the sole owner of the manufactory.*

Then there was the small matter of attaining social respectability. First of all, the man changed his name from Jamiel Chaviv Benyunes to John Charles Bestman. Then, about a year later, he disowned the faith of his fathers and converted to the Anglican Church (Catholicism, for all its attractions, was simply too Spanish an option). After that he divorced his first wife, the hapless and childless Lydia, and embarked upon a search for a new mate. His intention, at this stage, was to marry an 'English belle', someone who would consolidate his long-held dream of total anglicisation — but here my father run into a thorny dilemma. A most problematical setback, you could say. Most 'English belles' in Gibraltar, you see (at least most 'English belles' of any social standing) would have been seriously disinclined to enter into a nuptial contract with a Rock Scorpion of any sort, whether owner of one of the largest tobacco manufactories or not. It was just not the done thing, you understand. Scorpion men married Scorpion women, and English men married English women: anything less than this would have been *a violation of the long-accepted, time-honoured way of doing things.*

And yet, in spite of all this, my father remained undaunted. He stubbornly refused to budge. Scorpions and Britishers may have been at each other's throats since 1704, but he, John Charles Bestman, was going to marry an Englishwoman and *woe betide anyone who told him otherwise*! Soon, in fact, his eye fell upon Molly O'Callaghan, the daughter of a hard-up Irish ex-police sergeant who had been discharged from his duties for embezzling colonial government funds. Molly may not have been a true daughter of Albion and her religion may have only been of the papistical variety, but she also had some good qualities to commend her: she looked, for all intents and purposes, Anglo-Saxon; she had an English-sounding name; her father did not object to the proposed nuptials (quite the contrary, if truth be told!); and more important than any of all that, she spoke that brand of rough, cockneyfied garrison English so beloved by obsessively anglophilic colonials like my father.

There was only one slight problem with all this: Molly O'Callaghan, God bless her dear Irish heart, could not bring herself to share her bed with a wrinkled, leathery, overfed and overwined Rock Scorpion Jew. She positively baulked at the idea, preferring to slit her wrists, as she once confided to my maternal grandmother, than come anywhere near that 'crusty old Jewish baboon'. To overcome her scruples, John Charles Bestman resorted to some typical merchantman's behaviour: letting off thunderous curses one moment and then easing her conscience with a succession of pre-nuptial gifts the next. This, together with the constant threats from her ex-police sergeant father (for whom the marriage represented no less than a miraculous lifeline sent to rescue him from his impecunious ways), ensured that poor Molly was soon walking down the central aisle of the Anglican Cathedral of the Holy Trinity in the company of her new Scorpion husband. Jamiel Chaviv Benyunes had finally metamorphosed into Mr. John Charles Bestman.

**The thirteenth day of November, 1888**
I have a confession to make: I am running out of money. After the purchase of victuals and coal, as well as the handing over of the deposit monies demanded by the Jew Esadras, I now have just over fifteen Spanish dollars — that is to say, about seventy-five pesetas (roughly equivalent, if my calculations do not fail me, to five half-sovereigns and four shillings). I suppose I could go out and find somewhere to pawn my hat and greatcoat. Yet something within me rebels against the idea of walking around without those basic emblems of gentlemanly respectability.

In some ways, of course, I blame this state of impecuniousness on my own miscalculations. While trying to save up for this venture, I had assumed that four pounds would have been enough to keep me afloat during the initial four to five weeks that it would take to secure permanent employment within the colony. Since coming back, however, I have realised that prices have more than quadrupled or quintupled during my long absence. Such lack of discretion may seem most regrettable — but that, I am afraid, is what happens when you have been shut out from society for so long: you somehow lose all sense of proportion, finding yourself occupying a dream-world halfway between the present and the world you left behind all those years ago.

**The fifteenth day of November, 1888**
I did not write anything in my journal yesterday. I am not really sure why. Sometimes I am possessed by a most disempowering melancholy, the likes of which seriously depresses my spirit and sends me careening down into the very sloughs of laziness. Today, I am afraid, has been very much like that. During the early part of the morning I queued at the downstairs pump along with the other tenants, suffering their curious glances and stares in martyr-like silence. Afterwards I returned to the room with two buckets of water, one of which I accidentally toppled over as I was opening my door. I then spent the rest of the morning standing by the alley

window, my attention switching between the passers-by outside and the penumbral gloom of my unlit room. At some point it occurred to me that my present habitation shares many points of correspondence with my old cell at Pentonville. Sizewise it is about 13 feet long by 7 feet broad — roughly the same area as my old cubicle. The walls, too, are similarly rough-textured and covered with patches of damp. Even the furniture, I have to say, is likewise battered and decrepit.

**The sixteenth day of November, 1888**

I woke up this morning with another evil-looking bloodstain on my pillow. It possessed a greater thickness than last time, being reminiscent in form and colour to the powdery washings at the bottom of a port bottle. Upon clambering out of bed, I felt weak and dispirited, almost as if I was labouring under a debilitating fever or some obscure tropical malady. My first thought was to light a fire and return to bed, but, continuously dogged by the fear of insolvency as I have lately become, I decided to go out and carry on searching for employment. It was raining outside, yesterday's leaden greyness having given way to a fine, spray-like drizzle that humidified the atmosphere and made it difficult to walk without breaking into a sweat. Once I reached Main Street, I visited one or two establishments that I had not been able to fit within the course of my recent perambulations — most notably G. H. Cartwright the watchmaker and jeweller, and Solomon H. Cohen's 'White Flag' boot and shoe store. Unfortunately, neither of these firms had any vacancies and I soon found myself out in the rain again, my feelings of disappointment only staved off by the gnawing hunger pains that had been mounting inside my gut all morning.

After these first setbacks, I wandered down to the thin stretch of land behind the old Club-house Hotel. I then sat on a circular stone bench containing a palm tree growing out of its hollowed-out centre. I chose this bench because of the said palm tree, imagining that its leafy branches would serve to protect me from the rain which was now coming down in considerable quantities. As soon as I was settled, I brought out a handkerchief containing a partially cracked egg (or *huevo cascado*) which I had purchased earlier from a

Spanish *carretero* in Parliament Lane — *huevos cascados*, let me explain, being less than half the price of *huevos enteros.* I carefully peeled off a few pieces of loosely-stuck shell and then wolfed down the gelatinous mixture of yolk and white inside — an act which felt most satisfactory in passing, but which, in truth, did little to stave off the hunger that had been gnawing at my insides all morning. Following this, I stood up from the bench and wiped my mouth with my jacket sleeve. I then made my way down to nearby Irish Town and the site of my father's old manufactory. While I stood there, half-hidden from the rain under a shadowy doorway across the road, I found myself thinking about Messieurs Bergel and Ezequiel, the building's new owners. 'Who exactly are these people?' I wondered, scratching my chin. Probably Jewish merchants, one would have thought, judging by the Sephardic ring of their surnames. As I never heard my father mentioning their names back in the early 1860s, I assumed that they were just another pair of shady *nouveau riche* upstarts, taking advantage of another family's misfortunes to aggrandise their own position — just like Jamiel Chaviv had done at the expense of the unfortunate Ricardo Boselli in the 1840s. As the rain started to intensify around me, I wondered if either of the illustrious pair had any heirs and, if so, whether they were already being cultivated to vicariously fulfil their fathers' self-improving ambitions. This is something that all the respectable gentlemen Scorpions engage in: they gentrify their name with each succeeding generation, trying to distance themselves from the mud-encrusted origins that almost all of them without exception share. Consider all the big families with '*la Plaza*'[1]— the C_'s, and G_'s and F_'s. If you could draw a genealogical line far back enough in time, you would almost certainly find that the origin of their present wealth begins with some good-for-nothing *ratero*, some scruffy, penniless immigrant who probably double-crossed or smuggled his way into a higher plane of material existence. Messieurs Bergel and Ezequiel, I am sure, are no different in this respect. Soon, with all the money they have made out of the sweat and sacrifice of those miserable cigar-rollers employed under them, they will be sending their offspring to Eton, Harrow, Stonyhurst, etc.

---

[1] '*La Plaza*' – literally, 'the square' (a nineteenth-century Spanish term for Gibraltar).

— and before you know it, hey presto, all those shady stratagems of the past are replaced by a flurry of elegant postures and polished London accents, with no one able to take their heirs for the sons of the mongrel half-Spanish b_______ they really are!

PS: I forgot to mention something of great importance. On my way back home, I stopped at *el patio de sananes* on Bombhouse Lane and bought a quart of milk for only thirty-five centimes, the cheapest I have paid so far. I must not forget to carry on buying milk from here, as it is a good five centimes cheaper than elsewhere.

**The seventeenth day of November, 1888**

It is raining heavier today than during the last few days. I have been sitting next to the nailed-down window for most of the morning and afternoon, watching the raindrops slide down the cracked panes and the more voluminous body of rainwater cascading through the street outside. I am, of course, conscious that I should be out there seeking employ, but I find myself trapped in a most disempowering state of ennui, not knowing what to do with myself or where to next take my job-procuring mission. The irony of this is not lost upon me. Once upon a time, during the years when freedom of movement was denied to me, the thought of returning home (as I visualised this place at the time) fortified my constitution; it endowed me with the vitality to face the thousand and one affronts and humiliations that incarceration brings with it. Now that I am back here, though, I feel so flat and bereft of energy that I find it hard to understand how I could have *romanticised* this town to such a degree. In the words of some of my old inmates, I feel like a mug, a dupe, someone who swallowed a lie to keep himself going. Because the truth — make no mistake about it — is that I lied to myself. I turned Gibraltar into my supporting crutch, my guiding star, the one permanently-shining beacon that neither the taunts of my fellow prisoners nor the beatings of the screws could ever extinguish. That I had motives enough for doing so, of course, no one can deny; yet now, unburdened as I am by the need for any self-preserving lies, I feel let down and cheated, as if I had betrayed myself and my ambitions by clinging to such idealised fancies. Even when I was here all those years ago, the truth is, I was *never totally happy*. It was not that I lacked for anything, or that I was ever treated with any unkindness. Even during the giddiest years of my youth I was very much conscious of *that.* Standing half-hidden behind the crimson chintz curtains that draped my bedroom window, I would watch the unshod muleteer and *frutero* children shuffling through the street below and I would realise that I was very different from them, that I led an easy and carefree life by comparison. I was not, of course, able to understand that their state of indigence carried with it terrible hardships and suffering; at that age you merely register social inequalities like an amateur critic beholds a picturesque landscape — that is to say, as something lively and quite entertaining to watch, but which will cease to exist in your thoughts the moment you turn your back on it. Yet at the same time I was not so stupid as to look awry upon the gifts that fortune had been gracious enough to bestow upon me. Along with my parents, I lived in a grand patrician house with three floors and about fifteen rooms, the upkeep and running of which was entrusted to two major-domos, three domestick maids, four scullions and two liveried footmen. Our house, moreover, was blessed with all the best victuals and commodities that could be bought in Gibraltar at the time — finest Manchester linens, fresh fish from the market, succulent fillets of beef delivered straight from the cattle grounds in Campamento, figs and dates from Almeria, sweet and juicy Granadan oranges, first-rate cutlery from the silverworks in Bilbao. And yet, for all that, I cannot recall a time when I was ever *truly happy.* I realise that this may sound suspiciously close to ingratitude on my part — especially when one considers the world of hardship and pronounced wants that lay but a short distance from our Governor's Street residence — but happiness and affluence do not always make good bedfellows, do they?

All I can say here is that I was unhappy not because of any unkindnesses or cruelties that were being heaped upon my person — but rather because of what was being kept *absent* from me. Take my father, for example. As much of a provider and a *pater familias* as he undoubtedly was, he was also permanently locked away in his office in Irish Town — either trying to devise new ways to increase his by now substantial fortune or, what was more common as the years went by, hoping to impress his peers with his collection of whiskies and fine tawny ports. He had even fitted his office with a divan and one or two domesticating conveniences, thus enabling him to stay there several days without having to come home. Slowly but surely, what is more, these absences became longer and more frequent, sometimes stretching for days and weeks on end. In fact, by the time I reached my seventh birthday, you could say that my father had become almost like a stranger to me, occasionally sliding into my life (as he sometimes did) with all the unexpected and unwanted greyness of a Levanter cloud. Now and again, for example, he would suddenly present himself at our residence on Governor's Street and Mother and I would then be forced to endure one of those insufferably long and formal family dinners which Jamiel believed were the preserve of what he called 'the superior classes' — pitifully dull and tedious affairs which served no object, if I am to be honest, except to hear him ramble on about how well his business was doing or how he was expecting to be inducted into some traders' committee or the other. Even now, some thirty odd-years later, I shudder at their recollection — and not just because of the speeches we had to endure! Depending upon her mood, you see, Molly would either sit there looking cadaverously silent or else break into hysterical fits of giggling which Jamiel would suffer by gritting his teeth and momentarily looking at the ceiling — as if not knowing what on God's name he had done to deserve such lack of respect! — before carrying on talking about ledger books and profit margins and percentages and other meaningless tripe that no one apart from himself was interested in.

Besides these dinners, there was precious little else. Once or twice a year, perhaps, I would be walked over by one of the servants to my father's manufactory in Irish Town, where I would then be taken on a tour of the premises by my father and the six or seven yes-sirring lackeys who seemed to follow him like a clutch of faithful Praetorians wherever he went. 'This here,' Jamiel would say, stopping and looking at me with one of those psychotically self-satisfied smiles, 'this here is the smoking room or *el ahumador,* as we say in the Spanish tongue, a very important room in our factory, Charles . . . and this over here, this over here is the drying room . . . and this is the cutting room, the largest cutting room, *por cierto*, in the whole of *la Plaza.*' It was like that year in, year out – an endless round of affirmations and pointless declarations which were meant to prepare me for the role that I was supposed to play in the creation of the Bestman family dynasty, but which, starved of parental attention as I was, only served to make me hate Jamiel all the more for ignoring me during the rest of the year.

My mother was a different proposition altogether. Unlike Jamiel, she *did* spend long stretches of time in our grand patrician house, although her dreamy, somewhat solipsistic nature, as well as her penchant for surrounding herself with rich embroideries and expensive jewels, ensured that she devoted almost as little time to her son as Jamiel himself. That as a child I suffered and pined for her exceedingly I cannot, in all honesty, deny; yet, at the same time, I cannot help exonerating her behaviour. Consider the matter from Molly's angle, if you will. Once upon a time she had been forced to give up her name and maidenhood in exchange for financial security; now, having fulfilled her end of the bargain, she was not exactly going to start playing the role of happy, maternal housewife if she could possibly avoid it. That, at least, is how I have come to rationalise her behaviour. How else could you explain such consistent motherly detachment? From the moment I was first handed over to her by the midwife, it was clear that Molly did not really like me, seeing the hairy, blood-bespattered blob in her arms as a permanent, perpetually wailing reminder of her lost youth and the marriage she had been forced to enter with the 'crusty old Jewish baboon'. I was, shall we say, something of a symbol for Molly in this sense, constantly evoking memories of her girlhood wanderings through Buena Vista and the group of rowdy English garrison friends she had left behind. It was not (let me make clear) as if she consciously hurt me or did anything that would endanger my frail and sickly existence – that was not my mother's nature. Like most English people I have come across outside prison, she treated those she did not like with scorn and quiet indifference – rather than berating them with loud and publicly declaimed antagonism (as the more openly temperamental Rock Scorpions are wont to do). In this dispensation of silences, too, Molly was a consummate expert, driving my father, as well as most of the domesticks under her command, close to distraction with her sudden descents into glum irritability. It could have been the way her Darjeeling tea was poured by one of the servants; my father's reluctance to purchase a fifteen-pound diamond necklace that she had lately seen at Cartwright the jewellers; the failure of some Sevillian lace tablecloths to materialise on the appointed day of delivery: these as well as a whole host of other excuses would suffice to send her careering into one of those implacable, harpy-like silences that everyone within the Bestman household so dreaded.

Of course, no one hated these silences more than I did. Indeed, looked at from a certain angle, you could say that Molly was castigating me with one long unbroken silence, rarely suffering the perpetually sobbing two-year-old that I was to come anywhere near her. One reluctant peck on the cheek after breakfast and one even more disdainful kiss before she retired at night: that was the sum and total of the motherly tokens that I received from Molly Bestman (née Callaghan) outside the interminable hours she would spend locked up in her boudoir, either fanning herself with those large, hand-painted Sevillian *abanicos* of hers (which, despite her alleged detestation of all things Spanish, she loved so much), or else dreaming about the next piece of jewellery she would soon be badgering my father into purchasing for her. Later, of course, when she realised that I had inherited some of her introspective nature, she softened her attitude towards me somewhat and even suffered herself to come near me every now and then. This happened primarily during the times I was ill — extremely strange and dreamlike occasions when Molly would sit by my bed and even force herself to shed a few tears for the heavily-perspiring infant beside her. What exactly possessed my mother during those hours I swear I will never know. Did she momentarily lose her rationalising faculties? Was she perhaps worried about what the servants might think of her if she did not attend to her ailing son? Forgive me if I sound unnecessarily cynical and callous, but I always got the impression that her behaviour was prompted more by how she *thought* mothers were supposed to act than by any genuine sense of maternal tenderness. And yet I cannot pretend that I wasn't fond of these sudden, if somewhat theatrical bouts of unexpected affection.

(Give a dying man a glass of swamp water and he will lap it up like a life-giving elixir!) Consequently, I was *more or less constantly ill* – sometimes properly so, other times more in my head than anywhere else, but most of the time only in a purely make-believe capacity. Of these last bouts of pretend illness, I cannot remember much – except lying there gazing at Molly fanning herself in the musty silence and thinking that perhaps the world wasn't such a miserable place after all. My mother never held my hand or changed the sheets or performed any other ministrations during this time, that also is true – but, compared to the years of isolation that I had been subjected to, just lying there in her presence was enough for my young heart to overflow with feelings of the most tender kind towards the woman who gave birth to me.

Apart from these rare moments of sick-room interaction, I had very little human contact with anybody else. Again, there was a simple reason for this. In his effort to mould me into the perfect Anglo-Gibraltarian gentleman, my father forbade me any contact with anyone save our Spanish domesticks and the endless succession of British pedagogues who filed through our house with the intention of improving my character. The former came mainly from the slums of La Linea and lived along with their families in a small out-house near the back of our residence. As far as attire was concerned, they wore tailor-made clothes which my parents (in a rare example of conjugal union) had designed shortly after getting married – the women sporting velvety black dresses with white bonnets and pinafores, the men anachronistic, brass-buttoned jackets with white gloves and black trousers. My father, who throughout his life made it a point of personally interviewing every domestick in his employ, relied on the same contracting procedure that he used when handpicking his manufactory workers – making sure that they spoke enough English to be ordered about, but not so much that they could understand us when we talked about them. (This was one of the advantages of employing Spaniards; the other, of course, being that he only needed to pay them a mere fraction of what he would have had to pay an English person or even a native Scorpion!) If the candidates in question were lucky enough to fit this linguistic bill, they would then be employed and expected to adhere to the Bestman house rules. At this point my father's anglophilic particularities really came into their own. For a start all the domesticks were rechristened with ridiculously anglicised surnames which clashed most incongruously with their coarse, sun-tanned features — Sanchez becoming 'Sanders', Patricio 'Patricks', Ricardo 'Richards' and so on and so forth. Also, just as you would have expected from a man hell-bent on anglicising himself, none of our poor Linenses were ever allowed to speak Spanish within the house — *English being at all times the sole medium of communication.*

Naturally, the finest 'English' among our domesticks was spoken by my nannies. These women, Linenses each and every one of them, were entrusted with all the duties which my mother, being the rarefied and generally etherealised creature that she was, could not be expected to discharge: feeding me, bathing me, clothing me, preparing my food, taking me to the Alameda, watching over me so that I never came into contact with any children who could 'spoil' my upbringing — in other words, all the indispensable necessaries required for the cultivation of a young Gibraltar gentleman. My relationship with these fine ladies, if you must know, was cordial but decidedly unengaged. I was always 'Master Charles' to them, always the little lordling that had to be bowed and curtseyed to every morning. 'Yes, Master, Charles', 'no, Master Charles', 'whatever you say, Master Charles': I can almost hear their mechanical utterances even now.

At the time, of course, all this detachment seemed perfectly normal to me. More than that, it felt like a logical extension of everything that I had known and experienced in my own relationship with my parents. Later, of course, as I grew older and started to perceive how other children in the Alameda were being treated by their nannies, I began to question the extreme formality with which I was being regarded. Could all that excessive coldness, I now began to wonder, reflect some kind of secret working-class jealousy on their part? One of those unspoken resentments which low-born domesticks are said to feel, within their heart of hearts, towards their upper-class benefactors? Or did they, perhaps, resent my father's high-handedness and dismissive manner with those he deemed his social inferiors? Alternatively, was there something about my person – some glaring psychological failing, perhaps – which prevented them from engaging me in a friendlier manner?

For a long time I could not understand why it was that my nannies disregarded me in this way. Then, around the age of ten, I comprehended: it was because of my father. He had been behind it from the beginning. From the very day that I had been first entrusted to somebody else's care. To put it in plain and simple terms, he had ordered every one of my nannies not to importune me with any 'frivolities' unrelated to the course of their duties, believing that any 'Spanish mollycoddling' would drastically reduce my chances of ever becoming an upright English gentleman. That is why the maids had always been so cold towards me: not because they resented our wealth or because they had found my person disagreeable, but because they had been ordered to keep their distance from their young charge!

Only one domestick ever dared to break this code of interaction. The name of this woman, an amply-fleshed La Linean dame whose laughing manner I will never ever forget, was Bertha Partagas, and she had a habit, not altogether displeasing in itself, of pinching my cheeks and simultaneously calling me '*su pequeño angel*'. For about three months the splendid Partagas (or Paxton, as my father came to rechristen her) continued indulging me in this way, using every opportunity to kiss me and hold me and half-suffocate me by pressing me against her spectacularly huge bosom. I was, of course, very happy during this time, never having had my person enwrapped in so much human flesh before. Paxton's caresses, in this sense, came as a revitalising tonic to my soul, filling me with an ardour and a *joie de vivre* such as I had never known. Unfortunately for Paxton and me, however, such a pleasant state of affairs could not last long. One morning, while the voluptuous Paxton showered me with yet another volley of caresses, a pantry maid by the name of Delilah (this being the ridiculous anglicised appellation that my father had chosen for her in lieu of the untranslatable name of Dos Angeles) spotted her colleague in the tendering of her ministrations. This Delilah, being, like her biblical namesake, an altogether ambitious and scheming personage, reported what she had seen to Brown, the mistress of the house, who in turn reported it to Bartholomew, the house steward, who in turn, stuttering and nerve-ridden as I am sure he must have been, brought the matter to the highest authority within the Bestman household. Thus, by means of this series of interlinked communications (which, like a game of Chinese whispers, became more serious and damning as they passed up the chain of hierarchical command), my father came to learn of Paxton's transgressions and promptly and unceremoniously dismissed her.

Before I put my pen down for tonight, I should perhaps mention the only other group of people with whom I had any form of human contact: the tutors whom Jamiel had charged with the task of turning me into an English gentleman. These had started coming to our residence at the beginning of 1858. Although there had been a perfectly adequate private school just around the corner in Engineer's Lane, my father had one day resolved that conventional schooling was not suited to my temperament and promptly set out to find a more suitable alternative.

As usual, of course, it was a decision that came laced with a fair amount of snobbery. Having heard that the local school's fees were only £15 per annum, Jamiel immediately dismissed it as a school of no consequence and decided that my education would be better undertaken privately at home. 'There can be no other way,' he said gruffly one evening. 'He will be educated at home and have nothing to do with that *escuela de mala muerte* down in Engineer's Lane.' When my mother protested that closeting me at home like this would surely get on her nerves, Jamiel immediately put his foot down. 'You know, Mrs. Bestman,' he said, holding his hands behind his back and forcefully thrusting his chin out, 'that I will allow you practically anything for the sake of maintaining harmony within this household. But when it comes to my son's education, madam, things will be done my way, or no way at all, *sabes*?' And that, as they say, *was that.* Within only a few days, a troop of monocled, bow-legged English pedagogists suddenly began to descend upon our Governor's Street residence, carrying impossibly large and heavy copies of Bullion's

*Principles of Latin Grammar* or Charles Tilt's *Etiquette for Young Gentlemen* under their arms. Even to my untrained infant's eye it was obvious that they were a pretty conceited lot – slamming their books down on my child-sized escritoire with lordly arrogance and looking down on our Spanish domesticks as if they were mere *cucarachas* . . . just the type of behaviour, in other words, that would have endeared them to my wilfully eccentric father.

And yet, strangely enough, none of them ever remained long in our employ. Obsessed with perfection as he always was, Jamiel had a habit of firing my masters and replacing them with others he deemed more fit for the purpose – only to fire the latter in turn when he became convinced that there were better men and women out there waiting to take their place. Metaphorically speaking, one could say that our house on *la calle cordonero*[1] was like a continuously turning merry-go-round, the seats of which were continually being filled by different monocled educationalists and hefty-buttocked governesses. To continue with the same metaphorical conceit, many of those alighting from the same merry-go-around would be asked to climb back on it weeks and even months later – my father sometimes discovering that his new employees were not as proficient as those they had replaced.

About the teaching methods employed by these illustrious ladies and gentlemen, there is not much that I can say within these pages. My father, being the born fantasist that he was, loved to tell his bourgeois friends that he was providing me with an education fit for a lord, that he was 'aristocratising' me for the future, etc., etc. The reality, of course, was far less glamorous than that. Gibraltar, one has to understand, though a fairly refined place in comparison with the slum town of La Linea over in Spain, is essentially a trading post and not a place to attract men of high intellect. Allow me, if I may, to put it in a different manner: what sort of pedagogic masters could you possibly find in a colony known throughout Christendom for the intemperance of its military men and the perpetual contrabanding conducted by its civilian classes? Not very good ones, that much is certain. Take the fellows who Jamiel came to engage. Nearly all of

---

[1] An old-fashioned Spanish name for Governor's Street.

them were scruffy, ill-dressed chaps, their puffy, grog-red faces still bearing the pimples and burst blood vessels engendered by last night's drinking session (although with beautifully polished English accents and gentlemanly manners which would temporarily blind Jamiel to their sartorial and behavioural imperfections!). God knows what criminal pasts they must have fled to come to a place like Gibraltar! Even now, almost three decades later, I can still remember some of them: Mr. Alan Fenton-Paris, M. A., the grammar and deportment specialist who occasionally dozed off during my painfully stilted recitations of Cicero and Seneca; Mr. Herbert Rees-Clinton, the stout and heavy-limbed fencing master whose fat, podgy hands lingered somewhat excessively upon certain body parts of mine when teaching me the positions of *tierce* and *quarte*; Mr. Geoffrey Rose-Pringle, the old history master whose habit of picking his nose when bored led me to baptise him with the somewhat uninventive moniker of Mr. Good Old Nose-Pick. These and other learned gentlemen came and went, their combined efforts serving to turn me into a deeply diffident and insecure twelve-year-old polymath who laughed little and suffered from a somewhat hypochondriacal cast of mind. To this day I still carry the hallmarks of these gentlemen's handiwork. Thanks to their efforts, I can play the first twenty bars of Beethoven's *Für Elise*, conduct a thoroughly contrived conversation in French, more or less recognise Latin inscriptions on a church architrave and tell the difference between a *contre-dégagement* and a *contre-parade*. I am, in other words, what is popularly known as a jack of all trades and master of none — something which no doubt contributes to my present state of unemployability.

**The eighteenth day of November, 1888**

I overslept this morning as a result of last night's diary-writing labours. It must have been around half past ten when I woke up. A most disagreeable chill hung in the air, with both the nailed-down window and the one facing the interior yard frosted over with the overnight breathings of *Levanterous* vapour. For my breakfast I had a cup of cold tea (a grisly emetic concocted from some rainwater I had collected in a dish left out on my window ledge and the scummy dregs still left in the kettle from yesterday's morning brew) and some scraps of bread that I had been keeping under a tin bowl on the table. The bread was hard and a little tasteless, but it became softer after mastication and almost, dare I say it, edible. After finishing my tea, I re-read what I had written last night and then I found myself looking around the sad and dilapidated room which I am currently occupying. I found myself looking at all the chattels and possessions contained therein. Something akin to self-pity gripped me then, a feeling somewhere between disillusionment and out-and-out melancholia. I am not sure what exactly engendered this wave of sudden sadness within my breast, but I suspect that it had something to do with the tawdriness of the objects and possessions lying immediately around me:

1. A chair with a missing leg. 2. A pair of dirty old boots. 3. A mildewed leather coat. 4. A battered hat. 5. An unmade bed covered in a blanket of sack-rags. 6. A blunt knife. 7. A couple of bowls turned upside down to protect the food lying under them. 8. A mound of rat droppings next to one of the table legs, freshly excreted and laid out in perfect symmetrical formation — rather like the cannon balls you get beside the sixty-pounders on the Line-Wall.

In short, the room looked just the same as when I moved into it almost two weeks ago — with nothing of any real value save the lugubrious wood and pewter crucifix which still hangs, like some all-seeing eye, on the heavily-fissured wall behind the bed. The realisation filled me with an even greater sense of melancholy. Still dressed in my nightshirt, I sunk onto my knees and tearfully rasped out the following words:

*Let my cry come near before thee, O LORD: give me understanding according to thy word. Let my supplication come before thee: deliver me according to thy word. My lips shall utter praise, when thou hast taught me thy statutes. My tongue shall speak of thy word: for all thy commandments are righteousness. Let thine hand help me; for I have chosen thy precepts. I have longed for thy salvation, O LORD; and thy law is my delight. Let my soul live, and it shall praise thee; and let thy judgments help me. I have gone astray like a lost sheep; seek thy servant; for I do not forget thy commandments.*

I felt much better after this short prayer. I felt soothed in body, reinvigorated in spirit. From the foot of the bed, I looked up at the faintly glimmering body of the Redeemer on His wooden rood and I thought that I could see compassion across His roughly-chiselled features. I thought I could see fatherly concern. 'Even murderers are redeemed by the Lord's precious blood,' I whispered softly as my eyes filled with tears. 'Even ex-convicts are cleansed by the light of His grace.' The thought inspired me and calmed me down. Getting up to my feet, I picked up my coat and made preparations to go out.

It was bitterly cold outside. The Levanter cloud hung menacingly over the rooftops, and the ramps and gullies of the upper town were cloaked with a pitiless grey light. It is a constant companion to the *Levantering* of the atmosphere, this harsh and blazing grey light, quite beautiful in the way that it enshrouds the buildings and military fortifications, and yet, because of the clinging sense of humidity which invariably accompanies it, most oppressive to the optical and nervous faculties. My plan for the morning was simple: I intended to revisit some of the establishments that I had called upon during the last few days. I do not really know what I was hoping for — possibly to demonstrate my powers of persistence to my would-be benefactors and in this way ensconce myself into their affections. With this objective in mind, I visited two Main Street establishments, Thomas Gamble the Draper, and Hernandez the ironmongers. If truth be told, I was not expecting much from them — a few polite shakes of the head, perhaps, a couple of directorial shrugs. What I was *not expecting,* however, was the snarling and grimacing manner in which the owner of the second establishment, a small, thinly-moustachioed man with an ivory walking stick and a strong Gibraltar accent, made it indubitably clear that I was not welcome to call again under any circumstances. 'We have no vacancy, sir,' he said, brandishing his arms in a typical Rock Scorpion manner. '*Nada de nada.* I said to you other day, no? Didna me make clear to you, sir? No vacancy ees what I said — *como leche se lo digo, eh?*'

I became greatly dispirited after that. Consequently, I decided to retire to my usual spot behind Connaught House[1] and comfort myself

[1] Another name for the Club-house hotel.

with some of the bread and dried figs that I had brought along with me. On my way down to the seafront, however, I heard that a condemned man was about to be taken from his cell at the Magistrates court to the execution yard up at the castle. 'Quick, quick!' a woman in a frilly lace bonnet was saying to a rather frumpish bonnet-less friend. '*Si te alijeras*[1] we might even see him as he comes out of the courthouse.' I heard all this, I should perhaps explain, *in passing* – Main Street, because of its permanent state of overcrowding, being one of those places where news and gossip can veritably be plucked out of the air. The condemned man, the voices around me excitedly declaimed, was a Spaniard. A man by the name of Gonzalo Menendez Mendoza. A forty-three-year-old bachelor, proud and arrogant to a fault, who, on top of all the *miscreantish* attributes that his Spanish nationality had endowed him with, also happened to be the owner of one of the most villainously craggy and hirsute physiognomies. The wagging tongues said that Menendez Mendoza had worked at Mr. Francina's cigar manufactory for a while, but soon came to be dismissed on account of his smouldering *gypsified* temper. Of late he had been earning a living as a *frutero*, coming in every morning from the Lines[2] with a cartload full of artichokes and *higos chumbo* and then returning there in the evening with several bags of tobacco artfully sequestered within the nooks and crannies of his hand-truck.

The crime that was taking Gonzalo Menendez Mendoza this afternoon to the gallows was murder. Murder with a capital M, it should be said, seeing that his victim had not been a brawling redcoat or a double-crossing Spanish *contrabandista,* but a Gibraltar-born woman by the name of Elizabeth (or Eliza) Puertas. As to what exactly possessed the villainous Mendoza to batter poor Puertas with a butcher's cleaver, none of those around me could say with any certainty. Some said that there must have been some kind of romantic attachment (and subsequent disseverment) between the pair – there being no other reason, they maintained, for a man to murder a dame otherwise. Others, taking a somewhat different line,

---

[1] 'If you hurry up.'

[2] English name for La Linea de la Concepción.

speechified that Mendoza was drunk at the time of the crime and, as such, not wholly in control of his precariously balanced Spanish temperament. A few even maintained that Mendoza was innocent and that the whole thing had been engineered by Puertas' own family and, in particular, by her father, Mr. Robert Puertas — a devout churchgoer and *monaguillo* who disapproved of the way his daughter used to consort with smugglers, thieves and other garrison ne'er-do-wells.

Listening to all this talk made me remember the time that Jamiel took me to see an execution in Casemates Square. It happened in 1856 or 1857, back in the days when there were still public hangings in the colony. We had driven down to the square in one of the Bestman carriages, I remember, Jamiel, myself and Francis the head footman, the three of us sitting together in near total silence as the vehicle clipclopped its way down the macadamised road. Around fifteen minutes into the journey, Bryan the coachman informed us that he could only get as far as one of the narrow lanes adjoining the Square — there being, as he put it in his pidgin English, 'a big *á-conglomeración*, Mister Bestman sir, of many peoples in dee area.' 'Don't worry, Bryan,' Jamiel shouted in reply. 'We'll make our way to Burlington's by foot.' Presently we alighted from the vehicle and began to make our way through the accumulated throng. The first thing that struck me was the variety of smells around us. You could almost feel them rushing at you in individual waves of malodorousness: the bitter-sweet stench of sweat, the pungent reek of spilt wine, even the faint but unmistakable stench of human urine. I had never, so help me God, experienced anything like it and for a few moments I had to cling to my father's coat-tails to stop myself being swallowed up by the crowd. A veritable welter of emotions ricocheted through my seven-year-old brain just then. On the one hand, I felt disgusted and anxious, unable to believe that so many unseen hands and arms were bearing down upon me from all sides. At the same time, though, I found the experience liberating and oddly invigorating, as if conscious, in my own infantile way, that here was a world where appearances were not important and where being a Bestman mattered not one jot. 'Just hold on fast, Master Bestman,' Jamiel repeatedly urged me over the din. 'We'll be there soon! Just hold on fast for a bit longer!' Eventually, after three or four minutes of further manoeuvring, we made it to Crutchett's Ramp and the house of Mr. Burlington, my father's business partner and friend. Burlington, otherwise known as *El Scottish*, was one of the senior directors of the shipping company which brought Jamiel's tobacco over from the Cuban and Brazilian plantations. An unfailingly larger-than-life character, he was a tall, portly, rosy-cheeked, spectacularly-whiskered Scotsman who, unlike most Britishers on the Rock, enjoyed fraternising with the Scorpions and had even learned a few words of Gibraltar Spanish in the process. I had met him once or twice before at our residence on Governor's Street, where he was sometimes invited by Jamiel for dinner. *El Scottish* usually came dressed in an elegant white suit of corduroy and a broad-brimmed Stetson adorned with several strips of gold braid. He claimed that the hat had once belonged to General Zachary Taylor, commander of the American forces during the Mexican-American war and the twelfth President of the United States.

That day, however, Burlington was dressed in a simple grey suit and there was no Stetson in sight. Greeting my father with a firm handshake and myself with a pat on the head, he led us up the main staircase of his house to a large and elegant veranda which overlooked the square. In the middle of this balcony there was a table laid out with boiled hams, oysters, salmon, quail eggs and other delicacies. 'Please, gentlemen,' Burlington said, beckoning us over to the table with an affable wave of the hand. 'Help yourselves to whatever you wish. Be my guests.' Not wishing to offend our gracious host, we moved closer to the table and helped ourselves to some of the repast. The salmon, I seemed to remember, was good; the boiled ham even better. By my side Burlington and Jamiel continuing sipping wine and discussing business matters, their sombre murmurings only punctuated by those vigorous slaps to the back which Burlington, the quintessential man of action, loved to administer, and which Jamiel, the quintessential merchantman, always accepted with a scowling countenance. I watched them for a while with slowly diminishing interest; then I moved to the edge of the balcony and looked over into the square. About eight or nine hundred people had assembled around the gallows, with many more crowded on the rooftops of the surrounding buildings. Before leaving our residence, Jamiel had told me that we would be seeing a hanging and that I would profit ‘tremendously’ from the experience, but I still wasn’t sure what ‘hanging someone’ entailed. Certainly, judging from the reaction of the crowd down below, it had to be *something quite exciting*. Men laughed and tried to climb on each other’s shoulders. Native women sang *canciones* and waved their *mantones* above their heads. Redjackets — for once mixing with their Scorpion and Spanish neighbours — tossed their hats into the air and sang the coarse ballads that regulars love to sing:

I don’t want the Sergeant’s shilling,
I don’t want to be shot down;
I’m really much more willing
To make myself a killing,
Living off the pickings of the Ladies of the Town

At last, around two o’clock, the victim was led out onto the scaffold. Even at this late stage, I must admit, I had no idea of what was about to happen. In fact, I will say this much: even as the noose was being tightened around the victim’s neck, I found myself puzzled by it all, trying to wonder where all this d_____ silliness with the rope would eventually lead to. Indeed, it was only when the trap door was released and the hapless victim came to dangle from the end of the rope that I was struck by the reality of the situation, the dry-throated raspings of the dying man suddenly contrasting most shockingly with Burlington’s *sotto voce* remarks:

‘D___ it, Bestman! You were right! He’s not that much of a kicker, this one, is he now, old chap?’

Remembering all this now, some thirty-odd years later, left me feeling very confused. On the one hand, the memory unsettled me and made me recall the unspeakable horror of that grey autumnal afternoon when, right before my disbelieving young eyes, what had started out as a much-welcome journey in the company of my largely absent father suddenly metamorphosed into a scene of almost dantesque proportions. On the other, I was filled with a burning curiosity to walk down to the courthouse and see the murderer coming out of the building. I know, I know — 'tis most shameful to admit — but I just could not resist the general excitement in the air. Though public hangings are no longer allowed in this part of the world, people are still as fascinated with death as ever, dropping everything they are doing (just like they did this morning) to catch a fleeting sight of a murderer being led out of a court building. Perhaps it is because they are curious about witnessing something which in some ways presages the great unknown which is the moment of their own deaths. Or perhaps it is simply because death seems to stir up such contradictory passions within us. Consider my own time at Pentonville. While it is true that I never actually saw an execution during my term there — the cubicle that I occupied having had the misfortune (or good fortune, depending on how you may come to regard the matter) of looking out over Caledonian Road and not the hanging-yard — it is nonetheless equally true to maintain that I heard plenty of them from the inside of my cell and that I never, so help me God, enjoyed the experience. Moreover, I can safely say this much — there is nothing more blood-curdling than hearing men being dragged kicking and screaming to their deaths (only for everything to go eerily silent moments later). And yet I always listened to their cries, never covering my ears like I should have done, never turning away from the window till the last rasping croak had come to an end. What is the moral to be learned from all this? I think the answer is simple: death, whether we like it or not, captivates us all, it quickens the beating of our pulse and sanctifies our mundanity, adding a dark attraction to even the most commonplace of persons or events. It could be the doltish milkman's assistant who no one took any interest in until the day he stabbed his employer in the throat with a kitchen knife. The half-brained La Linean frutero who everyone dismissed as a drunken joke until the day he killed Lizzie Puertas with a butcher's cleaver. *Unknown one moment, infamous the next* — that is the cold baptism which death affords to all those who partake in its sanctifying mysteries. . . .

By the way, I almost forgot to say that when I finally got to the courthouse it was too late: the murderer Mendoza had already been spirited up to the Castle in a Black Maria.

**The nineteenth day of November, 1888**
It rained all day today. I sat beside the window most of the afternoon, hoping that the rain clouds would clear. I felt mightily dispirited.

**The twentieth day of November, 1888**
Again, more rain.

**The twenty-first day of November, 1888**
Someone must have died in our tenement block during the course of last night. The first indication that something was wrong came around two o'clock in the morning. I was cradled in Morpheus's arms, as the saying goes, when suddenly I was awakened by the sound of loud wailing. At first I thought that I was hearing the aftermath of yet another domestic quarrel, but as the minutes passed (and more and more voices joined the initial clamour) I had no doubts as to what had happened: someone must have passed away during the early hours of the morning. What else could have precipitated such loud and ever-increasing lamentations? Finally, at around eight o'clock, I heard the sound of a horse-driven vehicle pulling up outside the entrance to our building. Moving to the window, I was able to observe an open-backed carriage surrounded by a crowd of about twenty or thirty tenement dwellers.

Before long two burly fellows came out of our doorway carrying a small sack between them. From the form of the sack, as well as the ease with which it was carried, I was able to surmise that it must have contained the figure of a rather small person. A dead infant, most probably. This was confirmed a few minutes later when a young woman — short and dark-skinned and with her hair held in place by a cheap wooden *peineta* — lunged forwards towards the coffin and had to be restrained by a quietly weeping man by her side. '*No puede estar muerta*!' the woman cried. '*Mi chiquita no puede estar muerta*!'[1] As the carriage started to pull away, the assembled crowd erupted into applause and did not stop clapping until the vehicle was out of sight. I was a bit irritated at first by this collective show of emotion, but as the carriage disappeared down the street with the grieving parents trailing behind it I began to change my

---

[1] 'She can't be dead! My little one can't be dead!'

mind about what I was witnessing. During my years in Pentonville, I told myself, the demise of a fellow prisoner was something that neither the guards nor any of the inmates much bothered about. It was just a weekly irritation, an excuse for fumigating bed linen. Here, by contrast, the whole community rallies around those touched by bereavement with a very fierce and genuine sense of solidarity. Their clapping, it seems to me, is the symbol of this solidarity; it is their way of acknowledging and respecting their neighbour's pain. That cannot be such a bad thing, I suppose — even if it does feel a bit strange to someone brought up in the Anglican tradition.

**The twenty-second day of November, 1888**

Clear skies. Very light winds. Bought a *cuarteron* of artichokes from a street-seller on Cloister Ramp. Visited several establishments on Irish Town and nearby Parliament Lane, none of them proving favourable to my entreaties.

Things that I MUST unfailingly procure over the next few days:

1. Strong thread to mend my boots.
2. Firewood.
3. A cooking knife that can actually cut.
4. Some Calomel to mix with ordinary lard and then apply to the sores that have appeared on the left side of my neck.

**The twenty-third day of November, 1888**

I am not feeling well again. When I woke up this morning there was yet another encrustation of blood on my pillow, thicker and darker than the last time, the outline of which, it seemed to me, had been smeared across the cotton fabric in the form of two symmetrically-paired hearts. Also, I had very disturbing dreams all night, frightening and fantastickal sequences of images that are almost too obscene to be included in this journal. In the first dream, I found myself walking over to Casemates Square to witness the execution of an unknown criminal. When I got there it must have been about half past one and the square was already thronging with spectators. A sea mist had drifted in from behind the Waterport walls and hung like a gigantic wreath over the square, reducing the gallows, with its sinister combination of levers and pulleys and beams, to a ghostly Kraken rising out of the fog. Being unable, as I had done back at Burlington's, to occupy a position of panoramic vantage, I situated myself along the square's periphery and tried to raise myself up on my toes. In front of me there was a crowd of wild-eyed civvies, inebriated English soldiers and shifty-looking Campamento Spaniards, all of them shouting and swearing and singing and generally lapping up the festive spirit. Someone — I think it was a marine — shouted 'God save the Queen!' 'Yes,' a cheeky civilian voice immediately answered from somewhere in the crowd. 'And may we keep on hanging Spanish murderers in her name too, the damned Spanish b______!'

Somewhere at the back of my head, a voice kept on telling me that I had to be dreaming, that this was 1888 and no hangings had happened in the garrison for over twenty years — but at the same time I could not help being swept along by the atmosphere of contagious excitement circulating around me. Then, around two o'clock, a military-style drum roll sounded in the distance. *Tam-tara-ram-tam-tam, tam-tara-ram-tam-tam*! Raising myself up on my toes a second time, I see a tall man leading a manacled individual onto the scaffold. The manacled man is walking slowly, hesitantly; he has to be pushed forward by the man at his side. As I watch all this unfold, a most strange and awful fallacy suddenly seizes me. It occurs to me that the murderer looks just like my father! For a second this impression is so great that I actually convince myself that it is Jamiel standing there before the crowd, about to be executed for some unknown crime that he has committed in the past. It does not matter that my father has been dead for fifteen years or that the man who stands on the scaffold looks like my father did twenty-five years ago, thereby negating the possibility that it could be my actual biological father standing there being pushed around by the hangman. 'Father!' I cry as the murderer is ushered to the edge of the scaffold. 'It is I, Charles! Your only son! I've come back to see you! Let us embrace at least once before you die!' Obsessed with this idea, I begin to make my way through the cheering crowds, tearing bodies from my path, hoping against hope to reach the scaffold in time. Such is the state of emotional hysteria that I have whipped myself into, that even as I get closer to the scaffold I can still see Jamiel there before me. I can see him more clearly than ever now, no more than thirty or forty yards away, the same Jamiel that I used to know, with his receding grey hair and his swarthy Sephardic face.

'Father!' I shout once again, still trying to push my way through the crowds, ignoring the angry commands to go f___ myself which continue ringing around me. 'Do not abandon me like you abandoned me when I was in prison! Do not abandon your son when he most needs you!'

Soon I am halfway across the square and my heart is beating anxiously inside me. When I look up for a brief second, I can see that they are tightening the noose around Jamiel's neck. 'Oh no,' I silently whisper to myself at this point. 'Oh, no, no, no!' Knowing what is about to happen, I raise my arms and scream with all my might – but, alas, it is too late: a loud thwack suddenly echoes through the air and the crowd becomes silent, silent to the point where the lack of noise becomes a presence in itself – just like during that idolatrous moment in the Catholic Mass when the consecrated host is raised and the congregation plunges into the most awful state of reverential quiet. That instant something very strange happens: all my apprehensions suddenly come to an end. I feel myself floating, spinning, unable to concentrate on anything except the blood-thumping beat that still pulses through my veins. When I finally compose myself again, I turn around and, like in a dream where everything's eerily slowed down, I see everyone staring at the scaffold, their eyes riveted open, the words clogged up inside their open mouths. Then I shake my head and look in the same direction as them. There, no more than ten yards away, my father is dangling from the end of a rope, twitching frantically and most energetically, his tongue darkening, his eyeballs turned grotesquely inside out. . . .

In my second dream, the situation was reversed and this time I was a victim about to be executed at the gallows. I was standing before a braying crowd, with my hands cuffed behind my back and my arms held down by two officers of the law. Several yards away stood the executioner, a long-haired man dressed in a flowing black overcoat. He was bowing and waving theatrically to the crowd – somewhat, the fancy suddenly took me, like some kind of acrobatick circus performer.

'Charles William Bestman,' the executioner declaimed in a booming voice, 'you have been accused of betraying both your father and your family name, of failing to perpetuate the Bestman line and leading the life of a pitiful and *miscreantish* wretch. For these most base and ignoble crimes you have been sentenced to hang. Do you have anything to say before your sentence is carried out?'

At this point the executioner turned around and a feeling of cold confusion instantly swept through me. For even though the fellow had the hair and build of a man of twenty-five, his facial characteristics were just like those of my father. The sight immediately struck a chord of resentment within me.

'It was you who abandoned me all those years ago in prison,' I shouted, angrily struggling against the metal cuffs restraining my hands, 'you who cut me out of your will and who ignored me when I most needed you. How can you stand there and come up with such baseless accusations?'

'Did you hear what the ungrateful wretch is saying?' Jamiel, in his new guise as my executioner, swiftly said to the crowd. 'Can any of you comprehend such base ingratitude on the part of one so miserable and worthless? Is it possible that I could have progenerated such ungrateful issue, I ask you, my friends?'

He then turned around again and this time an even more fantastickal transformation had occurred – for even though it was still my father standing there, he had suddenly shrank in size and form, turning into an old man of around seventy or seventy-two, that is to say the age which Jamiel would have been had he been alive now.

'Why did you betray me, Charles?' this semi-cadaverous old man croaked in a pathetically thin voice. 'Why did you have to throw all my dreams away? I worked so hard to bring you up well, *hijo mio.* To help you achieve all that I could never achieve myself. Did you really have to spit into my face like you did? Did you really have to scorn and defile everything that was most sacred to me? Did you have to become the first MURDERER to bear our family name?'

I woke up shortly after that in what can only be described as a cold sweat. I was perspiring all over, my nightclothes clinging to my limbs and encasing me in a mire of my own creation. For a few seconds I remained panic-struck in bed, my sense of consciousness pivoted somewhere between the surrounding darkness and the memory of the dream that I had just been experiencing. Once I was able to determine that the blackness around me was part of my room and not the hell to which the hanging had consigned me, I got out of bed and began to pace frantically up and down the floor. I was nervous and anxious, still unsure of where I found myself. In my suitcase I had two bottles of gin that I had been given as a valedictory present by the London tannery where I worked for a few weeks before embarking on the *Zadane.* Though more than fifteen years had passed since alcohol had last touched my lips, I removed one of the bottles from where it lay half-hidden among old clothes and uncorked it. I then poured myself a glass, making sure that I filled it up to the brim. The gin tasted heavy and metallic, a distillation of the rudest, most unpleasant sort. Even so, I managed to quaff it down in one gulp, holding the glass stubbornly against my lips until every last drop was gone. I then put the bottle and glass on the table and walked over to the nailed-down window. It was raining outside, raining heavily. I watched the rain-drops slide down the cracked glass panes for some moments, quite fascinated by the way the rain water coalesced with the dirt encrusted in the cracks and then made its way down in streaks of rust-coloured brown. Then I returned to the table and poured myself a second glass of gin. It tasted just as bad as the first.

**The twenty-fourth day of November, 1888**

Was I right in coming back to Gibraltar, or should I have stayed in London? It is a question, I must admit, that has been gnawing away at my thoughts over the last few days. Even as I sit here this cold and rain-sodden afternoon next to my patio window, I cannot forget the day a few weeks ago when, suitcase in hand and with a clutch of half-forgotten memories in my head, I walked up the bridge-steps leading into the *S.S. Zadane*. Back then I was pretty much convinced that I was doing the right thing. Certainly, I had no doubts, no last-minute scruples of conscience. Gibraltar, for good or for worse, was my native soil, my *terra mater*, the only patch of God's earth that I could call home — even if everyone that I associated with the place had either passed away or disappeared to follow their own distant, offshore destinies. In this regard, I suppose, my feelings were very unlike the ones I had experienced when I made the journey in reverse, that is to say from Gibraltar to England, as a nervous and insecure thirteen-year-old. Then I was filled with a very different sense of certainty — the certainty that I was being uprooted from my homeland *completely against my will.*

Let me explain what I mean. From the age of seven, I had been told that at sixteen I would be sent to England to continue my education there. This proposition had been more or less drummed into me; it had been turned into one of those immutable and self-evident realities which childhood, with its unquestioning nature, cannot possibly hope to interrogate. At the age of sixteen, I would leave my masters and proceed to public school in England, where, so Jamiel never stopped reminding me, I would be transformed into a fine and upright gentleman. Why then did I find myself clutching the handrails on the fore-deck of the *S.S. Lothian* that grey, Levanter-shrouded day in 1862 at the tender age of *thirteen and a few months*?

It is a difficult question to answer. Before I can unravel it fully, I have to first describe the demographical and geographical layout of our residential quarters on Governor's Street. Situated in one of Gibraltar's up and coming localities, our building had formerly belonged to one of the Rock's richest landlords — an old Genoese codger by the name of Reginald Busifacio who, in keeping with the materialistic spirit of the age, had built the edifice with the idea of fitting as many people as possible within its walls. Essentially, the property could be said to have bordered on three fronts: Governor's

Street, towards the front; the dwellings of Mr. Brown and Mr. Lionel, two gentlemen of property and members of the Exchange, on each side; and a large backyard towards the rear which, though hemmed in by a cordon of buildings and very much open to the public view, belonged exclusively to us and contained the small out-house where most of our domesticks lived. Being a former hostel dwelling, our property had only two natural points of entry — the first, a grandly columned and porticoed entrance which my father had built to replace the original cramped doorway which led in from Governor's Street; the second, a small, double-bolted door which opened out into the already mentioned backyard. To this original scheme my father soon added a third entrance, or rather covered walkway of sorts, which had its point of access on Colonial Hospital Hill (the street parallel to and immediately behind Governor's Street) and led directly into the backyard out-house — thus diverting the servants away from the family entrance. As to the house itself, it had three floors — or rather, if we are going to be pedantic about it, two floors and a partly-submerged cellar. On the top floor there were the family living quarters: four sleeping rooms, two guest rooms, two bathrooms, the dining room, a parlour room and my father's permanently locked study. The floor immediately below (which, being on the same level as Governor's Street outside, could be designated the ground floor) housed what were referred to as 'the utility rooms' — namely, the kitchen, the washing and ironing rooms, the pantry, two bathrooms, two storage rooms and an additional two sleeping rooms for guests of a lower order. Finally, there was what was termed the lower ground floor, as the old subterranean cellar was known. Of all the floors this was by far the least habitable — principally because it contained no natural light other than that which came streaming through the three narrow, in-swinging windows, each of them shaped like horizontal arrow-slits and placed near the ceiling, which gave you an ankle-view, as it were, of the yard outside. Here my father kept all the assorted bits and bobs associated with his business — i.e., old ledger books, storage boxes, inkpots, unused keys, discarded promotional signs, weighing scales and other etceteras. The two higher floors were connected by means of a magnificently bannistered staircase which my father had modelled on a stairway he had seen at his friend Burlington's. The lower ground floor, by contrast, could only be accessed through a locked wooden door located near the main entrance. As I was discouraged from wandering through the utility floor and totally forbidden from entering the cellar, my movements were *in theory* limited to my room on the first floor and the patio attached to our house. Of these two traversable areas, I much preferred the latter, the length and breadth of which I knew as well as the markings on my Irish-Gibraltarian palm. I would make my way down to this little haven of mine whenever I had any spare time — in between lessons, whenever one of my masters was running late, just before retiring to sleep every evening — in short, whenever I got a chance to get away from my room on the first floor. As for the patio itself, there is not much that I can say here about it — other than that it looked just like any other patio in the vicinity. Clothes lines stretched from one end to the other, their sagging hempen cords burdened not only with the threadbare garments belonging to our in-house domesticks, but also the finer, more expensive Bestman apparel. From the petite size of some of these first garments, I knew that there must have been one or two children living in the servants' out-house (although I never did observe or even hear any of them during the entirety of my time in the patio). Also, there was an abandoned well squeezed into a corner of the yard — a ramshackle old thing composed of loose bricks and a half-corroded grating which had been there since God-knows-when. As this well could not be emptied or blocked off, my father tried to stop it from becoming a breeding ground for musquitoes by filling it with fresh water eels — there being nothing more appetising to those detestable sea snakes, as every Rock Scorpion will tell you, than the larvae of the common musquitoe.

Our patio, then, was no different from any other Gibraltarian patio — inasmuch as it reeked of bleach, it resounded with the swish of wind-dried clothes, and it was surrounded by a cordon of tottering, badly-maintained buildings. And yet, as I've already said, I loved that patio dearly. Inside that quadrant I could fence with the mace-wielding giants dangling from the clotheslines; I could throw stones at the slithering sea serpents that threatened to escape the well and attack the Bestman residence; I could run around with no particular direction, flapping my arms as if I were a kestrel or an eagle soaring high above the warehouses and crooked tenements of our ramshackle colonial town.

What else can I tell you about that thrice-blessed piece of land? That patio was my private sanctuary, my personal refuge, the only place within the Bestman residence where I could forget about life's burdens and constraints — even if in the end, rather paradoxically, it was here, in this very same patio, that began the long and fateful sequence of events that took me all the way to the foredeck of the *S.S. Lothian*. . . .

It all started with a game. A simple and enjoyable little game. At the time I never really had a name for it — I simply referred to it as 'the game' — but for the sake of clarity I will now call it the 'lava game'. Like the best sort of children's games, the lava game had very few rules to it. The first thing you had to do was to pretend that the patio was a lake of molten lava. Once you did this, you had to choose a 'safe haven' somewhere on the patio's perimeter. This safe haven was the point that you had to reach to attain ultimate victory, the lava game's equivalent to square 100 in a game of snakes and ladders. What made the lava game unique was that you had to make your way to the safe haven *without letting your feet touch the ground/lake of lava*. The only way you could do this, of course, was by going around the perimeter of the yard holding on to whatever you could find — pipes, window ledges, projecting bits of brickwork, iron clothes hooks, essentially anything that could stop you from sliding down to the ground. Also, just to make things that little bit more interesting, the safe haven could be changed as and when you saw fit. For example, sometimes it was the old well on the other side of the patio. Other times it was a first-floor window farther down the side of the house. On yet another occasion it might have been an old *tina*[1] which one of the maids had left near the entrance to the servants' out-house. The main thing, in each and every case, was to reach the safe haven without touching any of that horribly 'hot and scalding lava'. . . .

Throughout the summer of '62 I played the 'lava game' many times. I played it just after lunchtime and just before dinnertime, whenever

[1] A large metal tub.

one of my masters would fail to turn up for a lesson, on Sunday mornings after coming back from the English Cathedral with my Spanish Catholic nannies. I played it obsessively and yet, if I am to be honest, without much hope of ever triumphing, knowing that most of the time a combination of gravity and tired muscles would send me sliding all the way down into the abyss.

Then one day something altogether unexpected happened. While clinging to one of the external waterpipes, my boot accidentally touched one of the cellar windows and the latter swung open of its own accord! Intrigued, I climbed down from the pipe. Then I lowered myself on to my knees. Within seconds I realised that there was something wrong with the window's lock. Smiling at the thought, I reached out a hand and, after laying it tentatively against the glass, pushed the window in a little bit farther. A ten- or twelve-inch gap immediately opened. Through it I could see several piles of boxes, an ageing grandfather clock, and one or two cobwebbed printing presses. 'Good gracious Lord,' I found myself imitating my mother's Irish phraseology, quite bowled over by the limitless array of possibilities opening before me. 'What is *this*?'

That moment a daring thought entered my head. A most bold and audacious idea. *What if I squeezed my way through the window into the cellar? What if I threw caution to the wind and broke my way into the most forbidden place in the entire Bestman residence*? Although the window was no taller than two handspans, I was pretty sure — nay, I was thoroughly convinced! — that I could pull off the feat. All I had to do was lie on my stomach and then wriggle my way in sidewise. An easy enough operation, to be sure. From my kneeling position, I could see that there were some large cardboard boxes situated just a foot or two under the window — a perfect landing place, if ever there was one. Growing increasingly bold, I looked around to check if there was anyone espying my movements. No, not a soul in sight! Cheered by the realisation, I took a deep breath, laid down parallel to the window and began to wriggle my way in. . . .

I will not bore you excessively with what I found inside the cellar. Suffice to say that it was full of all the assorted paraphernalia that you would have associated with a flourishing business like my father's, as well as other things besides — boxes stuffed with old receipts, ten or twelve broken picture frames, a set of coalman's gloves, a brass sextant, a glass egg-timer, a large wooden mallet, a book called *Entomology for beginners*, three unused mouse-traps, an unframed copperplate engraving entitled 'Map and Prospect of the city of Gibraltar', an old-fashioned brass telescope that (upon closer inspection) proved to be missing one of its principal lenses, three or four boxes of old ledger books, a large chest full of rubber stamps, a set of ceramic thimbles commemorating the Great Exhibition of '58, two cobwebbed glass decanters, a pair of moth-eaten curtains, two rusted old safes, around seven or eight mildewed armchair cushions, a large colour poster advertising '*Bestman Numero Cinco, el sabor mas puro*' — the kind of junk, in other words, that would have left most rationalising beings full of indifference, but which, to a repressed and closeted child, represented no more and no less than an *Aladdin's cave of delights.*

**The twenty-fifth day of November, 1888**

It is about seven o'clock in the morning. I woke up approximately forty minutes ago with my face buried into my journal and a constellation of blood drops splattered across its ruled pages. For a while I was not sure where I found myself or what exactly I was doing — my head and arms having been drained of all feeling because of the extreme ungainliness of my sleeping posture. Soon, however, the rousing wind of consciousness blew over me and I realised that I must have fallen asleep while writing my journal. At this point I got up from my chair and made some tea. I then ate some hard malt biscuits. Now, having drunk my tea and finished my biscuits, I find myself sitting at my table again, ready to continue my story from where I left off last night. So, without further ado, as they say. . . .

After my fortuitous discovery of the faulty window, I began to secrete myself in the cellar whenever I got a chance. I was, of course, very careful when entering my new-found domain — always making sure that there was no one in sight whenever I made my descent and, likewise, arranging the window in such a way that it would always look closed from the outside. However, once inside the cellar all sense of caution came to an end and I was able to indulge in the most fantastickal childish stratagems. One day, for example, I would be a soldier in a Crimean trench, scuttling behind the boxes to avoid enemy fire. The next day I would be a rough and rugged explorer, clambering up the broken safes and the smashed-up chandeliers to reach the pinnacle of some as yet unconquered peak. A few days later I would become an Ottoman pasha, indolently reclining on my divan while a troop of eunuchs and semi-naked concubines stood to attention behind a haze of hashish smoke. . . .

Several happy weeks passed in this way. Then one day, towards the end of that same month, *all hell broke loose* — that is to say, I made the discovery which changed the whole course of my life. It all started one Friday morning — just after I had squeezed my way through the cellar window. If I remember correctly, I was sitting behind some boxes pretending to be an incarcerated musketeer. Suddenly I heard a scuttling sound from the other side of the cellar. At first I thought that it was a mouse or a rat — our residence, like most buildings in the vicinity of the colonial hospital, having a tendency to suffer from periodic infestations of vermin. However, when I heard the sound again moments later, I was filled with the instinctive certainty that it was too 'large' and 'substantial' a noise to have been made by a small-bodied creature. I therefore stood up and, just like the hero that I had been imagining myself to be, slowly made my way around the pile of boxes to where the sound was coming from.

What happened next, I daresay, almost brought my heart to a standstill. There, no more than several yards away, I was able to discern what looked like a human form. 'Sweet Mother of God,' I then thought, suddenly remembering all those tales of ghosts and hobgoblins which Mr. Fenton Paris, my master of grammatical composition, took great delight in reciting to me. 'The place must surely be haunted!' That moment I began to walk backwards and continued to do so until I crashed into some boxes and almost fell over. Then I heard a whimper. Yes, no doubt about it: it was a soft and high-pitched whimper, just like that made by a girl. Emboldened by this realisation, I got up from where I lay half-crouched and was able to confirm for myself that, yes, it was a girl and that she had retracted herself into a frightened bundle in a corner. The sight emboldened me even further.

'Who . . . who are you?' I said.

'*Lo siento, señorito,*' the girl mumbled rapidly through her tears in a soft voice which left me most affected. '*No me delates. No me delates. No vendre aquí nunca mas.*'[1]

For a few seconds I looked at her without saying a word. Who was this girl and what was she doing crouched in a corner of our cellar? The most logical explanation, it goes without saying, was that I must have been in the presence of a ghost. And yet something – I am not sure whether it was her high-pitched sobs or the look of woeful desperation in her eyes – convinced me that I was not standing before any mere ectoplasmic apparition.

'*Yo no malo,*' I finally said in the broken 'pidgin' Spanish which I had somehow managed to pick up from the servants' clandestine chatterings. '*Yo bueno.*'[2]

As ridiculous as I felt speaking in a language that I could barely comprehend, my words must have done the trick, seeing that the girl slowly began to calm down. She also began to uncurl herself, as it were, from her original position, removing her hands from her knees and sitting up against the wall behind her. Once she succeeded in this endeavour, I was able to perceive that she was slightly younger than me. About eleven or twelve years of age, judging from her petite form and her slender wrists. Her face, I noticed, was covered with innumerable streaks of dirt – just like the children of *carboneros* and other individuals of the lower sort. Nervously, I sat down beside her. By means of hand signs and the few Castilian words at my disposal, I was able to find out that her name was Lorena and that

---

[1] 'I'm sorry, little master. Don't tell on me. Please don't tell on me. I'll never come down here again.'

[2] 'Me no bad. Me good.'

she was the daughter of the widow Lozano (otherwise known as Lawrence), one of the washerwomen working for my father. She had been coming to the cellar for the last few weeks, she explained, having one day seen me clambering through the cellar window from the servants' out-house. She made this clear by pointing to her eye and then pointing at me, after which she made a diving gesture with her hands which I assumed to represent me going through the window. At this point I smiled and nodded. As there were still unshed tears glimmering in her eyes, I took out a piece of chocolate from my pocket and broke it in two, giving her the largest half. She looked at the chocolate for a few moments with a quizzical expression and then, seeing me put my own piece into my mouth, rapidly bit into it. A smile immediately lit up her features. 'It's called chocolate,' I said, smiling as the candy melted inside my own mouth. 'Cho-co-late.' 'Cho-co-lieht,' she repeated in that soft and fluty voice of hers. 'Yes,' I said. 'Chocolate. It's nice, isn't it? *Very bueno.*'

I brought out some more chocolate from my pocket and made a gesture indicating that she could have it. She took it without saying anything and put it in her mouth, smiling as she did so. To amuse her, I unbuttoned my waistcoat and brought out the gold pocket watch which my father had gifted me on my tenth birthday, dangling it from its chain like a pendulum. '*Que es eso?*' she asked with an enquiring frown. '*Es un* watch,' I gently replied. '*Como se dice?. . . Cosa* to find out the time. You know: *tick-tock-tick-tock-tick-tock.*'

We must have carried on exchanging ideas in this semi-intelligible manner for half an hour, maybe forty minutes. At the back of my mind I kept on thinking what my father would have said had he known that I was conversing with a washerwoman's daughter and within the limits of his own house to boot! Surely, I thought, he would have gone utterly mad with rage, descending into one of those episodic bouts of fury which not even my mother, with her constantly scornful and sarcastic rebuttals, would have dared to interrupt. Not that I really cared about what Jamiel thought just then. If truth be told, all that I could concentrate on was the girl Lorena and how gratifying it was to be sitting there in the darkness with her. That — and perhaps the stiltedness of my self-learnt Spanish, which at the time rose like an impenetrable barrier between us! How much easier, after all, things would have been had I been able to speak proper Spanish and not this bastardised 'monosyllabised' version of the language that I had picked up from the domesticks' involuntary nattering! Call me inquisitive if you wish, but there were just so many questions that I wanted to ask her: — what she thought of my family, where she came from, how she spent her days, how it was that I had never seen her before, what she had been doing in the cellar before we met that morning. Bringing out my pocket watch once again, I checked the time: it was already ten to eleven — just a few minutes, in other words, before Mr. Rees-Clinton was due to make his regular Friday morning appearance. That moment I came to a sudden decision: I would have to meet Lorena again. I simply had no option.

'You . . . *mañana* . . . here . . . *aquí*,' I said at last, nervously pointing to the floor space between us.

'*Perdoname, señorito*,' Lorena whispered, '— *pero no le entiendo*.' [1]

'You . . . *mañana* . . . *aquí*,' I again repeated, this time with an edge of desperation. 'Please come. I would like to see you again. *Aquí, por favor. Tu ven.* Come here again. I need to see you.'

'*Yo mañana aquí? Quieres que nos encontremos de nuevo aquí?*' [2]

'Yes, yes — *tu y yo*. Me and you. Tomorrow. *Aquí.* We meet again here. Same time. *Mismo tiempo que hoy. Entendido*? You understand?'

'*Si, señorito*,' she said, nodding. '*Le he entendido. Estaré aquí mañana si vos lo desea*.' [3]

---

[1] 'I'm sorry, little master, but I don't understand.'

[2] 'Me here tomorrow? You want us to meet here again tomorrow?'

[3] 'Yes, little master. I have understood. I will be here tomorrow.'

I could write at this point that things flowed very smoothly after this first meeting between us, but that would be a gross untruth: during the next twenty-four hours I found myself labouring under a most wearing state of nervous expectation, hardly able to sleep for sheer excitement. Like the eternal pessimist that I have always been, I thought that Lorena would not come to the cellar again, that she would misunderstand my instructions, that she would turn up at ten or earlier during the morning (when I would have been busy in the schoolroom) and not at eleven like I had asked her to. Again and again I thought the same thing: *how will she know at what time to come when all she speaks is Spanish and does not even know what a pocket watch is? Am I not being foolish in expecting so much from a mere servant's daughter*? In the end, however, all these idle apprehensions came to naught. Having wriggled my way through the unlocked window just before eleven, I found her sitting in a corner, looking as feeble and malnourished as a day earlier — although this time with her cheeks scrubbed clean and her hair collected in a tidy schoolmiss's bun. '*Buenos dias, señorito*,' she immediately said, extending towards me a vegetable that looked like a fat swollen pear. '*Se le apetece a usted la mitad de una chirimoya?*'[1]

After this first rendezvous, I began to see Lorena almost every day. Getting down to the cellar was never usually a problem, but finding a time when both of us were free was always a vexing matter — Lorena being occupied with the constant tasks that she had to do for her mother, and I, as ever, continually being importuned by my masters and their ridiculous lessons. And yet, despite all these assorted obstacles, we managed to spend twenty, perhaps thirty daily minutes together. We also began to get on famously well with each other. In spite of the linguistic barriers that had originally existed between us, our communication was improving by the day — Lorena slowly augmenting my limited Spanish vocabulary with different words and phrases, whereas I in turn tried my best to acquaint her with a few basic English expressions. From Lorena, too, I learned many things that served to open my eyes, as it were, against my father and his tyrannous ways. Among other things, for

[1] 'Good morning, little master. Would you like half of a custard apple?'

instance, I learned that he paid measly wages and that he treated everyone with extreme contempt; that everyone in the household feared him and knew him by the nickname of '*el hebreo feo*' ('the ugly Jew'); that he kept many *queridas* or mistresses in different quarters of town and that he sometimes entertained them within the set of rooms he had prepared for himself within the Bestman manufactory. Whether these stories were true or not, it is hard to say. Probably, thinking about it now, most of them were no more than empty fabrications, the type of mean-spirited, slanderous gossip put out by discontented workers who resent their masters' affluence. Still, at the time I had little trouble believing them all. *My father – a ruthless and tyrannical exploiter of the masses*? What could be easier to swallow than that?

Now, before I continue with my narrative, I must make one thing clear. From what I have written so far, one might perhaps get the impression that I began to see Lorena as something of a sweetheart, what penny novelists, in their attempt to divest the world of its humdrum mundanity, describe as a 'love interest' – but I am sorry to say that I never regarded her in that particular light. For a start, I have never been one to attach much import to womanly charms. Secondly, I do not think that Lorena herself, being no more than a child, had any idea about romantic love. In fact, as disappointing as it may sound to the reader of this diary, the simple truth was that Lorena was just a friend to me, someone whom I could talk to without fear of being judged, and who, in turn, chose to unburden herself before me without any misgivings of her own. All the same, I am prepared to admit, we must have looked a strange and most unlikely pair: the washerwoman's daughter and the young *señorito,* sitting together in the mouldy darkness and exchanging anecdotes about their respective lives.

Some four or five weeks passed and I was still meeting Lorena in secret at the cellar. If anyone would have observed me closely during this time, they would have surely noticed a certain *joie de vivre* in me, a most unusual sense of vitality which had not been there just a few months ago. But, of course, within the walls of the Bestman residence, no one noticed a thing. I was, in other words, allowed to continue leading my double life without impediments of any kind — the only disruptions to my routine, if you could describe them as such, being the one or two reports of unusual classroom lethargy which my good masters felt compelled to pass on to a slightly disappointed Jamiel.

Under these circumstances, it was not long before I became overconfident. That, I am afraid, is what often happens when you are caught in the grip of worldly happiness. You are so detached from life's worries that you actually forget that happiness, like life itself, is no more than a fleeting, temporary condition, a sliver of light in the long and often interlinked carousel of sorrows which lead from the cradle to the grave. In my particular case the bubble of happiness ruptured late one afternoon, as I was making my way down into the cellar. Unbeknown to me at the time, one of our servants was standing on the other side of the yard. She had been coming out of the out-house with a bundle of clothes that needed airing and had caught me, as they say, *in flagrante delicto* — with my legs already entering the window and the rest of my body about to follow.

What happened next, alas, is easy to imagine. Succumbing to that disgusting curiosity which possesses domesticks when faced with their masters' peccadilloes, the maidservant quickly crossed the patio and peered through the cellar window. Through the scratched and dusty panes she was able to perceive Lorena and myself, both of us sitting in languid repose while engaged in one of our curious 'translingual' conversations. Anger, shock, bemusement, jealousy that it was the widow Lawrence's daughter and not her own who was consorting with the young *señorito* in this way — it is difficult to know what feelings possessed this spiteful woman as she stood there contemplating the already mildewing fruit of our illicit friendship. All that is certain is that the domestick in question, a La Linean dame by the name of Richards (I cannot remember her original Spanish name right now), immediately ran into the residence and reported the matter to Brown, the mistress of the house, who in turn reported it to Bartholomew, the house steward, who in turn brought it to my father's attention later that same evening.

It did not take long before things took a turn for the worse. Early next morning, when I tried to slip into the cellar, I discovered that the window could not be pushed in like it used to. 'This is strange,' I thought. Had Lorena accidentally pushed something against the window when climbing through it earlier? Was she presently sitting somewhere in the cellar without realising that she had locked me out? If so, there was little I could do except wait until she resolved to leave the cellar. Shaking my head in disappointment, I lifted myself from the ground and decided to return to my room.

But that was only the beginning of my troubles. Later that evening I was told to present myself before my father in his study. When I arrived there just after eight, I found Jamiel standing before the fireplace with his back turned to me, his gnarled, podgy hands clasped together upon his overcoat.

'You, sir,' Jamiel said solemnly, still facing the fireplace, 'you, sir, are a rascal, you are.'

'What do you mean, father?' I asked as innocently as possible.

Jamiel immediately turned around and threatened me with a clenched fist. 'You, sir, are a rascal, I say! A very big rascal, what is more!'

I looked at Jamiel as he stood there like some portly, overfed pugilist and did not know whether to laugh or cry. In all the years of my youth, let me explain, my father had never hit me or so much as raised a hand at me. His preferred form of punishment, whether he had been aware of it or not — or should I say, *whether I deserved to be punished or not* — had always been silence, indifference, that cruel, last-minute turning-away of the eyes at the moment when you most needed solicitous reassurance. Taking all this into consideration, his current reaction scared me; it filled me with the horrible certainty that he was about to physically assault my person. And yet at the same, I must confess, I felt a secret contentment through it all, a kind of misplaced feeling of pride — knowing that such a blustery reaction was happening on my account, that I, as it were, was the sole reason for Jamiel's agitated state of vexation. I felt, in other words, *as if he were finally taking me seriously.*

'I still do not understand, sir.'

Jamiel glowered even more fiercely in my direction. 'You, sir, have been betraying my . . . my . . . my reputation with a . . . a . . . a *lavandera* . . . a washerwoman's daughter . . . a most base and most . . . most . . . *como lo digo?* . . . *bajuna* . . . of peoples. . . . You deny this, Master Bestman? You have the face to deny? Tell me, have you the little shame to maintain that this is not the case?'

'I do not understand you, sir.'

'Do not play *el inocente* with me, Master Bestman. You know perfectly well that I am talking about *the girl.* The Lawrence girl. You have been having a romantic affair with her behind our backs for many weeks.'

'A romantic affair?' I asked incredulously.

'Yes, Master Bestman. An affair. A romantic affair. Do not deny it now. I already have in my possession several handwritten depositions, signed by four different members of the Bestman household and translated by myself, in which it is stated, in plain and simple terms, how you entered the cellar in the company of the Lawrence girl on a number of occasions between the second and the fifteenth of this month and how, whilst there, you showered her with different declarations of love and romantic affection. . . . Do not pretend to look so shocked, sir,' he said, bringing out a small bundle of papers from his pocket and simultaneously affixing his reading glasses. 'It is all here written in black upon white. "I, Richards, charwoman under the employ of Mr. John Charles Bestman, solemnly swear how between the second and fifteenth of this month I did espy the young Master Bestman several times enter the cellar of the Bestman mansion in the company of the Lawrence girl. I also do solemnly swear that, from where I stood crouched next to the cellar window, I did hear Master Bestman in the pursuance of fancy-worded lovemaking, calling the Lawrence girl 'my most precious darling' and 'my most precious sweet' and promising how they would get married one day in spite of his parents and all those other ignorant fools upstairs, etc., etc. I did not bring this matter to Mr. Bestman's attention before for fear of provoking his ire, but, after seeing the free and most disgusting display of intimacy this morning between the *señorito* and that *malnacida* by the name of Lorena Lozano, I felt that I had no option but to come and disclose what I knew to be true. Signed. Richards the charwoman." What say you to all that, sir?'

'It's just lies, father!'

'Are they?' he said, bringing out even more papers from his coat pocket. 'What about these, then? Three more depositions signed by Sanders, Rodgers and Felicity, each of them claiming exactly the same thing?. . . Let me read one or two sentences from them for your benefit. . . . "I swear most solemnly that this morning the maid Richards called me to the patio, where she showed me, through one of the cellar windows, Master Bestman with his arm around the Lawrence girl in an attitude of great intimacy." Or how about this one: "To my surprise it became evident that Richards was right: Master Charles and the girl were embracing in a way that could only be described as wantonly amorous." Or how about this final one: "It was very dark inside the cellar, but I clearly saw Master Charles and the girl kiss and engage in other acts of lovemaking that common Catholic decency forbids me from describing."

'But I . . . I . . . I don't understand.'

'It is I that don't understand you, Charles,' Jamiel said gravely, turning once again towards the fireplace. 'If you would have come to me several weeks ago and told me that you had suddenly awakened to the charms of the female form, I would have made certain "arrangements" so that all these . . . these . . . *como lo digo?* . . . bodily energies of yours could have been voided discreetly and with the minimum of fuss. But *this*,' he said, turning around again and thrusting the papers angrily in my face, '*this* . . . this sullying of our family name and honour under my own roof . . . this ridiculous exchange of marriage vows in the most disgusting and most conspiratorial secrecy — this is something that I will never forgive as long as I live. *John Charles Bestman's son falling for the lies of a washerwoman's daughter*! And within his father's own house too! My God, I should have had those scheming Spanish *putillas* stripped and horse-whipped for their impudence instead of just dismissing them and sending them back to the Lines!'

Hearing this last piece of news, of course, pained me tremendously; it was, if I may indulge in a metaphorical fancy, almost like a dagger had been thrust in and out of my belly, taking with it all the happiness that had once resided in there. And yet, mark this, I did not weep. I could not bring myself to weep, you see — not with my father standing like a demented gargoyle beside me. Later, of course, when our interview ended and I got back to my room, it was another story altogether: the tears just could not stop rolling down my cheeks. 'Why did that b_____ maid betray us?' I kept asking myself between sobs. 'And why did all the others have to spread such vile calumnies about Lorena and myself?' I just couldn't understand what had possessed those d_____ women. Could it be because they begrudged that it was the widow Lawrence's daughter and not one of their own who had befriended me? Was it all just a conspiracy to get rid of Lorena and her mother? Persuading myself that some domestick skulduggery must have taken place, I dried my tears and calmed down. Then I did something that I had never done in all my life: I got one of the maids to send for my father. When Jamiel walked into the room some twenty minutes later, my calmness quickly evaporated and I found myself surrendering to that same wave of emotion that had previously engulfed me. With tears streaming freely down my cheeks, I told him that his depositions were a bunch of lies, that no act of lovemaking had ever passed between Lorena and I, that because of this, because of the undoubted Platonic purity of our friendship, he was honour-bound to rescue her and the good Lawrence from wherever they presently lay wallowing in their own homeless filth. . . .

It was all a dreadful mistake, of course. Not only did Jamiel fail to entertain my emotive entreaty, but he also looked at me with a cold and dispassionate eye throughout, unable to believe that his son, his own son, *blood of his blood and stock of his own stock*, as he often used to declaim, could have surrendered to such an unmanly outpouring of emotion over a mere *lavandera*'s daughter. Finally, he spoke the words that he had been dying all along to say:

'What a pathetic, snivelling *desgraciado* you are, Charles. How any son of mine could behave in this way I'll never know!'

Jamiel left shortly afterwards and I crawled back into bed. Over the next few days I stayed put in my room, hating myself for what had happened and trying my d______ hardest to get Jamiel to recall Lorena and her mother back from the Lines. I utilised all the tricks that my sad and lonely childhood had taught me could reverse parental neglect – refusing to eat, affecting to be ill, succumbing to 'dizzy spells' – but it was all to no avail: Jamiel just would not budge.

Then came the *coup de grâce.* One night, while I lay in bed in a disorientated and self-pitying state, Jamiel burst unannounced into my chamber and, catching me sobbing into my pillow, dragged me up to my feet. Presently he shook his head and told me to be *more like a man.* When I sobbingly told him that I could not help it, he shook his head again and declared that he had never felt as ashamed of his own son as he felt at the moment. He then turned his back on me. A long and tense silence followed. Finally, just as I thought that things could not possibly become any more unbearable between us, he coughed out loud and said that, after having weighed the *pros* and *cons* of the situation for the last few days, and seeing that time had not succeeded in knocking all these ridiculous romantic obsessions out of my head, I had left him with no option: *he would be sending me to England now and not in three years' time like he had originally intended.*

'It will be for the best, son, believe me,' Jamiel said, straightening his shirt collars in front of my bedroom window. 'You cannot carry on living here while you keep on thinking so much about a washerwoman's daughter.'

I could only look at him in astounded silence.

'I have already spoken to my *compadre* Burlington about it,' Jamiel continued, still standing with his back towards me. 'He says there is a capital school near London which is known for its efforts with *adolescentes mal-ajustados* such as yourself and which, he assures me, ranks among the finest schools *en la Inglaterra.* St Mary's College, I think 'tis called. Saint Mary's College in Winchester or something of the sort. I think one of old Burlie's nephews went there and received a splendid education. I have already made arrangements, through my friend Mr. Portsmouth of the London Chamber of Commerce, to have you admitted there forthwith.'

I will not lie: listening to Jamiel relate all this was like hearing something in a dream. From where I stood in the middle of the room, I could only gaze upon his shadowed form as one regards a daguerreotype or the flickerings of a magic lantern — that is to say, as something hovering between the corporeal and the illusional. *Could all this truly be happening? Was I really hearing what I was hearing?* If anyone would have told me just a few months back that I would soon be England-bound, I would have been almost delirious with joy, unable to believe that I was finally leaving behind the prisonhouse of the senses which for me had been the Bestman mansion. Yet now, having just discovered that my long-cherished dream of escape was about to finally come true, I felt thwarted and frustrated, pained beyond measure. . . . What else can I say about what happened that fateful night? I do not think that I have ever cried as much as I did in that cold and ill-lit bedchamber. Until that moment, you see, I had somehow clung to the hope that I would see my friend Lorena again. It was an infantile and somewhat illogical hope, I will grant you that much, but it was also a hope sustained by geographical proximity. Lorena was presently domiciling in the Lines and I in Gibraltar, and, while a mere league or two lay betwixt us in this way, there was always the possibility that we might one day meet again. Now, alas, all that was gone: I would be sent to England and I would never see my Lorena again. Saddened by the thought, I remembered my friend's smile and her gentle ways, her coal-black hair and the streaks of working-class dirt which sometimes besmirched her cheeks. I remembered all these things and then, like an old man reflecting upon his long-lost youth, found myself lamenting their loss, knowing that she was now *as good as dead to me. . . .*

That does not mean that I ever forgot poor Lorena or her ways. For the next five and twenty years I thought of her — at random moments, it is true, but always loyally, always devotedly, her memory resurfacing during those times when I most needed spiritual reassurance. I thought of her when I boarded the *S.S. Lothian* a few weeks later, when I found myself becoming the butt of the English schoolchildren's jokes, when I paid the ultimate price for my father's demented anglophilia. Even now, sitting here with an almost empty pot of ink beside me, I find myself thinking about you, my precious and long-lost friend, trying to work out what happened after Jamiel had so callously got rid of you, wondering if you and your mother ever managed to escape the poverty trap which, as sure as a hangman's noose, awaited you both outside the walls of the Bestman residence. Maybe, I tell myself, just maybe, you are out there somewhere, living in some squalid, upper town abode just like mine. Maybe our social circumstances have once again been equalised — the *señorito* and the washerwoman's daughter brought down to the same rung of life's ladder a second time . . . just like during those wonderful few weeks inside the Bestman cellar. Or maybe you expired many years ago, succumbing to one of the numerous diseases that would have surely lain in wait for a young girl dependent on a widowed and unemployed mother. Yes, that sounds more likely, I am sorry to say. *Dead and buried in some nameless, unmarked grave* — that is where you probably are now.

**The twenty-sixth day of November, 1888**

I woke up at two o'clock in the afternoon today feeling very tired and enervated. I was not really surprised by this, seeing that I spent most of yesterday writing this journal. After breakfasting on some bread and eggs, I quickly attired myself and made my way into town. This time I did not go to Main Street, but, acting on a rumour I had heard some days ago, proceeded instead to the port master's office at Ragged Staff, where, so promised the same rumour, several vacancies were up for grabs after three Mahometan boatmen had quit in protest at one of their own being horse-whipped by an over-eager English quartermaster. The hiring captain, a small, gnarled Englishman by the rather un-English name of Mick O'Flynn, was a hard-bitten old boy, about fifty years of age and six foot three in height. Something about his manner made me surmise that I was in the presence of an ex-convict. I know that this may be slightly hard to understand for those who know nothing of the incarcerated life, but there is something about ex-convicts, somehow recognisable to other ex-convicts, that separates them and distinguishes them from ordinary folk. It is almost like what the Rock-men say about being able to sniff out a Spaniard at twenty paces. Although superficially there is little to distinguish one conglomerate from the other (at least to the unpractised English eye), the Scorpion will tell you that there is a certain *je ne sais quoi*, an indefinable tangle of movements, gestures and attitudes, which enfolds the Spaniard and differentiates him from a son of Gibraltar. It was more or less the same with this fellow O'Flynn — there was something about him which reminded me of the 'magsmen', 'skittle-sharps', 'peter-claimers' and other types of criminal I met while locked up in the Pent.[1] Maybe it was the unflinching look in his eye — that dull and leaden gaze that convicts employ to hide any emotional or psychological frailties from each other. Maybe it was the scrutinous way he looked me up and down whenever I asked him a question — another typical characteristic, you will find, of the ever-suspicious convict.

But I am digressing. After reporting to O'Flynn in the area known as Lower Victuallers Yard, I was told that there were several vacancies available. I was then asked by my 'convict' friend if I was industrious and honest and did not mind working at different hours of the night, as well as suffering the scorn and disdain of certain over-haughty passengers for whom a boatman is no more than a sea-

[1] Magsman — a conman. Skittle-sharp — a passer of false jewellery. Peter-claimer — a stealer of luggage.

faring lackey. Naturally, I said that I did not mind. After that, O'Flynn asked me if I had any navigational skills or experience of sea matters. To this, too, I said yes – although with a hesitancy of purpose which caused O'Flynn to stroke his chin and look at me awry for a while. He then led me to a nearby pier and, pointing to a small mistico,[1] asked me to show him the sum and total of my navigational skills. I immediately got into the boat and rowed around for a while – not exactly like a master mariner, it is true, but not, so I thought, that deficiently either. Alas, by the time I came out of the vessel O'Flynn was shaking his head in that slow and thoughtful way of his. 'You're no boatman, fellow, are you now?' he said, taking my oar and positioning the boat near the pier. 'No, sir, I'm not,' I truthfully replied. 'A shame,' O'Flynn responded, with another solemn shake of the head, ' 'cos I liked you and would have employed you. There's too many Moors in this line of business, if you ask me.'

I thanked O'Flynn for his kind words and then set off home. I felt disappointed but secretly relieved at the same time, knowing, within my heart of hearts, that I could never have coped with the physical exertions demanded by the boating profession. Near the top of Castle Steps, I looked up at the sky and saw a cloud shaped like a human skull. The image filled me with a certain amount of foreboding, although it did not surprise me unduly. Of late I am seeing skulls and grimacing faces wherever I look. I perceive them in the most disparate of places – on my dust-encrusted window panes, in the clouds in the sky, even on the dark and jagged patches of damp bubbling up through my bedroom wall. In my days at prison, I remember, some of the inmates used to say that if you dream a lot about death it signifies that good things are coming your way. 'Death and funerals,' they used to declare, 'equals shilling bags and wedding bells, whilst laughter and hilarity, that'd be tantamount to widow's bawls and misery.' Could seeing skulls on walls and windows also count as a good omen?

**The twenty-seventh day of November, 1888**

I have decided not to write very much today. I feel tired and weak,

[1] A small sailing vessel traditionally used in the Mediterranean.

the result of having spent all last night coughing and bringing up bloodless but thickly-textured sputum.

**The twenty-eighth day of November, 1888**

Very bad nightmares all night. Probably a consequence of the fever which I have been enduring since late last evening.

**The twenty-ninth day of November, 1888**

I woke up this morning feeling really ill. I was coughing up blood and having difficulty with the in-flow of breath – it being a most prodigious effort to swallow without making a horrible rasping sound that grated all the way down my lungs and into my very bowels. My first thought was to stay at home and weather the storm, but the noise issuing from my bronchial tubes was so pronounced and so disturbing that I decided to make my way to the civilian hospital. It only took me fifteen minutes to reach the mentioned establishment, thanks to the precipitous gullies and steps that lead from my garret to that part of town. At the top of Chicardos Passage, an old woman with a shawl – crooked and hunchbacked, as almost all the old women around here are wont to be – asked me if I wanted my palm read. I was rather taken aback by this, I have to admit, and I hobbled on as fast as I could to get away from her.

Shortly afterwards, I arrived at the civilian hospital. Its lobby was a scene of almost dantesque chaos – with patients, relatives, orderlies, nurses and doctors all rushing around like decapitated *lagartijas*.[1] After enquiring, from a rather surly porter, what I had to do to be seen, I made my way to the new patients' counter. There was a line of people, three-deep in thickness, around the said counter, all of them pushing and jostling with each other in an effort to reach the lone clerk before them. For a second I contemplated turning around and going back home, the thought of mixing with such a plebeian crowd grating against my naturally misanthropic instincts – but then another volley of coughs swept through me and I knew that I could not turn back without first seeing a physician. Reluctantly, therefore, I joined the queue. When I finally managed to reach the front, I was handed a numbered slip

[1] 'Lizards.'

and told to make my way down a corridor to a second waiting hall. There I was to sit until my number was called out. Thanking the gentleman clerk for his help, I hobbled my way down the corridor until I reached the mentioned hall. It was large and spacious and its proportions were not dissimilar to that of a small-sized church. At the far end of the hall there was a wooden table behind which sat three wimpled nuns. Directly behind the nuns, there were three wooden doors, presumably, I thought at the time, leading to the doctors themselves. I calculated that there must have been some sixty, possibly seventy people in the hall. Despite the clear look of suffering on most faces, everyone was very quiet — with no more than the occasional cough or an imperfectly-suppressed sigh echoing through the hall. Every now and then one of the wimpled triumvirate would stand and call out a number, at which point some tubercular son of a w____ or some red-eyed mother with a child slumped on her shoulder would get up and make their way to the desk and there be told which door to go through.

Not exactly enamoured with the situation I found myself in, I coughed out loud and took my place at the back of the hall, still clutching my square of paper with the number 78 scrawled in a spidery hand next to a half-smudged hospital stamp. Everywhere I looked there were faces ravaged with suffering, an array of dark and sullen Scorpion faces which went all the way from the intensely dolorous to the quietly despondent. I tried to tell myself that these were my people, that I came from the same stock as them, but the thought did not exactly bring much comfort. Another thing that I noticed was that no one seemed to be there on their own — every patient being accompanied by a parent or a relative or a spouse or whatever other label could be applied to those infinitely bored-looking individuals sitting beside them. For a while I tried to disassociate from the scenes of human suffering around me by thinking of what I was going to eat later in the afternoon — but the smell of ordure and sweat circulating through the air made this an almost impossible task. Eventually, after waiting for about two hours, my number was called out and I made my way to the front of the hall. At this point one of the nuns instructed me to go through the door on the far left. Inside this room there was not a doctor as I had been expecting, but another wimpled nun. She was sitting behind a desk and writing on a large leather-bound book. As soon as I stepped into the room, this stern-faced nun ordered me, without looking up from her book, to sit down.

'Name?'

'Bestman, ma'am,' I replied. 'Charles Bestman.'

'Age?'

'Thirty-nine years of age, ma'am.'

'Place of residence?'

'10/a Angelo's Gully, ma'am.'

'Occupation?'

'None at present, ma'am,' I said with a nervous smile,'— although I am currently searching for employ.'

'Complaint?'

'I am coughing a lot, ma'am, and also bringing up blood. I also feel generally unwell.'

'Does your sputum — that is to say, what you cough up — have a strangely offensive smell, rather like stale beer?'

'No, ma'am,' I said. 'I don't believe so.'

'Could it smell of almonds, perchance, then?'

'No, ma'am. That neither.'

The nun looked up for the first time. ‘Can you cough some sputum now into this cloth?’ she said, extending a piece of white fabric towards me.

‘Yes, ma’am.’

‘I see no blood.’

‘It is not there all the time, ma’am. It comes and goes.’

The nun looked down again and started writing into her book. ‘I will make a recommendation that you be seen by Surgeon Nathaniel on the third of March, this coming year 1889,’ she said. ‘You must present yourself that day at the appointments counter at nine o’clock in the morning. You will then be given instructions what to do.’

‘The third of March?’ I asked.

‘Yes, the third of March,’ the Irish nun replied with very noticeable irritation. ‘That is the earliest date that I have available for Mr. Nathaniel. Would you like me to inscribe your name against that date, Bestman — yea or nay?

‘Yes, ma’am,’ I said.

I left the hospital shortly after that. I was feeling very dispirited and melancholic by this stage, unable to reconcile myself to the fact that I will now have to wait over three months before I will be admitted to the presence of a physician. I was also very angry that I had not remonstrated with the old nun. ‘Why did you just sit there, Charles?’ I reproachfully asked myself. ‘Why didn’t you tell her that the third of March simply wasn’t good enough? Could it be, perhaps, because you feared that arguing with her would make things even worse? That is what these middling administrative men and women are like, after all, is it not? If for some reason they like your face, they will hand you an appointment next week, right that very day if you are fortunate enough. If, on the other hand, you question their judgement or dare to remonstrate with them, they will make sure your appointment is delayed by a few weeks or that your records somehow go 'missing' just before your next hospital visit. That is what those petty, tyrannically-minded dictators are like: they confer life or death at the stroke of a pen, often without even being around to witness the consequences of their actions, may the Lord curse them and blight them for their monstrous, anti-Christian indifference.'

But I am digressing somewhat. After quitting hospital, my plan was to return to my abode and rest there awhile. I was intending to sleep for a few hours, perhaps to write a little in my journal. However, when I started walking up the first few slopes leading to the upper town, I felt so tired and devoid of energy that I decided to turn around and make my way down into the Main Street area instead. I know, I know: on the face of it this was a most foolish thing to do — particularly since, following the natural gravitational order of things, any pedestrianised descent into town now would have to be followed by an even steeper and longer climb later — but I was so tired and enervated at the time that I could only think in *praesens tempus*, as the saying goes, and, besides, I didn't exactly fancy the thought of going back to a room where all I could do was sit by a window and stare at the rats scuttling up and down the outside water pipes. Consequently, I gritted my teeth and soon found myself strolling down Main Street together with that endless, bustling throng of humanity which constantly walks on its cobbles. Here a really strange thing occurred: my mood and physical condition greatly improved. What exactly precipitated this sudden change I cannot really say. Perhaps the fresh air I took on the way down from the hospital had cleared my lungs, or perhaps the infectious dynamism of the Main Street crowd had rubbed off on me and somehow lifted me out of my previous despondency. Either way, I took advantage of this unexpected surge of enthusiasm by re-visiting three establishments that I had already been to during the last few days. At the third of these, an ironmonger's shop owned by a Sephardic Jew by the name of Mr. Serfaty, I was told that a vacancy would be opening at the beginning of the new year and then asked if I would be interested in applying for it. 'It is just an errand boy that I need,' the ageing Mr. Serfaty, seeing the look of astonishment that must have fallen across my face, said. 'You know, someone who will sweep the shop floor, run errands, manage the till – *esa clase de cosas.* But as you have already come to my establishment several times, and you remind me of my son Ishmael who died three years ago, well, what do you know, I think there's a strong chance I might just give the job to you!' By the time this news was delivered, I was in a state of the most feverish excitation. With my heart pounding wildly, I went outside into the street and lifted my eyes to the cloudy grey sky. Then I made the sign of the cross and softly whispered the words of Psalm 18:

*Lord, my rock, my fortress, my deliverer, My God, my rock of refuge, my shield, my saving horn, my stronghold! Praised be the Lord, I exclaim! I have been delivered from my enemies!*

Shortly afterwards, a feeling of great happiness possessed me and I was able to make my way up the steps and slopes leading to my abode with little, if any effort. 'Just imagine,' I happily whispered to myself. 'You'll be able to buy eggs and flour and potatoes and anything else that you want. No more *huevos cascados* for you, old chap!' In retrospect, I am not really sure why I got so excited – seeing that I am only twelve or thirteen days away from running out of money and the new job will not start until the beginning of the new year.

**The thirtieth day of November, 1888**

I am feeling very unwell again, hardly having the power to lift myself and sit upright against my pillow. I am also full of terribly resentful thoughts, unable to look back upon yesterday's episode at the hospital without feeling myself engorge with anger and hostility. The authorities here claim that free medical treatment is available to all, but we all know that it is only the rich who have the power to consult doctors instantaneously. Everyone else has to wait, to go through this horribly distended and time-consuming process where everyone treats you like scum and where you are made to feel that you are just a little cog that's no longer needed. If you happen to die before you get medically attended, then so much the better — it is one less bill that the colonial government has to pay.

Ultimately, it is only the lives of the rich that are important, the ones that must be preserved at all costs. I know because I have been on both sides of the divide, being important one moment and then expendable the next. When I was a child and I feigned illness to get attention, for example, I was constantly attended by doctors and nurses, all of them crowding around my bed with the most comical looks of concern on their faces. I had them all there, feeding from the palm of my hand, as it were, a gallery of smiling, grey-haired rogues who called me 'little chick' and 'precious little angel' and all kinds of other pet names designed to ingratiate themselves with my father and in this way obtain a few extra dollars from him. Now that I am an adult, however — now that I am coughing up blood and feeling as if my life were ebbing away with each passing day — I am told that I have to wait three months before being seen by a doctor who, chances are, will probably treat me with the contempt that men of his kind display towards the indigent and moneyless classes. This is not just ironical; it is positively criminal.

**The first day of December, 1888**

I got woken up again last night by my quarrelling neighbours. It is the second time that it has happened now in a month. I listened to their shouted exchanges for a while and then I moved to the window, where I sat for some time looking at the star-filled sky.

**The second day of December, 1888**

I had another strange dream last night. This time I dreamed that I was back at Saint Mary's, the school in Hampshire to which Jamiel sent me at the age of thirteen. 'Dog-eyes' Watson, 'Angryman' Jenkins, Thomas 'the pug' Waters, 'Bazza' Williamson: all my old tormentors were sitting once again at their desks around me — yet this time they were all smiling and treating me with the most unctuous civility, as if I no longer qualified as the unwanted interloper that I used to be. 'Here,' Dog-eyes suddenly said, extending towards me a bizarre metal object which, upon close examination, proved to be a crucifix in which the figure of Christ had been reduced to an armless torso, 'a little something for your delectation.'

When I woke up it must have been about five o'clock in the morning and it was raining outside. I could hear the rain hitting against the window panes and leaking in through the cracks in the roof. After climbing out of bed, I threw a blanket around my shoulders and coughed up some blood. Then I poured myself a glass of water and walked over to the window. As I gazed at the darkness outside, I found myself remembering those six months at Saint Mary's and everything that I endured there. Strange to think that all that is part of my past — the loneliness and the beatings, the humiliations and the nights without sleep, the unshed tears and the moments of suicidal abandon. You would have thought that none of it ever happened — so far away and distant from my present predicament does it all seem. And yet it did happen, that's for sure. All I have to do is close my eyes and I can see everything materialise in front of me. Suddenly twenty-five years no longer feel like such a long time; suddenly even the most obscure memories begin to open out and gain definition. Yes, it is true: by closing my eyes I can still remember the day that I first arrived at Winchester. I had been travelling for the last three hours in a chaise belonging to the London and Midlands Carriage Company. It was driven by a wild-eyed coachman by the name of Lackers, a *miscreantish* son-of-a-w____ who stank of gin and seemed to have taken an instant dislike to me the moment he was able to gather that I was not an Englishman born. When we finally reached our destination, it must have been close to five o'clock in the afternoon. The smell of pine trees hung in the air and I could hear the soft but beautiful sound of choral singing coming from afar. Stepping out of the vehicle, I saw this magnificent series of parapets and turrets and rising spires about half a mile away. A symphony of stone, no more and no less, set down on the Hampshire woodlands.

'Is this Saint Mary's College?' I asked my surly driver.

'Aye,' he replied, expectorating some mucus and spitting it a yard or two away from where I stood. 'Saint Mary's College it is. Home to our fine and dandy young scholar-boys *and other sorts.*'

I ignored the inherent hostility in his tone and turned once more towards the building before us. 'So this is Saint Mary's College,' I thought to myself. 'So this is the sort of college attended by the English gentry.' I have to confess it: I had never seen anything so grand or magnificent in all my life – my prior experiences with grandiosity having been strictly limited to the squat and pseudo-Arabic form of Gibraltar's Anglican Cathedral (a cross, as a celebrated garrison wit once described the edifice, between the Granadan Alhambra and a gunpowder arsenal!). 'Surely I will enjoy it here,' I thought as I started hauling my trunk down from the carriage unaided by the sneering Lackers. 'Surely one cannot be unhappy in a place as magnificent and marvellous as this!'

I will not bore you with a description of the bureaucratic formalities which preceded my induction into the college. Suffice to say that I was accepted as a freshman and soon found myself undergoing tutorial instruction along with the flower of England's youth. At this stage everything was going well – or at least *as well as one could have hoped for.* Like any other Johnny-come-lately, I was ignored by my classmates. I was pretty much left to my own devices. Even Jenkins, the boy who had the misfortune of sharing his desk with the new arrival, barely talked to me, preferring to chat with those on the other side of the classroom than dialogue with the sallow, undersized boy who sat hunched over his books beside him and who, so the story went, 'came from somewhere in the colonies'. This state of affairs, I am sure, would have upset most boarders and made them beg their progenitors for a speedy end to their tribulations. But, used to solitariness as I was and not exactly enamoured by the thought of seeing Jamiel again, I did not really mind. In fact, I quite liked it. Though sometimes I craved to take part in the rough and boisterous games that the others played in the schoolyard, I generally enjoyed being left alone. Indeed, in some ways you could say that I was doing what I had been doing all my life – seeking refuge from the world in my own interior worlds, forgetting my problems within the ceaseless carousel of my own imagination. Sometimes, it is true, there were moments when I did feel a little down at heart – such as when I used to lie in bed at night, or when I would find myself gazing through the classroom window at the misty, rain-soaked meadows outside (so different in character and appearance from the crooked, foul-smelling little ramps and alleyways of my native Gibraltar) – but generally speaking these never lasted long enough to *properly depress me*.

But then things changed. It all started when Jenkins' father pulled him out of Winchester. Although Jenkins himself never saw fit to disclose to me the reason for his sudden departure, I was able to determine from what he told everyone else that he was going to India – his father, the great Sir Barnaby Jenkins, KCMG, CB, DSO, MVO, etcetera, etcetera, having landed a job there as a colonial administrator. 'It will be absolutely stupendous,' Jenkins, a thin, indescribably dull little boy of fourteen, kept on saying. 'Good God, can you imagine how many elephants and tigers I'll be able to shoot while over there?' Whether or not Jenkins got to shoot all his elephants and tigers, of course, I cannot say. All I know is that a few days after these words were uttered the space at my side became vacant and I was now made to sit at the front of the class, near a lad named James Watson. A wiry, mop-haired youth with narrow, slit-like eyes that had a touch of the Mongoloid about them, this Watson was very similar to Jenkins except for one thing: unlike my former desk partner, who had never really bothered with me and seemed altogether indifferent to my person, he *positively despised me.* Even now, all these years later, I am not sure what exactly caused Watson, the son of a Manchester cotton merchant and an American-born socialite, to hate me so. Was it perhaps because my skin colour was slightly darker than everybody else's? Because, coming from Gibraltar, I mispronounced certain words which I knew from my reading but had never used before in actual conversation? Or because of the fact that I was not English and therefore, in Watson's warped xenophobic estimation, fundamentally different from everyone else in our classroom? I am not, in all honesty, able to say. One way or the other, the fact is that James 'Dog-eyes' Watson took it upon himself to torment me, making it his life's mission to find new and imaginatively cruel ways of irritating me and humiliating me in front of the others. If that were not bad enough, 'Dog-eyes' was approximately the same size and strength as me. What this, in practice, meant was that Watson and I could not easily slot into the age-old roles of bully and victim (which would have at least ensured that both of us knew our respective places and, by extrapolation, what we *could* and *could not* get away with), but instead found ourselves languishing in a universe of constant conflict, forever exchanging salvoes in an unending war of provocation and retaliation.

Every day, alas, it was the same: I would find myself having to fend him off, pushing him back, telling him to b_____ off, warning him not to come any closer, constantly having to check over my shoulder to see if he was there waiting to taunt me. Once, I remember, he stuck a pencil sharpener into my hand and I retaliated by kicking him in the shin. Another time he smashed an inkpot against my face and I took my revenge by spitting into his eye and calling him 'a no-good son of an Asiatic w____!' Yet another time he spat into my morning porridge and I, disgusted and dismayed in equal measure, felt compelled to scatter pepper into his eyes. Such was the attritional nature of our relationship, in fact, that any detached observer would have thought that Watson and I were a pair of inveterate troublemakers — *so frequently and so often* would they have witnessed us arguing and exchanging blows. This perception, what is more, would have been aided by Watson's intrinsically devious disposition. Like most agents of chaos, you see, James Watson was a master at hiding that critical first act of provocation: the rapid push in the back, the quickly-whispered 'you are a c___', the clinically-delivered stamp on the shin just as you walked out of the refectory. He would hide all these initial acts of aggression, let me explain, and then make out that it was you yourself who had callously provoked him into a confrontation! . . .

What else can I say in this journal that will do descriptive justice to the perverted incarnation of evil that went by the name of James 'Dog-eyes' Watson? If I were to write here that he was the type of figure that populates nightmares, it will probably sound too melodramatic. And if I were to claim that he was like some cankerous wound that refuses to cicatrize even with time, it will no doubt come across as too fanciful and poetic. For this reason I will resist the compulsion to indulge in any extravagant metaphors and finish by just saying this: truly and verily, James Watson, variously known as 'Dog-eyes', 'Chinkster' and 'Wat-wat', was simply a malevolent force of nature.

You will probably be wondering at this stage what the other boarders thought of my constant clashings with Watson. If that is indeed the case, let me tell you that at first they didn't seem to notice anything. Or perhaps they didn't really care about what was happening — it is hard to say. Slowly, though, all this began to change. At first it was just a few sniggers here, a few rounds of applause there. Certainly, nothing to suggest widespread classroom connivance. Before I knew what was happening, however, some of the others were assisting Watson with his dirty tricks — either by holding me down while he poured a pot of ink over my head, or else by helping him unscrew the legs of my cot before I went to sleep. Soon after this the whole class of thirty turned against me, laughing and swearing and pulling faces whenever Watson, now ably assisted by his faithful henchmen, launched upon one of his wanton attacks. At this point two things happened. First, I stopped retaliating like I had done in the past. Second, I retreated more and more into myself. In other words, I hardly bothered to speak to anyone if I could avoid it. This, of course, was difficult to sustain in a self-enclosed community dependent upon inter-personal relationships like that at Winchester. Even worse, it made me very unpopular with the school staff, especially with my masters, who mistook my reluctance to speak as a form of intractability or stubbornness. Countless were the occasions, for example, when Mr. Francois-Young, our black-cravatted master of French, would openly chide me for not being as '*enthousiaste*' as the others, or Mr. Landsholme, our cricket and P.E. master, would tell me off for skulking indifferently at the back of the sports hall.

Even more degrading, perhaps, were the times when Mr. Piper, our form master, would single me out during morning assemblies for not singing as loud as the others. 'You, boy,' he would say, dragging me by the ear to the front of the hall. 'Your lips are hardly moving. Come to the front of the assembly room, so that everyone can hear you sing!' What I went through during those moments, standing there with eight hundred boys laughing while I rasped out the words of some sanctimonious Wesleyan hymn, is hard to put into words. Something inside my breast, you could say, something inside there shrank and died, it withered away and turned into a ball of 'non-feeling', if that make any sense. And yet, despite all this, *I never sang out loud at morning assembly.* No, sir-ree. That I most surely never did. I tried a few times, it is true, but the words choked in my mouth even as the hateful Mr. Piper spotted me half-hidden among my fellow Wykehamists. At the time, of course, I hated myself for being like this. 'Why cannot I sing like the others?' I angrily used to think. 'Why do I have to make life so difficult for myself?' Now, however, I am able to understand. Refusing to sing out loud was my personal act of defiance; it was my way of clinging to the little independence of spirit that still remained, bedraggled and half-beaten to death, somewhere inside me.

Some three or four months passed in this way. By then my situation at Winchester had become something of a living hell, a prolonged and never ending form of torture. It was not just Watson's attacks that I had to worry about now; it was also the hatred which I had somehow began to inspire in all the others. Previously, for example, the question of my social background had never mattered. Now, however, for reasons unknown, it suddenly became common knowledge that I was not just the son of a foreign tobacco merchant, but the son of a Jew as well. In a school filled with baronets and marquesses, this, of course, was never going to go down very well. Worse than that: it was the sort of revelation that would have turned even the most saintly of schoolboy minds against me. In fact, shortly after my 'Jewishness' started to be publicly propagated, I began to wake up in the mornings to find the word 'JEW' smeared *excrementally* into my bed sheets, the stink of human faeces mingling with the laughter of those who stood there holding their noses and pointing mockingly at me: 'Look at the Jew-boy covered in s___! Looks like our little Hebrew pig has s___ himself again!' In vain did I protest that I was a born member of the Church of England, that I was as much of an Anglican as anyone else in the room. 'JEW! JEW! JEW!' they would all shout and stamp their feet on the floorboards every time I tried to remonstrate with them. 'You were born a JEW and a JEW you will always remain!'

On top of all this, there was the constant round of pranks and jokes that I had to put up with. Once, for instance, they tore off my breeches while we were getting ready for our lunchtime P.E. class and tied me to a clothes stand, where I remained for two hours until one of the school cleaners chanced upon me in my state of nakedness. Another time I was held by five or six of them in the exercise yard and forced to swallow the tail of a dead rat, the last thing I remember before passing out being Dog-eyes' gloating face suspended there above me.

It was more or less the same every day: tauntings, beatings, humiliations, the sound of Watson's cruel laughter ringing in my ears, the horribly disempowering feeling that comes from knowing that you can no longer fight back because the whole system is now turned against you. What else can I say here about my time at Saint Mary's? Every single day that I was there, if you must know, I wanted to break down and cry. Yet even that small consolation was denied to me, as I had nowhere to go within the school where I could shed my adolescent tears. Whether I was in the classroom or the dormitories, the assembly hall or the playing fields, the privies or the prop room: there was not a single place where I found myself unthreatened by their demonic machinations. Dread — that, in the final analysis, is the one quality that I most associate with my time at Saint Mary's. Dread of going to sleep at night. Dread of climbing out of bed in the morning. Dread of going to the early-morning assemblies. Dread of being picked upon by the odious Mr. Piper. Dread of waking up every morning with my bedsheets covered in excrement. Dread of finding myself alone with the others in the communal baths. Dread of falling asleep and waking up with my mouth stuffed with insects and spiders. Yes, that is the one quality which I will forever associate with my time at Saint Mary's College near Winchester: pure and simple dread.

**The third day of December, 1888**

I went to the Catholic Cathedral today and sat in its interior for a while. I am not sure why I did this, seeing that I am a born and bred Anglican and should naturally abhor the profusion of statues and rich gildings which adorn its every corner. I suppose that I felt a gnawing desire to see the church where my Irish mother used to regularly swallow her anti-Scorpion misgivings to worship alongside her southern Catholic brethren. To my surprise, the interior of the building was extremely quiet and peaceful, the whole of the nave enveloped in an incense-scented haze which seemed a million miles removed from Main Street and its assemblage of fast-shuffling pedestrians. For the next couple of hours I sat on one of the wooden benches near the entrance, watching the endless procession of worshippers come in from the street outside to pay their Catholic respects. It is a most curious thing to behold. First, they sprinkle themselves with holy water and then they proceed to their preferred piece of statuary, where, dropping to their knees and closing their eyes, they mumble soft words of prayer and adulation:

*Alma de Cristo, santifícame. Cuerpo de Cristo, sálvame. Sangre de Cristo, embriágame. Agua del costado de Cristo, lávame. Pasión de Cristo, confórtame. ¡Oh, buen Jesús!, óyeme.*

Again and again I heard the same prayer. Although part of me felt slightly repelled by these idolatrous murmurings, another part of me, deeper within, wished that I, too, had the capacity to derive such spiritual nourishment from my material surroundings. At around three o'clock a young priest came out of the vestry and began to guide the small crowd of worshippers in what appeared to be a rosary recitation. The service was very long and repetitive (consisting, principally, of lengthy priestly prayers followed by '*amens*' and '*salve reginas*' on the part of the congregation) – yet, paradoxically, seemed to have a soothing and almost salutary effect on the nerves, the likes of which I found most enjoyable. Halfway through the ritual, a drunken redcoat stumbled through the doors and made his way down the main aisle to the altar. The priest, a gaunt-faced young man with a juvenile moustache across his upper lip and the tortured look of a Zurbaran penitent, seemed most unnerved by this development. He coughed and scratched his head and then spent the next few minutes nervously glancing between the missal lying on the lectern and the soldier who tottered idiotically near the altar railings. Finally, the clergyman could not stand it any longer: he walked over to the young redcoat and, in accented but perfectly understandable English tones, told him that this was not the most appropriate way to conduct himself in the House of God and that he should either sit down with all the other worshippers or make his way out of the building. The soldier, who looked like he could not have been older than eighteen or nineteen, stared at him for some moments without saying a word. Then he raised his hand to his forehead in a military-type salute and said, 'Aye-aye, Mr. Spanish Priestman, sir.' Subsequently, he turned around and staggered out of the building, much to the relief of the moustachioed young priest and the worshippers in general.

**The fourth day of December, 1888**

I have computed that I only have seven or eight days left before I completely run out of money. What I will do then is anybody's guess. If I had been favoured with a different disposition, I could of course have bought some *picadura* tobacco and smuggled it across the frontier into Spain, where I could have then sold it for twice the amount that I originally purchased it for. This is what almost everyone in this place does: they buy one or two *cuarterones* (or quarter pounds) of *picadura* from the tobacco manufactories, hide it under the fold of a dress or inside an expertly hollowed-out handcart, then make their way into Spain with the clandestine goods. Unfortunately, I do not think that I am capable of such openly felonious behaviour. At Pentonville, I promised Pastor Michaels and the other gospel-grinders that I would never again succumb to criminal temptation — and I do not intend to break this pledge of faith after all these years. And, yet, I have to say, a feeling of great uncertainty has taken hold of me. What shall I do when the money runs out? And where shall I go? I don't really know. Esadras, the old Jew, is due to call at my abode any day now and I am sure that he will not be overjoyed when he hears that I do not have enough money to pay my next rent instalment. Again, I am forced to ask the same critical questions: what shall I do? and where shall I go? In the Bible it says that we should trust the Lord in times of indigence, seeing that even the little sparrows derive sustenance from Him, but we all know that these are anachronistic words, written at a time when men were not as avaricious or perhaps as materialistic as they are at present. And yet maybe I shouldn't be so cynical. 'The Lord upholdeth all that fall, and raiseth up all those that be bowed down.' Isn't that the promise which is written in the blood of our Saviour? Just a few days ago, while walking past the Exchange, I overhead a rich, elegantly-attired gentleman say that one should not bother too much about the Gibraltar poor — there being more than enough *higo chumbos*[1] scattered across *el monte*[2] to keep them going for a few years. Perhaps I could avail myself of nature's bounty in this way, could I not? And yet the truth is I am not so sure. Can you imagine an ex-convict like me, with little experience of nature's ways, foraging for berries and other edibles? It seems highly unlikely, don't you think? All I know — and this much I can say with complete certainty — is that I am becoming more and more desperate by the day and that something needs to happen if I am not going to slide into a state of irrevocable indigence. On a separate, more cheerful note, I am happy to say that I feel much better today than I have for some time. This morning I awoke without any encrustations of blood on my pillow and almost the entirety of my day has passed without any coughings or any other manifestations of sickness.

**The fifth day of December, 1888**

Another perfectly salubrious day. In the morning I strolled down to *el pueblo*, as people here commonly refer to the centre of Gibraltar town. First of all, I went to the premises of Avelino A. Sanguinetti, Leather Merchants and Athletic Outfitters, and then on to Schembri and Co., Grocers and Provision Merchants — only to discover that there were no vacancies at either establishment. Afterwards I toyed around with the thought of visiting the good Mr. Serfaty and asking him for a small loan, the entirety of which could be deducted from my first salary, but in the end I resolved that this would probably

---

[1] 'Prickly pears.'

[2] 'The mountain' – a local term for the wooded area near the top of the Rock.

annoy him and, quite possibly, make him retract the offer which he made a few days ago. I then retired to the gardened area behind the old Club-house hotel, where I spent a long and altogether relaxing hour contemplating the boats and steamers anchored in the bay. As it was a fairly cloudless day, there were quite a few people occupying the other stone benches – mainly nurse-maids with their young charges and one or two unemployed and unsalaried individuals such as myself.

**The sixth day of December, 1888**

Esadras came this morning to my room. He was very polite at first, but, when he realised that I did not have the money that I owe him, he became very angry and insulting, calling me 'a miscreant son of a w____' and 'a d_____ dog of an Englishman'. I tried to calm him down, telling him that he would have his rent money very soon, but this only seemed to increase his ire. 'You, sir,' he hissed most resentfully, 'are *un pájaro de mala cuenta*, that is what you are, sir. A most contemptible oath-breaker.' Not knowing how else to get rid of him, I offered him a glass of gin and then told him that my weekly allowance from my great-uncle in London had been delayed in the post and would surely get here within the next two or three days. This totally fabricated item of news seemed to appease the old dog somewhat, although he could not stop himself from letting me know that he would call the police and have me evicted if I am unable to procure the money when he comes back in a week or two.

Once Esadras departed, I sat by the window for an hour or so, wondering what I could do to come up with the twenty-five pesetas that I owe him. I was, needless to say, in a very anxious and fretful state of mind throughout this time, constantly besieged by the twin demons of depression and loneliness. Again and again it occurred to me that my life has been one long unbroken period of worry – there never having been a time, apart from possibly my short interludes with Lorena and Paxton, when I could be said to have been *truly happy.* The thought upset me and filled me with something akin to self-pity, although I managed to stave off these feelings by thinking of the good Mr. Serfaty and his job offer. Finally, at around half past eleven, I got up and attired myself and started heading down into

Main Street. Being a Friday morning, the streets were relatively quiet and empty, with little more to be heard other than the creak of the fruit and vegetable carts on their way around the houses. From a one-legged man standing at the top of *el callejon de los masones*, I bought a *cuarteron* of salted chestnuts for twenty *centimos* — something which I immediately regretted, as most of the chestnuts were filled with small worms. About ten or fifteen minutes later, I found myself walking past *The British Pharmacy* on Main Street. Now, just as in the days of my youth, *The British Pharmacy* boasts the most eye-catching of window displays — always stocked with famous pharmaceuticals like Beecham's cough pills and Clarke's blood purifying syrups. Often you will find small groups of Linenses huddled next to its window, the poor b______ marvelling at all the wonderful things that you cannot find in their own filthy, pox-ridden town. Today, however, all of these products had been removed and replaced by a single item: a dark green bottle sitting atop an assortment of crimson drapes. Directly below this artistically-assembled tableau one could discern a large printed sign:

**SAVE YOUR LIVES BY TAKING**
**OWBRIDGE'S LUNG TONIC**

*Save your Lives by taking Owbridge's Lung Tonic. It has a power over disease hitherto unknown in Medicine. Are you at all weak-chested or inclined to be Consumptive, with just a touch of Cough now and then? Try this wonderful medicine! The Cough and Weakness will disappear like magic, and you will feel a strength and power you never had before. . . . Available inside for only five pesetas a bottle!*

I have a confession to make: I was very tempted to buy this wonderful preparation. However, after considering the matter for some moments, I decided that I could not really afford to part with five pesetas and promptly gave up on the idea. I then walked down to the Line-Wall and sat on an old stone bench facing the sea. Across the bay there was a frigate making its way towards the coaling depot, its gigantic metal shape cutting a fine figure through the cold, lead-grey waters. I watched it for a while, marvelling at the miracle which is modern man's ingenuity. At half past one, I thought about walking down to the coaling station to see if there were any jobs on offer, but I subsequently determined against the idea and began the long tramp up to my room instead. From a shop at the *calle comedia,* I purchased some salt beef and a pound of half-rotted onions, having earlier decided to boil up some broth in the evening. The shopkeeper, a rotund, red-faced Scorpion by the name of Casares, was an exceedingly talkative individual. While he served up my order, he told me that one of his customers had recently found an Afghan war medal near Scud Hill in the South district. He had found it lying next to a drain, the old *dependiente* said, adding, somewhat unnecessarily in my opinion, that the said object had been 'completely covered in s___.' Being a conscientious and upright fellow, the finder decided to take the medal to the *Gibraltar Chronicle*'s office in the hope that it would be reunited with its rightful owner.

'Now guess what happens then?' the Scorpion shopkeeper said at this point, momentarily pausing from his beef-slicing with a sour-faced grin. 'The *Chronicle*'s editor, sir, he makes some investigations of his own and, *crèeme lo que le digo, señor,* discovers that the medal actually belongs to his best friend, one Captain Reginald Primson of number 12 Scud Hill, *un caballero muy apuesto pero un poco despistado,* as it is said round these parts, and that the gentleman in question, being, like most English gentlemen, a man of fair and equitable disposition, wants to find the person who had handed in his medal and recompense him to the tune of *quince dólares españoles.* Life is mighty lucky for some, don't you think, my good sir?'

After leaving Mr. Casares' shop, I recommenced my walk up *la calle comedia* and finally reached my abode around half past two. For the next two or three hours I sat by my window without doing much, my thoughts alternating between Esadras' rent payment and the simmering pot of broth suspended from a hook just inside the fireplace.

**The seventh day of December, 1888**
Rain and more rain.

**The eighth day of December, 1888**

More rain. The doorway leading into our block has completely flooded.

**The ninth day of December, 1888**

I did a very foolish thing last night: I drank a whole bottle of gin. Even now I am not exactly sure how this monstrous act of intemperance came to pass. At around half past nine, finding myself trembling under my blankets, I opened my suitcase and carefully retrieved the bottle from where it lay swaddled among old rags. My intention, at this stage, was to drink a nip or two of gin - just enough, in other words, to warm me up and take my mind off the mounting December cold. Within minutes, however, some secret demon must have buried itself into my soul . . . as I find myself drinking with no aim other than to get intoxicated. Again and again I am conscious of what I am trying to achieve: to lose myself in alcohol, to bludgeon my sorrows into insentience.

Soon, rather unsurprisingly, I am totally and utterly drunk. I know that this must be so — *as I am suddenly possessed by the desire to talk with someone, to unburden myself of my problems in front of another human being.* It is like a stake that needs to be ripped out from my heart — this yearning for company that has suddenly mushroomed within my soul. Stuffing the bottle of gin into my jacket pocket, I open the door and stagger out into the night. I do not know where I am going or what I intend to do. Around me the streets are dark and empty, divested of the emblems of diurnal life. Everything is quiet and lonely, just as it always is in Gibraltar at night, enfolded in that thick and heavy blanket of darkness which falls over everything here after twilight and which is only broken by the tremulous blue glimmerings of the gas lanterns standing at intervals of twenty or thirty paces to each other. First, I walk down Angelo's Gully and then I enter the twisting, crooked alley known as *el callejon de nadie*. Along the way I chance upon one or two passers-by, probably policemen or home-returning coalmen, shadowy and ill-defined figures whose features, because of the lateness of the hour and the state of drunkenness I find myself in, I cannot make out with any accuracy. I want to stop and talk to these people, to reach out and engage them in conversation — but I dare not approach anyone, so frightened am I of the darkness and the things that come with it. Soon I am walking down Colonial Hospital Street, trying to negotiate its broad, unlit *escalones* without falling. Nearing the end of the steps, where the street forks out into four different directions, I become aware of a light hovering up ahead. It is blue and faint and it seems to belong to some kind of tavern. As I get closer to the source of the light, I can make out a shadowy entrance and a handpainted sign above it which says 'Jack of the Ramps'. I know this place: it is one of the most notorious public houses in the colony. I have often heard about it during my walks through Main Street. I am tempted to go inside this tavern and see what it is like, but instead I take the first turning on the left and find myself entering a long and poorly-lit alleyway with dark and cavernous doorways on each side. From the corner of my eye I see strange shapes moving in the doorways, half-drawn silhouettes and shadows that float and tremble in the musty-smelling darkness. At first I think that I must be hallucinating, but then I realise that I am walking through Serruya's Lane, *la calle peligro,* the street of the thousand and one temptations. My father, God rest his Jewish soul, was always complaining to his friend Burlington about this same alleyway, saying that it was a shame that an avenue like this existed no more than five minutes from Waterport Street and just a stone's throw away from our residence on Governor's Street. 'How can you allow a quarter like that to develop within the heart of the community?' Jamiel used to say, shaking his greying head and almost making himself sick at the thought. 'I just don't understand this colonial government of ours. To disregard the complaints of the lower classes is one thing. But to disregard the complaints of the well-to-do just so that the soldiers can carry on indulging in their fornicatory practices simply beggars belief!' As I find myself remembering his words, I am aware of something moving by my side:

'Hey, Mister. You want good time? *Quieres pasar un buen rato?*'

It is the voice of a woman. And it is coming from one of the doorways. Through the darkness I can see that she is no more than fifteen or sixteen years old, her hair pinned up in a ribboned bob in the manner of a schoolgirl.

'Look,' she says, sliding down her chemise to reveal the alabastrine contours of a juvenile breast. 'For you. You want. *Tu quieres?*'

For a second I am tempted to follow the girl through the doorway. The compulsion is so strong and so intense that I find myself marvelling at my own thoughts. *My God, Charles,* I tell myself. *What are you thinking? Have you lost your wits or something? Can you really be contemplating doing such a thing?* It is indeed a most incredible piece of reasoning, I have to say. I hardly have any money to give away and, besides, just the thought of female flesh fills me with an uneasy sense of repugnance. Why then should I even be contemplating such a course of action? *Maybe it is the loneliness,* I tell myself. *The loneliness that burns unseen within my breast.* What else could drive a man like me to such a beastly thing?

I shake my head at the young girl and continue walking down the lane. More women begin to appear, materialising out of recessed doorways and archways like unholy apparitions. I can hear their sultry cries in the darkness: 'Hey sailor-boy. You looking for a good time?', '*Ven paca querido mio,*' 'Where you going so fast? *No va a llegar a ninguna parte corriendose de esa manera!*' Desperately, I increase my pace. I can feel the sweat growing cold on the back of my neck. I can feel a floating hollow opening inside my stomach. 'What is wrong with me?' I ask myself. I feel sick at the thought of going with one of these women, yet once again I am seized by the urge to stop and surrender to their entreaties. The temptation is almost too great. *To hold another human being for an hour, to hold and to be held at the same time, to share soft words against the flickering light of an oil lamp*: would it not be better than these vampirical wanderings through the night? Once again I feel like a criminal. Worse, I feel like a villainous wretch. And yet I am not doing anything wrong in wanting to kill off my loneliness, am I? Could it not even be said that I am *merely being human*? That I am simply trying to quench a part of me that has remained unquenched for so many years? *Oh sweet and merciful Lord! What is wrong with me? Why am I like this? For God's sake, I am a lifelong bachelor who has never shown the remotest interest in women. What on earth is possessing me?*

In the end I manage to survive the gauntlet of Serruya's Lane and stumble out onto the adjoining set of steps. It is much quieter there, the only sound coming to ear being the soft splutterings of a gas lantern some twenty or thirty yards away. Nervously, I retrieve the bottle of gin from my jacket pocket and hold it up to the outlying light. There is still about a finger or two of liquid left inside. The alcohol, I soon discover, is bitter and most acidulous in taste, but manages to spread a pleasing warmth through my entrails. Once reconstituted in this way, I make my way down the steps and then stagger through a series of narrow lanes until I am in the vicinity of Main Street. Again there is no one around, the normally busy walkways looking strangely sepulchral under the thin, blue glow produced by the gas lanterns. Up ahead in the distance I can see a bright yellow light. I am not sure where it is coming from, but as I start walking towards it I realise that it belongs to another tavern. A sign hanging above the doorway says *The Ape's Tail.* Smiling drunkenly, I make my way to the entrance and then proceed to stagger in. There is no one inside except a small, sallow man, clearly of Spanish or Scorpion origin, standing behind a counter. The floor is covered with wood shavings — just like you would find in a barber shop. On the wall there is a picture of the Queen during the time of Lord Melbourne — yellowing and crumpled with age and set behind a cracked pane of glass. I empty one of my pockets on the counter and manage to count eighty-five centimes. I hand part of this amount over to the bartender and ask him for a bottle of grog. When he brings it to me, I finish it in one gulp and then I order another. The bartender does not like this. 'You're drunk, mister,' he says.

'So much the better,' say I, stifling a cough.

'So much the better for you, sir, but not so much the better for me — seeing that it is I who will have to clean up this place should you not stomach your grog.'

'Fear not,' I rasp out between coughs. 'I will be no trouble. I am merely here to drown my sorrows, as they say. . . . By the way, why is everything so quiet today? I thought that the taverns here in Gibraltar are always supposed to be full.'

'It is eleven-thirty on a Sunday evening, sir,' the bartender says, taking out another bottle and this time pouring it into a glass. 'The taverns are out of bounds to the soldiery on Sundays between ten-thirty at night and two o'clock afternoon-time the next day. Don't you know garrison regulations, sir?'

I scratch my head at the revelation and then take hold of the glass. 'So the taverns are out of bounds on Sundays. . . . By the way,' I suddenly say, turning again to the olive-skinned bartender, 'where are you from? You don't sound from these parts?'

'I'm a Rock-man, mister,' says the bartender, this time with an edge of defiance. 'Born and bred.'

'You don't sound it particularly,' say I.

' 'Tis my profession, sir. I have to deal with many English gentlemen such as your good self, so their way of speaking naturally rubs off on me. Ask around town *si no me crees*. You will find I am known as Juan Sevilla, the bartender from the *Tail*.'

'That may be very true, Juan,' I half-splutter back, 'but in one respect you have erred. I am no Englishman. No, sir. *Assuredly I am not.* I'm a Rock-man too, such as yourself.'

The barman crosses his arms over his chest and grins. ' 'Tis difficult to believe, sir – judging from your London intonations – but as you're a paying man, and it is no business of any barman to doubt paying men, I will, as your compatriots say, take you at your word.'

'Ask me where I was born, sir,' quoth I then, 'and I will prove it to you.'

'Where were you born, then?'

'I was born in Governor's Street, just up the road from here.'

'A good answer, sir. Aye, indeed. Did you by any chance walk through Governor's Street on your way down here and see a sign bearing its name?'

I put my glass down on the counter and look at him for some seconds. 'I was sent away to England at the age of thirteen, Juan. My half-mad father wanted to improve my schooling and turn me into a true English gentleman. *Un verdadero caballero ingles* — isn't that how you say it?'

A scornful look suddenly besmirches the barman's countenance. 'What was the name of your father then? He must have had *mas pesetillas que centimos* to fund such an enterprise.'

'Our ancestral name was Benyunes, although you may have- '

'Benyunes?' the bartender interrupts me with a dismissive laugh. 'That name be as common round here as Smith is where you come from, sir.'

'I was about to say that you may have known us better by the name of Bestman, that being our adopted family name.'

'You mean like that old tobacco? What was it called again? Bestman's number five?'

'That is the one, sir.'

The bartender looks thoughtful for a few seconds. 'What happened to that old brand? I haven't seen it around for years.'

' 'Tis a long and convoluted story, sir,' I cough out my reply. 'A veritable saga, as they say.'

'You mean you do not wish to tell us about it?'

I look at him steadfastly for a few seconds, then look down at the counter again. 'Have you heard about Newton's law of universal gravitation, Juan?' I finally say. '*Every particle of matter in the universe attracts every other particle with a force that is directly proportional to the product of the masses of the particles and inversely proportional to the square of the distance between them.*'

'What's that got to do with anything, mate?'

'Or, as it is more commonly expressed, *what goes up must come down.*'

'Meaning?'

'Meaning, sir, that everything, from great Empires to large companies like *Bestman's Tobacco Products*, must come to an end.'

'You're telling me that the company went bust or something like that?' says he.

'Sold out, sir,' say I, taking a quick sip from my glass and trying to stifle yet another volley of coughs. 'My mother sold out. She woke up one day shortly after my father died, walked down to our old manufactory at Irish town, thought "enough is enough" and put the whole company up for sale.'

'She must have made a lot of money, for sure,' Juan says, picking up a glass from behind the counter and wiping its rim with a stained cloth.

'Oh, aye. That she did. A whole lot of money, for sure.'

The bartender's face suddenly distorts into a malicious grin. 'What happened then, if I may be so bold to ask? No disrespect to you, sir, but I never saw a scruffier, rougher, more *pordiosero* son of a w____ than yourself this present night!'

I smile sadly. ‘Twenty-five years, Juan. That is what happened. Twenty-five long and difficult years.’

‘I do not follow.’

I look at him for a few seconds and then gaze down into my glass. The liquid inside looks dark and heavy, its scummy, tar-like surface covered with a smattering of iridescent purple and gold swirls. I decide it is time to *let it all come out.*

‘It was meant to be five years at first,’ I say, swallowing hard. ‘That’s how long my father said it would take. You go abroad for five years and then you come back all polished and refined, snorting snuff and reciting lines from Ovid and Catullus. No use in simply staying in Gibraltar and playing out the role of the rich little colonial. That may have been good enough for the children of other rich merchantmen, but not for the son of Mr. John Charles Bestman. “If you want to make a real mark in life” as my father used to say, “you have to follow the paths untrod by the crude majority, you have to diverge from the ways of the contentedly ignorant.” That, at least, was the plan, the way he had conceived it all. Little Master Bestman would go to Winchester public school for boys and come back five years later a fine British gentleman, ready to perpetuate the Bestman dynasty and take it to new heights of grandeur.’

‘I still do not follow.’

I unclench my hands within my pockets and look at the barman across the bar counter. What a strange fellow this Juan Sevilla is! Possessing a head as large as a twenty-five pound *sandía*[1] and eyes the size of croquet balls, he speaks English almost as breezily as a Cockney market-hag and yet, because of the thick tangle of hair that sprouts from his neck and face, still manages to look as Spanish as a tight-trousered Toledan toreador. Only in Gibraltar, for sure.

‘Can I ask you something quite strange, Juan?’ I say, once again redirecting my attention upon the glass.

---

[1] Watermelon.

The bartender nods stiffly.

'Have you ever heard of a medicine called *Owbridge's Lung Tonic*?'

'*Owbridge's Lung Tonic*? No, never. Why do you ask?'

'No reason, really,' I reply, looking up again with a smile. 'It's just that I saw it advertised inside a shop window some days ago and I was wondering whether a man such as yourself, being in constant communication with all sorts of people as you are, might have heard some reports regarding its effectiveness.'

Juan Sevilla does not look very amused. 'You are confusing me, sir,' he says. 'One moment you are talking about being sent to school in England, the next you are asking me about some fancy Lung Tonic type of medicine. What has all this got to do with them twenty-five years you talked about earlier?'

He is right, of course. I am merely babbling about inconsequential drivel, trying to defer the re-opening of old wounds. It is an old speciality of mine.

'Okay, Juan,' I finally say. 'Okay. Let's forget all that and start again. Imagine a corridor. Twenty or twenty-five yards in length. With beautiful walnut panelling just like you see in great mansions and palaces. The corridor leads from Chernocke House, which is the name of the house dormitory for junior boys at Winchester, to the main assembly hall, where the boys gather every morning for prayers and notices. Along the walls of this corridor there are little niches with busts of famous Old Wykehamists. Thomas Otway – dramatist, Robert Lowth – Bishop of London and English grammarian, Joseph Warton – literary critic and Headmaster of Winchester. . . . Strange, isn't it? Even now I remember their names. I remember the names and the order of the statues and even the different expressions of hauteur on each of those marbled physiognomies. It is the little details that stay with you in the end, isn't that what they say? *Los pequeños detalles*. . . . I'm sorry, Juan. I have started to digress again, haven't I? . . . I do it all the time.

Something of an ingrained habit. . . . I guess it's because I don't have much contact with people these days and conversation doesn't come easy to me. . . . Anyway, as I was saying, there is a corridor. Every morning it has to be walked. It takes roughly about thirty seconds to go from one end to the other. A matter of no consequence, you could say. A simple stretching of the legs. And yet every morning I cannot bring myself to do it. I shudder at the thought. I am overcome with fear. I am literally quaking in my boots. And do you know why I am like this, my good Juanito? I will tell you why. It is very simple. Every morning, you see, my companions pounce on me as I walk down that corridor. It is almost like a tradition. A public school ritual. *Beat the dago,* they call it. *Wallop the blackie.* Sometimes even the prefects join in. You are walking down the corridor when suddenly seven or eight of them surround you and start pushing you about. One of them punches you. Another kicks you. Three or four of them tear down your breeches. Yet another spits upon you. It is like that every day. A bright and cheerful way to start the morning. *Beat the dago before the dago gets to the assembly hall.*'

The barman looks at me pensively for some moments. 'Were you the only foreigner in your school, sir?'

'Aye,' I reply quietly. 'I suppose you could say that. There was another boy called Hooton whom everyone called "the Indian", but he had only got that appellation on account of having formerly lived in Calcutta or some other colonial outpost with his military father. The guy was as much of a Hindoostani as I am a Chinaman from Macau.'

Juan sighs out loud and then starts pouring himself a glass of grog. 'I think I have an idea of what you must have gone through,' he says, casually angling his head to one side to make sure he fills the glass right up to the brim. 'The soldiery here, they've always been quite resentfully inclined towards us Gibraltar men and women. They call us blackies, darkies, apes, blackamoors, mongrels, rock baboons, ourang-outangs, *gazpacho*-swillers. In their estimation we are not just another race; we are members of a lower life form. I guess your fellow scholar-boys must have been prejudiced towards you in a similar way, wouldn't you say?'

Juan says these words and then brings the glass up to his lips, slurping the first few drops to avoid any wanton spillage. Afterwards he puts the glass down and smiles at me. A perfectly harmless and docile smile, it occurs to me, the smile of a man who knows nothing except wiping glasses and sweeping up floors and getting drunk from time to time in the company of his military clientele. Make no mistake about it, I think to myself at this point: this chap may sound English, but he is a Scorpion all right. He endures one or two scornful English looks in his little bar and he equates that to getting punched and kicked in the head every day of the week. It is the same old story as always, I'm afraid — that whiny old tale that has been repeated *ad nauseam* since the day that some stout-hearted Englishman first planted the Union flag upon some patch of foreign soil. *If you're a colonial, you will make sure that you sing loud about your oppression.* Nothing less than this will do. Listen to any Scorpion prattle on about the government here, for example, and you'd think that all his family and friends were being shackled and manacled and sold off to the highest English bidder. It's the Scorpion's last and best line of defence against Westminster: playing out the role of the little defenceless colonial. Mind you, I'm not saying that the English are the incarnation of governmental saintliness — that is not my intention. God knows how they have mistreated the native population over the years and robbed them of everything that is rightfully theirs. But listening to some of the complaints being aired by the Scorpions, you'd have thought that the military junta were crucifying the natives upside down or something in that vein. . . .

'Do you know what the worst thing was, Juan?' I suddenly say, looking down at the counter. 'The worst thing was waiting in the dormitory in the mornings. That, in many ways, I have to say, was even worse than the corridor beatings: the sitting there and doing nothing, knowing that the time was coming, that it was fast-approaching, that I couldn't escape what lay ahead, that I'd soon be lying in the corridor face-down trying to protect myself from their blows, that I'd soon be squirming and wriggling under their feet and asking for mercy like I always did — without mercy ever being granted to me.'

The bartender goes quiet for a long time. 'What did you do in the end?'

'What did I do in the end? Let me think about that one for a second. Running away? Not very realistic. Suicide? Went against my religion, didn't it? Complaining to my masters? Something of an unlikelihood, seeing that many of them hated me as much as my short-trousered tormentors. Begging my father to pull me out of school? There'd be more of a chance of a man flying to the moon, don't you think?'

'So what happened?'

'What do you think happened, Juan?'

'I don't know.'

'Go on, Juan — have a guess.'

'I don't know — you fell ill or something?'

'Not quite, Juan Sevilla, although a pretty perspicacious answer in its own right. Go on — try again.'

'I don't know — you were badly hurt and had to be taken to hospital?'

'No, no that either. Give it another shot, if you will.'

'*Yo que se*![1] You complained to the authorities and they transferred you somewhere else?'

'No, sir. I killed one of them.'

---

[1] 'What do I know!'

'What?'

'Not just any of my tormentors, it has to be said,' I quickly reply, 'but the main instigator himself, the same d_____ b______ who had started it all, all those months back. A wretch by the name of Watson. A most villainous and shameless cur whose life was so empty that he could only bring vicarious meaning to his existence by inflicting pain and suffering upon others. '

'And how did you kill this Watson fellow?'

'With a knife, my dear *señor* Sevilla. A table knife, to be precise. I stole it from the dinner table one day and hid it under my jacket. That same night I crept up to his cot in our dormitory and I stuck it in his throat. Just like this. . . . Oh, sir, it was a most prodigious sight, I assure you. A most prodigious sight.'

'What was?' the bartender asks with a fearful look.

'Why, the blood, Juan. The blood. 'Twas everywhere, soaking his sheets and his pillow and spurting in thick red gushings even while he gurgled in his throat and looked at me with sad and imploring eyes.'

'*Virgen Santísima*. . . !'[1]

'*Virgen Santísima* indeed,' I reply with a contemptuous smile. 'Do you know what the scariest thing was, Juan? The scariest thing was that I thoroughly enjoyed it – seeing him gurgle like that, making those awful noises in his throat. It was like . . . like . . . I don't know . . . like I was . . . I don't know how to quite put it . . . like I had forgotten everything about who I was during that single, searing moment of glorious violence. Does that make me a bad person, I ask you, Mr. Juan Sevilla? Does it make me what ordinary Christian folk such as yourself would call evil?'

---

[1] 'Holy mother of God!'

The bartender rapidly picks up the empty grog bottle by my side and puts it under the counter. 'Did they come and arrest you after that?'

'Aye, sir. That they did.'

'And then you were sent to prison?'

'Aye, sir. That and all — though I did, in all fairness, spend three years at a juvenile correctional facility before being transferred to what could be termed prison proper.'

'And what did your father the old Mr. Bestman in Gibraltar say?'

'My father the old Mr. Bestman?' I reply with an ironic smile. 'Not much. Or perhaps nothing at all. I will never know, will I, seeing that I never again heard from him.'

Juan Sevilla looks at me with an incredulous expression. 'You mean your old man never spoke to you again?'

'He disowned me, sir. Totally cut me out from his life. I had betrayed his sacred plan, you see. Torpedoed his designs for an all-powerful Bestman dynasty. For that, alas, he was never able to forgive me.'

'But he must have spoken to you again, surely?' the bartender says. 'Maybe some time later? After his disappointment was over? You were his son, *despues de todo.*'

'Not once, sir,' I reply. 'Not once. Although I did receive a letter shortly afterwards from Prescott and Lequich, lawyers and notaries, informing me that John Charles Bestman, proprietor of *Bestman's Tobacco Products*, had formally disinherited me and removed me from his will. That's the way my father liked to do things all his life — cleanly and surgically, with minimal human contact.'

'But that doesn't make sense,' the bartender says. 'The man must have been *medio loco* or something!'

'Possibly,' I reply, calmly stroking my chin. 'Quite possibly.'

'What about your mama? What did she say to all this?'

'You mean the woman who gave birth to me? Not a word, sir. Not a single b_____ word. She was never really interested in me, you see. Never had been. I was the fruit of a marriage that had been forced upon her, a permanent reminder of everything she had most come to hate. Consequently, she never really stomached me that much. As a matter of fact, she only wrote to me once. About ten years later. Just after my father had died of some kind of cancerous cerebral malady. She said that she had sold off the company and that she was moving back to Ireland, back to the village where her family originally came from, along with some fireman sergeant friend of hers. She said that she was starting a new life and that she did not want anything to do with Gibraltar any more. She did not say so explicitly, but reading between the lines you could tell that she did not want me to contact her. In the envelope there was a cheque for five pounds, sir. Five pounds. Out of the ten thousand or more that she must have sold the company for, Mrs. Molly Bestman sent me five pounds!'

Juan Sevilla looks down at the counter. 'That's tough. I'll say that much. Exceeding tough.'

'Mind you, Juan,' I say, taking another sip of my grog, 'there was at least one consolation. In the letter that my mother wrote, she said that my father had never been the same again after hearing about the Watson murder. She said that he had grown quiet and withdrawn, that he had started drinking regularly at night. . . . So I guess that in his own way he *did care* about me and what had happened. Enough to make him turn to the bottle at any rate. At least that's what I tell myself.'

'And how long again did you say you spent in jail?' the bartender asks.

'Twenty-five years altogether, sir. Twenty-five long and terrible years during which my only sustenance was the word of the Lord and the books of philosophical and religious instruction which I borrowed from the good Deacon Gowan.'

'You make it all sound so very scary, sir. Truly you do.'

I nod affirmatively and then look away. 'What can I say, Juan? There are things embedded in my past that no man should have to talk about in the *first person possessive.*'

'I take it from that that you don't want to be asked about your time in jail?'

'And you take it right, sir.'

A curious glint then lights up the bartender's eye. 'What was so bad about it then?'

'You are funny, sir,' I say.

'Not funny, Mr. Bestman; just curious.'

'Either way, I think you're overstepping yourself somewhat.'

The bartender smiles and uncrosses his arms behind the counter. 'Oh come on, mister,' he says. 'I have to at least try to get an answer from you. You won't begrudge me that. That is what us Scorpions are known and justly famous for. Delving into all those familial nooks and crannies, trying to uncover each other's business. 'Tis the national pastime here – don't you know it?'

I raise my glass and take a quick swig. 'I will tell you one thing,' I subsequently say, putting the glass on the counter. 'It's something that I have never mentioned to anyone before, but seeing that you are so persistent, and that I will probably never see you again after tonight, I might just as well. . . . In Pentonville there was a man named Harry Stanson whom everybody knew as Harry Molasses. This Harry Molasses was a Flower and Dean Street man,[1] a

[1] A street in Whitechapel known during Victorian times for its concentration

professional magsman[1] who had been wheeled in on account of a failed job somewhere near Margate. He used to sing songs at night, old Harry did, even though we were all supposed to be quiet as tombstones. You know the sort – bawdy music hall songs with the innuendo piled on thick and deliciously expressive. No one really knew why he did it. Some said that he missed his missus something terrible, like, and that he sang his songs to remind himself of her caresses. Others that he was just a crazy old a___ who had no idea why he sang or what his songs were about. Myself, I wasn't too sure about any of that. Every man has his own way of coping with life inside and I guess that singing was just Molasses' way of making things that little bit more endurable. The problem, of course, was that singing, whether of the bawdy or the more uplifting Wesleyan variety, was not allowed in Pentonville. I will go farther than that: it was the type of thing that could easily cost you a severe beating. Still, Harry did not seem to mind any of this. They could shout at him. They could put him on half-rations. They could thrash him within an inch of his life. None of this would stop him from singing his music hall arias whenever it took his fancy.

'But then one day something very strange happened: Harry Molasses suddenly stopped singing. He went quiet just like that. Everyone on our floor, you can imagine, was very relieved at first – thinking that at least now we would get a decent night's kip. But after a few days had passed we all started wondering what had caused old Harry to stop. Finally, one of the more affable screws explained what had happened to one of the prisoners, who in turn told everybody else.

'One day, you see, Harry's wife had come to tell him that she was thinking of hitching up with somebody else. She said that she was sick and tired of being alone and that she was having trouble surviving on the three or four weekly shillings that she earned as a seamstress. "How's I going to carry ern feeding arr children and payeen for summun to look after thar wights?" she told poor Harry. "If I don't latch meself onto this new man, I will be turned out into

---

of criminal types.

[1] A magsman, in Victorian rhyming slang, is a conman.

thar street and then who's gonna take care of arr Billy and arr little Nelly?" Being a sentimental man, Harry did not take this very well. His wife, his precious darling wife, was going to leave him for somebody else! How could he possibly endure life's degradations knowing that he was being cuckolded in this way? That same evening Harry made up his mind: if Florence was going to run off with some unknown guy, why, he might as well kill himself that very night! To this end, he got up later that evening on his stool and tried to hang himself with an elastic cord that until moments before had held up his prisoner's trousers. . . . But then fate intervened: the cord proved too weak to sustain Harry's frame and he came crashing down to the ground. Not to be outdone, Molasses smashed the legs of his wooden stool and then used one of the splinters to open up his veins. This seemed to do the trick – but unfortunately all that smashing up of wooden bits attracted the screws' attention and, before you knew it, Harry was being spirited down to the prison's medical dispensary on the ground floor. There they cleaned up his wounds and patched him up and then tied him down to a chair. They also, it goes without saying, socked him once or twice for having had the temerity to cause such a fuss after visiting hours.

'They then left him there, thinking that tied down to the chair Molasses couldn't get up to any more mischief. Unfortunately, someone had forgotten to put away the bottle of *Ingwersen's Phenyle* which they had used to clean up his wounds. Harry, being the observant type, noticed this and shifted his chair as best as he could towards the table on which stood the uncapped bottle. He then knocked the bottle over with his forehead and proceeded to lap up its deadly contents, hoping by this means to dispatch himself from this world to the next. Sadly for Harry, though, the phenyle did not kill him. No, sir, that it did not. It just caused irreparable damage to his stomach and his lungs, as well as damaging his vocal chords for ever. Harry Molasses, from that day onwards, became known to us all as "Harry No Voices".'

I put my glass down and smile at the bartender Sevilla. Something tells me that he is not impressed, that he was expecting to hear some shocking tale of sodomy and merciless establishment brutality; but I do not care less — I do not intend to dredge up any further scabrous little anecdotes for his benefit.

'When were you released from jail?' the bartender presently asks.

'I was released on the sixth day of this February past, at ten minutes past ten. Twenty-two years to the day when I first walked in through the grand marble archway leading into the Pent,' I say and then pause awhile for dramatic effect. 'True clockwork precision. That's what makes the British Empire great, that is.'

'And what did you do then?'

'After my release?' I ask, casually picking up my glass. 'Not that much, if truth be told. I travelled here, I travelled there. Went up to Oxford. Came back to London. Spent a few days in a tree-house habitation in a forest in Kent. Did a little bit of oyster-picking along the banks of the Medway. Slept inside an abandoned chicken farm on the Isle of Grain. Picked up a few 'pures' for the gardeners at Ranleighs. The wild and wonderful ways of the newly-released prison convict.'

'And then, I take it, you came here?'

'Not immediately,' quoth I. 'First, I worked at a tannery in Highgate for two months. Needed a few more pounds to add to the sum my mother sent me before I could purchase my passage ticket.'

'Which you finally bought one day and then, next thing you know, lo and behold, you suddenly find yourself sitting in *The Tail* with Juan Sevilla telling him all about your sundry infelicities?'

I smile and put my glass back on the counter. 'Yes — something like that — with a couple of days in between tossing and turning in some seaborne repository of disease and a few weeks struggling to make ends meet in some flea-pit s___-hole in Angelo's Gully. 'Tis a great story, don't you think? Worthy of being turned into a novel and all. *A Returning Colonial's Tale* — that would be its title. The most fantastickal story of a man who was forced to leave his hometown and who had to endure twenty-five years of tortures and unremitting buggery before he was able to wind his way back to his beloved Rock.'

The bartender does not seem to appreciate my self-mocking tone. 'I'm not so sure about that. I mean, about it being a great story and all. I may not be much of a reading man myself, but this much I know and that is that novels are supposed to end well, with all the characters happy and greatly contented.'

'Well, I am here now drinking with you, sir. Isn't that a happy end in itself, my *bartendering* critic of the Literary Arts?'

Juan Sevilla once again shakes his head. 'Maybe so — but look at you, Mr. Bestman: you are as poor as they come and you have been hoodwinked out of a fortune that should have been rightfully yours. That is not the kind of end you find in a novelistic book, sir. You know the type I mean: where the fellow gets married to his sweetheart and inherits a fortune and suchlike rubbish.'

'Ah, sir. You are a *most* discerning critic,' I say, grabbing my glass and tilting its contents into my mouth. 'A most discerning critic. Why don't you bring out another bottle from under the counter and be so kind as to join me for another drink?'

I do not, in all fairness, remember much about what happened after the third bottle appeared. I think we talked about the kind of things that men talk about in Gibraltarian taverns: what the soldiers of the 58$^{th}$ had been doing last week, who had been captured at the frontier smuggling tobacco and who had got through, what Governor Hardinge had said about Maltese immigrants during a private conversation with the Chairman of the Exchange, whether all this talk about a new dockyard should be taken seriously or not — the usual stuff, in other words, that men talk about when there's nothing else left to say. Finally, at some point between one and two o'clock, I must have staggered my way back home. I write 'I must' because I do not have any actual recollection of undertaking that particular journey, the only thing that I can recall with any certainty being standing in front of my door struggling to fit the key into its lock. Apart from that, I can't remember anything else.

**The tenth day of December, 1888**

For the second time in two days, I have woken up with a feverish distemper and a garland of blood drops on my pillow. I feel weak and desperately tired, a state of affairs made all the worse by the furious headache that has been pulsing between my eyes since the morning after my drunken escapade at *The Ape's Tail*. My first thought this morning was to stay in, but I knew that I could not justify such inactivity in the light of my financial situation. Therefore, I breakfasted on eggs and a little bread and then, donning some garments and gritting my teeth, went outside. The sky was grey and miserable as far as the eye could see, with the Levanter hanging like soupy Whitechapel factory-fumes over the terraced rooftops. After visiting a few establishments along Main Street, I went down to the Line-Wall, where I watched some ships anchoring at the Coaling station. I was feeling rather glum, but my spirits quickly picked up when I discovered that someone had left a half-eaten breadstick on the bench next to mine. The bread was soft and tender too, as if it had just been baked a few hours earlier. After I had finished it, I told myself that I would return to Main Street at one o'clock and continue looking for employ. But when the time came I grew disenchanted with everything and decided to return home. As I reached the top of *la Calle Comedia* some ten or fifteen minutes later, I came across a woman who seemed vaguely familiar. She had coarse, grey-flecked hair that fell down to her shoulders and eyes that shone like shards of obsidian. An archetypal Scorpion woman, if ever there was one. I cannot explain how, but I somehow got it into my head that she was none other than Lorena Lozano, the daughter of our old washerwoman and my secret *camarada de armas* in the Bestman residence. I was positively and totally convinced that this was so. 'Lorena,' I said, staggering towards the woman and grasping her by the shoulder. 'It's me, Charles, Charles Bestman. Don't you remember me?' For a second the woman looked at me without saying a word — her eyebrows raised in a V across her forehead, a mixture of fear and curiosity glinting across the dark and bottomless pools that were her eyes. '*No hablo ingles*,' she then said, quickly turning away. '*Por favor no me molestes mas. Soy casada y madre de tres niños. . . .*' [1]

**The eleventh day of December, 1888**

I got a note delivered today saying that Esadras will be coming soon with a bailiff to collect his tenancy monies. The note was written on fine vellum paper and signed with a flourishing hand, its inflated loops and triple-crossed Ts (his surname is Tudela Tartas) more suited to a duke than a gnarled little skull-capped man. Jamiel would have got on splendidly with him, I am sure.

**The twelfth day of December, 1888**

Not much to report. On my way back from buying bread this morning, I stopped at a cafe and partook of some refreshments. I should not have done this, seeing that I am down to my last few *centimes* — but it was very cold and I was very tired and I desperately needed some *revitalising*. The cafe I chose was the *Universal* on Main Street. It is a strange little place, I have to confess, this rundown but highly popular cafe on the Rock's main thoroughfare. Its walls are splattered with a curious array of English and Spanish advertisements - one for *Bass's Ale* here, another for *Brandy Tamarindo* there, yet another for the *Gibraltar Chronicle* just a few yards away. The waiters are nearly all Spaniards from La Linea - dark-skinned, indolent types who slouch near the serving counter smoking cigarillos and doing their best to ignore their customers. Across the floor, meanwhile, you find a truly cosmopolitan array of characters: a group of Scorpions, sitting at their tables with their hats by their side and their *capas* flung over their chairs; one or two military men, drinking and guffawing out loud; three or four Musulmans, sitting quietly with just a solitary tea on the table between them. At hourly intervals a small, bow-tied man by the name of Castro comes out from behind a screen and begins to play some Spanish music on the piano. This Castro individual is very popular with the patrons, judging from the rapturous applause and the cries of 'bravo, maestro' which greet his appearances. After a few notes, he is joined by several Spanish girls, who start dancing

---

[1] 'I don't speak English. Please stop following me. I'm married and a mother of three children.'

and playing the castanets around him. From the coquettish manner these *señoritas* throw roses at some of the patrons, you'd be forgiven for thinking that something altogether indecent is unfolding before your eyes — but you could not be more mistaken. No, sir, the *Universal* is an utterly respectable establishment. 'A place fit for the whole family', as the advertising blackboards by the entrance proudly proclaim. If you are looking for musical entertainment of a different kind, you are better off heading to some of the less discriminating venues in town — such as *The Glass Barrel* on Cornwall's Parade, or *The London Bar* at the junction between Governor's Street and Governor's Parade.

**The thirteenth day of December, 1888**

I feel very ill and debilitated once again. There are thick, wine-red slivers of blood mixed in with my sputum and I am having trouble just sitting at the table and writing. Also my chest is hurting and gripped by an oppressive sensation, as if some invisible spectral hand had closed itself over my heart. For what it's worth, I have resolved to disregard my scruples and smuggle some *picadura* tobacco into Spain. I am not very comfortable with the idea, but there is just no other way left to escape the present slide into indigence. I will start by smuggling two pesetas' worth of the stuff and then selling it on the other side for about ten. I will then return to Gibraltar with the profits accrued and buy more merchandise, which I will in turn smuggle back into Spain. It is said (or so at least I have heard) that the Spanish *aduaneros*[1] are not as observant in the discharge of their duties with English members of the garrison. I will therefore pass myself off as an innocent tourist on his way to a pic-nic at the Cork Woods — trying to look as lost as possible and asking a few questions in English just to reinforce this illusion.

I already have the tobacco with me; it is currently lying in seven brightly-coloured pouches on the table. I bought it this morning from the shop attached to my father's old manufactory. A sad old business, as you can imagine. I have already unstitched the seams of my coat, so as to produce a thin compartment between the lining and the leather. I will insert the tobacco into the said compartment

[1] Customs agents.

tonight, pinning it downs by means of hooked little wires and trying to distribute it evenly to avoid the sight of any telltale bulges on the outside. It is not the most foolproof method of concealment, I know, but it is all I can aspire to at the moment. Besides, the smuggling of goods into Spain has always been something of a lottery – dependant not so much on how well you conceal the goods, but on whether you are unlucky enough to get stopped and searched by the Spanish customs men. I must cease writing now, as I feel sick and faint and need some rest. May the Lord grant me the strength to succeed in my endeavours tomorrow. Well does He know that I am only turning to this deplorable business because I am hungry and thoroughly out of sorts. 'We are troubled on every side, yet not distressed; we are perplexed, but not in despair; persecuted, but not forsaken; cast down, but not destroyed.' (II Corinthians 4:8)

**The sixteenth day of December, 1888**

It was my last chance. My final opportunity. And now it is gone. Now there are no more chances left. And yet it could have all turned out so differently, could it not? After crossing the frontier, I thought that I was there, that I was finally on my way towards economic salvation. Why not, after all? Why not? Why b_____ not? The hardest part had already been achieved and I was about to be recompensed for my efforts. And yet I was duped, tricked, betrayed by my naivety. A man appeared from nowhere. I can see him now: grey-haired, unshaven, a typical scoundrel from the Lines. He asked me in Spanish if I was selling tobacco and I said yes. '*Entonces venga usted por aquí*,' he said, leading me down one of the hundreds of labyrinthine alleys that the Lines is famous for.[1] Accursed be the moment that I first set sight on him, *maldita la sangre que corre en sus venas.* Yes, I was tricked. I was duped. I was led to the most recondite corner on earth and then set upon by a gang of Linense thugs who took my tobacco and beat me for the privilege. '*Maldito ingles*!' they shouted at me even as I was being kicked and punched. '*Vendiendo tabaco como uno de los nuestros*! *Quien te crees que eres*?'[2] It must have been my accent which betrayed

---

[1]'Then come with me this way.'

[2]'Damn Englishman!Selling tobacco like one of ours! Who does he think he is?'

me, that stupid, useless intonation which has left me straddled between two worlds, unable to belong to either. Or maybe they already saw me coming — so nervous and unsure of myself did I feel just then. Whatever it was, they did not stop kicking and punching me until I was left there, lying in a pool of my own blood, the same precious blood that is now slowly being extracted from me with every accursed, lung-shredding cough. Just how long I remained lying there either I cannot say. Maybe it was an hour. Maybe it was two hours. Lying in that godforsaken corner of that godforsaken town, time no longer meant anything. Reality slowed down. Experience itself imploded and contracted into a spinning gyroscope located outside my own senses. All that mattered instead was the wind, its ebbing and flowing, its chorus of broken sighs. Again and again it blew over me, passing over my inert body like a susurrated benediction, gently stirring the blood-encrusted hairs on my wounded head. Voices, flickering lights, moving figures, two calloused hands clasped behind a grey overcoat, a granite headstone with no name, a feeling that I am being watched by some gigantic blood-filled eye in the sky: did I really dream about these things or have I retrospectively superimposed them on my dream-memories? One thing I will say, one thing I know for certain: someone must have helped me to my feet. How else could I have got up and managed to stagger back through the frontier? I remember a presence, a living shadow. I turn to one side and it is there, fuzzy and indistinct, almost unreal. I wish I could register a face, the curve of a supporting shoulder, but all that I am aware of are shadows, movements, a silhouette that is constantly being redrawn against the flickering haloes of luminosity behind it. Who is carrying me unbidden in this way? Who is it that is dragging me through the desolate marshlands of the neutral ground? A voice inside me says, 'It is your conscience that is dragging you, Charles. It is the memory of Godliness in you that has come to rescue your wounded soul.' I want to believe this, I want to believe it with all my might, but I know that a conscience cannot carry someone's weight. Maybe it is someone who has taken pity on me, I tell myself. Maybe it is my guardian angel. Maybe it is a wicked demon who does not want me to die before I have lived through my pre-allotted sufferings and tribulations. I do not know. All I know is that I somehow made it back to Gibraltar and that for the last two or three days I have been lying here in my bed, alternating between consciousness and the world of dreams. Sometimes I have been able to look up from my pillow; other times I have been too powerless to do even that. All during this time I have been coughing up blood — so much blood that my sheets are covered in dark and petal-like patches of red, just like the bridal sheets of a devirginated bride. There is blood on the floor too, scattered here and there like that in a butcher's abattoir. On the table, incidentally, there is another letter from Esadras. It must have been delivered yesterday, or the day before yesterday — it is hard to tell. Outside it is raining. I think it is rain at least, but perhaps it's the sound of the wind. I am, needless to say, very confused. And I am very tired. Even as I write these words, the world keeps on spinning and spinning. I do not know if this makes any sense, but I feel like a lifeless shadow, a mound of broken stones, something beyond the limits of ordinary terrestrial consciousness. I am also very scared, but I am trying to hold on to the promise that the Lord has made to the believer. 'Thou shalt not be afraid for the terror by night; nor for the arrow that flieth by day; nor for the pestilence that walketh in darkness; nor for the destruction that wasteth at noonday.' (Psalms 91:5)

**The seventeenth day of December, 1888**

Made my way to the hospital this morning. Felt very sick and faint, constantly bending down and vomiting thick spurts of black blood. At the hospital I got told to come back on Monday as there were no surgeons currently available. When I told them that I urgently needed to see someone, they became very arrogant and dismissive, as if they could not believe that I, an indigent beggar of no importance, was daring to question their hallowed words. 'Cursed be the man that trusteth in man,' I promptly whispered the words of the Prophet Jeremiah. 'For he shall be like tamaric in the desert, and he shall not see when good shall come.' Subsequently, I made my way back home very slowly and with faltering step, as if carrying a deadweight strapped to my shoulders. Somewhere between the ramp known as Chicardos Passage and the next sequence of steps beyond it, I came to a decision. If there is a hell and I am consigned to it for my crimes, I will come back to haunt them. The nurses and the surgeons, the porters and the high-collared officials: all those unsmiling bureaucrats who look upon you as if you were a cockroach crawling into their daily salad bowl. You know who you are, you money-driven beasts. My blood will drip down onto your heads and stain the colour of your eyes. My tombstone will be as a stake driven into your black and charcoaled hearts. Yes, I will haunt you, do not doubt that. I will follow you wherever you go, leering at you during your every waking hour. I will taunt you, I will mock you, I will be the shadow that besmirches your innermost thoughts. When you wake up, I will be there. When you go to sleep, I will be there. When you look into the mirror, I will be the shadow that creeps out of the surrounding darkness and buries itself in your soul. An eye for an eye and a tooth for a tooth. So it was written and so it shall come to pass. . . . But what am I saying? Why am I so full of vengeful thoughts like these? Is it right that a man teetering across life's threshold should be driven on by so many hatreds? I do not understand myself sometimes. Here I am, clinging to the edge of hope, and yet I persist in buttressing myself with bitternesses and cold hatreds. Is this the way that a man should prepare to meet his maker? Should I not be considering another way? Remember the Lord's own words while sermonising on the Mount: 'Ye have heard that it hath been said, Thou shalt love thy neighbour, and hate thine enemy. But I say unto you, Love your enemies, bless them that curse you, do good to them that hate you, and pray for them which despitefully use you, and persecute you. That ye may be the children of your Father which is in heaven: for he maketh his sun to rise on the evil and on the good, and sendeth rain on the just and on the unjust.'

**The eighteenth day of December, 1888**

I went to bed last night thinking that I would die in my sleep. Very strange sensation. You are lying there listening to your own breathing, floating in a vacuum that has been fleshed out from your own [______].[1] Sometimes it is quiet; sometimes you can hear the rush of your own blood coursing through your veins. You look to the ceiling one moment and you see demons, mischievous, grimacing gargoyles with lubricious eyes and gaping mouths that clamour for the trembling flower-petal that is your soul. Then you look again a

---

[1] Indistinguishable word.

few seconds later and you see angels, quiet and gentle-faced seraphim with hands extended imploringly towards you. What else can I say? I have become a diffused bundle of consciousness, a receptacle of random sensory impressions. Everything outside this coil of feeling has long since been forgotten: Mr. Serfaty, the job that I was promised, Esadras's rent money, my years of exile. 'What else can I say apart from this?' I ask you. I cannot visualise the future. I cannot recreate the past. I cannot even imagine things outside this room because my imagination has been cut down and compressed into the capillaries of my diseased body. Does this make sense, I wonder? Can anyone who-is-not-me really understand what I'm saying? I don't know. I am not really sure. Once upon a time, for what it's worth, I read that you are only ready to die when you stop being able to imagine your future. Sounds too black upon white, if you ask me, too reassuringly compartmentalised. And yet it's strange, nevertheless, isn't it? This sense of passivity? This submissiveness of the spirit? If someone would have told me months ago, for example, that I would have been at death's door and felt so passive, I would have found it hard to believe. Death is fear, I would have said. Death is anxiety. Death is the silent scythe that one day suddenly begins to swing above our heads. How can you just sit there and calmly wait for it to pass?. . . And yet look at me now – sitting here on this filthy bed, doing nothing other than spitting blood and wiping the sweat across my forehead, slowly surrendering to the illness which is gnawing away at my spirit. Ultimately, that is the way of all flesh, I suppose. We think that we will rage and fight against the reaper's coming, kicking and screaming like a newborn being dragged into the light, but in the end we go out with a noiseless whimper, a downward movement of the eyes. That does not mean to say that I am not frightened. No, do not mistake my passivity or lack of reaction for equanimity or composure. I am frightened, let it be said. I am sweating fear through every pore of my body. In fact, I will go one step farther and say that I cannot imagine a world without me in it, unable to conceptualise what it must be like to have my all-too-human thoughts and frailties suddenly and everlastingly replaced with an empty chasm of blackness. Why is it then that I am able to sit here without giving vent to the cowering fear that I feel inside? It is very simple. I am scared and passive at the same time, knowing that no histrionics or curses or prayers or ritual invocations on my part can delay the execution of the grim inevitable. That is the ultimate truth about those caught on the threshold between life and death: we are so bereft of hope and expectation that even fear stops following its usual cycle.

**The nineteenth day of December, 1888**
'And I will bring the blind by a way that they knew not; I will lead them in paths that they have not known; I will make darkness light before them, and crooked things straight. These things will I do unto them, and not forsake them.' (Isaiah 42:16)

**The twentieth day of December, 1888**
I am doing very well again. I feel most refreshed and full of vitality. Jamiel came in to see me this morning and said that he had been wanting to write to me, but that he had fallen ill and died shortly after he had reached this decision. That is why you never heard from me, he said. He also told me that he had done the things he did because he was totally mad. I told him not to worry and then I made two cups of tea. We drank them together next to the lit fire. He was most courteous throughout, telling me about his plans for his new tobacco manufactory. He says he is going to sell a new brand of cigars. *Bestman's Number Thirteen* — that's what he will call them.

**The twenty-first day of December, 1888**
Periods of lucidity, alternating with feverish delirium. Dull throb just above the eyes and extremely tightened neck and shoulder ligaments. Esadras must have let himself in at some point during the last five or six hours, for there is another envelope on the table. I haven't been able to get up and open it. I wish I could — I hate the thought of a sealed envelope.

**The twenty-second day of December, 1888**
The rain is still falling against the window panes and the *tina* under the leaking ceiling has once again overflowed. I want to get up to clear the mess, but even writing these lines is a terrible struggle.

**The twenty-fourth day of December, 1888**

Jamiel came in this morning and told me not to worry. He brought me a bottle of cough syrup and said that we would talk again when I get better. I must make sure to buy some more *huevos cascados* tomorrow. There is a place at the bottom of Rodger's Ramp where they are only eighty centimes a dozen. That's really cheap for *huevos cascados*. Really, really cheap.

**

## Editor's note

The journal of Charles Bestman was discovered behind some loose brickwork in a house in Arengo's Palace Gully in August, 1997. The person who discovered the notebook, a Moroccan labourer by the name of Idrissi Ben Mohammed, handed it over to Mr. Francis Cuenca, a retired shop steward who had taught him how to read and write in English at the beginning of the 1980s. For the next five or six years the journal remained in Cuenca's sole possession. Then, towards the end of 2003, I was introduced to Cuenca by my friend Steven Kenneth Cloud. While the three of us sipped coffee together at the *Piazza Grill*, Cuenca revealed to me that he was in possession of a handwritten diary dating back to the late nineteenth century. He assured me that the diary did not deal with very interesting things — '*mayormente algun enrollo de familia*' was how he described it — although, perhaps, he conceded, it could have some latent historical value. Rather intrigued, I asked him if I could have a look at the journal. Mr. Cuenca agreed without hesitation, although he warned me not to expect anything too interesting.

About six o'clock the next day, I met Mr. Cuenca at his apartment in Humphrey's Estate. After a cup of tea and some small talk, he led me from his kitchen to the spare room. From a chest of drawers he produced a badly tattered notebook tied with a pink ribbon. As he carefully untied the ribbon and opened the book, I noticed that the diarist's hand was small and crabbed, quite unlike the flourishing hand you would have expected from a late Victorian. The writing also seemed to get smaller and more crabbed as the diary progressed, as if the author were labouring under a progressively worsening malady. My curiosity piqued, I asked Cuenca if I could take away the journal and examine it for a few days. At first the retired shop steward resisted this idea — saying that the notebook was in too fragile a state to be taken anywhere — but eventually he agreed on the proviso that I returned the diary by the end of the week. Over the next few days I read

Bestman's journal and carefully transcribed its contents into my computer. I also conducted some background investigations of my own. From the Gibraltar government archives, for example, I was able to ascertain that Bestman died two days after his last journal entry, on the twenty-sixth of December, 1888. The cause of death was listed as unknown, with the word 'tuberculosis' added in parenthesis next to a question mark. I also checked the *Gibraltar Chronicle* archive in the Garrison library and found one or two items of news that corroborated the journal's contents — including the arrival of the *S. S. Zadane* on the seventh of November and the reported loss of an Afghan war medal in the Scud Hill area some weeks later.

Overall I do not think the diary is as boring as Mr. Cuenca made out. Although not the most scintillating piece of Victorian literature, it still offers us a very vivid glimpse into the trials and tribulations of fin-de-siècle colonial life and also helps us understand the relationship between Gibraltarian merchants and their military overlords. For once, too, we have in our possession a nineteenth-century text written by a native Gibraltarian (rather than by some mildly amused, parasol-brandishing Englishman). This is something that has eluded us for many years and it would be a shame indeed if such a seminal text continued to remain unknown to Gibraltarian scholars and educated readers in general. With this in mind, I approached several Gibraltarian cultural bodies at the beginning of 2005 to see if they were interested in publishing Bestman's journal. Their response, however, was extremely disappointing. Some said that the diary was too morbid; others that it did not contain enough topographical or historical detail to warrant publication; others (perhaps even more remarkably) that it did not talk about Gibraltar in an appropriate light. Consequently, I decided to forget about officialdom and see if the private sector would be interested in sponsoring the diary's publication. I tried all the mercantile groups and organisations that I could think of: banks, lawyers, accountants, betting companies, foreign multinationals. Unfortunately, the private sector's attitude was equally unenthusiastic and is best summed up by the response I got from a member of the Gibraltarian banking fraternity: 'If this was a cookbook of local recipes or something like that, then yes, *por que no* — we'd be happy to fund publication. But the diary of an alcoholic murderer who hardly lived here anyway — that's just not something we would like to associate with.' In the end it was only thanks to Rock Scorpion books, a small independent Anglo-Gibraltarian publishing company based in the UK, that things finally got going. Although Rock Scorpion foresaw that Bestman's journal would probably never become a bestseller, they recognised its historical value and decided to publish it and distribute it in both Gibraltar and the UK. In the words of Rock Scorpion's director of marketing, Ms. Danielle Bryant, 'isn't it about time that we Gibraltarians, who celebrate a version of Gibraltarian history in which our ancestors seldom appear, should start to acknowledge and read about our own past instead?' As a Gibraltarian historian and commentator, I have to agree. Even if history does not always reinforce the myths we invent for ourselves, we should always strive to uncover its hidden truths. To refuse to do so is not just academically reprehensible; it is an insult to the generations that struggled and suffered so that we can enjoy the privileges of today.

E. E. Pedroso,
University of Strathclyde,
23-10-2006.

# Costa Cuttings

## A modern tragi-comedy in sixty cinematic scenes

### 1.

*A Costa del Sol beach. The sound of crashing waves. There are six or seven bodies lying on the sand, most of them face down. A man in a dark blue uniform is going around laying blankets over them. A large crowd watches behind a hastily erected police line. Somehow or the other a small toddler has got past the line and has waddled his way towards one of the bodies. For a few seconds he stands there, quite entranced by the shapeless figure lying before him. 'Alejandro, Alejandro,' a woman's voice suddenly shouts from somewhere in the crowd. 'Come here right now. What do you think you're doing? Come back here right now!' That moment a Guardia Civil walks up to the boy and leads him back to the mother. 'I'm so, so sorry,' the mother, a blonde woman with a pink sarong tied around her waist, says to the Guardia. 'He's always running off. Don't know what I'm going to do with him.' 'Don't worry,' the Guardia replies, patting the young boy on the head while staring down at the woman's breasts. 'It's not his fault that these "moros" launch themselves out into the Straits in their ridiculous little boats. Someone should tell the idiots that it's a dangerous sea out there.' Presently the camera pulls back and we are shown a panorama of a crowded beach. The camera then weaves its way in and out of different beachgoing types [a geriatric with glasses licking an ice cream, a young woman applying suncream to her breasts, a little brat sulking next to his parents] until it reaches the wall that separates the beach from the adjoining road. Three Spanish youths, Chus, Juanjo and Rafa, are sitting on this wall.*

Juanjo: Look at the tits on that. Just look at them. I'd gladly quit my studies just to get a feel of those lovelies.

Chus [meditatively]: They're not bad, are they? Not bad at all. . . . What nationality do you think these chicks are, Juanjo – Swedish, German or English?

Juanjo: Not sure. They don't look pale enough to be Scandinavian. Probably German or English, I think.

Rafa: *Cristo Dios*, can't you two do anything other than look at women's breasts? Do you have to act like a pair of stereotypical Iberian *pervertidos* wherever we go?

Chus [ignoring Rafa's comments]: Look, I think that one of them is looking at us. Yes, yes, she definitely is. Look, Juanjo. She's smiling. She's smiling at us!

Juanjo: Yes, you're right. [Smiling back at the girls; between his teeth.] *Carry on smiling, you little 'guiri' bitch. Carry on smiling. I'll give you something to smile about when I get hold of you and fuck your ass tonight*!

Rafa: Christ almighty!

Chus [very excitedly]: Look, look! She's waving at us. The blonde one's waving at us!

Rafa: You guys just freak me out, do you know that? There's half a dozen dead illegal immigrants lying on that beach and all you can think of is copping off with the first girls you see.

Chus [ignoring Rafa again]: I think you should go down there on a reconnoitring mission, Juanjo. Try and see what they're up to tonight. Maybe you can convince them to come with us to *La Pequeña Lulu.*

Juanjo: Yes, maybe you're right. Let Captain Juanjo go and reel the three little bitches in. I'll tell them that we've got some free drink tokens for tonight or some other bullshit. You know what these *guiri* bitches are willing to do for a few drinks.

[Juanjo hops down from the wall and starts making his way to the girls. Chus immediately leans forwards, trying to get a better view of what is happening down below.]

Rafa: You guys are just unbelievable. Simply unbelievable.

Chus: What was that again?

Rafa: I said you guys are just like . . . I don't know . . . walking barrels of testosterone or something.

Chus: Come on, Rafa. It's just a bit of fun. Life's not just about stethoscopes and abdominal examinations, *tio*.

Rafa: Yeah, whatever.

Chus: You should try and relax, man. Go with the flow for a while. Smoke a few joints, drink a few *cubatas*, chat some birds up. Remember the old proverb about all work and no play. . . . [Getting excited all of a sudden.] Look at Juanjo. He's getting all cosy with them. What a fucking cool customer. We'll be having a drink with these *furcias* at *La Pequeña Lulu* before you know it.

Rafa: Jesus, if you guys are the future of the Spanish medical profession, I might just as well emigrate now!

Chus [totally focused on the beach]: That's it, Juanjo: give them a little bit of the old Latin charm. Flex your pecs and put on your pretty-boy smile. Get them all lathered up inside their G-strings. [Rafa shakes his head despairingly at this last comment.] Show them what they could be getting their grubby little hands on tonight.

Rafa: And to think that you guys will probably be taking the Hippocratic oath in a year or two!

Chus: Look, look! He's already touching the blonde one on the shoulder. The guy's sure got balls.

Rafa [disgustedly]: *Joder*!

Chus: That's it, Juanjo — charm them into submission, boy. Knock them down with our legendary Andalusian charisma. . . . Look, the all-conquering hero approacheth.

[Juanjo appears moments later sporting a wide smile.]

Chus: Well, what did they say?

Juanjo: They said they'd come. I told them that we'd treat them to a few drinks tonight and they agreed to meet us at *La Pequeña Lulu* at half-nine. [Punching the air behind the wall.] Captain Juanjo reels them in yet again, *muchachos*!

Chus: Where are they from?

Juanjo: Don't know. Didn't ask. English, I think. Fuck knows. [Slapping Chus on the thigh.] Let's go somewhere and have a drink, shall we? Don't want to give the bitches the impression that we're drooling over them, do we?

Rafa [under his breath]: Yeah, right.

Chus [hopping down from the wall]: Sure. I wouldn't mind knocking down a few *jarras* of *San Miguel*. . . . Did you say that all three of the girls are coming?

Juanjo: Yes, all three. Do you know what that means? [He turns towards Rafa.] Even Einstein here might get laid.

Rafa [matter-of-factly]: I wouldn't be so sure about that, Juanjo.

Juanjo [grabbing Rafa by the neck and playfully ruffling his hair]: I was only joking, you silly fuck. Stop taking things so seriously, will you?

[Juanjo and Rafa tussle goodnaturedly with each other. After a few seconds, the three lads start walking away from the wall.]

**2.**

*A busy Costa nightclub. Loud techno music. Smoke-filled semi-darkness. Juanjo and Chus are on the dance floor with two of the young Englishwomen. Rafa is sitting at a table with the remaining girl, looking detached and somewhat uncomfortable. After a very long pause, the girl turns to him.*

The girl [shouting above the din]: Do you like it here?

Rafa: No, not very much. Do you?

The girl: Not particularly. . . . What did you say your name was again?

Rafa: Rafa.

The girl: Say again?

Rafa: Rafa.

[A long pause.]

The girl: I'm going to go outside for a bit of fresh air, Rafa. Do you want to come?

[Rafa nods.]

**3.**

*A large balcony overlooking the sea. Loud music coming from inside the building. Rafa and the girl are looking out over the balcony. The girl is lighting a cigarette.*

The girl [after a while]: Do you smoke?

[Rafa nods. The girl offers him a cigarette and lights it for him.]

Your friends won't get anywhere with Judy and Trudy, you know. They both have boyfriends back home.

Rafa: I think you're telling the wrong person.

The girl [after an even longer pause; turning slightly towards him]: You're not like the other two, are you?

Rafa: Like Juanjo and Chus?

[He smiles.]

I should hope not.

The girl [looking out over the balcony]: Look, there's *Alpha Canis Majoris*. The 'dog star'.

Rafa: I can't see anything.

The girl: There, directly above that belltower. Just trace an imaginary line upwards until you see a fuzzy, sort of bluish speck of light. It's one of the closest stars to earth — just 8.57 light years away. It is visible from every inhabited point on the earth's surface.

Rafa: You seem to know a lot about stars.

The girl: I'm studying Philosophy of Science at college.

Rafa: Are the three of you studying the same thing?

The girl: Judy is doing Media Studies and Trudy Packaging and Design.

Rafa: Packaging and Design?

The girl: You know – designing packages for foodstuffs and things like that.

Rafa: Oh.

The girl: People study shit like that in the UK.

Rafa: Right.

The girl: You guys are students too, aren't you? Juanjo — or whatever his name is — was saying earlier.

Rafa: Yes. We're studying at the University of Málaga.

The girl: What are you studying?

Rafa: Medicine.

The girl: All three of you?

Rafa: Yes. Hard to believe, isn't it?

The girl [looking at the sky again]: I can imagine you as a doctor, but not the others.

Rafa: I'll take that as a compliment.

The girl: I tend to avoid doctors if I can. I find them too patronising. Have you read Michel Foucault?

Rafa: Michel Foucault?

The girl: He's a French cultural philosopher. He writes about power relationships between doctors and patients. Every doctor should read his works, in my opinion.

Rafa: I'll try and remember his name.

The girl [after a pause]: Do you know — your English is something else!

Rafa: What do you mean?

The girl: I mean it's fucking bloody brilliant, that's what I mean.

Rafa: Thanks. I've worked really hard to reach this level. I'm hoping to do a post-doc in America after I finish here.

The girl: Really? Where exactly in the States?

Rafa: Cleveland. They're supposed to have the best neurosurgery department in the world there.

The girl: Interesting. . . . [Turning towards him and smiling.] Anyway, I'm going to go back to the hotel: it's getting really cold out here and this is not really my kind of scene. Do you mind walking me there, please? It's just round the corner from this place.

**4.**

*A narrow, cobbled alley on the way back to the hotel. Rafa and the girl are walking along the alley about a metre apart. A metal lamppost illuminates their movements.*

The girl: If it was up to me, I'd force every aspiring medic to sit in front of a rotting corpse for a few days. Get them to stare at death in the eyeballs and reflect on their own mortality. Maybe then they would stop being so goddamned arrogant and condescending when they qualified as doctors.

Rafa: Sounds a bit extreme.

The girl: I just don't like the medical establishment's collective attitude. At the moment I'm seeing this doctor in Leeds because of a recurring ear infection. Can't be much older than thirty, thirty-one. What an arrogant, pompous, conceited, self-satisfied little bitch, I tell you. You'd think that she shits diamonds and pearls from the way she looks down on you, the silly cow.

Rafa: I think doctors are like that everywhere. You should see some of the ones that lecture us in our *facultad* in Málaga.

The girl: Foucault was right, you know. Medical knowledge carries an associative risk of megalomania. I'm surprised that you haven't read him yet.

Rafa: Don't be so surprised. I'm afraid that I don't know much apart from the subject I'm studying. Chus and Juanjo and the others have somehow got it into their heads that I'm some kind of mad, eccentric, scientific genius, but the truth is I'm just some average, ordinary guy who just happens to study very, very hard.

The girl: Why do you think you are like that?

Rafa: What do you mean?

The girl: Why do you study so hard?

Rafa: I don't know. Family pressure, I suppose.

The girl: Family pressure?

Rafa: I have three older brothers and they're all doctors. I don't want to be the exception.

The girl: Fear of failure has made you obsessively single-minded?

Rafa: Something like that.

The girl [reaching the hotel entrance]: I've got the opposite problem. I'm always reading outside my subject. I'm distracted by all kinds of things, me. History, geography, literature, art, poetry, politics – basically, whatever takes my fancy. . . . Well, I'd better go. Thanks for walking me back here: it was very nice of you. . . . Remember the name again: Michel Fou-cault. F.O.U.C.A.U.L.T. Think of 'fuck off' said with a French accent and you won't go wrong. I'm sure they'll have some copies of his books in your library.

Rafa: Yes, I'll have to keep it in mind. Sounds like an interesting subject.

The girl: Well, goodbye then.

Rafa: Yes, goodbye.

The girl [pausing by the hotel entrance]: Listen, I'm going on a trip to a place called Casares tomorrow. It's supposed to have some kind of really spectacular medieval hilltop fort. I tried to get Judy and Trudy to come with me, but they wanted to spend the day at the beach. Would you like to come with me?

Rafa: Sure. How are you getting there?

The girl: I think there's a bus from here to Casares. I was planning on catching the one that leaves at 9.30.

Rafa: How about if we go on my scooter? I could pick you up from here at 9.15 if you want.

The girl: Will it take long to get there by scooter?

Rafa: About twenty or thirty minutes, I'd imagine.

The girl: Okay, then. That sounds fine. See you tomorrow at 9.15.

Rafa: Yes, see you tomorrow.

**5.**

*Outside the girls' hotel. Half past nine in the morning. Rafa stands astride his scooter, anxiously checking his watch and wondering whether the girl will turn up. Close-up of his face, perhaps, or of his fingers tapping against the scooter's handlebars. After about thirty seconds, the girl appears. She is wearing a flowery summer dress and her features are shaded by a broad-brimmed straw hat. Your classic 'English Rose look', in other words.*

Rafa [shyly]: Hello.

The girl: Hello.

Rafa [still shy]: You're looking nice.

The girl: Thank you. Have you been waiting long?

Rafa: No, only about ten minutes.

The girl: Sorry about that. I had a bit of a rough night and struggled to get out of bed this morning.

Rafa: Really? How come?

The girl [shaking her head]: Trudy and Judy.

Rafa: What happened?

The girl: Have a guess.

[Rafa shrugs his shoulders.]

They came back to the room at half past four. Totally fucking pissed. Wanted me to start watching a DVD with them. Some Flamenco aerobics bollocks that they bought yesterday morning. At fucking half past four in the morning! Can you believe that shit?

Rafa: How come you are on holiday with those two? You don't really seem like them.

The girl: We used to share a flat in our first year at Leeds. They're actually quite nice girls once you get to know them.

Rafa: I'm sure. Anyway, do you want to hop on?

The girl [climbing on the scooter]: Cool.

Rafa [turning his head slightly towards her]: I'm going to take the main road for a few kilometres before heading up the mountains. Is that okay?

The girl: Sounds fine to me. Shall I put my arms around you?

[Rafa nods. He kickstarts the scooter and slowly rides off.]

**6.**

*On the main highway. Heavy traffic, exhaust fumes, etc. Rafa is concentrating hard on the driving; the girl is smiling behind him. Suddenly a gust of wind blows her skirt halfway up her leg. A swarthy, unshaven guy in a passing truck shouts some obscenity at her.*

The girl: What did he say?

Rafa [turning around]: What?

The girl: The guy in the truck? What did he say?

[Rafa shrugs his shoulders.]

**7.**

*On a mountain road. The scooter's engine is spluttering noisily. Down below we can see the Costa del Sol, with its beaches and high-rise hotels.*

Rafa [shouting above the din]: Do you see that building over there?

The girl [shouting back]: What?

Rafa: That building over there? Do you see it?

The girl: You mean the one with the copper-coloured roof?

Rafa: Yes, yes, that one. That's the school that I used to go to as a kid. *El Colegio de Educación Infantil y Primaria Miguel Hernández.*

The girl: You what?

Rafa: *El Colegio de Educación Infantil y Primaria Miguel Hernández.*

The girl: I can't hear what you're saying.

Rafa: Don't worry. It's not that important.

**8.**

*At Casares. The girl is running through the medieval ruins with her straw hat in her hand. Rafa follows behind with a forbearing smile, looking a little embarrassed.*

The girl: Wow! Isn't this amazing? It's so desolate up here, so . . . so monumentally barren! [Turning towards him.] Is it always like this? So empty, I mean?

Rafa: Well, it's the middle of summer now. Most people are down at the beach.

The girl [running towards an old building]: That must be the church that was badly damaged by the Anarchists during the Civil War. I was reading about it in my *Lonely Planet Guide* last night. It was built in 1505 by order of the Catholic Kings and remained in use until 1845. . . . And that must be the place where the Fascists used to hurl their enemies down into the gorge below during the Civil War.

Rafa: You really are interested in History, aren't you?

The girl [excitedly]: Yes — can't you tell?. . . Look, that cross over there must mark the spot where the "hurlings" took place. . . . Jesus, isn't that scary? Can you imagine being prodded over the edge by someone's rusty bayonet?

Rafa: Doesn't sound very nice.

The girl: God, just think about it. Less than seventy years ago some poor bastard must have stood there thinking 'Shit. This is it. I can't get out of this one now.'

Rafa: Yes, it is difficult to imagine.

The girl [meditatively]: I wonder what thoughts must have crossed his head before he was pushed.

Rafa: Hmmm.

The girl [sadly]: Probably thinking about his wife and children, wondering what on earth he'd done to deserve this. . . . [In a changed tone; glancing teasingly back at Rafa.] Or maybe just lamenting that he would never have sex again. That's more like you Iberian lot, isn't it?

[She smiles and jogs to another part of the fortifications.]

That must be the old Islamic gateway. It's the only architectural feature left over from the days when Casares used to be a Moorish fort. . . . I'm surprised there are no information plaques anywhere around here. There's so much of historical significance in this place.

Rafa: Maybe we Spaniards don't want to be reminded of all the tragedy and bloodshed in our past.

The girl [running a hand over the gatehouse wall; lost in thought]: Maybe. . . . You know something? You haven't asked me what my name is yet.

Rafa: Haven't I? I'm sorry. I'm always doing things like that.

The girl: Well, then? Are you going to ask me or what?

Rafa: What's your name?

The girl [still lost in thought]: My name's Isabelle. Just like the Queen who ordered the Moors to be expelled from Spain. [In a very harsh English accent; with a slightly demented look.] *Is-a-be-la la Cat-ol-ica, la mad-re de Esp-a-ña.*

[She laughs all of a sudden and starts running away from him.]

Now come and do your Queen's bidding. I want to see every nook and cranny of this place before we go!

[He shakes his head with a smile and follows her to the other side of the ruins.]

**9.**

*Rafa's bedroom. About eight o'clock in the evening. Rafa is lying in bed, pensively staring at the ceiling. Suddenly the phone starts ringing in the corridor outside. A few seconds later, Rafa's mother enters the room with the cordless receiver in her hands. 'It's your friend, Juanjo,' she says, walking over to the bed and handing him the phone. Rafa waits until she leaves the room before speaking.*

Rafa: Hi, Juanjo. What's up, *tio*?

Juanjo's voice: Hey, Einstein, where've you been? We haven't seen you since last night at the club. Have you being abducted by aliens or something?

Rafa: I've been kind of busy, Juanjo.

Juanjo's voice: Busy, eh? Trudy and Judy told us all about it this morning at the beach. Taking that Isabelle girl on a romantic date somewhere up in the mountains. You're a sly one, aren't you, Rafael Esteban?

Rafa: It's not like that, Juanjo.

Juanjo's voice: What do you mean – it's not like that?

Rafa: We're just friends.

Juanjo's voice: Come on, Rafa. You're not expecting Captain Juanjo of the *Culos and Tetas Club* to believe that, are you?

Rafa [very serious]: Perhaps not, but that's the way it is.

Juanjo's voice: Listen, don't start acting again as if someone's just stuffed a stethoscope up your ass. I know how incredibly touchy you future neurosurgeons are. What are you doing tomorrow afternoon? Me and Chus are thinking of driving up to Red Xanadu for a few beers before heading down to the beach. Do you want to come with us?

Rafa: I can't.

Juanjo's voice: Why not?

Rafa: I'm taking Isabelle to the Tivoli amusement park at five.

Juanjo's voice: You what?

Rafa: She's a big fan of amusement parks.

Juanjo's voice: Wait a minute. Wait a minute. Am I really hearing this right? You're telling me that you're taking your bird to the Tivoli in the middle of an August afternoon?

Rafa: She's not my bird, Juanjo. I've already told you.

Juanjo's voice: But you're going to fry, man! It'll be about 40 degrees in the shade at the Tivoli!

Rafa: I tried telling her, but she said she didn't mind.

Juanjo's voice: Jesus Christ, you do know how to get a woman all hot and bothered, don't you?. . . How about the day after that, then? Will you condescend to have a beer with your mates, or will you be taking your little floozy on some other crazy-arsed August afternoon expedition?

Rafa: I don't know. That's the day the girls are leaving, isn't it?

Juanjo's voice [sarcastically]: So I expect you'll be wanting to see her off at the airport, right?

Rafa: I don't know. Haven't actually thought about it. . . . Anyway, stop bugging me with all these questions. How about you and Chus? How are you getting on with the other two girls? [In a mocking tone.] Have you slept with them yet?

Juanjo's voice: Not yet, mate, but we're getting closer and closer all the time. We're actually thinking of having a farewell barbeque for them down at the beach tomorrow tonight. Get them all tanked up with Bacardi Colas just before they leave. Can't see the little *putillas* resisting me and Chus's charms when they're staggering around the beach up to their eyeballs in rum, can you?

Rafa: You know that they've both got boyfriends back home, don't you?

Juanjo's voice: Oh, yeah. We know all about that. The fat one kept on telling Chus about her boyfriend after she gave him a blow job last night. Must have gone on some crazy, fucked-up guilt trip or something. Chus says she just couldn't stop telling him how loving and caring *'el muy cabrón'* is. Can't believe these *guiri* girls sometimes, can you!

Rafa: That's disgusting. I thought you said that nothing had happened between you guys and the girls.

Juanjo's voice: I said that we hadn't fucked them, mate, not that nothing had happened. Do you think that me and Chus would still be hanging around them if we hadn't already caught a whiff of their vinegary vaginal juices?

Rafa [pulling a disgusted face]: Jesus, Juanjo! I'm supposed to be having my dinner in a minute!

Juanjo's voice: Sorry, mate. I always forget that you're not a filthy fucker like the rest of us. . . . Anyway, better leave you if you're going to be having dinner. You're welcome to join us down at the beach tomorrow night – even though I get the feeling that you'll end up taking your bird to the cinema or something equally 'Rafa-like'. Take care, mate. I'll call you in a couple of days.

Rafa: Take care, Juanjo. . . . And don't get the girls too drunk. It won't be fun for them flying with a hangover.

Juanjo's voice [laughing]: You're such a dick sometimes, do you know that?

[Juanjo hangs up. Rafa smiles for a second, then gets up from his bed and leaves the room.]

**10.**

*Outside the Tivoli amusement park. Intense sunshine. Crickets chirping somewhere in the background. Rafa is sitting on a bench, looking at his watch. Some moments pass before Isabelle appears.*

Rafa: I thought that you wouldn't come.

Isabelle: Don't be silly. Whatever gave you that idea?

Rafa: I don't know. I thought that maybe you had forgotten our appointment or something.

Isabelle [playfully slapping him on the shoulder]: You silly little Spaniard! Thinking that I wouldn't come! You said the same thing yesterday morning too, didn't you? I hope that you'll buy my entrance ticket just because of that!

[Rafa nods and begins to walk to the ticket kiosk.]

Hey, I was only joking! You don't have to get me the ticket.

Rafa: No, no, it's okay. I insist. Let me get them. [To the ticket seller.] *Dos adultos, por favor.*

**11.**

*Inside the amusement park. Typical fairground sounds and sights. Isabelle is almost jumping up and down with excitement.*

Isabelle: Wow! Look at this: there's absolutely no one in here! We're the first people in!

Rafa: It's a bit early still. Most people don't come until about seven because of the heat.

Isabelle: That's good for us, isn't it? This is so . . . so . . . I don't know . . . so surreal. It's almost like something out of a film set. Something out of . . . I don't know . . . *The Third Man* or something. You know the film that I'm talking about, don't you?

Rafa: I'm sorry – I'm not a big movie fan.

Isabelle: Oh, come on – you must know *The Third Man.* Everyone knows *The Third Man.* Joseph Cotten and Orson Welles. Set in Vienna after the Second World War. You must have heard the theme song, surely?

[She begins to whistle *The Third Man's* theme tune.]

Rafa [apologetically]: I'm sorry – got no idea.

Isabelle: Anyway, it's not important. [Handing him her camera.] Here, take my camera. I'm getting on the merry-go-round. Try and get a few pictures as it comes around. . . . [She starts running towards the attraction, but then catches sight of an ice cream kiosk and changes her mind.] Wait. Actually, I'll get an ice cream first. I could do with something cool and refreshing. Would you like one too?

Rafa: No, thanks. I'm fine as I am.

Isabelle: Are you sure?

Rafa: Yes, thanks.

[She approaches the kiosk and asks for a 'Neapolitan Suprise' with raspberry sauce. The vendor nods and starts scooping out the ice cream. As he is doing so, he turns around to his assistant and mutters '*Valiente par de tetas.*' Rafa, who is standing behind Isabelle, overhears him and stares at him coldly. The ice cream seller realises that Rafa must be Spanish and throws him a half-apologetic, half-defiant wink.]

Isabelle [licking her ice cream]: What did he say?

Rafa: He made some comment about your breasts.

Isabelle: Really? What did he say about them?

Rafa [embarrassed]: I don't know – something about them being nice or something like that.

Isabelle: Did he? That's funny! [Running off towards the merry-go-round again.] You should have got yourself an ice cream. They're lovely!

**12.**

*Some moments later. Isabelle is on the merry-go-round. We see her go around about six or seven times. Every time she comes into view she is striking a different pose [one hand behind her head, licking her ice cream, blowing a kiss, etc]. Rafa looks just as uneasy as he did at the medieval ruins in Casares.*

**13.**

*A little later still. Isabelle and Rafa are walking together through the amusement park. A few people can now be seen in the background.*

Isabelle: Where did you say you were from again?

Rafa: Benalmadena.

Isabelle: Is that far away from here?

Rafa: We are practically in Benalmadena now. The town begins just down the hill.

Isabelle: Really? I thought we were in Torremolinos.

Rafa: They're very close together, Benalmadena and Torremolinos. Sometimes it's hard to tell where one finishes and the other begins.

Isabelle: Anyway, I bet it must be lovely where you live.

Rafa: It's okay.

Isabelle: You don't sound too convinced.

Rafa: Your hometown's your hometown – isn't it?

Isabelle: Still, it can't be worse than Walsall where I come from.

Rafa: I thought you came from Leeds.

Isabelle: Leeds is where I'm studying; Walsall is my hometown.

Rafa: What's it like – this Walsall place?

Isabelle: Shit. That's what it's like. Absolute, pure shit. Tattooed roughnecks everywhere, cocky little shits at every street corner, beggars that follow you and threaten you with rusty syringes. A town full of useless, ignorant, tattooed, foul-mouthed, baseball cap-wearing daytime television viewers: that's what it is.

Rafa: What's a daytime television viewer?

Isabelle: Someone who doesn't want to work and who sits on their arse all day fleecing the taxpayer.

Rafa: I don't understand.

Isabelle: A yob, a fucker, a nasty, good-for-nothing scumbag who thinks that the state owes him a debt of gratitude just for being born.

Rafa: Okay, I get it now.

Isabelle: God, I sound so reactionary, don't I? I'm actually quite a liberal person, you know.

Rafa: Don't worry. Everyone's got something or the other against their hometown. You've got these daytime television viewers; we've got Antonio Banderas.

Isabelle: What?

Rafa: Antonio Banderas. Or 'Anthony Flags', as he would be called if he was English. . . . Doesn't sound quite right, does it?. . . If you ever get a chance to visit the centre of Benalmadena, you'll see what I mean. Street names, apartment blocks, town squares, pet shops, grocery stores: you'll find señor Banderas's name painted across every place you look.

Isabelle: You mean Antonio Banderas was born in Benalmadena?

Rafa: Born here, lived here for the first fifteen years of his life, then got the hell out and was never seen again. Something for the rest of us in Benalmadena to be eternally proud of, don't you think?

Isabelle [laughing]: You and I have more in common than I first thought.

Rafa: I know that most people in Benalmadena would rather castrate their first-born son than slander the great Antonio, but I'm kind of tired of seeing his name all over the place, to be perfectly honest.

Isabelle: We should form a political party. *The Anglo-Spanish anti-Antonio Banderas coalition* it would be called. Dedicated to removing Mr B's name from every single name plaque in Benalmadena.

Rafa [laughing]: Yes, that would be a good idea.

Isabelle [pointing to one side]: Look, it's the 'Swinging Longboat'! I've always wanted to go on one of those. [Starting to walk towards the attraction.] Do you mind if I go for a quick ride?

**14.**

*Eight o'clock that same evening. At the park's refreshment marquee. Rafa and Isabelle are sitting at a table facing each other. After a while, a waiter brings them a jug of Sangria and two little plates of tapas.*

Rafa [pouring out two glasses]: Mmmm. That looks good, don't you think?

Isabelle: What's in Sangria exactly? I've always wanted to know.

Rafa: Not totally sure. Fruit, lemonade, wine, a few cinnamon sticks, a bit of cognac, I think.

Isabelle [pointing to one of the side dishes]: What's in that dish over there?

Rafa: '*Angeles a caballo.*' Bacon and rice wrapped in . . . what's the word in English? . . . let me think . . . leaves of wine?

Isabelle: Vine leaves?

Rafa [trying one]: Yes, vine leaves. That's it.

[He picks up the plate and offers her a stuffed vine leaf.]

You should try one: they're very nice.

Isabelle [without touching the vine leaves]: Has anyone ever told you before you've got really beautiful eyes?

Rafa [looking uncomfortable; putting the dish down]: No, not really. . . . [Picking up the other plate.] Would you like to try these? They are called '*gambas al pil-pil*'. Prawns in a garlic and almond sauce.

Isabelle: Okay. Should I use one of those little forks, or can I pick them up with my fingers like you picked up the vine leaf?

Rafa: Use a fork. They're quite oily.

Isabelle [stabbing a prawn with her fork]: Do you mind if I ask you a personal question?

Rafa: No, of course not.

Isabelle: You promise you won't be offended.

Rafa: Don't be silly. Do I look like the type who gets easily offended?

Isabelle: Actually, yes. . . .

Rafa: Go on. I promise I won't be offended.

Isabelle: Are you gay?

[All of a sudden Rafa looks away, a pained expression across his face.]

I'm sorry. I haven't offended you, have I?

Rafa: No, no: it's just that. . . .

Isabelle: . . . . just that what?

Rafa [regaining his composure and looking straight at her]: Everyone thinks that I'm gay at the medical faculty.

Isabelle: And are you?

[Rafa shakes his head.]

So why would they think that you're gay, then?

Rafa: I don't know. I think it's because I don't go chasing women like all the others.

Isabelle: But is that reason enough for them to think that you're gay? I mean. . . .

Rafa: You don't understand: this is Spain. The land of the *macho Ibérico* and all that silly bullshit. If you don't whistle at beautiful girls and brag about the 'bitches' you've slept with, you might as well hang a sign saying '*Maricón*' around your neck.

Isabelle [opening her bag and bringing out a packet of cigarettes]: Can't you pretend to be like that just to shake off these rumours?

Rafa [shaking his head]: It's just not me . . . all that *machista* rubbish.

Isabelle: But you do like women, don't you?. . . I mean, I'm assuming that if you're not gay, then you must like women?

Rafa: I do like women. Of course I do. It's just that . . . I don't know . . . I kind of . . . I don't know how to explain it in English. . . .

Isabelle [lighting herself a cigarette]: I'm sorry. I shouldn't have started this conversation. Don't feel obliged to carry on.

Rafa: No, no, it's okay. I want to tell you. [Looking straight at her again.] Have you ever felt like there's some . . . how can I say? . . . this dark force inside you that no one can see?

Isabelle: What do you mean?

Rafa: People look at you and see some boring, clumsy, four-eyed idiot, but all along there's this savage force inside. This *dark thing.* Torturing you, hurting you, poisoning your every minute. Like some kind of interior fire.

Isabelle: I don't understand what you mean.

Rafa: Okay, how can I say this differently? There's something inside me . . . something which . . . I don't know . . . maybe it's a special kind of awareness or something . . . which makes me feel kind of . . . I don't know . . . different to everybody else . . . and stops me from behaving the same way as the others. Does that make any sense to you?

Isabelle [offering him a cigarette]: Not sure.

Rafa [accepting the cigarette]: I mean, I like women. Don't get me wrong. There's nothing that I would like more than to find myself . . . well . . . a girlfriend. But I'm scared. I'm scared of what will happen. Do you understand what I'm saying? It's almost like this thing, this force inside me, will grow and take control over me.

Isabelle [leaning forwards and lighting his cigarette]: You really are a dark horse, aren't you?. . . Listen, I don't think that I would worry too much if I was you. I know that you are probably really fed up with everything and I don't want to trivialise what you're going through, but I think you're just sexually frustrated, that's all.

Rafa: Do you think so?. . . God, I can't believe that I'm sitting here talking about all this with you! I would rather pluck out my teeth than tell anyone about these things — and yet here I am discussing all this with someone I met only a few days ago!

Isabelle: Chill, man. Flush out all that macho Spanish bullshit from your head. People in England are not as judgmental as you dogmatic Iberian hotheads. My advice as a liberal, forward-thinking modern Englishwoman is simple: find yourself a girl you fancy, tell her that she's the best thing since sliced bread and wait for things to evolve naturally. I mean, there must be someone you fancy, surely?

Rafa: Not, really. . . . [Looking directly at her again.] Well, maybe there is.

Isabelle [with a knowing smile]: Well, then? What are you waiting for?

Rafa: She might not like me as much as I like her.

Isabelle: That's something you've got to find out for yourself.

Rafa: What if she takes offence when I approach her?

Isabelle: I somehow doubt that very much.

[He smiles and awkwardly reaches for her hand. They kiss.]

You really are a silly bugger. You could have the world at your feet if only you had a bit more confidence.

Rafa: It seems like I have the world at my feet already.

[They kiss again.]

Isabelle: See? One kiss and you're already starting to talk like some natural-born Iberian charmer. Was that really so difficult?

[He smiles. They kiss for the third time.]

**15.**

*Night time. Isabelle and Rafa are walking out of the amusement park arm-in-arm. Stars are glittering across the evening sky.*

Isabelle: I wish I wasn't leaving tomorrow. It feels like I'm just beginning to get to know you.

Rafa: Strange, isn't it? The way people's destinies are suddenly brought together and then torn apart again.

Isabelle: That's a bit poetic for a boring old medic who supposedly has no interest in anything apart from his own medical books. My, my, my – you're learning very fast, aren't you?

Rafa: In Spain we say '*una mujer hermosa puede transformar un príncipe en un idiota, y un idiota en un príncipe.*' A beautiful woman can change a prince into a fool, and a fool into prince.

Isabelle: Christ, and I thought that English proverbs sounded cheesy!

[He smiles. They carry on walking arm-in-arm in silence for some moments.]

I wish Trudy and Judy didn't always go out so late. We could have gone to my hotel room now.

Rafa: Don't worry – we'll find some other place.

Isabelle: I know. It's just that I'm getting tired and I need to sit down for a while. Plus I don't really feel like going to some shitty, overcrowded sports bar. . . . I have an idea. Why don't we go to the beach?

Rafa: The beach?

Isabelle: Yes, why not?

Rafa: I don't know. It can get quite crowded on the beach at this time.

Isabelle: Crowded? At nine o'clock at night?

Rafa: Okay, then. Let's go to the beach.

**16.**

*The beach at night time. Isabelle is walking through the sand about ten paces ahead of Rafa. A full moon can be seen in the sky.*

Isabelle [stopping and looking back at him]: Over here?

Rafa: Just a little bit further. We're still quite near that group of people over there.

[They walk another twenty or thirty paces and then Isabelle stops again.]

Isabelle: How about over here? This is secluded enough, don't you think?

Rafa: Maybe just a little bit further.

[She walks another twenty or thirty paces and then stops again.]

Isabelle: Here?

Rafa [gauging the distance between them and the nearest set of people]: Yes, I think this is fine now.

Isabelle: Thank God for that! I thought you were planning to walk all the way down to Gibraltar!

[She throws her bag on the sand and begins to strip off.]

Rafa: What are you doing?

Isabelle: I'm going for a swim.

Rafa: What?

Isabelle: Come on, don't be such a prudish, Spanish little scary cat. Aren't you going to join me or what?

Rafa: But I don't have any swimming trunks.

Isabelle [already naked and beginning to run towards the sea]: Who needs clothes? It's the middle of the night, for Christ's sake!

[After a few moments of indecision, Rafa takes his clothes off and follows her into the sea. For a few seconds they splash water at each other and generally fool around. Then they gravitate towards each other and begin to get passionate. Suddenly he draws back.]

Isabelle: What's wrong?

Rafa: Nothing.

Isabelle: What do you mean — nothing? It's not that 'interior fire' thing again, is it? I've told you: you've got nothing to be scared of.

Rafa: No, it's not that. It's just that I was thinking about all those dead bodies lying on the beach the other day. Do you think we should be doing this sort of thing here?

Isabelle: Don't be such a silly boy. The sea has no memory and no past. *As if it were too great, too mighty for common virtues, the ocean has no compassion, no faith, no law, no memory.*

Rafa: Nice lines. Where do they come from?

Isabelle: Some writer called Conrad. You won't know him. . . . Anyway, the point I was trying to make is that whatever happened here the other day has already been washed out by the waves. . . . So just stop being silly and come here, will you?

[She draws him close to her and they begin to kiss again. Within minutes they are making love.]

**17.**

*About ten minutes later. Rafa and Isabelle are lying together on the beach. The camera should be nestled between Isabelle and Rafa in this scene, giving us a fisheye view of the heavily-starred sky.*

Isabelle: There's Saturn. Can you see? And over there the constellation of Gemini with Castor and Pollux. . . . If you go a bit further down to your left, you can see Canis Minor and then, just underneath it, Canis Major. And then Orion just next to them on the right. . . . Can you see the three stars which make up Orion's belt? Alnitak on the left, Alnilam in the middle and Minatka to the right. Aren't they beautiful?

Rafa [as if in trance]: Yes, they are.

Isabelle [smiling; turning towards him]: What's wrong with you? You sound as if you've popped a Valium or something.

Rafa: It's just the stars. They are so . . . so. . . .

Isabelle: . . . . hypnotic?

Rafa: Yes, hypnotic.

Isabelle [looking at the sky again]: I know what you mean. It always makes me feel a bit sad when I look at them. Makes me wonder what the hell we're all doing down here. Just imagine: they've been shining there for millions of years. Not a thousand or ten thousand or even a hundred thousand years, but millions and millions of years. It kind of puts a different perspective on human history, don't you think? The Egyptian Pharaohs, the rise of the Roman Empire, the medieval crusades, the First World War: all these things have come and gone and yet the night sky is virtually identical to what it was back at the very beginning. Orion still stands there with his sword, his hunting dogs still crouch obediently at his feet.

Rafa [after a long silence]: This is so perfect.

Isabelle: What is?

Rafa: This moment. I wish that I could somehow freeze time and capture this moment forever. *This is how it should be, how things were meant to be.* Compared to this instant, everything that has gone in my life so far has been a stupid, silly joke.

Isabelle: Don't be so harsh on yourself. You've achieved quite a lot with your life.

Rafa: Yes, but it never felt right, never felt like this. This sense of peace, this sense of . . . how can I say in English? . . . oneness with everything around you. Don't you ever get the feeling that you're not living your life the way it's meant to be?

[Pause.]

I wish that all this could last a bit longer.

Isabelle: Well, maybe that's not so difficult.

Rafa: What do you mean?

Isabelle: Didn't you say earlier that you still have a few weeks left before starting college again? Why don't you come to Leeds for a few days? I know that we won't be able to lie on a beach like this and stare at the stars, but we'd have a real laugh all the same.

Rafa: I wish that I could, but I wouldn't be able to afford it.

Isabelle: It's not that expensive. You can catch a cheap flight from Malaga to Leeds with *Jet 2* for about sixty pounds. Just imagine: in a few days' time you could be sitting with me in my living room in Hyde Park.

Rafa: I don't know. I should be preparing for my September exams.

Isabelle: Take your books with you then. I work part-time at a supermarket most mornings. You could study then.

Rafa: I don't know. There's only a few weeks left before the next set of exams. And they're quite important ones. . . . Although it would be nice, wouldn't it?

Isabelle: You bet it would.

Rafa: And I could study every morning while you're at work.

Isabelle: Of course you could. Just imagine the things that we'd be able to do. [Whispering suggestively.] You and me. Together in my bedroom. I can almost visualise it now.

[She begins to giggle. They start to kiss again.]

**18.**

*Outside Isabelle's hotel. Very late at night. Isabelle and Rafa appear walking arm-in-arm.*

Rafa: Well, the moment of truth has come. I really don't know what to say.

Isabelle: Don't say anything just yet. You said earlier that you'll be at the airport tomorrow morning. Leave all that farewell business until then. Just turn round and walk away now. It's better like that, trust me.

Rafa: Don't I even get a kiss?

Isabelle: No, not even a kiss. That way both of us will sleep with the expectation of seeing each other tomorrow — and not feeling like we've left something really precious behind.

Rafa: I suppose that you're right.

Isabelle: I know that I'm right. Just go now. We'll be seeing each other again in a few hours.

[He opens his mouth to say something, but she puts a finger to his lips and shakes her head. Then she turns around and walks away.]

**19.**

*Rafa's bedroom. Rafa is asleep in bed. On his bedside table there is a digital alarm clock. Suddenly he opens his eyes and looks at the alarm clock. He stares at it for some seconds, more asleep than awake, then realises that he has overslept and jumps out of bed shouting 'Mierda! Mierda! Mierda!' He rapidly gets dressed, leaves the house and then sprints across the street to where his scooter is parked.*

**20.**

*On the highway to Malaga airport. Rafa is swerving perilously in and out of traffic. Occasional beeping of horns, etc.*

## 21.

*Malaga airport. A dishevelled Rafa appears running across the departure hall. He stops before the main flight information board and nervously scans it until he manages to track down Isabelle's flight. He then sprints towards desk no 56, but finds that there is only one person checking-in there. Angrily shaking his head, he turns around and runs towards the immigration control area. Upon reaching it, he finds a long queue of people waiting to go through. He walks down the side of the queue, shaking his head and frowning all the time. Just as he is about to give up looking for them, he sees Isabelle and her friends.*

Isabelle [running towards him and throwing herself into his arms]: Rafa!

Rafa: I'm sorry. I overslept. . . . God, I'm so glad that I made it here in time!

Isabelle: I'm so glad too. I thought you'd never come. . . . [Taking out a pen and notebook from her handbag.] Quick, give me your address and telephone number and I'll give you mine.

[He starts to write his details in her address book.]

Rafa: *Mierda*! This pen's not working!

Isabelle [taking out another pen from her bag]: Here, use this one.

[He finishes writing and hands the notebook back to her. She tears a slip of paper from it and quickly writes down her own details. They are almost at the front of the queue now.]

Isabelle [with tears in her eyes]: You're lovely. Do you know that? Please don't let anybody else tell you otherwise! You're really, really lovely! . . . And remember if you want to come to Leeds, you are more than welcome. Anytime. Just call us and let me know.

[They embrace and kiss again. Trudy and Judy remind Isabelle that they need to get moving. Reluctantly, the couple disengage. At the first security point, Isabelle turns around and blows Rafa a kiss. Then she goes through the metal detector and disappears from sight.]

## 22.

*A succession of interconnected scenes showing Rafa on his way home: (a) walking through the interior of the departure hall (b) heading towards the airport car park with a plane flying overhead and (c) riding along the highway on his scooter.*

**23.**

*Rafa's bedroom. Rafa is lying on his bed, staring at the ceiling.*

Rafa's mother's voice [from the corridor outside]: Rafa, the food's ready!

[Long pause.]

The food's ready, Rafa! Come and get it before it grows cold!

Rafa [after another long pause; getting out of bed]: Okay, okay. I'm coming!

**24.**

*A few days later. The promenade next to the beach. Chus and Juanjo are sitting on the wall overlooking the beach. Rafa comes walking past them.*

Juanjo: Hello, hello. Look who's here. If it's none other than our friendly neighbourhood loved-up neurosurgeon. Where've you been, man? You're more difficult to locate these days than a *guiri* who doesn't like showing off her *tetitas.*

Rafa [with his hands in his pockets]: Been at home. Couldn't be arsed going out.

Juanjo: Tut-tut-tut. That's not what Mummy Esteban told me when I called the other night. Said that you weren't feeling too well and that you didn't feel like talking to anyone. Me and Chus have been really worried about our loved-up little neurosurgeon, you know.

Rafa: I just needed a little time to think, that's all.

Juanjo [no longer sarcastic]: Oh, fuck. You're not still thinking about that girl, are you? She's been gone almost a week now.

Rafa: The voice of the perennial romantic. . . . By the way, how did you guys get on with the two girls the other night at your beach barbecue? I've been meaning to ask you for a few days now.

Juanjo [nudging Chus lightly in the ribs]: How did we get on? Tell him, Chus.

Chus [matter-of-factly; bringing out his packet of cigarettes]: Juanjo fucked Judy and Trudy, while I fucked Judy and got Trudy to give me a second blow job.

Juanjo: *The Judy and Trudy fucking and sucking show*: that's what it was like.

Chus [lighting his cigarette]: Bet you the bitches' pussies are still mashed to a pulp.

Rafa: Is that so? I'll have to ask them if they're feeling any better when I see them next week.

Juanjo: What do you mean?

Rafa: I've decided I'm going to fly up to Leeds to spend a few days with Isabelle.

Juanjo: You must be joking. You'll freeze your ass off up there. Besides, the internal medicine exams start in a few weeks. How are you going to study for them in bloody England?

Rafa: I'll be taking my books with me, won't I? Isabelle's got a part-time job in the mornings, so I can study then.

Juanjo: Man, you're really smitten, aren't you? You should be careful, you know. Holiday romances are like corpses on the dissecting table – they start rotting in your hands before you know it. Ain't that so, Chus?

Chus: Sure it is. Look at me and that Claire girl I met in Estepona when I was nineteen. I even went to Hastings in the UK to see her for a few days. What the fuck was I thinking about I'll never know!

Rafa [full of curiosity]: What happened between you and her? I've never heard you talk about this before.

Chus: She had a boyfriend back home, that's what happened. A big, tattooed, bull-headed crew-cutted *hijo puta* who got told that I was Claire's 'linguistic interchange partner' and who didn't stop asking me questions about Real Madrid and Zinedine Zidane every time I met him.

Juanjo: Sounds like a real *pesadilla, tio.*

Chus: You can say that again, brother. If you would have placed that Claire bitch to one side with her legs wide open and her cunt dripping love-juice, and Zinedine Zidane on the other with his bald patch and his ball juggling skills . . . you can guess which of the two that football-loving fool would have gone for. That was some real fucked-up, creepy shit, I tell you.

Juanjo: Well, I hope that you at least did your duty as a *macho Ibérico* and fucked her well and proper!

Chus: Man, what sort of question is that! I was knobbing her senseless while that fucking thug was driving his delivery van or doing whatever he was doing. I wasn't going to go all the way to *guirilandia* just to talk about the size of the Bernabeu and the intricacies of the offside trap, was I?

Juanjo: That's the spirit, my man. Fuck 'em and forget 'em. Which reminds me. [Turning to Rafa.] I hope that you fucked that Isabelle girl before she went back home. Wouldn't want the neurosurgeon letting the side down now, would we, Chus?

Rafa [smiling]: Maybe I did. Then again, maybe I didn't.

Juanjo: What do you mean – maybe you did, maybe you didn't? Don't forget you're among mates here. Did you knob the bitch or what?

Rafa: I'm not going to tell you that, am I?

Chus: Oh come on, Rafa. What are you trying to do – protect Miss *guiri* bitch's modesty. Be straight with your mates, will you? Did you screw her – yes or no?

Rafa: Jesus, you guys just don't know when to let things drop, do you?

Juanjo: Not where mates are concerned, Einstein.

Rafa [suddenly annoyed]: Well, if you must know, I did screw her! Is that okay? Are you happy now? Does that make me more acceptable in your eyes? Am I one of the gang now?. . . You mindless, half-witted pricks! Jesus, has everything got to be so fucking 'biologistic' with you lot?

[He walks off in an angry huff.]

Chus: What's got into him?

Juanjo: I don't know. I think that little English bitch is really messing with his head. I don't think he should be flying out to see her like he wants to.

Chus: I bet you she's even got a boyfriend at home like that Claire bitch had. Those English girls are like *demonios*, man. They'll fuck anything in sight.

Juanjo: I know. But I don't think the poor old neurosurgeon has realised that yet.

## 25.

*A street phone at night. Rafa is making a call.*

Rafa: Hello. . . . Yes. Can I speak to Isabelle Green?. . . This is Rafa Esteban here. . . . Rafa Esteban. . . . Yes, Ra-fa Es-te-ban. . . . From Spain. We met recently. . . . Okay, thanks.

[A long pause. Rafa lights himself a cigarette, puts more coins into the phone.]

Hello, Isabelle?. . . Yes, it's me. . . . It's so nice to hear from you too. Who was that guy on the phone?. . . Oh, okay. I forgot you shared your house with other people. . . . Listen, do you remember what you said that night at the beach?. . . What do you mean – 'what did I say?' You know – about me coming over for a few days. Were you serious when you said that?. . . It's just that I've been thinking and I think that you're right: I could do with a few days away from here. . . . Within the next few days, if that's okay with you. . . . Really? That's great! I'm so glad to hear that! I wasn't too sure if you really meant what you said! . . . Oh no, no, no: don't take it the wrong way. It's just that . . . you know. . . sometimes people say things without really meaning them. . . . especially when they're on holiday in a place like the Costa del Sol, if you know what I mean. . . . How about this Thursday afternoon, then? I went to the travel agents this morning and they told me there's a cheap flight on Thursday that gets into Leeds at six. . . . Fantastic. That's really great. I'll go and see them tomorrow morning and get the flight booked. . . . Yes, yes. Everything's all right here. Saw Chus and Juanjo today at the beach.

[He puts more coins into the phone.]

Yes, they're okay. Just being their usual selves. Lazing around at the beach. Trying to spot their next victims. You know what those two are like. . . . Yes, I know, but they are not that bad either. Juanjo, especially, has always been very kind to me. I've known him since we were together at infantile school. . . . Yes, that's what I meant: infant school. . . . We're actually kind of related, you know. He's my third or fourth cousin or whatever you call it when you have the same great-great-grandparents. . . . Anyway, I better go. I'm calling from a phonebox and I'm already running out of money. . . . No, no: it's okay, don't worry. That's why I came to a phone box in the first place. I didn't want my Mum to overhear our conversation. I'm sure she would try to persuade me not to go anywhere if she found out. She's a typical Spanish Mum. Very *posesiva*. . . . Anyway, the phone's already making beeping noises, so I guess I'd better be going. . . . God, I can't believe that I'm doing this! Can't wait to see you again. . . . Are you sure it won't be a problem meeting me at the airport?. . . Okay, that's fine. See you then. Bye-bye. . . . Okay, bye.

## 26.

*Malaga airport. At the flight check-in desk. Rafa is in a queue composed almost entirely of English people. He is soon called forwards by the attendant.*

The attendant [in a bored, expressionless tone]: Passport and flight ticket, please.

[Rafa hands the documents over.]

How many items are you checking in?

Rafa [placing his suitcase on the conveyor belt]: Just this one here.

The attendant: Any items of hand luggage?

Rafa [holding up a small shoulder bag]: Just this.

The attendant: Do you mind popping it on the scales for me, please?

[Rafa does as he is told.]

Okay, that's fine. I'm now going to ask you a few security questions. Is that all right?

[Rafa nods.]

Did you pack your suitcase yourself?

Rafa: Yes.

The attendant: Are you carrying anything on someone's behalf?

Rafa: No.

The attendant [pointing to a card propped up on the counter]: Could you just have a quick look at the items pictured on this card? Can you confirm that you're not carrying any of them?

Rafa: No, I'm not carrying any of them.

The attendant: Okay, then.

[He looks down and starts typing on his keyboard.]

Would you like an aisle or a window seat?

Rafa: A window seat, please.

[More typing.]

The attendant: Okay, then. Here's your boarding ticket. You will be boarding your plane today at Gate B12 at approximately twenty-past three. Make sure you're there at least twenty minutes before boarding, okay? [Without the slightest trace of enthusiasm in his voice.] Have a pleasant flight, sir.

**27.**

*Inside a duty free shop. Rafa is being shown a bracelet by the shop assistant.*

Rafa: How much is it?

The assistant: Twenty-five euros.

[Rafa picks up the bracelet.]

It's made with real Swarovski crystals and it comes with this free Dolphin key-ring.

[Pause.]

It's also guaranteed against any manufacturing or material defects for a period of two years.

Rafa [after examining it for a few more seconds]: Okay, I'll take it.

**28.**

*Inside the plane. Rafa is sitting next to a very rough-looking middle-aged English couple. The man is wearing a Manchester United shirt and a Burberry baseball cap. The woman wears several gold medallions around her neck and a T-shirt which says 'Anyone hotter than me is a hustler.' Rafa gazes at them for some seconds, then rapidly looks away when the man notices him. He nervously picks up the in-flight magazine.*

**29.**

*The arrivals hall at Leeds Airport. Rafa comes out into the hall, pushing a luggage trolley. He stares around him apprehensively for a few seconds until he sees Isabelle in the crowd. They rush to each other and embrace. No words are spoken for about thirty seconds; they just cling to each other in a state of quiet emotion. Finally, she says 'Welcome to England.'*

**30.**

*In a taxi. Rafa and Isabelle are sitting in the back of the vehicle, holding hands.*

Isabelle: How was your flight?

Rafa: Not bad. I was sat next to this very strange couple. Must have drunk about ten beers between them, but didn't say a word to each other the entire flight. . . . Apart, of course, from the times when the woman had to go to the toilet and the man had to let her out. [Trying to imitate a rough Northern accent.] 'Need to go the loo,' she would say. 'All right then,' the guy would reply. And that was it: nothing else was said.

Isabelle [laughing]: That's the English for you. More interested in their beer than in each other.

[She looks down at the Swarovski bracelet on her wrist.]

This is so sweet of you. You shouldn't have got me anything.

Rafa [a little embarrassed]: It's nothing, really.

Isabelle: You may think so, but it still means a lot to me.

Rafa [looking through the window]: It's very green out here, isn't it?

Isabelle: Yes. Don't expect it to be too green where we're going, though.

Rafa: Where is it that we're going exactly?

Isabelle: Hyde Park.

Rafa: Not the famous Hyde Park in London, I hope.

Isabelle: No, Hyde Park in Leeds. Otherwise known as 'Studentville'. Terraced houses, council tenants, Indian take-aways, gangs of thieving little kids and about ten or fifteen thousand university students all crammed into two or three square miles.

Rafa [sarcastically]: Sounds a bit like Torremolinos, right?

Isabelle: Almost, but not quite.

**31.**

*The outside of a terraced house. The taxi pulls up nearby. Isabelle can be seen paying the taxi driver inside the vehicle.*

Isabelle [stepping out of the taxi]: Well, here we are. Home sweet home. [Picking up Rafa's suitcase.] Jesus, what have you got in here? This thing weighs a ton!

Rafa: Sorry – it's my medical books. I brought them with me so that I could study in the mornings.

Isabelle: Did you bring your whole library with you by any chance?

Rafa: Very nearly.

[He helps her drag the suitcase up the front steps. While they are engaged in this operation, a group of three or four pre-pubescent kids starts heckling them from across the road.]

Rafa: Who are they?

Isabelle: Oh, don't pay any attention. They are just some little shits from the council estate down the road. Can't stand students.

Rafa: I don't understand. Why are they like that?

Isabelle: It's only what they hear from their bastard parents.

[She opens the front door.]

I wonder who the ignorant fuckers think will be treating their kids for multiple stab wounds and defending them in court when they grow older.

**32.**

*Inside the house. Isabelle and Rafa are walking down the entrance corridor.*

Isabelle [pointing towards the first room on the left]: That's our living room. Bit scruffy, I know. And I do apologise. But that's what you get when you share a house with three pigs. . . . That's our kitchen in there. Bit of a shit tip as well, I'm afraid. By the way, are you hungry? I can cook some Spag Bol now or we can order a take-away later. Whatever you prefer.

Rafa: I'm fine for now, thank you.

Isabelle: Okay, then. I'll have to introduce you to the delights of the good old-fashioned English take-away a bit later.

[She leads him up the stairs.]

That's the bathroom. And that's Billy's room. That's Andy's room. And that's Dawn's room. And this . . . is my room.

[She beckons him inside. It is a typical young woman's room. Posters, plush drapery and candles everywhere.]

Do you like it?

Rafa [looking around him]: Yes, it's very nice.

[He walks to the window]

Isabelle: Oh, I forgot to tell you. We've got a panoramic view of the local mosque. Or more accurately: what will soon become the local mosque. 2.5 million pounds, that's costing. Funded almost entirely by some rich restaurateur from Bradford. I wouldn't mind it so much if I didn't have to see the local builders regularly pissing in every corner of the site. I wonder if the millionaire from Bradford knows how they are consecrating his hallowed Muslim turf.

[She walks up behind him and embraces him.]

I'm glad that you're here.

Rafa [turning around and kissing her]: So am I.

[She smiles and leads him to the bed. They tumble on it and begin to kiss.]

**33.**

*Isabelle's room. Early morning. A large pizza box and some empty cans of beer are strewn across the floor. Suddenly the alarm clock starts ringing.*

Isabelle: God, I feel rough.

Rafa [waking up too]: What time is it?

Isabelle [getting out of bed]: Half past seven. I've got to be at the bus stop in ten minutes.

Rafa: I'll come with you.

Isabelle [getting dressed]: No, no: it's okay. I told you last night: you can stay here and study.

Rafa: It's okay. I want to go with you. Plus I don't feel like studying today. I want to go for a walk around Leeds instead.

Isabelle: Okay, then. Whatever you prefer. [Throwing a baggy, military-style coat at him.] Here, make sure you put this on. It'll be cold out there.

**34.**

*The inside of an overcrowded bus. Harsh, expressionless faces all around. Isabelle is sitting next to a sober-looking businessman, while Rafa is standing about three or four yards way. From time to time they glance at each other and smile.*

**35.**

*Outside Morrisons Supermarket.*

Isabelle [tying her 'Morrisons apron' behind her back]: Well, I better go. I'm a few minutes late already.

Rafa: Okay, see you later.

Isabelle: Remember the places that I told you about earlier. The Victoria Quarter, the Corn Exchange, the Town Hall. There's not a lot to see in Leeds, so you might as well start with the nice places.

Rafa: Okay.

Isabelle: And, whatever you do, don't leave the city centre. There's some really rough areas which are only twenty or twenty-five minutes' walk from here. I don't want you to be mugged on your first day in Leeds — okay?

Rafa: Okay

[She leans forwards and kisses him.]

Isabelle: Better go, then. I'll see you here at around one-thirty. Have a nice morning.

Rafa: You too.

**36.**

*A succession of interconnected scenes showing Rafa in different parts of Leeds: (a) window shopping at the Victoria Quarter (b) walking around the inside of the Corn Exchange (c) sitting on a bench at City Square, drinking a can of Coke.*

**37.**

*Outside Morrisons again. Isabelle walks out of the supermarket, untying her apron.*

Isabelle: Had a nice morning?

Rafa: Yes, it was really interesting. I went into this little museum near the town hall and saw an exhibition called 'British *surrealismo* since 1945'. Didn't understand a thing, but it was good fun. . . . How about you? Did you have a good morning too?

Isabelle: It was all right. They moved me from the till to the deli counter to cover for a woman who's off sick with pneumonia. Been slicing salamis and honey roast hams all morning. . . . Anyway, what do you fancy doing now?

Rafa: I don't know. Shall we go back to the flat?

Isabelle: Back to the flat?

Rafa: Yes, I'm a bit tired after walking all morning. You don't mind, do you?

Isabelle: No, of course not. We can go back to the flat and have some of that nice homemade apple pie that my Gran sent me.

**38.**

*Isabelle's bedroom. Rafa and Isabelle are under the covers, making love very frenetically — obviously an ironic counterpoint to Isabelle's last comment in the previous scene.*

**39.**

*Isabelle's living room. Mid-afternoon. Rafa and Isabelle are watching 'The Jerry Springer Show' or some other mindless television programme. Noises can be heard from the corridor outside, as if someone is coming through the front door. Moments later, a tall, muscular lad with a sports holdall over his shoulder walks into the living room. He is Andy, one of Isabelle's student housemates.*

Isabelle: Hi, Andy.

Andy [speaking with a strong Newcastle accent]: Hi, Isa. Who's this?

Isabelle: This is Rafa. My friend from Spain.

[She stands.]

You fancy a cuppa? I'm just about to put the kettle on.

Andy: Nah, it's all right. I'm playing roogby down at Meanwood in hoolf oon hour.

Isabelle [turning to Rafa]: Rafa, this is Andy. The guy who lives opposite me. He's studying P. E., aren't you, A?

Andy: Sports Science oond Coaching. [In an exaggeratedly slow voice.] Nice to meet you, pal. You here long?

Isabelle: Give over, A. Rafa speaks very, very good English. You don't have to talk to him like he was five and a half years old.

Andy: I wor just trying to be polite, that's ooll. Jesus, one cannie do anything right these days! . . . Anyhow, I best be getting off. I only gor ten minutes to get ready. [To Rafa.] Catch you later, pal. . . . By the way, we still having them people come over toneet, like?

Isabelle: Yeah, I don't see why not? [To Rafa.] You don't mind meeting some of our friends, do you, Rafa?

Rafa: No, of course not.

Andy: All right, then. I'll try and get a few beers on me way boock from roogby. . . . See you later, pet.

Isabelle: See you later, A.

[The rugby player leaves the living room.]

He's a real top bloke, Andy is. Probably the nicest of my housemates. . . . How many sugars did you take with your coffee again? Was it one or two?

Rafa: Three, please.

Isabelle [exiting the room]: All right. Be back in a second.

[Rafa continues watching *The Jerry Springer Show* for some seconds, then picks up the remote control and changes the channel].

**40.**

*A dirty and badly dilapidated bathroom. The shower is on and Rafa is deliberating how to get in without brushing against the mouldy shower curtain. Suddenly there is a knock on the door and we hear Isabelle say 'Can I come in?' Rafa wraps a towel around his waist, opens the door and finds Isabelle standing on the landing wearing nothing but a pair of knickers.*

Isabelle: Quick, quick — let me in before someone sees me!

[She slips past him and Rafa closes the door.]

Rafa [quite shocked]: What are you doing?

Isabelle: I'm coming to have a shower with you, aren't I? It's much more fun than having a shower on one's own.

[She takes off her knickers and jumps into the shower.]

Well, are you going to stay there and stare at me like some kind of psycho perv — or are you going to jump in with me?

[Rafa nods a little sheepishly, then walks into the shower cubicle.]

**41.**

*Isabelle's living room. About ten or twelve people are scattered here and there. Smoke, music, chatting voices. Rafa is sitting at the far end of one of the sofas, with Isabelle on his knee. He looks alienated and somewhat uncomfortable; she is talking animatedly to a guy on the other side of the room.*

Isabelle [somewhat drunk]: Oh, come on. Don't defend the indefensible, mate. You can't say that the Americans didn't have it coming. Have you actually bothered to look at what they've been doing in the Middle East for the last twenty or thirty years?

The guy: I'm not defending the indefensible. I'm just saying that someone should stand up and tell these little Arab fuckers that we're not prepared to take any of their shit, and, since no one else has got the balls to do it, it might as well be us and the Yanks.

Isabelle: Listen, mate, you're living fifty years in the past. What are you going to do next — stand up and sing *Land of Hope and Glory*? Claim that we are morally obliged to support the Americans because they baled us out in 1941?

The guy [becoming more and more defensive]: I don't think you understand what I'm trying to say. All I'm saying is that at this moment in time we need strong political leaders who won't back down in the face of the terrorist threat.

Isabelle: Yes, of course. Just like Donald fucking Rumsfeld. He personally sells barrel-loads of Anthrax to the Iraqis while working as Reagan's Middle Eastern Envoy and now he has audacity, the sheer fucking gall, to turn around and accuse Saddam Hussein of harbouring weapons of mass destruction. Are these the kind of political strongmen that you are referring to?

The guy: I'm just saying that tyranny must be resisted at all costs and that the forces of freedom won't back down until their job is done.

Isabelle: Where did you get that quote from — George W. Bush's handbook of clichéd, smile-like-you're-a-dumb-fucker aphorisms? What a dick you are. Who do you think put this evil tyrant Hussein in power in the first place? Lex Luther and the 'Legalise Kryptonite Now' Alliance? Doctor Moriarty and his gang of Chinese Opium addicts?

[Three knocks on the front door. Isabelle gets up and walks to the door, glad to get away from her verbal sparring partner. Rafa stares at her quietly from the sofa. Suddenly the guy sitting beside the Spaniard turns towards him. He looks very, very stoned.]

The stoned student: You're Isa's Spanish mate, aren't you?

Rafa: Yes.

The stoned student: Which team do you support — Real Madrid or Barcelona?

Rafa: Neither. I don't really like football.

The stoned student: But you're Spanish, aren't you?

Rafa [getting up]: Excuse me — I've got to go to the toilet.

**42.**

*The bathroom. Rafa stands urinating into the toilet bowl. All of a sudden someone starts banging on the toilet door. Rafa looks over his shoulder and shakes his head, but carries on standing before the toilet. More loud banging. After he has finished and washed his hands, he opens the door. A young couple can be seen on the landing.*

The young man: Jesus, what've you been doing in there, mate? I was about to dial 999 on your behalf.

[Rafa smiles uneasily.]

The young woman [rowdily]: Come on, mate. You've pleasured yourself enough in there. Now let others have their turn, will you?

Rafa [slightly confused]: Excuse me?

The young woman: Come on, come on. Just get out of the way, will you?

[They barge their way past him and lock the door. We can hear the woman giggling a few seconds later.]

**43.**

*Back in the living room. Rafa is looking for Isabelle, but she is nowhere to be seen. After a while, he approaches the stoned student on the sofa and tries to grab his attention.*

Rafa: Have you seen Isabelle?

The stoned student: You what?

Rafa: Isabelle? Have you seen her?

The stoned student: Oh, yeah. She went out to score some gear with Cookie and the lads, I think. Should be back soon.

[Rafa nods and wearily walks out of the room.]

**44.**

*Isabelle's room. Rafa is lying in bed and the lights are switched off. Over the next few minutes he switches on the bedside lamp several times to check the alarm clock by his side. Each time he does this the clock reveals a different time: 1.45am, 2.17am, 3.03am. Shortly after he has switched off the lamp for the third time, drunken voices can be heard coming from the street outside. Isabelle's voice can be distinguished among them. At this point Rafa switches on the lamp and once again looks at the alarm clock: it is 3.57am. Visibly annoyed, he shakes his head and switches off the lamp.*

**45.**

*Isabelle's room. Early morning. Streams of light are flooding through the window. Isabelle is sleeping in bed fully clothed. Rafa is lying awake next to her, staring at the ceiling. Ten or fifteen seconds pass in silence.*

**46.**

*Isabelle's kitchen. A kettle is boiling. Isabelle stands next to it in her dressing gown, dishevelled and plainly hungover. Rafa is sitting at the kitchen table, looking away from her.*

Isabelle: Look, I said I'm sorry. I called the house but someone said that you had gone to sleep. I didn't think it would be a good idea if we came back and woke you up just to drag you to Little Jakey's.

Rafa: I felt so stupid here on my own.

Isabelle: I just wanted to let you sleep in peace, that's all. I know that you're not into pot-smoking and all that shit.

Rafa: Maybe – but I'm not into being treated like an idiot either.

[She walks to the table and sits down facing him. Her dressing gown rides up her legs, exposing her knickers underneath.]

Isabelle: Don't be angry with me. I was only thinking about you.

[Rafa looks at her for some seconds, then smiles. They interlace hands.]

You forgive me, don't you?

Rafa [nodding]: Yes, I forgive you.

[Isabelle smiles and runs a hand through his hair.]

Isabelle [suddenly looking away]: God, I feel so sick. Shall we go out and get some fresh air?

**47.**

*Ten or twenty minutes later. Isabelle and Rafa are walking hand-in-hand through Hyde Park common. The sun is out and small pockets of students can be seen here and there.*

Isabelle: Isn't this beautiful? I can already feel my head clearing!

Rafa: Are all these students?

Isabelle: Yes, isn't it great? Almost everyone's back from the holidays now. . . . Look, they've put up one of those bouncy castles.

[She points to where the 'bouncy castle' is located. A few students are happily jumping around inside.]

Rafa: Don't tell me that you're thinking of jumping up and down on that, are you?

Isabelle: Me? Go on that now? Do you want to see me puke my heart out or something?

Rafa: Well, I know how crazy you are sometimes.

Isabelle: When I'm drunk, yes. Maybe even when I'm sober. But certainly not when I'm hungover.

Rafa: Discretion is the greatest part of valour. Isn't that a famous English expression?

Isabelle: Yes – something like that. Shall we go and get a bite to eat? My stomach's crying out for some oily, greasy junk food.

Rafa: Sure — what would you like?

Isabelle: How about a fat, disgusting, ketchup-covered hot dog from that burger van over there? I need something to line my stomach if I'm going to be okay for tonight's party.

Rafa: Tonight's party?

Isabelle: Oh, yeah. I didn't tell you, did I? Don't worry — it'll just be a quiet little gathering. Some other friends of ours have arrived back in Leeds and they're coming round tonight to our place for a couple of hours.

Rafa: I hope you won't drink as much as last night. You really stank of alcohol this morning.

Isabelle: Don't worry, Daddy. It'll be a quiet one tonight. I wouldn't be surprised if only Trudy and Judy and one or two others turn up. . . . Come on. Let's get over to that burger van. I'm absolutely starving!

**48.**

*Isabelle's living room. Very loud dance music. All the lights have been switched off except for an old-fashioned lava lamp. About thirty or thirty-five people are crammed into the room; many of them are dancing. Rafa is on his own, trying to make his way through them. After a while, he finds Isabelle talking to Andy by the stairs.*

Isabelle [throwing her arms round him]: Isn't this crazy! We were only expecting three or four guys and look what we get — a whole *housefull* of party animals!

Rafa: Isabelle, I'm not feeling very well. I think I'm going to go and lie down for a while.

Isabelle: What's wrong, my darling?

Rafa: I just feel a bit sickly, that's all. Must be that hot dog that I had at the park.

Isabelle: Oh, my poor darling. Do you want me to come upstairs with you?

Rafa: No, no: it's okay. You stay here and enjoy yourself. I'll be okay on my own.

Isabelle: Are you sure?

Rafa: Yes.

Isabelle [throwing her arms around him again]: You're an angel, do you know that?

[Rafa nods glumly and moves away. Halfway up the stairs, he turns around and sees Andy lean over and say something to Isabelle which makes her laugh.]

**49.**

*Isabelle's room. Loud music coming from the floor below. Rafa is sitting on the bed, holding his head in his hands. After a while, he gets up and walks over to the window. He opens the curtains and looks at the half-built mosque for some seconds. Then he closes the curtains again.*

**50.**

*Isabelle's room. Early morning. Rafa wakes up and discovers that Isabelle is not lying next to him.*

**51.**

*A few minutes later. Rafa is looking for Isabelle around the house. He tries the bathroom and the kitchen before walking into the living room. It is a complete mess in there, with beer cans and pizza boxes and plates of food strewn everywhere on the floor. There is someone asleep on the sofa.*

Rafa [trying to wake up the sleeper]: Have you seen Isabelle?

The bloke [waking up]: What the fuck?

Rafa: Isabelle? Have you seen her?

The bloke [shaking him off]: Get off me, you weirdo. What the fuck are you talking about? Who the fuck is Isabelle?

Rafa: Isabelle. The blonde girl who lives in this house.

The bloke: You mean Andy's mate? I don't know — and I don't fucking care. Go ask Andy. The fucker spent most of the night trying to get into her pants, didn't he? Now go and let me get some kip, will you?

**52**

*Outside Andy's room. Rafa is deliberating whether to knock on the door or not. He looks at his watch: it is 7.32am. Finally, he plucks up courage and knocks on the door. There is no response. He knocks again. Still no response. He knocks even louder.*

Andy's voice [very sleepily]: Yeah?

Rafa: Andy, can I talk to you for a moment?

Andy's voice: Who the fuck's there?

Rafa: Rafa, Isabelle's friend. I need to talk to you.

Andy's voice: Mate, it's half poost seven on oo Soonday morning! Cannie it not wait till oo bit later?

Rafa: It's important.

[Some moments pass. We can hear Andy getting out of bed. Finally, the door opens a few inches.]

Have you seen Isabelle?

Andy: Aye, she's in here.

Rafa: What?

Andy: Easy, easy. Don't take it wrong way, mate. She wor puking all over place and she didn't woont you to see her in such oo state, so I told her that she could stay in me room for night, all right.

Rafa: And you expect me to believe that?

Isabelle's voice [waking up]: What's wrong?

Andy [turning around]: It's yar foreign mate, Isa. I don't think he's too hooppy with you, like.

Isabelle's voice [drowsily]: Oh, fuck.

Andy [turning towards Rafa again]: Listen, pal. Me and Isa are just mates, okay? I'm starting to feel a bit offended, like, that you should doubt me word like you obviously do.

[He opens the door a bit further and puffs his chest out in a threatening manner. Isabelle can be seen through the gap between the door and the frame — lying in bed and holding her head in her hands. Rafa looks at the rugby player for some seconds, then shakes his head and walks back into Isabelle's room.]

## 53.

*Isabelle's room. Rafa is standing by the window, staring at the mosque. Isabelle has just entered the room, looking very bedraggled and disorientated.*

Isabelle: What's wrong?

Rafa: What do you think?

Isabelle: Come on, Rafa. You don't seriously think that I'm going to be sleeping with Andy right under your nose. What kind of a trollop do you take for me?

Rafa: I don't know, Isabelle, I don't know.

Isabelle [looking very upset]: What do you mean – you don't know? How can you say that? What's got into you?. . . Look at me, Rafa. Look at me. What do you notice? Yes, I'm fully clothed.

Rafa: So?

Isabelle: What do you mean — so? How long have I taken to come from Andy's room to mine? Ten seconds, fifteen seconds, maybe twenty seconds at the most? What does that tell you?

Rafa: You tell me.

Isabelle: Jesus, have I got to spell it out for you? Do you think that I would have been able to change into my clothes in fifteen seconds if I had been sleeping with Andy like you think that I was.

[She starts to cry.]

This is how I slept in his bed, Rafa — *with all my clothes on.* I just didn't want you to see me in the state that I was in. Is that such a fucking crime?

[Rafa turns around and sees her crying. For a second he looks at her tenderly, almost as if he is about to forgive her — but then he becomes stern and unforgiving again.]

Rafa: I'm sorry, Isabelle, but in my country girlfriends sleep together with their boyfriends — not in the bed of the guy next door!

[He walks angrily out of the room. We can hear him going down the stairs and then slamming the front door on his way out.]

**54.**

*Rafa is walking through the streets of Hyde Park. It is very early on a Sunday morning and there is no one around. From time to time he blows on his hands, trying to ward off the cold. We can hear Isabelle's voice in the background — as if Rafa were thinking of what she said earlier and already regretting his actions.*

Isabelle's voice: Jesus, have I got to spell it out for you? Do you think that I would have been able to change into my clothes in fifteen seconds if I had been sleeping with Andy like you think that I was. . . . This is how I slept in his bed, Rafa – with all my clothes on. I just didn't want you to see me in the state that I was in. . . . Is that such a fucking crime? *Tell me, is it such a crime?*

[He shakes his head and turns round.]

**55.**

*Rafa is standing outside Isabelle's house. He hesitates for some seconds, then knocks on the front door. When nobody answers, he tries the door and discovers that it is unlocked. He decides to go in. As he walks past the living room, he sees that the unknown guy is still sleeping on the sofa. Upstairs, he finds that Isabelle's room is empty. He also notices that Andy's door is slightly ajar and that there is nobody in his room either. As he is about to go back down into the living room, he hears Isabelle giggling inside the bathroom. He walks over to the bathroom door.*

Andy's voice: I think you're still drunk.

Isabelle's voice [drunkenly]: No, I'm not.

Andy's voice: What about your foreign mate? What's he gonna think of this, like?

Isabelle's voice: He's not going to be thinking anything, is he, 'cos he's pissed off and he's gone out for a walk. . . . In any case, I've gone off him big style, the possessive little shit.

Andy's voice: Well, if you say so, who oom I to complain? I never liked the coont anyhows.

[Shocked, Rafa staggers down the stairs and then runs towards the front door. As he leaves the house, he almost crashes into a little Asian kid who is riding a tricycle down the road.]

The little boy [waving a fist at him]: You fucking idiot! Watch where you're going, you fucking asshole!

[The camera continues focusing on Rafa's anguished face as he carries on running down a succession of streets.]

**56.**

*A secluded part of Hyde Park common. Grey sky, abandoned shopping trolleys, empty beer cans scattered all over the ground. Rafa sits on a metal bench, sobbing. A half-drunk bottle of whisky pokes out of his jacket pocket.*

**57.**

*Around two or three o'clock that same afternoon. Rafa is wandering through a street in Hyde Park. Further down the road we see four middle-aged locals coming out of a pub.*

Man 1 [approaching Rafa]: 'ere, mate. You got a light?

Rafa: Excuse me?

Man 1: 'ere, Flinny. Look what we got 'ere. A proper tanked-up asylum seeker [Putting his arm around Rafa.] Where you from, matey?

Rafa: Spain.

Man 1: He's from Spain, lads — 'ave you heard? I bet you his name's Manuel — just like that dumb cunt in that old comedy with him off *A Fish Called Wanda.* [Turning towards Rafa again; in an exaggeratedly slow tone.] Lis-ten, me mate here Flinn-y, he's try-ing to le-arn Fla-men-co danc-ing, in't he? Do you mind show-ing him some of your fan-cy su-per-fly moves? You know, a bit of the old spinning-about olé-olé stuff. I'm sure Fli-nny would be most grate-ful . . . [To Flinny; in his normal voice.] wouldn't you, you useless, drunken cunt?

[All the locals start laughing except Flinny.]

Flinny [coming up to Rafa; very aggressively]: You're from Spain? What are you doing round here, you fucking foreign cunt? First of all you con our Becks into joining Real Madrid and now you lot come here trying to steal our jobs from us. Jesus fucking Christ, what the fuck is wrong with this fucking country?

[Man 1, Man 2 and Man 3 laugh even louder.]

Flinny [to Rafa again]: What are you looking at, eh? What the fuck are you looking at? You want a piece of me, do you? Is that what you want, you dago piece of shit? Cos if you do, I'll knock your fucking block off. Do you understand me, dickhead? Am I making meself clear? I'm going to rip out your head and bury your headless corpse with me own two hands!

Man 3 [grabbing Flinny by the shoulders]: Give over, Flinny. He's just a little student shit. Let him go back to his fucking hovel. [Waving Rafa away.] Clear off, mate. Fuck off before we let Flinny 'mad dog' Bairstow loose on you.

[More drunken, hysterical laughter. Flinny shakes off Man 3 and tries to punch Rafa. The others quickly restrain him.]

Man 1 [holding Flinny down together with the others]: Just fuck off, mate. Get yourself away before he breaks loose. . . . He may look and talk like some screwed-up little spaz, but he's got the strength of ten men, our Flinny here has!

[Another outburst of drunken laughter. Rafa continues walking down the road.]

**58.**

*Early evening. Rafa is staggering through the maze-like streets of Hyde Park. It should be clear by now that he is totally drunk — and utterly lost.*

**59.**

*At a street crossing. Eight or nine adolescent kids are sitting on some railings. Rafa is walking across the other side of the street. After a few seconds, one of the kids gets up and approaches the Spaniard.*

The kid [in a loud voice; so that his mates can hear him]: Gee'us a pound, dickhead. I want to buy meself a packet of crisps.

[The other kids start laughing across the street. Rafa carries on walking regardless.]

Haven't you heard what I said, you fucking drunken knobrash? Gee'us a quid before me and me mates *pummelise* you well and proper.

[The kid waits for some seconds and then tries to hit Rafa. Though extremely drunk, the Spaniard manages to push his assailant away. Suddenly there is an uproar across the street and all the other kids come scampering in Rafa's direction.]

**60.**

*A few seconds later. Rafa is running away from the kids. He looks distressed and extremely disorientated, all memory of Isabelle and his maudlin afternoon having been erased from his face. Turning around a street corner, and finding himself momentarily hidden from his pursuers, he sprints down a narrow alleyway. For some moments he remains still, gasping for breath and standing with his back against a brick wall. We are painfully conscious of the panic rushing through his veins, the almost unbearable effort he is making to stifle the rasping sound of his breathing. Finally, he emerges from his hiding place and starts heading down the road. He looks visibly shaken and is stopping every few paces to gaze behind him. Not more than ten or fifteen seconds later, as he is going around a street corner, he comes face to face with the kids again. This time they pounce on him and drag him into the nearest alleyway, where they start attacking him from all angles. Within seconds Rafa collapses on the ground.*

The kid [finally waving the others to a stop]: Wait! Let's see if he's got any money on him.

[He bends down and rummages through Rafa's pocket until he finds his wallet.]

Nothing. Just some fucking, toilet paper foreign money. Useless, motherfucking knobrash.

[He gets up and kicks Rafa very violently on the head.]

Now, let's get the fuck out of here.

[The kids rush off. The camera continues focusing on Rafa's motionless body lying on the ground. Ten, maybe fifteen seconds pass in this way. Sound of crashing waves in the background. Fade-out to end.]

# Roman Ruins

## I.

Termini Station, Rome. 9 March, 2002. 9.47 am. The sky is grey, threatening rain. Commuters are scuttling in and out of the building. A young woman has just left the train at platform 9 and is making her way towards the concourse. She is wearing an expensive suit and carrying a large leather briefcase. The name of this woman is Giulietta Giordano and she is a barrister with *Baroni and Baroni,* criminal law specialists and purveyors of last-minute redemption to the well-heeled Roman classes. Earlier that morning, her Audi convertible had not started and she had been forced to take a train to get to work. If that wasn't irritating enough, the train had arrived half an hour late and she would now have to miss the company's monthly boardroom meeting. . . .

Once outside the train station, Giulietta opened her briefcase and retrieved a mobile phone from the inside. She prised its front panel open and began to dial her secretary's number: 'Hello, Marla. . . . Yes, it's me, Giulietta. Look, I'm going to be a bit late. Had a spot of car trouble this morning. . . . No, nothing serious — just your average, run-of-the-mill mechanical breakdown on the day of the partners' boardroom meeting. You know the kind of luck I've been having lately, don't you? I'm outside Termini right now, so I guess I'll be another twenty to twenty-five minutes, okay? Tell Rocco not to worry about the Patroni case — I've got the amended documents with me in my briefcase. See you soon.'

It was only when she switched off the phone that Ms. Giordano became aware of the beggar beside her. He was standing just a few yards away, an amorphous grey mass, a formless shadow loitering menacingly nearby. Instinctively, Giulietta tightened her grip on the phone and increased her walking pace.

'Please, madam,' the beggar's voice soon echoed behind her, 'do you have some spare change? Can you spare a few euros so that I can get myself a coffee? Please, please, my lovely, lady, don't let Zoran go without his regular morning espresso.'

Something about his voice made Giulietta stop. Maybe it was the slight foreign accent, maybe it was because he sounded submissive enough to be told to fuck off, maybe it was just simple, self-sabotaging curiosity. Whatever it was, the moment she turned around Giulietta saw exactly what she had been expecting to see: a tramp. A filthy, stinking, shit-encrusted tramp, as the Roman saying went. He was wearing a scruffy woollen hat and his cheeks were darkened by a layer of curly, dirty-looking stubble. A handful of plastic bags hung from his belt, each of them tied with intricate bow knots and filled with assorted bits of rubbish. An illegal immigrant, more than likely – judging from both the tell-tale tufts of throat hair and the Slavic squareness of his jaw-bone. 'Fancy being frightened by this piece of shit,' Giulietta Giordano thought for a second before pivoting on her Gucci stilettos and continuing towards the station's taxi rank. It was then that the tramp spoke for the second time:

*'E per pensare che gli occhi bei siano supposti per essere il portal ad un'anima bella.'*

The words caused Giulietta to stop in her tracks and turn around again. ' "And I thought that beautiful eyes were the portal to a beautiful soul." Those lines are from the medieval poet Giulio d'Este,' she said.

'Yes,' the tramp replied with his eyes half closed and a trail of saliva sliding slowly down his chin. 'I believe they are.'

Giulietta studied the tramp for a few moments without saying a word. He could have been anything between twenty-five and fifty-five: it was hard to tell with someone as fucked-up and as grimly undernourished as him. His face had a frighteningly sickly and cadaverous pallor (think chemotherapy; think dark, satanic mills), while his eyes had the glazed expression of an intractable glue sniffer. Even at five paces' distance Giulietta could pick out the smell of shit and dried urine wafting out of his clothes. For a second the lawyer could only look at the man in silence, trying hard to overcome the urge to throw up. Then, without knowing what strange emotion possessed her, she took off a thin sapphire ring from one of her fingers and flung it on the ground beside him. 'There you go,' she said sneeringly. 'Let's see how many espressos that will get you!'

**

Giulietta Giordano quickly forgot about the beggar and her spontaneous act of altruism. The ring had been a present from her ex-boyfriend (a man she would have gladly castrated, had she been given the chance), so there was nothing particularly charitable about her actions. But Giulietta was not destined to completely forget about the beggar or her ex-boyfriend's ring. About three weeks later, as she sat moodily in her office with a cup of strong black coffee, she looked at the calendar on her desk and saw that it was Thursday the twenty-ninth. 'Damn!' Giulietta muttered softly, putting down the espresso and buzzing her secretary through the intercom. 'Look Marla. I've just realised I've got an hour's legal aid this morning. Is there anyone out there wanting to speak to me?'

'Yes, Miss Giordano, there is a . . . person out here.'

'Send him in then, will you?'

Giulietta waited for some moments, slowly sipping her coffee and scanning through the documents of an important case that she had to deal with later that afternoon. When the door finally opened, she signalled with one hand to whoever had come in to sit down while she finished looking through her papers. 'Look,' she said, still gazing down at her documents. 'Let me make one thing clear. I don't do this because I believe in justice or anything like that; I just do this because my company feels that it is good practice to devote a small percentage of our time to helping the government. At the moment I have some very important cases on my hands, so if you are guilty — which I am not saying you are, but you might very well be — I would very much appreciate it if you pleaded guilty at your trial and we got this over and done with. Time, as they say, is money and I've got better things to do with my time at the moment than to get involved with a convoluted legal aid case.'

Giulietta looked up from her papers and found herself staring at a small, shabbily dressed man of about thirty or thirty-five. He was standing by the door with his hands in his pockets, looking dazed and generally disengaged from his surroundings. Something about him seemed familiar. Unnervingly familiar.

'Excuse me,' Giulietta said. 'But do I know you? I mean, have I represented you before?'

The bearded man shook his head and smiled. 'You gave me your ring two and a half weeks ago. Remember?'

Giulietta closed her eyes for a brief second and then swore under her breath. 'Look,' she finally said, 'I don't want you to get any funny ideas. I gave you that ring because my ex gave it to me and I hated his guts so much that I didn't want it anywhere near me. Is that clear?'

The man nodded quietly. 'I understand.'

'I just don't want you to believe that I'm a very generous or charitable person by nature, because I'm not. Okay?'

The man nodded once again.

'I'm actually a cold, materialistic, egotistical bitch who thinks like a lawyer, acts like a lawyer and cares about nothing except making heaps of money. Do you understand what I'm saying? Am I making myself clear?'

'You have made yourself perfectly clear,' the bearded man said.

'Also, please be aware that under the Italian government's *aiuta legale* scheme we are only able to carry out legal aid work to an upper limit of fifteen hundred euros. What this in practice means for you is that you are entitled to roughly two hours of legal advice and assistance. In our experience we find that this time is best utilised when divided between an hour-long fact-finding session and an hour of actual court representation. If we go above this two-hour limit, you will be liable to pay for your legal fees yourself. Therefore, I suggest that we start as soon as possible and that you try and answer my questions as truthfully and as cooperatively as possible. Do you understand what I'm saying?'

The man nodded yet again. 'Yes. I understand.'

'Right, then. Take a seat. I'm going to switch on my Dictaphone and you can tell me exactly what we are dealing with here.'

**

**Transcript of a conversation between Miss Giulietta Giordano, self-assured Roman lawyer, 33, and Zoran Vujovic, itinerant tramp of unknown origin, 37**

Zoran: It was because of the ring.

Giulietta: What do you mean?

Zoran: The ring you gave me.

Giulietta: I'm not following you.

Zoran: The ring. They found the ring on me.

Giulietta: Who did? What are you talking about?

Zoran: The Roman *Carabinieri*. That same night.

Giulietta: The *Carabinieri* found the ring on you?

Zoran: Yes.

Giulietta: The day I gave it to you?

Zoran: Yes.

Giulietta: At the station?

Zoran: Yes. They sometimes come down to Termini when they have nothing better to do. It's kind of like a game to them. Harass the homeless and terrorise the tramps. Great fun for all to have. Mega thrills guaranteed. You know what bastards coppers can sometimes be like.

Giulietta (abstractedly): You speak very good Italian, by the way. How come?

Zoran: I've been here for a few years now.

Giulietta: And you've learned to speak like this in a few years?

Zoran (shaking his head): My stepmother was Italian. She used to swear at me and my brother in Italian while we were growing up. '*Catso*' and '*pezzo di stronzo*' and shit like that.

Giulietta: Where was she from? Your stepmother, I mean?

Zoran: She was from Bologna.

Giulietta: That's funny. My father's from Bologna originally.

Zoran (very sarcastically): You could almost say that we're related, couldn't you?

Giulietta (coldly): Anyway, carry on. You were saying something about the *Carabinieri*?

Zoran: Yes. Some policeman fucker told me to turn out my pockets and then he found the ring. Said that I had stolen it. 'I have not stolen it,' I said. ‘A beautiful young lady gave it to me as a present.’ ‘Yeah, yeah, yeah,’ the arsehole then said, laughing to his mates. ‘I suppose you’re gonna tell us she gave you a blow job too? Tell us what really happened, you little shit,’ he said, ‘or we’ll lock you up for the night!’ ‘But I’ve told you the truth,’ I replied. ‘I got it as a present!’

Giulietta: I suppose they didn’t believe you.

*Zoran shakes his head.*

Giulietta: So you are being done for possession of stolen goods, then?

Zoran: Possession and assault.

Giulietta: Assault?

Zoran: I bit one of the guy’s ears when he was trying to push me into the van.

Giulietta: You what?

Zoran: I bit one of the guy’s ears when he was trying to push me into the van.

Giulietta: But why?

Zoran: He was punching me on the back of the head. It was kind of . . . hurting.

Giulietta: I see. Is there anything else that I should know? Any other crime that they’ve charged you with?

Zoran: No, that is all.

Giulietta: Are you sure?

Zoran: Yes.

Giulietta: Okay, Mr. . . .

Zoran: . . . Vujovic. Zoran Vujovic.

Giulietta: Okay, Mr. Vujovic. Let me ask you a few questions for my personal records. Try and be truthful, please. I need to know as much as possible about you before we go to court. . . . Date of birth?

Zoran: Three — nine — sixty-four.

Giulietta: Place of birth?

Zoran: Caglavica, a small village near Janjevo.

Giulietta: And where is this grand old place by the name of Janjevo?

Zoran: Kosovo. It's in Kosovo.

Giulietta: So you're a Kosovan?

Zoran: I'm a Kosovan Serb. . . . Don't look so surprised, Miss Giordano. (Is that how you pronounce your name?) In spite of what the media tells you, not all of us Serbs are raping, torturing monsters.

Giulietta: That is not what I was thinking. Please don't assume that just because I go silent for a second I have to be having those sorts of thoughts.

Zoran: What were you thinking then, if you don't mind me asking?

Giulietta: Just about Kosovo in general. Nothing interesting and certainly nothing we should be wasting any more time on.

Zoran: Are you sure, Miss Giordano? Perhaps I might enjoy hearing what RAI and CNN have taught you about my native country.

Giulietta (sighing quietly): You really are a grade-A pain in the ass, aren't you?

Zoran (with his hands outstretched before him): I just want to know what you think about us, that's all. (Putting on a thick foreign accent.) Juu knoh whart aih'm saj-een?

Giulietta: Don't tempt me because I might just do that.

Zoran: Be my guest, Miss Giordano.

Giulietta: Okay, in that case, seeing that you're so insistent, I'll tell you what I know about Kosovo. Kosovo, although part of Serbia, was full of Albanians. The Serbs didn't like this and started to throw the Albanians out. Next thing you know the Americans step in and start bombing the place to bits. Before long most of Kosovo is reduced to rubble (just as you would have expected from anything in which the Americans are involved) and for the second time in a few years you have thousands upon thousands of displaced people trudging all over Europe. You can see them every day wandering through the streets of Rome and other European cities — Muslims, Serbs, Gypsies, Bosnian Jews, Kosovan Albanians, each with their different stories, each pointing accusatory fingers at each other. Just who is right and who is wrong is difficult to tell, but one thing is pretty sure: the presence of all these immigrants on Italian soil makes for some strange political bedfellows. On the one hand, there are those who argue that these people have no home to go to and that it is Italy's moral duty to take them in. Among these you find Marxist town mayors, paedophilic Vatican priests, caviar-guzzling left-wing MEPs who claim they cannot act against their social conscience, Yankee-loving members of Berlusconi's *Forza Italia* for whom taking an anti-immigrant stance would be tantamount to criticising their own support for the American "liberation of Kosovo". On the other hand, there are those who will stop at nothing to keep the immigrant hordes at bay — working-class Italians (never much enamoured of immigrants, as they have always been), extreme rightwing groups such as *Fiamma Tricolore* or *Destra Protagonista* (who complain that these refugees are nothing but bloodsuckers running amok through the streets of Rome), and even hard-line anti-American Marxists who feel that by accepting the population overspill caused by *Operation Allied Force* Italy is tacitly condoning the US's wars of imperialistic aggression. . . . That, more or less, is what the Yugoslavian situation means to us ordinary Italians: a total first-class fuck-up. . . . Anyway, why am I telling you all this? It is you who's supposed to be answering my questions and not vice versa. How did you get to Italy?

Zoran: I walked.

Giulietta: You walked?

Zoran: I crossed over into Hungary from Serbia and then I made my way into Slovenia and on to Trieste on the Italian side. From there onwards it was very easy to get here.

Giulietta: How long did all that take you?

Zoran: I don't know. A month, maybe two. I can't really remember. My mind was too occupied with other things to register what was happening around me.

Giulietta: Are you here legally or illegally?

Zoran: You mean here in your office or in Italy in general?

Giulietta: Spare me the comedy routine, will you?

Zoran: I received my P34 three months ago, but I am still waiting for my P36, if that's what you're asking for.

Giulietta: That's not good. Do you realise that a court conviction could seriously derail the asylum application process? You could either be sent back to an internment centre for refugees or even, under certain circumstances, find yourself being forcibly deported?

Zoran: I am aware of that.

Giulietta: Okay, as long as you are aware, that's fine. Let's carry on. Do you drink alcohol?

Zoran: Yes, I do.

Giulietta: How much?

Zoran: I don't know — whatever I can find.

Giulietta: What would be a typical week's consumption, would you say?

Zoran: Look, I already said I don't know. Do you think I take down notes of what I find in rubbish bins?

Giulietta: Okay, in that case, let me ask you this – do you consider yourself an alcoholic?

Zoran: No.

Giulietta: Are you sure?

Zoran: Yes.

Giulietta: What about drugs?

Zoran: What about them?

Giulietta: Do you take them?

Zoran: Yes.

Giulietta: What sort?

Zoran: Heroin, amphetamines, coke, hashish. Basically, whatever I can get.

Giulietta: Would you describe yourself as a drug addict?

Zoran: Depends.

Giulietta: Depends on what?

Zoran: On how you define being a drug addict.

Giulietta: A drug addict is generally someone who can't live without drugs, who needs to chemically prop up his existence either with stimulants or depressants.

Zoran: In that case, yes, I'm probably a drug addict.

Giulietta: Do you have a fixed address in Rome?

Zoran: Do I look like I have a fixed address?

Giulietta: What if someone were to come looking for you? Where would you be normally contactable?

Zoran: In and around Termini Station, I guess. That is where I spend most of my time.

Giulietta: Okay, then. Let us proceed. Have you ever, now or at any other moment in time, been engaged in fulltime employment?

Zoran: What do you mean?

Giulietta: Have you ever worked? Either in Italy or before you came here? It will look good if we can link you with a profession of some sort before we go to court.

Zoran: I used to paint for a while.

Giulietta: You used to paint?

Zoran: I could use the word artist, but I don't think that painting newly-weds or university graduates posing with their parents justifies the use of the term.

Giulietta: So you're a professional artist?

Zoran: Was. I haven't painted or drawn anything for years.

Giulietta: Okay, in that case I'll write down 'artist — not practising.' Any family, relatives or dependants with you in Italy?

*He shakes his head.*

Please answer 'yes' or 'no', Mr. Vujovic — my Dictaphone is not built to pick up a shake of the head. Do you have any family relatives or dependants with you in Italy?

Zoran: No. I have no family or dependants.

Giulietta: Okay, that's enough for now. . . . Just one more thing. How come you knew who Giulio d'Este was? Don't tell me now that the old Tuscan rhyme-spinner is big in the Balkans?

Zoran: What the hell are you talking about, lady?

Giulietta: Giulio d'Este. The medieval poet. Don't you remember? You quoted a line from him about beautiful eyes being the portal to a beautiful soul. I had to study him at school.

Zoran: Oh, that. It's a line I picked up from some old tramp called Bebo. Never fails to reel in the ladies, if you know what I mean. A real vanity tickler.

Giulietta: A real vanity tickler?

Zoran: Yes, a real vanity tickler. Kind of like a verbal dildo. That's how old Bebo described it. Always catches them by surprise and makes them give you a few coins.

**

Zoran's court case was held about five weeks later in a small *Tribunale Ordinario* on the Via Triboniano. It was very hot inside the courtroom — the air conditioning having been out of order now for the better part of two weeks. As expected, the chamber was empty except for the main protagonists in the case: the testifying *Carabinieri*, the defence and prosecuting lawyers, the defendant, and, of course, the *iudice* — the last of these looking splendidly old-fashioned in the gold-tasselled robe and box-like hat worn by members of his profession. From the moment the trial opened, Giulietta chose not to mention anything about her encounter with Zoran at Termini, stressing instead that the defendant was a tolerant, good-natured and cheerful individual who had no previous criminal record and had only come to Italy to escape 'the whirlwind of chaos and destruction' which for some time now had engulfed his native Kosovo. 'You can ask any of the assorted men and women who congregate every day around Termini station,' the thirty-three-year-old lawyer said, taking a moment to glance over in Zoran's direction. 'Zoran Vujovic is the kind of man whom everyone confides in, they will tell you. A true people's person.' As regards the ring that was supposed to have been stolen, Vujovic had no memory of how it came into his possession. If he had indeed stolen the ring (something which could never be proved anyway), it was only to feed his drug addiction and not because he wanted to steal anything as such. A matter of simple self-preservation, to put things in their proper context. As far as the alleged assault against the *carabiniere* was concerned, the defendant's state of intoxication prevented him from being fully conscious of his actions and therefore absolved him *in sua mente, se non nell'azione* from the charges laid against him. This did not mean that the defendant was unaware of how serious his conduct had been. Quite the contrary. For the last seven weeks he had been torturing himself with the thought of what happened that night at Termini and now wished to take this opportunity to extend his most sincere and heartfelt apology to the officer concerned. ('I'm sorry that I bit you on the ear, officer Castellani. I just got a little nervous, that's all. You know what I'm saying?') At last, at around quarter to twelve, the judge banged his gavel and cleared his throat. He then pushed his square-rimmed spectacles up the bridge of his nose and looked at the small group of people assembled before him:

'After considering the different particulars of this case, I have decided to turn down the prefecture's request for the deportation of Zoran Vujovic. I am taking this decision on the grounds that, under present-day Italian law, there is insufficient evidence to identify him as a menace against the state and against the Italian people in general. I therefore declare that the defendant can, should he so wish, continue with his ongoing application for asylum. Similarly, considering the fact that no one has claimed ownership of the ring which was supposed to have been stolen, it remains unclear whether Vujovic was peddling stolen goods at the time of his arrest or not. Therefore, I am also forced to absolve him of that charge. However, Vujovic *did* assault an officer of the law – and this is an offence that cannot remain unpunished. Moreover, considering that Vujovic is currently enrolled in the P36 asylum application programme, I am obliged to impose a custodial sentence that will make him realise that, in this country at least, assaulting a police officer is a very grave and serious matter. Consequently, I sentence *il accusato* Vujovic to a term of six months imprisonment in C.C. Roma Berbieri commencing from this very day, from which the seven weeks he has already spent in custody will be deducted. All rise. *La sessione ora è chiusa.*'

It was not the kind of verdict that the state-appointed lawyer had been anticipating. Normally, whenever she lost a court case, Ms. Giordano would glance back at her clients and shrug her shoulders with the slightly apologetic air of someone who has tried her very best against heavily stacked odds. But that day, much to Giulietta's surprise, all her confidence abandoned her and she felt as small and overwhelmed as the first time that she had stepped into a courtroom and found herself surrounded by a gathering of people hanging on her every word. For a brief moment she clutched the wooden handrail in front of her and gazed at the defendant seated by her side: he was staring at the judge without saying a word, looking faintly ridiculous in the pinstriped suit that she had bought him from a charity shop a few days earlier. And then something happened that had never happened in the seven years that the *signorina avocata* had been practising as a barrister: she blamed herself for sending someone to jail.

'I'm sorry,' Giulietta mumbled as one of the uniformed officials began to handcuff her client. 'I really don't know what happened.'

'Don't worry,' the Serbian drug addict replied. 'You tried your best. That's all that matters — isn't it? You said so yourself earlier, remember?'

'Yes,' Giulietta said. 'You are right: that is what I said earlier.'

**

The days passed. Giulietta's Audi was fixed and she could now drive to the law firm again. Not only that, but towards the end of that same week she was assigned a fat case involving three businessmen accused of smuggling several container loads of tobacco from Gibraltar to Sardinia. ('Congratulations, Giulietta,' one of the senior partners at *Baroni and Baroni* had said to her as he handed the case documents over. 'Get out there and show them what you're made of!') Under normal circumstances this sort of event would have left Giulietta in a state of considerable elation — but this time around things were not quite that simple. 'What have I done?' she asked herself again and again, unable to stop thinking about Zoran mixing with all those murderers, rapists and paedophiles who were supposed to be locked up inside C.C. Roma Berbieri. 'Why did I have to give him that ring? Why did I have to act so impulsively?. . . *Madre di Dio,* why do things always have to get so bloody complicated?'

**

To get to C.C. Berbieri you had to drive to San Tiburtino, a municipal district some twenty kilometres outside Rome. The prison had been built in the late 1960s by Pierre Tomasso, a Piedmontese architect who claimed to have studied under Le Corbusier and who took pride in describing himself as a 'Functional Futurist'. Locals referred to the Piedmontese's creation as '*il testiculo de Tomasso*' – a nickname that mocked the building's singularly squat and formless appearance. Originally intended as a centre for rehabilitation and social integration, the prison had lost much of its credibility since its much-vaunted opening in 1967, becoming a byword for overcrowding, insanitary conditions and establishment brutality. In 1983 the Pope visited Berbieri to meet and forgive Mehmet Ali Ağca, the Turkish extremist who had previously tried to murder him. That same year, Adolfo Mancuso, a thirty-nine year old Neapolitan criminal serving a fifteen-year sentence for armed robbery and attempted rape, seized one of Berbieri's seniormost prison officers, his excellency *Ispettore Superiore* Achille Alberto Simone, and did not release him until the authorities had delivered to his cell two *Melanzane e Prosciutto* pizzas, the last three editions of *Playmen* magazine and a bottle of his favourite grappa. When questioned by journalists later about his rather idiosyncratic choice of demands, a broadly smiling Mancuso, who, according to his psychological profile report card, suffered from 'pronounced neurotic and psychotic tendencies', was reputed to have said, 'Well, it wasn't as if they would have agreed to send over a helicopter or a *puttana tettona*, is it? One learns to be realistic in a place like Berbieri, *capisce?*'

When Giulietta Giordano drove into the visitors' car park at Berbieri prison on Sunday, 14 May 2002, it had just gone half past one in the afternoon. A faded orange sun could be glimpsed behind the low-lying clouds, its refracted rays occasionally seeping through the toxic Roman smog and inundating the plain below with a strange otherworldly light. From the outside the prison looked functional and uninviting, tinged with that utilitarian soullessness which tends to engulf most government buildings built in the sixties. Looking at it now made Giulietta feel slightly sick. 'Am I doing the right thing coming here?' the lawyer all of a sudden thought. 'Or am I just blaming myself for something that has nothing to do with me?' Certainly, one thing was clear: if she hadn't given him the ring, Zoran would have never ended up in Berbieri. That much of a causal chain could be established. And yet, had she not acted in good faith? Could she really be held responsible for something that lay outside her direct field of control? Was she not going against her lawyerly instincts by trying to undo what could no longer be undone?

The car park at Berbieri was connected to the visitors' waiting room by means of a long underground corridor. Although no more than ten or fifteen metres long, the passageway was very brightly lit and its walls were plastered with 'No Smoking' signs and posters telling you not to smuggle drugs or weapons into the building. At the end of the corridor there was a set of concrete steps which led into the waiting room itself – a low-lit, low-ceilinged hall that stank of piss and dried vomit. The moment she stepped into this area, Giulietta was confronted by a gallery of different human types: the respectable and the not-so-respectable, the deeply mortified and the deeply uncaring, the sparklingly clean and the outstandingly dirty, all of them fanning themselves furiously with out-of-date newspapers and magazines in the stifling heat. For a second the thirty-three-year-old looked at the multitude around her and thought about using her lawyer's identity card to expedite proceedings. That would have been the easiest option, the most logical course of action. And yet something – a sense of guilt, perhaps, a lingering feeling of doubt – made her sit instead between an unshaven old man and a turbaned woman breastfeeding her baby. There she remained for approximately ninety minutes: chewing some gum, fiddling inside her handbag, scratching the side of her neck, examining the state of her nails, trying to look unconcerned when a fist fight erupted some yards away. Finally, at around quarter past three, she was asked to advance to the main security checkpoint.

'Excuse me, madam,' a *polizia penitenziaria* blurted out with all the charm of a bored shitless government functionary. 'Do you mind if I ask you a few routine questions?'

Giulietta turned to one side and saw a young, overweight woman of twenty-eight or twenty-nine, her corpulent frame squeezed in a navy blue uniform one or two sizes too small.

'Do you know that it is illegal to carry drugs, money or weapons into this prison?' the prison officer asked.

'Yes, I'm perfectly aware of that.'

'And do you know that anyone caught bringing in any of these things might be liable to spend up to five years in prison?'

'Yes, I'm aware of that too.'

'Good,' the prison officer suddenly replied with a self-satisfied smile. 'You may carry on now.'

But Giulietta, being the 'cold, materialistic, egotistical bitch' that she was, was in no mood to 'carry on' just then. 'Wait a minute,' she answered hastily. 'Do you mind if I ask *you* some questions of my own now?'

'What do you mean, madam?'

'Do you know that I've been sitting in a dingy, poorly ventilated waiting room for about ninety minutes? Do you know that in this room there were about three hundred other people (that's about one person for every three square metres, in case you're not mathematically-orientated) and that about one third of them were kids bawling and being sick inside their perambulators? Do you know that I've had to sit next to these people and listen to their crude jokes, their swearing, their sobbing, their threats of committing suicide, their complaints about the heat and about the amount of time they had been sitting there waiting? Do you know that all during this time I was dying for a cigarette but I couldn't actually bring myself to smoke one — not because of the 'No Smoking' signs (which no one paid much attention to, anyway), but because the only seat I could find was next to a bronchial old man and a turbaned gypsy woman breastfeeding her baby? Finally, do you know that I'm a lawyer, and that I'm seriously, seriously pissed off, and that what I've experienced this afternoon contravenes Article 55, Subsection 3a of the Prisons Maintenance Ordinance and that, if anyone carries on pissing me off, I will be lodging a complaint directly with the Minister of Justice himself? *Do you understand what I'm saying, lady?*'

The prison officer looked visibly perturbed. 'I'm sorry, madam, that you've been experiencing such problems. You should have said that you were a lawyer when you . . . well . . . when you first came in. You could have used the entrance for *avocati* and *magistrati*. You could then have come straight through to the security and search area without having to wait.'

'I'm here on a fact-finding mission,' Giulietta replied curtly. 'I have been asked to check what conditions in the visitors' waiting room are like. Haven't you heard of the Ministry of Justice's *Secret Shopper* programme?'

'In that case, I'm very sorry about your experience,' the prison officer said. 'I truly am. It's just that half of our staff are on strike now and we're badly understaffed. You know how it is with government departments these days. Please follow me, madam, and I'll see that you get to meet your client immediately.'

The prison officer ushered Giulietta out of the security area and into a long, narrow corridor. Upon reaching the end of the corridor, they entered a large white-tiled hall. It was brightly lit and divided by a reinforced perspex wall in the middle. There were also one or two old-fashioned revolving fans on the ceiling. Across her own side of the divide Giulietta was able to recognise some faces she had seen earlier in the waiting room: a woman with the words *Una femmina pericolosa* tattooed down the side of her neck, an old man wearing an SS-style leather overcoat, two teenagers holding hands and chewing gum, a young man with both eyebrows shaved off and a tattoo of a teardrop on his cheek. Before Giulietta had time to examine who these people had come to visit, she was led to a chair marked 'no. 46' and told to sit down. 'Your client will be with you in a few seconds, *signorina avocata*,' the female prison officer said.

When the Serbian drug addict finally appeared, Giulietta had to rub her eyes to make sure that she was not hallucinating. Though no more than two weeks had passed since their day in court, Vujovic looked older and thinner now, with wine-red swellings under his eyes and greasy curls of hair that fell over his forehead and partially obscured his eyes. Even his skin tone had drastically changed, going from the greying, cadaverous pallor of a drug addict to the parched and shrivelled dryness of someone who was being forcibly deprived of his addiction. In a word: he looked totally and utterly screwed.

'*Gesu*!' Giulietta exclaimed as the prisoner sat down in front of her. 'You look like something out of *L'Exorcista,* you do!'

Vujovic looked up with an expression of undisguised contempt. 'Thanks for that.'

'I've brought you some cigarettes and some chocolate, Zoran,' the lawyer said in a much quieter voice.

'I don't smoke and I don't like chocolate.'

'Well, give them to somebody else then. Or sell them. I'm sure you can get quite a few euros for them.'

The prisoner smiled unenthusiastically.

'How are you doing, anyway?' she asked.

Zoran raised his left hand in the air — it was shaking violently, twitching like it had a life of its own. 'You can see for yourself,' he said.

Giulietta looked down uncomfortably. 'Is there anything you need?' she said quickly and almost under her breath. 'Tell me, and I'll try and bring it for you.'

'I need money. About two thousand euros.'

The *avocata* looked up again. 'What do you need that much money for?'

'What do you think? I need to buy myself some lollipops and chocolate.'

Giulietta shook her head and bit her lower lip. 'I'd get into real trouble if I tried anything like that.'

'Bring the money inside you,' the prisoner said, looking her straight in the eye. 'You're a lawyer — they'll never search you.'

'What do you mean?'

'You heard. Bring it inside you. Four notes of five hundred. Either in front or behind — it doesn't matter as long as they're well wrapped up.'

Giulietta looked down and bit her lower lip again, this time almost drawing blood out of the soft, lipsticked-flesh. 'You know what?' she finally said in a hushed but extremely angry tone. 'I'm going to forget you said that to me. I'm going to forget it even though you've made me very angry. Fancy asking that of me? Who the hell do you think I am? Some slut out of *Midnight Express* or something? Tell me! God, I don't know where you people get the fucking effrontery from!'

Zoran smiled apologetically, but not without a hint of mockery. 'I'm sorry,' he said. 'You asked me whether you could help and that's the only way I could think of.'

'Yeah, well,' Giulietta replied, already hating herself for having come to Berbieri, 'just you thank your fucking lucky stars that I'm not going to tell on you!'

Zoran uttered a soft sigh and then forcibly clamped his trembling hand on to his lap. Watching him do this made Giulietta feel even more furious.

'Why do you take drugs in any case?' she angrily asked. 'Why are you poisoning yourself in this way?'

'It's a long story'

'Oh, is it now?' the thirty-three-year-old *avocata* sneered contemptuously. 'Let me try and guess. Your wife ran off with your best mate and you decided to become a bum? Or maybe you were a rich millionaire who one day converted to Buddhism and decided to slum it with his less fortunate 'brothers'? Or maybe you couldn't stand the strain of modern living and decided to pack it all in, just like that? Or maybe, being a Serb, you are just full of guilt for what your people did in Kosovo to everyone who was not Serbian?'

The prisoner carried on holding his hands and looking down at his lap, seemingly unconcerned.

'Answer me, Goddamit!' Giulietta hissed angrily. 'You had the nerve to ask me to carry money up my ass-hole for you — at least I deserve a bloody answer!'

That moment Zoran looked up. 'My family got killed several years ago by masked commandos belonging to the pro-Albanian KLA,' he said quietly. 'They shot my four-year-old son in the head and gang-raped my wife and my twelve-year-old daughter before shooting them in the head too. It happened just ten yards in front of me — roughly the same distance as from here to where that prison officer stands casually picking his nose. The only reason they didn't kill me was because I was hiding behind the boiler in my garage and I was too goddamned scared to come out and confront them. Because I didn't have the guts to stand up for my own flesh and blood. Do you think that you could have guessed *that, signorina avocata*?'

'Is all that true?' Giulietta asked in an almost inaudible voice.

'No, I just like making up fucked-up little tales to shock female Roman lawyers!'

Giulietta looked into his eyes and saw that they were staring straight into hers, the pupils still and noticeably dilated. She also noticed that his left hand had stopped trembling. It lay limp and lifeless on his lap, like some kind of inanimate object, *like something that did not really belong to him.*

'I'm sorry,' the lawyer suddenly said, quickly getting up to go. 'I'm really, really sorry.'

**

When Giulietta went to work the next day, everyone noticed how pale and sickly she looked. Soft purple bags had puffed up under her eyes and her skin had acquired the texture of cheap handbag leather. Old Signor Baroni, one of the two brothers who had founded the firm back in 1947, even stopped her outside the boardroom and asked her if something was wrong. 'Are you all right, Giulietta?' he said in his soft Milanese accent. 'You look rather pale, my dear.' 'I'm fine, Umberto,' Giulietta responded, trying to shrug off her boss's genteel apprehensions with a tired smile. 'I've just got a bad cold, that's all. No need to worry about me.'

The morning dragged by like Monday mornings do. At ten-thirty Giulietta had a preliminary meeting with Angelo Cappuccito, the pony-tailed representative of the three businessmen who had been caught smuggling tobacco from Gibraltar to Sardinia. For the next ninety minutes Signor Cappuccito, a small, dark-skinned man whose handtailored clothes contrasted quite spectacularly with his crud-encrusted fingernails, sat with his feet propped on the boardroom's coffee table, smoking *Montecristos* and talking about what he described as the three men's 'social consciences'. 'Look at Don Claudio,' he said theatrically at one point, pausing to puff at his hand-rolled cigar. 'That man has donated money to thirty-three different charities, including seven orphanages, two convents and an institution for the mentally infirm. How could we possibly allow such a pillar of society to go to jail, I ask you, signorina? It is necessary — more than that: it is *vital* — that the jury be made aware of how important these men are to their native Calabria. This, after all, isn't simply a question of tobacco smuggling,' he added as he tipped some cigar ash into a *Baroni and Baroni* ashtray. 'This is about a large number of people who'll have no one to provide for them if these Calabrian gentlemen are sent to jail. Do you understand what I'm saying, signorina?'

When the meeting finally finished at around one, Giulietta walked back into her office and told her secretary that she was taking the rest of the day off. 'Make sure you cancel all my appointments, Marla,' she said, taking a couple of Paracetamols from one of her desk drawers and swallowing them without any water. 'I'm not feeling that great today.' 'You sure you want to do that, Ms. Giordano?' Marla asked. 'You have Vince Tomassini and Michael Cabezuto coming in this afternoon, remember?' 'Get Rocco to deputise for me for an hour,' Giulietta responded with half her body already out of the door. 'He knows the ins and outs of the Ameritalia case better than anyone else in the office and he owes me a favour after I sorted out that David Trentino fiasco for him.'

It took Giulietta Giordano about an hour to drive home. Coming in through the door, she took off her jacket and her high-heeled shoes and then threw herself on the black leather sofa in the centre of her living room. For the next five or six minutes she remained totally motionless on the sofa. She could feel her heart beating against her ribcage, pumping anxiety all over her body. What I need is a good pick-me-up, she finally decided. She could almost picture it in front of her — a nice Cosmopolitan, with a little bit of lime juice to tickle the palate. 'Yes,' she told herself, getting up, 'that's what I need. A bit of the old Cosmo magic. Forget uppers and downers and the kind of shit that the others in the office take. Nothing like a Cosmopolitan's restorative powers when all's said and done.' Growing more and more excited at the thought, she walked over to the drinks cabinet and began to pour herself a glass, quietly whispering the formula she knew so well: 'One part Cointreau. Followed by three parts Vodka. Followed by three parts Cranberry juice. Followed by a few drops of lime juice.' However, just as she took her first sip of the drink, she noticed her reflection in the kitschy art nouveau mirror that hung above the cabinet. What she saw there really shocked her. Despite the innumerable face creams that she applied every morning and evening, she looked pale and haggard – with splodgy traces of lipstick smeared across her chin and clumps of mascara on her eyelashes. Also, if that wasn't bad enough, the skin around her neck had grown red and coarse, covered in tiny goose pimples that brought back the memory of an undercooked chicken dish she had once tasted in a Taiwanese restaurant in the Trastevere. That moment a wave of self-understanding suddenly flooded over Giulietta. 'I have no option,' she whispered to herself, smoothing down one of her eyebrows with a finger she had dipped into the glass. 'I have to do what he wants.' Then she did something that really surprised her: she brought the glass to her lips and finished the Cosmopolitan in one quick gulp.

**

The following day Giulietta Giordano woke up with a dry throat and a strong migraine. She had spent most of the night pacing up and down her house and going to the bathroom, unable to think of anything except her impending visit to Berbieri. 'What if they discover me?' she once again asked herself, this time sitting in the kitchen with an untouched glass of orange juice by her side. 'What if they catch me red-handed?' She could almost visualise the headline in the *Corriere della Sera* – **Top lawyer caught in prison smuggling fiasco, sentenced to three years' imprisonment.** 'Jesus Christ,' Giulietta suddenly whispered to herself, 'can you imagine what everyone will think? Rocco, Marla, old Mr. Giordano, even that dickhead Angelo Cappucitto? She must have gone off her rocker, they would say. Must have flipped out with stress. Happens all the time to these young lawyers, you know. They push themselves to the limit day in day out and then suddenly, pouf!, out goes their sanity and their health!' Shuddering at the thought, she looked at the small ball of greaseproof paper resting on the table beside her. Stuffed inside it were two thousand euros. Lying on the table the thing looked innocuous and meaningless, a crumpled-up piece of wastepaper that someone had forgotten to throw away. 'Could anything be more fucked-up than this?' she wondered.

**

The journey from Giulietta's village to Berbieri took about fifty-five minutes. Giulietta drove slowly and with great care, always stopping at traffic lights and never exceeding the constantly changing speed limit that the authorities had set to plague the suburban driver. When she finally got to her destination, it had just gone midday and the sun could be seen shining dimly through the sulphur dioxide haze. A temperature post in the street gave a reading of 33. 5 degrees; a billboard nearby declared 'Life is much more fun if you drink Moretti beer.' Just before she got out of the car, Giulietta rapidly scrawled a note and then positioned it on the walnut-panelled dashboard: 'To all those concerned: sorry for everything. Some things are just too complicated for simple explanations. Guess that life wasn't as predictable as I first thought. Please don't judge me too harshly. xx Giulietta.'

**

She was taken to chair number 27 in the visiting room. She had already been sitting there for nearly twenty minutes, one leg crossed over the other, dreaming about the cigarette she could not have and simultaneously regretting having overdone it with her Cosmopolitans the night before. 'Be calm,' she whispered to herself from time to time. 'Be fucking calm. You're a lawyer and no one's gonna mess with you! Don't forget that, Giulietta! Don't forget it!' She repeated these and other similar words again and again, but they didn't seem to be having the desired effect – judging from the drops of sweat that kept on trickling down her forehead and into her eyes. Presently, during a lapse of concentration, she turned around and saw that the wall behind her was lined with prison officers. Even worse, they were all staring directly at her! 'Shit!' Giulietta thought, immediately sinking her teeth into her lower lip. 'What am I supposed to do now? What am I supposed to do?' It was at that moment, just as she was about to pick up her handbag from the floor and rush out of the visiting room, that Zoran appeared on the other side of the screen and sat down opposite her:

'Did you bring the money with you?'

Giulietta looked at Vujovic for a few moments and saw that he was sweating profusely, his long and greasy curls matted down the side of his face like those of some unholy messiah.

'Well, *have you, or haven't you?'*

Giulietta nodded silently. Across the other side of the perspex divide Zoran gritted his teeth and muttered something under his breath.

'What . . . what's wrong?' Giulietta nervously asked.

'Nothing, nothing. . . . I'm just glad you brought the money, that's all.'

'Are you sure?'

'Yes. . . . Yes, of course.'

Giulietta smiled uneasily and then clasped her hands together on her lap. 'By the way . . . speaking about the money . . . what I mean is . . . how do I manage to-'

'Don't worry about that,' Zoran Vujovic replied, waving her silent with a dismissive gesture of the hand. 'All you have to do is wait for a few minutes and then say to one of the guards that you'd like to go to the bathroom. You can retrieve it then. Keep the money hidden inside your sleeve on the way back. When you get here, just pass it to me through this little speaking vent before you.'

Giulietta looked at him directly in the eye. 'Are you really sure this will work, Zoran?'

'Totally sure. That's the way everyone does it.'

'What about the guards? Won't they notice anything?'

'The guards know that it happens. They just ignore it. Otherwise the inmates would be up in arms and this place would be impossible to control.'

'Are you sure?' she asked. 'That doesn't sound very convincing to me.'

'Totally sure. It's one of those unwritten laws. Don't you know anything about Italian prisons or what?'

'I don't know. You make it sound so simple.'

'Come on,' Vujovic suddenly growled between his teeth, 'stop fucking about. You know you owe it to me, Miss Hot-Shot fucking lawyer. If it wasn't for that ring, I wouldn't have ended up here trying to stop all these Italian "lover boys" from screwing my hairy Balkan ass. Just do what you are supposed to do and then we can call it quits, okay?'

'But won't they see me passing the money to you? There are so many guards in the room.'

'Don't be silly, woman,' Zoran whispered angrily. 'The guards don't even look. Just pretend you're going to kiss me through the glass or that you're going to show me your tits or something like that. No one will bat an eyelid.'

'I'm still not sure.'

'Oh, for fuck's sake, woman, have you come here to torture me or something? Can't you just do this little favour for me after all the shit you've put me through? '

Giulietta gazed down for about ten seconds, her attention focused on the shiny yellow buckle on her designer stilettos. Then she looked up and nodded slowly. Subsequently, she turned around and asked one of the prison guards if she could go to the bathroom. The guard looked to the other side of the hall and made some kind of coded signal with his fingers to one of his colleagues. Shortly afterwards, a female officer walked over to Giulietta and asked her to accompany her through a small door behind the row of uniformed prison officers. The lawyer nodded and began following the woman down a succession of narrow, fluorescent-lit corridors that smelled of damp and industrial-strength disinfectant. Finally, after walking through what seemed like a labyrinth of passages, the warden slowed down and pointed to a door with the letters WC stencilled across it in black paint. 'You have two minutes,' the uniformed woman said, propping herself against a nearby wall and glancing at the black Casio watch strapped around her wrist. 'Any more and I'll have to open the door and fetch you out. Is that understood?'

## II.

Zoran Vujovic served only two of the four and a half months that he was sentenced to. He did not particularly like the experience of being locked up in an Italian prison (he especially hated the gelatinous mixture of rice and potatoes which he was served every day), but then again he did not find it that bad either. With the two thousand euros that Giulietta had smuggled into Berbieri for him, he could more or less buy anything that he wanted from the guards and the convict black marketeers – heroin, cocaine, speed, chewing gum, grappa, porn mags, the odd bottle of imported Heineken beer. On one occasion he was even able to procure a fully-charged portable DVD player for the evening. The property of one of the prison guards, it was smuggled into his cell in between some towels and bed linen and had two Sylvester Stallone films and an old porn movie sellotaped to its aluminium underside. . . .

All during this time Giulietta Giordano carried on visiting Zoran at regular weekly intervals. She always brought him chocolate bars and Lucky Strikes (even though he kept on telling her that he did not like chocolates and that he hadn't smoked for ten years) and never seemed to mind that Zoran spent most of the visiting hour looking bored and picking at the festering purple scabs on his forearm. If you'd asked Giulietta why she continued visiting him, she would have probably shrugged her shoulders and told you that she did not have the faintest clue. Maybe she was lonely. Maybe she was bored. Maybe it was just an escape from everything else. You never really knew with the sort of routine that she followed, constantly being pushed to meet deadlines and commission targets, never having the time to relax and do the things that ordinary people did. What was it that Rocco at the office always said about criminal lawyers? 'We are a cursed breed,' he was always saying, shaking his head and sighing in that slightly camp way of his, '— always having to make excuses to the people we love, always being forced to spend hours with the people we inwardly despise. Sure, we make a lot of money, no one can deny it. We own nice houses, drive expensive cars, fly business class when we go on holiday. But what comfort is all that when we can't even take a shit without thinking about how much money we're going to squeeze out of our next clients!' Rocco was right, of course: most of the lawyers she knew were greedy bastards who overworked themselves to the point of mental collapse. That is why so many of them had what could be termed their irrationalities, their counterbalancing moments of madness. In her firm, for example, there were crossdressers, aircraft spotters, paintballing fanatics, historical battle recreators. Maybe seeing Vujovic every week was something like that — a counterbalancing irrationality, something designed to thwart the humdrum predictability of her daily life. How else could you explain the way she had acted at every stage — telling herself that she would have nothing more to do with him and then still seeing him all the same? First it was the ring, then the trial, then the first visit to Berbieri, then the episode with the two thousand euros. If all this didn't equate to a counterbalancing irrationality, *then what exactly did*?

Zoran Vujovic was no less puzzled by the lawyer's behaviour. 'Why does she continue visiting me when we barely speak to each other?' he often wondered. 'And why does she carry on bringing me those bars of *Pernigotti* or *Pernigotto* or whatever you call that disgusting Italian chocolate? Surely, there has to be something wrong with the broad!' Not that Vujovic minded her visits that much. Actually, he found her quite amusing, this scatty, power-suited Roman lawyer who somehow blamed herself for his going to jail. Like most people with money, she pretended to be very hard, but underneath all that she was quite a soft and malleable broad, with something of a martyr complex to boot. He had a hunch that she was the type of woman that men were always taking advantage of, something which he found sad and amusing at the same time. Just before his jail term ended, Giulietta promised him that she would be waiting for him outside the prison gates on the day of his release — and, sure enough, the first person that Zoran saw upon regaining his freedom was the criminal lawyer standing next to her Audi TT. She was clutching her hands behind her back and smiling uneasily, almost as if she were not sure of what she was doing. Despite it being a bright summer day, she looked even paler than usual.

'Hello, Zoran.'

'Hello, Miss Giordano.'

'Good to be out?'

'Yes, very good.'

'How was the checking out procedure? Did you get all your possessions back?'

'Yes. . . . Look, Miss Giordano,' he said, stiffly shaking his head, 'there's no need for any of this. You really shouldn't have bothered coming down here. I told you, I can cope on my own.'

'Yes, but I wanted to be here, Zoran. . . . I felt that I could at least give you a lift to wherever you're going. . . . Besides, I'm off work today and I've got nothing else to do.'

'Are you sure?'

'Come on,' Giulietta said, unclasping her hands behind her back and turning towards the car. 'Dump your bag in the boot. Where do you want me to take you?'

'I don't know. Anywhere near Termini will do.'

'Termini train station?'

'Yes. That is, if it isn't too much out of your way. If not, drop me off wherever — I don't mind.'

Termini station lay about thirty to thirty-five minutes' drive from the municipal district of San Tiburtino. To get there you had to follow the S-567 into the *rioni* of Campo Marzio and then, after negotiating the mishmash of traffic cops, 'lane-hoppers' and aggressive gypsy beggars which usually accumulated at the Roma-Campo Fiore zonal interchange, turn left and then right onto transurban highway 68 (not to be confused with transurban highway 67, which involved two lefts and a right turn and which brought you back into the north Roman suburbs through the districts of Revola and Campitelli). As their journey took them briefly through the centre of Rome, they could see the usual sprinkling of famous Roman landmarks along the way — the Coliseum, the arch of Constantine, the monument to Vittorio Emanuele, the Castel Sant'Angelo — the kind of Rome, in other words, that everyone from Timbuktu to Tennessee knew.

At Termini, Giulietta once again rediscovered her lawyerly sense of self-control. Parking her Audi between a Coke delivery van and the unoccupied end of a taxi rank — an action which immediately provoked loud wails of protest from the *tassìstas* stationed at the front of the queue — she stepped out of the car and helped Zoran retrieve his bag from the boot. She then extended her hand towards him. For a second or two the criminal law specialist held his bony hand in hers, surprised not only by the sandpapery roughness of its texture but also by the extraordinary limpness of its grip. (What did the deputy senior partner at *Baroni and Baroni* used to say about men with a limp handshake? Something about them having little dicks and no sense of business acumen?)

'Well, I'd better get going,' Zoran finally said, starting to inch away. 'Thanks for all your help. I won't forget it.' He walked a few more paces and then stopped again. 'You know, I've been meaning to tell you: I never thought that lawyers like you existed. I mean, you've got to be mad, haven't you? Mad or suffering from some kind of martyr complex, perhaps? Do you know what I'm getting at? Or maybe, just maybe, there was more to those stupid lines of poetry than I first thought. . . . Anyway, I think I've talked too much already.'

He turned around again and started to walk away. Giulietta watched him without saying a word. He was wearing the same tattered pinstriped suit that he had worn all those months ago at his trial, looking every bit as pathetic and ridiculous as he had done that day in the courtroom. Goddamn that cream-coloured pinstriped jacket, Giulietta suddenly thought. Goddamn that Giulio d'Este. Goddamn that fucking stupid ring and that Kosovan war. Goddamn Giulietta Giordano for being so ridiculously over-sentimental at times like these!

'Zoran!' the lawyer suddenly cried out. 'Zoran, wait!'

The drug addict stopped on the other side of the street and turned around.

'Listen,' Giulietta shouted over the sound of the running engines and chatting pedestrians. 'Didn't you once say you were a painter of some sort?'

'What?' Zoran yelled back from the other side. 'What was that again?'

'I said, didn't you used to be a painter or something?'

He shrugged his shoulders and pointed to the side of his head to indicate that he could not hear. Giulietta swore under her breath and started crossing the road towards him.

'I'm sorry,' Zoran said as soon as the lawyer reached him. 'I couldn't hear you.'

'No, no,' Giulietta replied quickly and rather nervously, 'don't be sorry. It's just that . . . well . . . you see . . . well . . . didn't you once say you were a painter? Well, I've been thinking about it and maybe . . . maybe . . . who knows . . . maybe, if you want . . . if you feel comfortable with the idea . . . well . . . you might . . . well . . . you might want to help me decorate my house in Veruccio. It's in a bit of a mess at the moment . . . well, a total mess really, come to think of it . . . and I need someone who can help me sort things out. You know, paint a few ceilings, finish tiling the kitchen, put up a few cornices, that sort of stuff. I'll pay you well and you can stay in one of the spare rooms upstairs while working for me if you want.'

Zoran shook his head. 'I don't think that's such a good idea, Giulietta.'

'Why not?'

'I'm a drug addict, remember? I need my fixes to keep going. . . . Besides,' he added with a half-smile, 'I said I was an artist, not a painter.'

'Same thing, isn't it?'

'Trust a lawyer to say something like that.'

Giulietta smiled back and then lowered her eyes slightly. 'I don't mind you taking drugs,' she finally said. 'As long as you don't do it in front of me, I'm fine with it.'

'Jesus Christ, Miss Giordano, *you're even crazier than I first thought*!'

'No, honestly — I don't mind. As long as you don't take drugs in front of me, I'm fine.'

'But you don't even know me, Giulietta,' Zoran protested. 'I could turn out to be a rapist, a pervert, a psychopathic axe-murderer. How can you let me into your house just like that?'

'Let's just say I have a very strong feeling that you aren't any of those horrible things. . . . Besides, it's not like I don't know you, really, is it?'

'You're crazy, do you know that? You're totally fucking crazy!'

'Maybe — but you'd be even crazier if you turned down an offer like this!'

Zoran looked down for several moments, a frown darkening his already dusky features. 'Are you really sure about this? I don't want you to be getting into something which you might later regret.'

'I'm sure. I know what I am doing.'

'That's what Slobodan Milosevic said to us Serbs when he decided to turn up the heat in Kosovo,' Zoran said, looking up at her with a semi-serious expression. 'A bit of caution isn't always a bad thing.'

'Yes, but I am no Sloban Milosevic and employing you in my house is no genocidal military operation — is it now? So what do you say, then? Deal or no deal?'

**

Giulietta Giordano lived in la Residenza Mare d'argento, a small residential complex some sixty or seventy kilometres north of central Rome. The development had been constructed by *Rossellini i Tedesco*, a large, trans-national company which specialised in building luxury houses and apartments in prime residential areas. It lay just ten minutes from the village of Veruccio, one of the prettiest and most historic villages of the so-called *'cintura verdi di Roma'* and the fourth stop on the Termini-Ghibberti suburban train line. Out of the five types of home that were originally on offer, Giulietta had settled for a 'class D' property — a two-storey, five-bedroom house with an underground garage and a village-facing balcony. She had purchased the deed two years ago, shortly after having been promoted to the post of junior director within her firm. In the last year and a half the property had more than doubled in value — although, like many other luxury developments in and around Veruccio, la Residenza had lately began to suffer from the crime wave currently sweeping through the north Roman suburbs. Recently there had even been reports of armed Albanian gangs targeting some of the more luxurious houses within the complex. The local *polizia* referred to them as *'il chloroformeri'* — owing to their habit of drugging their victims with chloroform just before each late-night burglary. The *chloroformeri's* operational methods had a frightening predictability about them: they would shoot your guard dogs with tranquilliser darts, break into your house, drug you and your family while you were still asleep, and then help themselves to all the Rolex watches and Chopard necklaces that you were stupid enough to keep stashed inside your dresser. After the first spate of crimes, *Rossellini i Tedesco* had beefed up security throughout the development – adding dog patrols and armed guards to their already extensive array of protective measures. They had even installed twenty-four CCTV cameras at different points across the twelve acre site, hoping to catch the Albanian outlaws *in flagrante delicto.* Unfortunately, none of these prophylactic strategies had so far been of any value. In the last month alone the *chloroformeri* had struck twice – ransacking the property of Dr. Makuso Rinaldini, a young plastic surgeon from Cremona, in the first instance, and then breaking into the complex's mini-golf club and roughing up two Libyan gardeners who were doing some overnight topiary work. On both occasions the same handwritten note had been found at the scene of the crime: 'Rich Roman pigs. Prepare yourselves to get fucked by the fine gentlemen *chloroformeri.* You have been warned.'

Zoran and Giulietta arrived at la Residenza just before half past seven in the evening. After going through the gated entrance, the lawyer slipped down a couple of gears and took off her sunglasses. She then switched off the car's AC unit. Through the passenger window Zoran observed the usual hallmarks of middle-class living – garden sprinklers, immaculately trimmed hedges, uniformed security guards, a variety of 'No Trespassing' signs. He also noticed a distinct lack of pedestrians.

'Is it usually as quiet as this?' Zoran asked.

'Yes, things have become a bit weird here after what the Albos have been doing.'

'The Albos?' he asked.

'The Albanians. A gang of them has been going around breaking into people's houses and drugging them with chloroform. By the time they wake up there's not so much as a light bulb left in the house!'

'That's what happens when you allow Albanian scum into your country, I'm afraid.'

'It's not just the fact that things are getting stolen that's worrying people,' Giulietta said, slowing down even further. 'A woman just down the street, for example, woke up to find herself surrounded by several Polaroid snaps of her that had been take while she had been *chloroformed*. They were compromising to say the least.'

Zoran smiled grimly. 'Albanians and sexual molestation. Why am I not surprised about what you're telling me?'

'Look,' Giulietta said, discreetly trying to change the subject. 'See that house over there. That's where I live.'

'Nice. Very nice.'

'That's what everyone says when they first see the house,' Giulietta confessed as she descended into first gear and drove into the underground garage. 'But it is not so nice inside. In the two years that I've been living here, I've hardly done any work on it. Wait till you see what it's like. You might just regret having accepted my job offer — that's how shitty the place looks inside!'

**

Zoran Vujovic started working on Giulietta Giordano's house on the first of July, 2002. Although he had been out of work for a few years, it took the Serbian surprisingly little time to get used to his new routine. Each morning he would wake up at half past seven and inject himself with about 150 mg of heroin. Shortly afterwards, he would join Giulietta in the downstairs dining room for tea and toast (decaffeinated and milkless, with only the thinnest scrapings of margarine). As soon as the lawyer left at quarter past eight, he would return to his room and sniff a quick line or two of Coke — just enough to shake off the heroin's 'downing' effects and get him going for the day. He would then slip into a pair of overalls and begin to work on the cornices in the different rooms. Between 11.45 and 12.45 he would stop and fix himself a bite to eat. Some frozen microwave meal, most probably, or maybe some half-eaten refrigerated pizza left over from the day before. After lunch, it was time for a little more cocaine or a couple of cold Moretti beers from the fridge — something, in other words, that would keep the morning 'high' from fading. The remainder of the afternoon was occupied with a variety of jobs — cutting the kitchen tiles, fixing the wiring, applying artex to the walls. These would carry on until the lawyer arrived home at around eight or nine, at which point the Serbian would lay down his tools and retreat back into his room upstairs, ready for some food and his second heroin fix of the day. Apart from this, there is not much else to relate about Zoran's new life in Veruccio. Sometimes, when he was really bored in the evenings, he would switch on the little black-and-white portable in his room and sit in front of it till the early hours of the morning. He would watch whatever was on: the nine o'clock RAI news, dubbed American sitcoms, National Geographic documentaries, a daily quizshow programme called *soldi e cervelli.* Occasionally — whenever Giulietta took it upon herself to cook an evening meal — he would be forced to leave his room and join her at the dining table. There he would sit for an hour or two, patiently listening to her whinge about her workload or the self-centred tendencies of her current boyfriend:

'You know what he did yesterday?'

'What?'

'He asked me if I minded him going with his mates to Amsterdam next week for a few days. Can you believe that? Does he think I was born yesterday or something? Does he think that I don't know what men get up to on these stag nights in Amsterdam? Do you know what I said to him then?'

'What did you say?'

'I said if you go with your mates to Amsterdam, don't expect me to be waiting for you when you come back. I may tolerate your constant flirting and your never ending lies, but I'm not going to be here for you once you come back from drug-infested whore-central bloody Amsterdam. That's what I said to him.'

That was on the *good days.* On the bad days, when Giulietta was tired and didn't feel like talking much, they would sit facing each other without saying anything — just like they had once done on opposite sides of the perspex divide at the visiting room in Berbieri. He would be picking at his *Insalata Caprese* or his *Linguini alla Romana* with a bored, slightly angry look; she would be staring into space and thinking about some contract that had to be hammered out before the close of the week. In the end, just when it seemed that no words would ever pass between them, she would suddenly ask him something about his past:

'Why don't you ever talk about it?'

'Talk about what?'

'About what happened.'

'What do you mean?'

'You know: what you went through, the feelings you had to deal with. . . . You *should* talk, you know. Talking's good.'

'Sure it is.'

'I mean it, Zoran: talking about it would help you more than you think.'

'Yeah, I'm sure.'

And then one day, totally out of the blue:

'Do you know what that fucking idiot of an American president said in an interview today, Miss Giordano? He said — and I'm almost quoting him word-for-word here — "We are in Kosovo because we care about saving lives and we care about the character of the multi-ethnic, post-Cold War world. We have been fighting against the idea that statehood must be based entirely on ethnicity." That is what the American president said. Bit ironic, don't you think, considering what is currently happening between Kosovan Serbians and those so-called Kosovan Albanians?'

'I don't understand what you mean,' Giulietta said, crossing her knife and fork on her plate.

Vujovic shook his head with noticeable irritation. 'That's the problem, Miss Giordano. You people don't understand anything. You never will. You hear what is said on pro-American channels like RAI or CNN about Serbian atrocities against Muslims and you forget that abuses like that are rarely committed by one side alone.'

'I still don't understand you, Zoran.'

Zoran looked at Giulietta in silence for a few seconds. 'Let me tell you a little story, Miss Giordano,' he said. 'When I was a young boy, two Albanian men came to our farm. They came asking for work. When my father told them that there were no vacancies currently available, they went away. Later that same evening, while we were sitting in the lounge watching TV, we heard the sound of laughing voices coming from outside, but didn't think too much about it. When we walked out of the house next morning, we found out that Whisky, Banditi and Mr. President, our three Alsatians, had been shot and had had their heads hacked off. Across a nearby wall someone had used their blood to write "*Kraj isključivo za srbin klešta.*" Death to all Serbian dogs. Or to translate it exactly as it was written, "To all Serbian deaths some dogs". '

He reached for his glass and took a sip of water. After doing this, he turned to Giulietta again:

'I will tell you something else, Miss Giordano: one day the West will come to regret having installed what is practically an autonomous Muslim state within the Balkans. It will come to pass — just as sure as we are sitting here talking over this plate of *penne puttanesca.* You cannot betray six hundred years of Christian heritage without causing the Heavens to bleed.'

Giulietta could not help a smile from forming on her lips. 'You sound very apocalyptic today, Zoran, if I may say so.'

'Apocalyptic?' Zoran angrily replied. 'Look at the way your Western governments use propaganda to further their own territorial and economic ambitions. That's what's really *apocalyptic* here, Miss Giordano. It could be Kosovo, Somalia, Kuwait, Nicaragua: it's always the same formula in the end. First, you switch on the television and you are bombarded by the usual images. You know the ones I mean: tearful children being spirited away in trucks, corpses lying in between piles of rubble, heavily moustachioed men shouting and firing machine guns into the air. Next thing you know U2 or some other bunch of limelight-hugging do-gooders are bringing out a song about human rights abuse. That's the way it always goes: first there are the newsreels, then there are the songs and then there are the torch-lit rallies led by victims of these so-called human rights abuses. Same old pattern again and again. That's the way it always goes these days, you see, Miss Giordano. If you're an American president and you want to start a war of imperialistic aggression, then make sure that you bring out the old ploy of human rights abuse. That way everyone will fall for it. *In the name of human rights, we will bomb and maim and leave a blood-smeared trail of orphans and widows in our wake.* That is what you Westerners ultimately believe — isn't it, Miss Giordano?'

'But what about Sarajevo?' Giulietta asked with a piece of penne stuck on the tip of her fork. 'What about Zvornik? What about those eight thousand men and boys who were murdered by General Mladić and his forces in Srebrenica? Are you trying to tell me that military intervention wasn't justified on those grounds alone?'

Zoran looked down at his plate for some seconds. 'If you would have asked me back in 1995 whether NATO forces were justified in using military force to stop Mladić and the nationalist militias from terrorising the Muslim frontier towns along the border between Serbia and Bosnia, I would have probably said, "Fuck you. This is the Federal Republic of Yugoslavia and we will do whatever it takes to maintain the territorial integrity of our state." '

'But if I asked you about it now, *this very moment,* in 2002?'

'If you asked me about it this very moment — knowing what I now know about what happened in places like Srebrenica — I would of course tell you that it was all a big mistake, that we should have never allowed Mladić and the other fanatics from doing what they did to the Bosniaks. . . . Still, that doesn't mean that what happened in Bosnia

Herzegovina in 1995 can be compared to what happened in Kosovo in 1999.'

'What do you mean?' Giulietta asked.

'The first set of NATO bombings in 1995 was ordered for a very specific reason — to stop the Bosnian Serbs from violating UN-designated safe areas in Bosnia. The second set of bombings, by contrast, was no more than a callous act of political and military depredation.'

'Meaning?'

'Meaning quite simply that in 1999 the Americans used the pretext of so-called human rights abuse in Kosovo to bomb our country back into the Stone Age and establish Uncle Sam's hegemony in the region.'

'Oh, come on, Zoran,' the lawyer said. 'What are you trying to tell me now — that the same Serbs who tried to ethnically cleanse Bosnia in 1995 were suddenly the victims of an American-orchestrated conspiracy less than four years later. That's a bit simplistic, don't you think!'

'Simplistic?' Zoran almost shouted back. 'Look at the way that a US-dominated Yugoslavia now forms a convenient bulwark against the Russians. Look at the way that our decimated republics are now being rebuilt by good old-fashioned American steel and concrete. Yes, I admit that a few Serbian hotheads overreached themselves when trying to defend the rights of their Serbian comrades in the neighbouring republics of Bosnia and Croatia (that is something that no decent, fair-minded Serb can deny), but at the same time you can't deny that the Americans had their own cynical reasons for bombing Milosevic and the rest of Serbia to shreds, can you?'

Giulietta decided that moment that there was no point in continuing with the conversation.

**

Then there were the times when Giulietta's boyfriend would drop in unexpectedly at the house. His name was Antonio Claxton and he was one of the partners at *Pizzolota, Berti and Claxton,* Italy's foremost experts in company law. He was about six foot two and two hundred pounds, a stocky, overbearing hulk of a man who was always immaculately dressed and was supposed to have represented his country at rugby while a law student at the University of Trento. Despite his rather un-Italian name (allegedly inherited from an Irish great-grandfather), he looked every inch the rich Italian lawyer – handsomely tanned but with a cruel aquiline nose, with jet-black hair that clustered in thick unruly curls upon the nape of his neck. Zoran hated the way he normally swanned in through the door – smiling and dangling the keys of his Ferrari Testarossa from his middle finger. Just after the two men were first introduced, something really strange happened: Claxton dragged Giulietta by the elbow into her bedroom and kicked the door shut behind them. Left alone in the living room with his paintbrushes and his plastic bottle of turpentine, Zoran could not help hearing every single word that passed between the two quarrelling lovers:

'Is this the guy you were telling me about? What the fuck's wrong with you – *letting a complete bum like that* into your house? Have you gone fucking mad, Giulietta, or what?'

'He's not a bum,' Giulietta replied defensively. 'He's a drug addict and he's a friend of mine, all right?'

'A drug addict?' Antonio shouted irately back. 'For fuck's sake, Giulietta, who do you think you are – *Mother Teresa of fucking Calcutta*? What the hell's wrong with you?'

'Nothing's wrong with me, Tonio. Zoran's just a friend who I'm helping out, that's all. Is that so difficult for you to understand?'

'Yes, of course,' the company lawyer retorted sarcastically, 'a "friend" who you're helping out! Just you be careful, sweetie-pie, that your fucking "friend" doesn't fucking rape the shit out of you one night or batter your brains out through your nostrils or steal every single fucking thing that you've got in the house!'

Zoran continued eavesdropping for a while, but then grew bored and went back up to his room. With meticulous care he prepared himself a large 250 mg fix of heroin and then shot it into one of his right radial veins, wincing momentarily as the liquefied powder entered his bloodstream and slowly worked its way into his system. 'Fucking piece of Italian shit,' he thought, briefly visualising Antonio's tanned face before slipping into a state of drug-induced mindlessness.

From that day onwards Antonio never talked to Zoran about anything other than the state of the weather or the mechanical precision of his Ferrari. He seemed like a pompous, conceited, unreservedly ignorant type of man, the kind of arrogant, Rolex-wearing fool who couldn't have a conversation without throwing in some self-glorifying detail about the territory he owned or the state of his finances. Even so, Zoran tried his best to ignore him. For the first time in years, he had money and a job, as well as a roof over his head. He also had drugs. More drugs, if truth be told, than he had ever laid his hands on. Cocaine, heroin, crystal meths, ecstasy, amphetamines, little pre-prepared doses of speedball. On top of that, he no longer had to go through all the old hassles and inconveniences associated with getting hold of the stuff. Nowadays it was the easiest thing imaginable. Every ten or twelve days, he would put one hundred and fifty euros into an old leather wallet that had belonged to one of Giulietta's ex-boyfriends and then stroll down to the nearby rail station. On arriving there, he would take one of the frequent shuttle services into Termini and then walk to the very end of platform 16, finally coming to a stop next to the small kiosk that sold flowers and newspapers. There, under a rotting corrugated iron ceiling through which large stretches of the Roman sky could be seen, he would buy his drugs from a fat, goggle-eyed Azerbaijani whom all the drug addicts in and around Termini knew as '*il Signor Elefantoni.*' He would receive them in fifteen, individually wrapped doses, tucked between one of the unsold newspapers that the newsagents behind them regularly discarded. He would then walk back to platform 9 and board the next train to Veruccio, silently laughing at the fact that he was back at Termini dressed in a shirt and tie of all bloody things. *What did he care if Antonio 'cornuto' Claxton had money shooting out of his goddamned arse-hole*?

**

Several months passed. Autumn came and the hills around Veruccio slowly divested themselves of their last remaining foliage, turning the same colour as the desiccated fields surrounding them. Around this time, too, the *policia locale di Veruccio* made a historic announcement. Three Albanian brothers, Uran, Valbon and Xhevat Qafa, aged twenty-nine, thirty-two and thirty-seven respectively, known locally as '*il chloroformeri*', had been arrested while trying to break into a private residence within the Residenza estate. They were currently being detained in Veruccio, the official press release said, and would soon be transferred to a detention centre in south Rome. If anyone knew anything about these individuals, they were kindly requested to call *Ispettora* Alessandra Gobi of the Veruccio local police force on 022-2368-5917 or 022-6650-2231. All calls, needless to say, would be treated with the utmost confidentiality.

Not long after this famous announcement, Giulietta knocked one evening on Zoran's door and asked him whether she could talk to him downstairs. 'Sure,' the Serbian drug addict responded from inside, rapidly shoving a bag of drugs under his mattress and wondering what could be wrong. When he entered the downstairs living room a few minutes later, Zoran found Giulietta sitting by the dining table with a glass and a bottle of Baileys. She was wearing a silk kimono with a pelican embroidered in red and gold thread across the back. She looked visibly stressed — more so than normal.

'Ah, Zoran,' the lawyer said, rising from her chair, 'there you are. Please, take a seat. . . . How's things?. . . Incidentally, I like the way the bathroom is shaping up. It should look quite stunning by the time you finish, don't you think?. . . And as for the cornices in the first guest room — those are looking quite spectacular too.'

'I'm glad you like them,' Zoran slowly replied, by now extremely curious to see where this sudden interest in his handiwork was leading to.

Giulietta smiled uneasily and walked over to the balcony window. A strong wind was blowing outside, sending dust clouds racing through the streets and rattling the terracotta flowerpots hanging from her balcony wall. Across the road one of her neighbours was standing with his back to his living room window. From his hunched position he seemed to be either masturbating or fiddling with his trouser fly — it was difficult to tell which. Unable to repress a shiver of discomfort, Giulietta took her hand out of her dressing gown pocket and turned the latch on the window.

'Okay,' she said, suddenly turning around with new resolve. 'Enough messing about. The reason I've called you down here is because Antonio and I have been talking and we've decided that it would be a good idea if you enrolled in a drug rehabilitation clinic. It's one of the best clinics in the country and you won't have to pay a single euro. Antonio's arranged it all himself. What do you think?'

Zoran lifted his gaze from the floor and looked straight into the lawyer's eyes.

'Well?' Giulietta said enthusiastically. 'What do you think? Isn't it a great opportunity to bury your habit once and for all?'

'It would be — if I wanted to kick my habit.'

'What do you mean?'

'Not all drug addicts necessarily want to kick their habit.'

He could sense that his words had really annoyed her. He could feel it in the air, a sudden chill, an almost palpable feeling of *atmospheric turbulence.*

'So what you're trying to tell me,' Giulietta suddenly shouted, 'is that you want to spend the rest of your life like this? Is that it? Pumping all that fucking shit into your body? Waiting until you collapse one day and die? Is that what you're trying to tell me?'

Zoran looked down at the floor again and shrugged his shoulders. Giulietta immediately muttered something under her breath and then slumped down on a leather armchair.

'If I go,' he said, 'who will finish the kitchen and the bathroom?'

'Antonio says he'll finish them.'

'What about the different types of cornices throughout the house? Will he be able to handle them?'

'I think so. He's very good with his hands.'

'Are you sure?'

'Yes. He fixes classic cars for a hobby. Old Ferraris and shit like that.'

Zoran gazed up and saw that the lawyer was clasping her head between her hands, a look of quiet melancholy across her eyes.

'This is all Antonio's doing, isn't it?' he said.

'No, it's not. Don't be silly.'

'Please don't bullshit me,' Zoran said grimly. 'I know he doesn't like me being around. I'd be the same if I was in his position.'

'Okay, so what if it's his idea?' Giulietta almost shouted back. 'At least this way you'll get to kick your habit. Is that such a bad thing? Do you always have to react so negatively to everything? Can't you at least pretend to be happy that he's trying to get you into one of the best addiction clinics in the country?'

He looked at her again and saw that she was almost crying, the tears threatening to spill at any moment down her cheeks. He also noticed that her kimono had crept up the side of her legs, exposing part of her left upper thigh.

'Okay. Okay,' he whispered softly, turning away. 'If it means so much to you, I'll go to this clinic of yours.'

'What was that? What did you say?'

'I said okay: I'll let you book me into this drug rehabilitation place of yours. . . . Just give me a few days to finish the cornices in the guest room and the utility room, and paint the balcony,' he added with an awkward attempt at a smile. 'I don't want Antonio messing the rooms up after I worked so hard on them – you know what I mean?'

**

The clinic of Santa Lucia dell'acqua lay fifty-five kilometres north of Rome, midway between junction 78 and junction 79 on the E-35 to Orvieto. It was situated on ten acres of sunflower fields and its windows and balconies all faced the imposing rocky façade of *la parete di Santa Lucia,* a cluster of mid-range basalt mountains which started just one and half kilometres away and extended for ten kilometres northwards. The clinic, a small, multi-turreted building that looked like a whitewashed fire station, had opened in 1978 and specialised in the treatment of drug addicts, alcoholics, gamblers and other victims of obsessive-compulsive behaviour. Among its list of past clients were film stars, rock singers, Roman Catholic priests, supermodels, Serie A footballers, Communist MPs and, if we are to believe the rumours circulated by the Italian tabloid press, a former Vice President of the Italian Republic itself. On the day that Giulietta Giordano and Zoran Vujovic arrived at the clinic, the adjoining mountains were covered by a thick, low-lying mist and the sunflowers were withering in the fields. It was Wednesday the fourteenth of October, 2002, the same day that Serbian and Albanian leaders were meeting in Vienna for their first face-to-face talks since the end of the Kosovan troubles.

'Well,' Giulietta said, removing the key from her car ignition, '*il momento del destino* has arrived. Shall we go inside and get things going?'

The Serbian drug addict nodded and got out of the car. Within minutes they found themselves walking through a large and spacious lobby which reeked of floor polish and was totally dark except for a few dust-speckled rays which came filtering in through the main entrance. On the wall immediately to their right there was a large sign which said 'Santa Lucia dell'acqua — the home of new beginnings'; to its left, a very heavy and imposing metal crucifix. Some ten or fifteen yards away, a woman could be seen typing behind an enormous wooden desk. She was about fifty or fifty-five-years old and had small, rodent-like eyes that kept on nervously scanning the sheet in front of her. She also had an elaborate perm which reminded Zoran of Dustin Hoffmann's character in the film *Tootsie.* As they got closer to her desk, he spotted a name badge pinned on her blouse – 'Mari Dorio, Communications and Visitor relations officer.'

'Welcome to Santa Lucia dell'acqua,' the receptionist suddenly said, looking up. 'My name is Mari Dorio and I'm the Communications and Visitor relations officer here at the clinic. What can I do for you today?'

'Zoran's here to check in with you,' the lawyer said, taking out a letter of admission and placing it on the desk.

The Communications and Visitor relations officer looked at the letter but made no attempt to pick it up. 'What did you say the name was again?' she said.

'Zoran. Zoran Vujovic. He's registered for the Peace and Internal Calm programme.'

'Okay,' the receptionist said, looking down at a large printed spreadsheet on the table 'Let me just check a few details. Zoran Vuj-o-veech. Yes, here he is. Peace and Internal Harmony candidate number 31. Registered as a cross-referral for the substance and behavioural dependencies programme. Age: 37. Nationality: Serbian. Food and lodgings plan: superior economy. That's the one, isn't it?'

Giulietta nodded with a touch of irritation.

'Okay, then,' the receptionist said. 'In that case, would you like to follow me to the induction hall, please? We will initiate the admissions process right away.'

The receptionist stood up and escorted them to a metal door on the other side of the hall. They then entered a long and very brightly lit corridor. Just like in the lobby, the smell of floor polish was very strong here — only this time it was mixed with a few pungent medicinal odours that were difficult to recognise. After walking for ten or fifteen seconds, they reached a second metal door. A security panel could be seen on a nearby wall, along with a brass sign saying 'New Patient Induction Hall.' Shielding one hand with the other, the receptionist tapped some numbers into the panel and waited until the doors swung open. She then swivelled around and positioned herself in front of the newly opened gap — in order to block out the view behind her.

'I'm afraid no visitors are allowed beyond this point,' the receptionist said, shaking her head. 'It's part of the clinic's rules.'

Giulietta turned towards Zoran and saw that he was scratching his left elbow rather manically. She decided not to prolong the moment more than was appropriate.

'Well,' the lawyer said, trying to muster a smile, 'I must go now. I'll come and visit next Wednesday. I can come then, can't I?' she said, turning towards the Communications and Visitor relations officer.

'Certainly,' Mari Dorio rapidly piped out. 'Visitors can come to the clinic at any time between 3 to 4 on weekdays; and between 12 to 1 on Saturdays. Just make sure you do not bring the patient any drinks or chocolates or sweets or any other consumables. Patients are only allowed to consume the nutrient-rich foods which the clinic specially prepares for them.'

Giulietta smiled coldly at the woman and then looked at Zoran again. 'Well, I guess this is it, Zoran.'

'Yes, I guess it is.'

'Funny how time flies, isn't it?' she said a little nervously. 'One moment we are sitting in my living room talking about this, the next you are here about to go in.'

'Yes,' he responded flatly, 'it's *very funny*.'

'Anyway,' she said, leaning forwards and giving him a quick peck on the cheek. 'I'd better get going. Get them to call me at the office if there's anything you want.'

'Don't worry: I will.'

'Oh, one more thing,' Giulietta said, turning one last time towards Mari Dorio. 'Can I bring Mr. Vujovic some magazines and newspapers during my next visit?'

'Yes,' the receptionist replied. 'Provided that they contain non-stimulating content and that they are approved by the duty psychologist, you should have no problem at all bringing magazines and newspapers into Santa Lucia dell'acqua.'

**

**A conversation between Giulietta Giordano and Zoran Vujovic held exactly fourteen days after the latter checked in at the Santa Lucia dell'acqua rehabilitation centre**

Giulietta: How's it going?

Zoran: You did not come last week like you said you would.

Giulietta: I'm sorry. I was busy with work. The Don Claudio case is winding to its conclusion and everything's a bit mad at the moment. . . . Anyway . . . how's everything going? Do you feel you're getting something out of this?

Zoran: It's all right.

Giulietta: You don't sound too convinced.

Zoran: Well, what can I say?. . . How about you? You look quite stressed today.

Giulietta: Do I?

Zoran: Yes. Most noticeably.

Giulietta: I had an argument with Mr. Claxton some days ago. I suppose that's the reason why I look a little bit stressed.

Zoran: I should have guessed.

Giulietta: Turned out that some ex-girlfriend of his was trying to get in touch with him and he never mentioned it to me.

Zoran: I'm sorry to hear it.

Giulietta: Still, we talked about it and everything is okay now. It's all patched up.

Zoran: I'm glad for you.

Giulietta: Listen, let's not talk about me and Antonio, shall we? Let's talk about life here. What have you been doing? What about the methadone? How are you coping with it?

Zoran: I'm coping fine.

Giulietta: That's good. Do you want to elaborate a bit on that?

Zoran: The doctors said that it could bring some problems in the beginning, but I've been all right up to now.

Giulietta: That's great. I'm really pleased to hear it. What else have you been doing, then? Anything interesting to report?

Zoran: Nothing much — just the usual stuff.

Giulietta: What do you mean?

Zoran: You know, talking about your experiences, writing them down, sharing them with others. That kind of thing.

Giulietta: What about lectures? Antonio told me that they get different people to come and talk to you. Is that true?

Zoran: We had some Buddhist monk come in the other day.

Giulietta: What did he talk about?

Zoran: Raju-something he was called.

Giulietta: What sort of things did he say?

Zoran: He said he was Indian, but he looked European to me.

Giulietta: What did he tell you?

Zoran: Oh, you know. Buddha, Karma, how to overcome suffering, how to let go of things: all that.

Giulietta: Was it good?

Zoran: Yeah, I guess so.

Giulietta: I'm glad to hear it.

**

**A conversation between Antonio Claxton, law firm director and restorer of classic cars, and Giulietta Giordano, tired, disgruntled and mildly depressed lawyer, held later that same evening**

Antonio: Well, how did it go?

Giulietta: Okay.

Antonio: You don't sound too convinced.

Giulietta: You know what he's like.

Antonio: What do you mean?

Giulietta: '*Taciturno*' should be his middle name.

Antonio: '*Ingrato*' would be a much better choice, if you ask me.

Giulietta: It's like squeezing blood out of a stone – talking with that one. Christ, he doesn't half irritate me at times!

Antonio: I've already told you time and time again: just forget about the guy.

Giulietta: I'm not so sure about that.

Antonio: Not so sure about what? Just drive up to the clinic tomorrow and tell him that it's best if you stop seeing him. Tell him that I'm pissed off with the whole thing and that I've threatened to leave you if you carry on visiting him. That should sort the little bastard out.

Giulietta: I don't know, Tonio.

Antonio: Come on, Giulietta. You're being too soft again.

Giulietta: Do you think so?

Antonio: Do I think so? *Gesù Cristo*, Giulietta, how many other Italian lawyers would cancel important meetings so that they could go and visit some immigrant Serbian drug addict in rehab?

Giulietta: I never cancelled a meeting; I just rescheduled one or two appointments with people I didn't particularly want to see anyway.

Antonio: That makes everything so much better, doesn't it, darling?. . . I tell you, Giulietta, if I was a less confident sort of guy, I'd almost be tempted to think there was something going on between you and Mr. Serbian scumbag.

Giulietta: Don't be so stupid.

Antonio: Then start acting like a mature, responsible adult and tell this guy to go hang. Don't you think you've done enough for the little shit already? Just tell him how much of a burden he's become and *that's that*. And if he doesn't like it, well, tough shit! You can't let this fucking idiot carry on controlling your life the way he does.

Giulietta: You reckon?

Antonio: Trust me on this one, will you? Just take a couple of hours off work tomorrow and go tell him to piss off. Be firm with the guy for once. . . . Now pass me that Rolex catalogue over there and come here, will you? I want to show you something that I saw earlier.

**

Giulietta Giordano arrived at Santa Lucia dell'acqua at three o'clock the next day. On her way there she had been caught in a traffic jam near the Campolino/ Sant'Ippolito interchange, one of north Rome's most notorious bottlenecks. To while away her time, she had switched on the car radio and started listening to a discussion programme on the recent Congressional elections in the United States, swearing violently every time one of the studio panellists, an anti-Communist MP from Treviso Bresciano, began extolling the virtues of the American Republican party. Now, having just arrived at Santa Lucia dell'acqua, the Roman lawyer found herself enduring what was possibly an even more stinging affront: the middle-aged receptionist, who during her last two visits to the clinic had been a model of annoying officiousness, seemed to be purposefully ignoring her.

'Excuse me,' Giulietta finally said, knocking loudly on the receptionist's desk, 'I've come to see Zoran Vujovic. Could you please lead me to the visiting room — or are you going to make me stand here for another five minutes while you sort out your paperwork?'

'Zoran Vu-jo-veech?' the woman said without looking up from what she was doing. 'Just a minute, please.'

The receptionist picked up her phone and held it about three centimetres from her ear. 'Doctor Barman?' she said at last. 'It's me, Mari on reception. Are there any updates reference Vu-jo-veech by any chance? You know, the TT3? I've got this person here who's come to visit him. . . . Oh yes, yes. Now I remember. Don't worry, Dr. Barman. I'll tell her that you're on the way. . . . Dr. Barman will come down shortly to see you,' she then said, turning to Giulietta. 'He'd be grateful if you took a seat in the lobby in the meantime.'

Giulietta threw the receptionist one last angry look and then sat down. As she placed her handbag on the floor, she noticed a magazine rack by her side. After a moment of hesitation, she picked up a magazine called *Amici* and started flicking through its pages, but quickly got bored with it and put it down. Then she sighed out loud and looked at her watch: it was already twenty past three. 'Damn,' she thought. 'Why does everything have to take so long when you're in a rush?' Shaking her head, Giulietta took out a packet of Lucky Strikes and lit herself a cigarette. She puffed at it slowly, meditatively, letting the smoke escape in soft, grey swirls from the sides of her mouth. As soon as she finished the cigarette, she flicked the butt on to the wooden floor and crushed it with her left heel. Moments later, a tall, Asian-looking doctor appeared before her. He was about forty-five and very well dressed, sporting one of those elegantly coiffured bouffants rarely seen outside American TV soaps like *ER* or *Falcon Crest*. He was also smiling from ear to ear.

'Smoking is not really allowed inside the building,' the Asian doctor said in an extremely posh Roman voice.

'But being harassed by a rude and incompetent receptionist is?' Giulietta asked.

The man toned down his smile and extended a hand. 'I'm Dr. Barman. You must be Mrs. Vujovic?'

'No, no,' Giulietta replied, standing up. 'I'm just a friend of Mr. Vujovic's.'

'Well, Miss. . . . '

' . . . . Giordano,' she answered quickly. 'Giulietta Giordano.'

'Well, Miss Giordano,' Dr. Barman said, his gaze moving from Giulietta's breasts to her face, 'I'm afraid you can't see Mr. Vujovic right now.'

'What do you mean — I can't see him? Is there something wrong?'

Dr. Barman rapidly shook his head. 'Oh no, no, Miss Giordano. Nothing's wrong. It's just that Mr. Vujovic's detox programme is going through a bit of a . . . rough patch at the moment.'

'What do you mean — a rough patch? Would you please care to explain yourself?'

'Certainly, Miss Giordano,' Dr. Barman said. 'You see, when a patient is taken off drugs and given methadone — or, in Mr. Vujovic's case, a compound of clonidine and methadone — he usually experiences withdrawal symptoms at some stage or the other. Basically, this is because prolonged use of opiates like heroin affects an area of the brainstem known as the *Locus Coeruleus.* This, if you like, is the brain's fear-alarm system, the part which controls the range and intensity of our emotions. Normally, the withdrawal symptoms start immediately after the drug has been stopped and tend to last between a week to ten days. However, in some cases — because of a variety of complex factors — there is a delayed reaction time and the symptoms don't start until two or three weeks later. This, I'm afraid, is what has happened to your friend Mr. Vujovic. He is basically experiencing withdrawal symptoms two weeks later than normal.'

'But I don't understand,' Giulietta said, shaking her head. 'Zoran seemed to be doing really well yesterday.'

'I'm sure that he was, Miss Giordano. But different patients experience different reaction times when it comes to withdrawal. Besides,' Dr. Barman added gravely, 'there is also the matter of the patient's own . . . how can I say? . . . psychological peculiarities. Seen in this light, excessive or abnormal withdrawal symptoms could indicate a deep-seated reluctance to terminate current patterns of behaviour.'

'You mean he's having this bad reaction because he doesn't want to get well?'

'Possibly. Quite possibly.'

The Roman lawyer forcefully bit into her lower lip. 'Can't I just go and see him for a few minutes? I have something very important to say to him.'

'I'm afraid that won't be possible,' Dr. Barman said, suddenly putting on a reproving face. 'A patient suffering from withdrawal is hardly in the mood or condition to talk with anyone, please understand.'

'You mean that he is totally out of it right now? Is that what you're trying to tell me?'

'Not exactly how I would put it myself, Miss Giordano,' Dr. Barman said with a smile, 'but I think you're finally getting the picture. . . . Don't worry, Miss Giordano. In a few days' time your friend will be able to take visitors again, you'll see. . . . Look,' he added, all of a sudden leaning forwards, 'I'm starting my afternoon break in a few minutes. Would you care to join me for a cup of coffee in our canteen? We can go over Mr. Vujovic's case in detail there, if you wish.'

**

When Giulietta returned home later that evening, she went straight to the drinks cabinet and started preparing herself a Cosmopolitan. She chose the biggest glass she could find for it — a highball tumbler engraved with the words 'World's Most Rapacious Lawyer' and a cartoon of a geeky-looking man sitting on a tall pile of dollars. The glass had been a Christmas present from her personal secretary. It was the kind of gift that people in the office normally gave you — some 'specially chosen' item which left you feeling unsure whether they were 'having a laugh' or simply paying you back for all the shit they took from you during the rest of the year. Presently Giulietta removed the cocktail stirrer from her glass and tossed it to one side. She then walked over to her sofa and sat down. Unhooking her mobile from its waist-clip, she began to dial Antonio's number.

'Hello, Antonio. It's me, Giulietta.'

'Hello, Giulietta. How's it going?'

'Look, Tonio, I'll get straight to the point — I've had a bad day and I need someone to cheer me up. How would you like to come over to Veruccio and stay the night? I bought a nice bottle of Barolo on the way home. We can drink it together by the fire and have some naughty fun afterwards. What do you say?'

'I don't know, Giulietta,' Antonio replied. 'I'm very busy right now with some important work stuff. I mean, you just can't expect me to leave everything I'm doing and come running to you at the drop of a hat. Especially on a weekday like today. We've already talked about this before.'

'Look,' Giulietta said, suddenly close to tears, 'I'm not asking you to marry me or anything like that. It's just that I've had a really awful day and I'd like to be with you. Is that too much to ask?'

'Was it something to do with your visit to Berbieri?'

'Yes,' Giulietta replied in a hoarse whisper, '*it bloody well was.*'

'Okay, okay, you don't have to start blubbering over the phone. If it's that bad, I'll be there in an hour.'

'Thanks, Tonio,' Giulietta said, stifling a sob. 'I really appreciate it. I really, really do.'

**

Antonio Claxton arrived at la Residenza just after half past seven. He came dressed in one of his hand-tailored Armani suits, the double-folded cuffs of a pink shirt poking stylishly out of his jacket sleeves. A rolled-up copy of one of the classic car magazines – *Quattroruote,* perhaps, or maybe *Auto Italia* – could be seen tucked under his arm; a pair of Oakley wraparounds hung from a fluorescent green cord around his neck. Ignoring the look of irritation in his eyes, Giulietta jumped up from the sofa and ran straight towards the company lawyer.

'I'm sorry, Tonio,' she said, quickly burying her head into the scented collars of Claxton's shirt. 'I shouldn't have made you come all the way here. But I felt really, really bad.'

Antonio smiled wearily and started stroking the back of Giulietta's head. 'It's all right, Giuliettina, it's all right. I'm here now.'

He continued caressing her hair for a short while, then disengaged himself from her embrace and walked over to the drinks cabinet. For a minute or two he rummaged around in its interior. 'Do you have any whisky other than this cheap shit?' he finally said, holding up a bottle of Vat 69.

'I'm sorry, Tonio. That's all I have. You know that I don't really drink whisky.'

The lawyer dug his chin into his chest and let off a quietly disgusted sigh. 'In that case, Vat 'rat piss' 69 will have to do, won't it?. . . Would you like anything from the bar now that I'm here?'

'No, thanks,' Giulietta replied dreamily from the sofa. 'All I want is for you to come and sit beside me.'

The company lawyer smiled stiffly and made his way back to the sofa. He then removed his shoes and sat down. Soon after this Giulietta laid her head on Tonio's lap and started telling him about the horrible bitch at the clinic and the insufferable Pakistani doctor who had stared continuously at her breasts. ('It was as if the guy was transfixed, Antonio. He just couldn't stop staring at my tits. He must have been a *mammophiliac* or something.') All during this time Antonio listened with poorly feigned attention, limiting his participation in the conversation to a few assenting nods and a couple of strategically placed monosyllables. Soon he lost interest altogether and began to massage her shoulders and neck. Gradually, by the tiniest of degrees, his fingers abandoned her neck and started moving towards her breasts . . . until Giulietta's blouse was undone and the tops of her nipples were peering out of her bra. 'What exactly are you doing?' the criminal lawyer laughed at this point. 'Are you also obsessed with my tits or what?'

That night Antonio Claxton and Giulietta Giordano made love until two o'clock and then fell asleep in each other's arms. But their nocturnal union was not destined to last long. Just a few hours later – at around five-thirty in the morning – the doorbell rang downstairs and woke them both up.

'Can you go see who it is, darling?' Giulietta murmured drowsily. 'Must be that damned paperboy again. Only a few days ago he woke me up at six to say that he couldn't fit one of my magazines through the letterbox.'

'All right, all right,' Antonio groaned huskily. 'Just give me a minute. I can't go down starkers, can I?'

'Thanks, darling. You're a real treasure, do you know that? *Un vero tesoro.*'

The company lawyer got up and wrapped himself in a black silk kimono which he kept on a peg behind the bedroom door. He then started making his way down to the living room. A frothy, resinous aftertaste – the kind you normally get after having imbibed half a bottle of Vat 69 the night before – clung to the inside of his mouth and he had trouble descending the stairs because of his state of sleep-induced lethargy. He felt seriously – more than that: he felt *dangerously* – pissed-off. 'Who the fuck could it be?' he wondered as he rubbed his eyes and tried to shield them from the morning light filtering through the living room window. He looked at his watch: it was five-thirty. Five fucking thirty on a Friday morning, for Christ's sake! 'If this is the paperboy,' Antonio told himself as he approached the door, 'I'm going to murder the little runt with my own hands!'

But it was not the paperboy who greeted him on the other side of the door; it was the Serbian drug addict Zoran Vujovic.

**

'What are you doing here?' Giulietta asked Zoran with a look of barely disguised aggravation. 'I spoke to one of the doctors at Santa Lucia dell'acqua yesterday and he told me you were experiencing severe withdrawal symptoms.'

'I che-che-checked out of-of-of the cli-cli-clinic last night. I've come to fi-fi-finish the ki-ki-ki-kitchen.'

'You mean you've quit your rehabilitation programme?'

Zoran Vujovic nodded slowly, an involuntary smile forming on his lips.

'Have you been taking drugs, Zoran?' Giulietta asked.

'No, no, no, Miss Giordano. No drugs for Zo-zo-zoran today. Zo-zo-zoran only had a few dri-drinks to celebrate che-che-checking out of the cli-cli-clinic. That is all. A few dri-drinks to celebrate getting out of that te-terrible place. And now Zo-zo-zoran, he is here, isn't he: ready to finish your lovely cornices and your lovely ceilings. That's what he-he-he is here-here for.'

Giulietta made a gesture with her eyes and Antonio stepped aside to let Zoran through. The addict nodded gratefully and stumbled into the lounge. As he reached the centre of the room, he tried turning around, but rapidly lost his balance and walked straight into the coffee table, knocking over two glasses and an empty bottle of wine from the night before.

'Oh, shit . . . fu-fuck . . . shit. I'm so so-so-sorry ab-ab-about this. I will pi-pi-pick your gla-gla-glasses up now.'

'Leave it,' Giulietta hissed quietly but determinedly. 'Just go up to your old room. I'll clear it all later.'

Zoran straightened up and then smiled at her through half-closed eyes. 'You're my gua-guardian angel,' he said hoarsely. 'Do you know that? You're my *anđeo čuvar.* Has anybo-bo-body ever told you that? You're my beautiful, kind, generous *anđeo čuvar.* Do you know what I me-me-mean?'

'Just shut up and go to the guest room, will you?'

'Sure, my *an-an-anđeo čuvar.* Sure. Your word is always my-my com-com-command.'

He staggered up the stairs and entered his old room. Then he closed the door behind him and flung himself on the bed. Although he was suddenly possessed by the most uncontrollable lethargy, he thought he could hear the sound of shouting voices. He wasn't sure where they were coming from at first, but then he realised that it was Giulietta and Antonio arguing downstairs. 'You must be goddamned fucking stupid!' the company lawyer was shouting in a loud and irate voice. 'All I needed was one word from you, just one word, and I would have slung him out of here! Kicked the fucking piece of shit out once and for all!' 'Oh shut up, will you?' Giulietta countered agitatedly. 'Look at the state he's in. I can't just sling him out like that, can I?' That instant Antonio began to laugh sarcastically: 'You're an idiot, Giulietta! I hate to say it, but you're just an idiot! That good-for-nothing piece of Serbian trash is taking the piss and I can't do a single thing about it! It's fucking pathetic – that's what it is!' After this there was a five or six-minute silence. Then someone slammed the front door shut, the impact of the crash momentarily reverberating through the guest room's window. Filled with curiosity, Zoran dragged himself out of bed and moved towards the window. Through the half-drawn blinds he saw Antonio's open-top Ferrari coming out of the underground garage. Giulietta and the company lawyer were occupying the front seats, looking like a married couple after an argument. 'So this is the bourgeois dream that everybody aspires to,' Zoran whispered grimly as the car zoomed down the road. 'The quintessence of Italian consumerism.' Shaking his head, he closed the blinds and walked back to the bed. Then he got down on his knees and began to rummage underneath the mattress. Yes, the drugs were still there, thank God. Five cellophane-wrapped 100 milligram bags, still tucked between the throwaway newspaper sheets from the newsagents down at platform 16. *The best mind-blowing, life-warping, reality-busting shit that you could possibly hope to find,* according to 'Signor Elefantoni' the Azerbaijani. Grinning at the thought, Zoran took out his discharge file from his jacket pocket and placed it alongside the drugs. Then he slid the mattress back into place again. No, he was not going to take any drugs today. Today he was going to work. He was going to finish the cornices that still needed doing. That is what he had promised Giulietta and that is what he would do. First, though, he decided to lie down and rest for a while. Just to get some energy back, he thought with a yawn. . . .

When he woke up twelve hours later, it was dark and silent and a cold draught was blowing in from somewhere. For a few seconds Zoran lay in bed listening to his own heartbeat, wondering where he was and why the inside of his mouth felt so horribly dry. Then he began to remember everything that had happened earlier: the crash against the coffee table, the pieces of glass on the floor, the look on Antonio's face, the hard slog up to his room, the argument raging downstairs. In particular, he could not stop thinking about Antonio's words: 'That good-for-nothing Serbian piece of trash is taking the piss. That low-life piece of scum is messing up your life and I just can't do anything about it.' 'Is that right?' Zoran now wondered. 'Am I taking the piss?' Certainly, they had paid for him to attend a drug rehabilitation unit and he had let them down by running away. In that sense, yes, perhaps he had taken the piss a little. *And yet how could you say that when he hadn't wanted to be cured in the first place?* I mean, what was the point of getting cured, after all? What was the fucking point? He didn't take drugs because he liked the chemical high; he took drugs to forget, to block out certain memories, to stop old wounds from re-opening and bleeding again.

Sighing softly, Zoran rolled over and got out of bed. He then switched on the black-and-white television. To his surprise, he knew the place that flashed up on the screen. It was the main square in Janjevo, his hometown back in former Yugoslavia. 'What the fuck is this?' he thought, suddenly filled with panic. 'Every day they screen those brain-dead shows with mini-skirted hostesses and plump-cheeked peasants in the audience, and yet today, of all days, they have to be showing *something like this*. . . . Could I still be fucked? Did I inject an unusually large dose of heroin before falling asleep? That could be it, couldn't it?'. . . And yet it didn't *feel* like he was imagining things. That *was* Janjevo on the screen. Not Janjevo as it was now, with its loud-talking Yankee contractors and its dithering, dumb-ass Blue Helmets, but as he had left it back then. A town buried in its own ruins. A community raped by the forces of progress and modern civilisation. The square, in particular, was just as he remembered it: bombed and covered in mounds of rubble. Two or three dead bodies could be seen amid the debris, surrounded by pools of dark and congealed blood. As the camera zoomed into a close-up, he noticed that one of the bodies was that of a little boy, about nine or ten years old, with long blond hair that was being continuously swept back by the wind. The boy's eyes were wide open and a large fly was crawling across his heavily bruised forehead, stopping and then starting again in that jerky and deceptively swift manner that insects have of moving.

'Why is it that the dead's eyes always look so white?' Zoran suddenly found himself thinking. 'So white and so open, as if, having had the first glimpse of the afterlife, they wanted to turn back around and communicate the awful, hellish reality of what had just been revealed to them on the other side?'

He could not understand it. He had seen eyes like that before — the dead and fearful at the same time, lifeless and yet bearing the agony of seeing their owner's last living moments. He had seen them and carried on flashbag them still — in his dreams, in his moments of solitude, in the other ti cks he occasionally suffered. If he had seen this blond boy at any slowly sime, he would have probably closed his eyes and let the images had been k to the back of his subconscious. That, after all, is what he smothering doing for the last few years: suppressing, containing, and other fo the past under a never ending round of drugs and alcohol ms of self-abuse. But on that particular day, the thirtieth of October, 2002, Zoran was caught somewhat off guard. Violently hungover, unable to forget either Giulietta's resentful looks or the memory of Antonio's cruel words, he found himself gazing at the television and thinking about the one thing that he did not want to think about just then: the day in 1999 when his wife and children were shot outside his garage. He found himself remembering little details that had lain locked for a long time within his subconscious: facial expressions, half-forgotten smells, the brand of cigarettes one of the gunmen had been smoking, the trickle of urine oozing down his son's legs, the smell of rust and moisture that impregnated the area where he was hiding behind the boiler. He found himself wondering why it was that he remained alive when his wife and children were dead, he found himself thinking how crazy and fucked-up the idea was, *how utterly fucking mad.* He found himself constantly reliving the moment of their deaths, continually trying to see where he had gone wrong, forever alternating between the memory *of what was* and the possibility of *what could have been.* He found himself shutting his eyes, biting his tongue, trying all along to stem the flow of memories that gushed like blood and pulverized flesh out of a freshly opened bullet wound. Finally, he found himself repeating the same prayer that he had once prayed in the garage:

*Oce nas koji si na nebesima, da se sveti ime Tvoje, da dodje carstvo Tvoje, da bude volja Tvoja i na zemlji kao na nebu; hleb nas nasusni daj nam danas; i oprosti nam dugove nase kao sto i mi oprastamo duznicima svojim, i ne uvedi nas u iskusenje; nego izbavi nas od zla.*

**

Giulietta returned to Veruccio about half past ten in the evening. She had spent the last fifteen hours locked up in a cramped, badly ventilated office that reeked of coffee and cigarette smoke, unable to stop worrying about what had happened that morning. Neither Antonio nor herself, the truth was, had said much as they drove into the city, both of them sitting next to each other in stubborn silence during the entire fifty-five minute journey. Later on he had tried phoning her a couple of times — but Marla, dutiful and reliable as ever, had kept on telling him that her boss was in a meeting and 'currently uncontactable'. As Giulietta now reached into her handbag for her house key, she wondered whether this had been a wise move or not. What was she, after all, without Antonio? Just an overpaid lawyer with no meaning in her life? An Audi-driving bitch who earned more than she could spend and whose only comfort lay in seeing how much commission was piled upon her already substantial salary at the end of every month? Yes, he could be a bastard sometimes and, yes, he had something of a womanising streak inside him (he was Milanese, after all, wasn't he?) — but he was also the only 'real thing' that she had, the only ray of light that shone in her spiritually-impoverished existence. *Better the devil you know than no devil at all* — isn't that what people in this city said?

When she opened the door, the first thing that hit Giulietta was the smell of shit and urine in the air. It stung her like an unexpected slap — throwing her mind into temporary disarray and almost making her lose her balance. Quickly switching on the light, she saw Zoran sitting on the ground with a blanket thrown around his head and shoulders. He was rocking slowly on his haunches, his expression distant and barely conscious of her presence. A few yards away lay a couple of syringes; beside them, two metal spoons and a dark, slimy coil of excrement. Giulietta instinctively clasped her hand to her mouth in horror.

'Sorry, my *anđeo čuvar,*' Zoran whimpered softly. 'I couldn't help it. . . . I just couldn't help it. . . . The town square. . . . The little boy with the hair. . . . That horrible fly . . . *dalke crnilo i grozan* . . . crawling across the eyes . . . those beautiful and silent eyes . . . so silent . . . so still . . . just like Gavrilo's . . . just like Gavy's. . . . You understand me, don't you? You understand what Zoran is saying?'

She saw the look of supplication in his eyes. She saw the trails of saliva sliding down his chin. Just a few weeks ago, perhaps, she would have been touched, maybe even moved to pity. But pity and sympathy had long since been wrenched out of her.

'The camera,' Zoran continued, still rocking on the floor. 'The eyes. . . . The young boy's eyes. . . . They were so . . . so . . . so . . . *beznade'zan i tu'zan. . . .* Do you understand me? Do you understand what I'm saying, my *anđeo čuvar?*'

He stared at her with an imploring expression, but a look of venomous revulsion suddenly darkened Giulietta's face:

'Get out of my house! First you ruin my relationship with Antonio and now you ruin my living room! Get out of here before I call the police and they take you back where you belong!'

'But you don't understand,' Zoran said, his eyes suddenly filling with tears. 'That camera. . . . That face. . . . The fly that crawled and crawled . . . *crnilo i grozan . . . crnilo i grozan. . . .* Surely you understand, my *anđeo čuvar*. Surely you can see what Zoran can see.'

'Just get out!' Giulietta shouted, pulling him up by his shirt collar. 'Get out or *I will drag you out myself*! Is that understood?'

Zoran nodded tearfully and began to make his way towards the door. Twice his knees buckled under him and twice he fell on the floor, the second time landing just inches away from the door and Giulietta's feet. Seeing him lying there like this made the lawyer even more furious. 'Never come back here again!' she screamed at him as he slowly dragged himself over the threshold. 'Do you understand me? I don't want to see your face for as long as I live! Is that understood? Am I making myself clear? I don't want anything to do with you or your stinking goddamned Serbian past! Do you hear me? I've had enough and I can't stand it any more. Just go away and leave me alone! Do you hear? Go back to Termini or wherever you please! Just fucking leave me alone! Do you hear me? I just want to be left alone! Do you understand? FUCK OFF AND LEAVE ME ALONE!'

**

The weeks passed. On the fifteenth of December 2002, Giulietta Giordano defended Messrs. Claudio, Casagrande and Alfredo, the three men accused of smuggling tobacco from Gibraltar to Sardinia, and, much to everyone's surprise, managed to quash every single charge levelled against them. ('Did you hear that?' Signor Casagrande whispered to Signor Alfredo as soon as the verdict was announced. 'That fucking old *cornuto* of a judge has just fucking released Plinio, you and me. Is the world going nuts or what?') That same afternoon a flushed and euphoric Giulietta phoned Antonio Claxton for the first time in six and a half weeks and asked him whether he wanted to accompany her to the restaurant party which Messrs. Claudio, Casagrande and Alfredo were holding later that evening to celebrate their unexpected release. After going quiet for a second, Antonio said that it was very nice to hear from her and that he would have loved to accompany her to *Il Gambero Rosso*, but unfortunately he was having dinner with his new girlfriend that same evening and could not therefore accede to her request. 'Give me a call some other time, Giulietta,' he said before putting the phone down. 'We've got to get together again one of these days and *reminisce* about old times.'

Giulietta went out alone that night and did not get home until quarter to four. She had spent most of the evening fending off the amatory advances of the moustachioed Signor Casagrande (who had discarded his sober courtroom suit in favour of a fluorescent yellow Hawaiian shirt which he wore unbuttoned to his navel), while at the same time drinking voluminous amounts of *Dom Perignon* champagne and stuffing her face with canapés. On balance, it hadn't been the best of nights – not only because Signor Casagrande had felt personally insulted that his defence lawyer had refused to slip with him into the gentlemen's toilets, but also because she had missed Antonio more than she had done during the last few weeks. On top of that, old Signor Baroni, the venerable founder of *Baroni and Baroni* who shuffled around with a silver-tipped walking stick and whom everyone took for an unimpeachable model of rectitude, had squeezed her buttocks on two – yes two! – separate occasions. 'What is it with men?' Giulietta presently thought, switching on the living room lights and flinging her fur coat carelessly on the dining table. 'You think you know what they are like and then they go and do something which totally wrecks your opinion of them.' Perhaps what Marla had said earlier that evening about men all being a bunch of perverts was right. 'If you want to know what a man is really like,' her secretary had said, delicately nibbling into an olive that she had just fished out of her Martini glass, 'then try and imagine him banging his thingey. If you can't imagine him banging his little todger, then you will probably never know the entirety of the man standing before you – you know what I'm saying, Giuliettina?' Was that right, Giulietta now wondered. Could every man out there, from her father to his Holiness the Pope himself, carry embedded within them the negative image of a secret masturbator? If so, she wasn't being very perspicacious, was she? Perhaps that is why she always fucked-up in her relationships: she just didn't have the capacity to visualise the 'entirety of the man' standing there before her. Maybe, when all was said and done, that was the root of her problem. She just didn't know enough about men. She just couldn't see beyond their handmade suits and their sophisticated posturing.

Giulietta walked over to the drinks cabinet and started preparing herself a Cosmopolitan. As she opened the bottle of Cointreau, she remembered Antonio and his suggestion about getting together and 'reminiscing' about old times. 'That is so typical of the asshole,' she thought, filling her glass to the brim. 'So bloody typical. He's fucked me a few times and now he thinks he owns me for life.' That's what all these Italian corporate types are like, Giulietta reflected: they think that going out with someone for a few months is the same as a lifelong certificate of ownership. Growing more and more angry at the thought, she shook her head and shoved the Cointreau bottle back into the cabinet. Then she noticed something lying on the floor. 'For fuck's sake,' she thought, squatting rather unsteadily down on to her haunches. 'Can't that fucking Ethiopian cleaner I employ ever clean the place right!' As she bent down even further, she realised that it was an old button which had lodged itself into a crack between the skirting board and the floor tiles. From its size and shape, she was sure that it must have belonged to Zoran – probably coming from one of the paint-splattered overalls he used to wear. The realisation unnerved Giulietta slightly and took the edge off her drunkenness. Although several weeks had passed since Zoran had left the house, she still hadn't ventured into the room he once occupied. She was not really sure why she had acted like this. Perhaps she did not want to be reminded of bad times. Or perhaps she was scared of uncovering something vile and repulsive inside the room. 'You really are a funny one, Giulietta Giordano,' she now whispered to herself, standing upright again and bringing her Cosmopolitan to her lips. 'Why don't you just go up there *this moment* and prove to yourself how silly you are!?'

It took her less than thirty seconds to reach the first floor landing. For a while Giulietta held her glass in her hand and gritted her teeth, unable to believe that she was still nervous of going into the room. Then she turned the doorknob and went inside. As she switched on the light, she could not help picturing some of the scenes that must have gone on within the room – the sound of heroin being boiled up in a spoon, a needle entering a swollen blue vein, a pair of bloodshot eyes swirling within their sockets. Feeling a little dizzy, Giulietta sat down on the single bed and wrapped herself with the blanket, rubbing her arms vigorously to counteract the shiver that suddenly ran down her spine. As she did so, she moved the mattress slightly out of place and caught sight of what looked like the edge of a newspaper under it. Overcome with curiosity, she slid her hand under the mattress and discovered that she was right – it was a copy of the *Corriere della Sera*. Tucked between its pages were five or six bags of a fine, greyish substance similar to talcum powder, along with a small bundle of papers held together by an elastic band. Leaving the drugs to one side, Giulietta loosened the band and began to examine the papers. To her surprise, she realised that, apart from three or four typed sheets that had been stapled together, most of them were drawings – fine and boldly coloured pictures that showed signs of careful draughtsmanship. The drawings were all of the same person: a young woman with a tentative, rather vulnerable expression. She had been drawn in different poses — sleeping, eating an apple, sitting on a sofa, gazing down at her hands, holding a butterfly. Giulietta looked at them for some seconds, filled with the uncanny certainty that she was gazing down at someone she knew really well. Then the truth suddenly dawned upon her. 'My God!' she thought, quite astounded by the thought, '— it's me! He's been drawing pictures of me!' Not knowing whether to feel flattered or repelled by the idea, she put the drawings down and turned to the typed sheets:

## Six cathartic exercises, designed to uplift, embolden and rescue us from the clutches of mental despair

**Exercise 1. Write down the first ten words that come into your head.**

1. Red
2. Black
3. Crimson
4. Night
5. Despair
6. Gun
7. Smile
8. Face
9. Pick-axe
10. Black

**Exercise 2. Now write down the first word that you associate with each of those ten words.**

1. Red: mouth
2. Black: bullet
3. Crimson: head
4. Night: me
5. Despair: ghost
6. Gun: agony
7. Smile: betrayal

8. Face: murder
9. Pick-axe: flower
10. Black: gangrene

**Exercise 3. Now write down whatever comes into your head. It could be a story, a poem, a description of an event that has happened to you, a phrase stuck in your head. You can be as brief or as elaborate as you wish. Don't feel restricted in your choice of subject matter.**

Betrayal. It's difficult word. A hurtful one. Somehow I knew that it was my fate all along, that one day I'd end up betraying them and turning my back on them. Call it intuition. Foreboding. A sense of premonition. One day, I thought, there will come a time when you will be found wanting. I knew it all along. I could sense it coming. You see, from the beginning I knew that I *didn't really deserve them.* Sure, I stood up for them plenty of times when the *going was good.* Telling some drunken idiot to stop staring at Jovana in a crowded bar, carrying Miloska in my arms to the hospital when she was ill with meningitis. But that was not the real thing, was it? Somehow, at the back of my mind, I knew that I was going to end up betraying them one day. I had this fear, this intuition, this sense of damnation foaming up in the blood. And I was right, wasn't I? I was right in the end.

**Exercise 4. Now answer the following multiple-choice questions. Try to be as honest as possible. Place a tick against the answers which you feel are most appropriate.**

**1. If you could choose the way you died, what would be your preference?**
a. to be smashed-up in a traffic accident [ ]
b. to be beaten to a pulp by a burglar [ ]
c. to slip down from a cliff while rock climbing [X]
d. to catch AIDS from a beautiful prostitute [ ]

**2. If you had to kill someone, which weapon would you use?**
a. a gun [ ]
b. a knife [ ]
c. a pair of scissors [ ]
d. your hands [X]

**3. Which of the following words, in your opinion, is most closely associated with death and destruction?**

a. incidental [ ]
b. fundamental [ ]
c. elemental [ ]
d. chronological [X]

**4. If you could wish for anything in the world, what would you wish for?**

a. a night with Raquel Welch [ ]
b. a bottle of the most expensive French champagne [ ]
c. the severed head of your greatest enemy on a silver tray [ ]
d. none of the above [X]

**Exercise 5. If you had to choose a word to describe how you felt right now, which word would you choose?**

Directionless.

**Exercise 6. A tape recorder is now being switched on. In your own words, complete the following phrase: 'Once upon a time there was. . .**

. . . a beautiful little boy and a beautiful little girl. Once upon a time there was an angel whose eyes were like silent clouds drifting through a quiet Mediterranean horizon. Once upon a time there were blue skies and intensely lived moments and the promise of constantly renewed tomorrows. . . . And now, you might ask? What is there now? I will tell you what there is now. Now there is just this: a photograph. A tattered photograph. I carry it in my pocket all the time. It is not more than five or six years old, but it is already scratched and yellowing. In it there are four people. They are standing on a beach promenade, smiling and laughing. . . . Every time I look at this photograph, I feel a sickness spreading inside me . . . a sense of unbearable oppression. . . . Sometimes photographs are like that, I guess. You look at them and you cannot help wondering how you could have looked so innocent, how you could have been so unaware of what was to come next. . . . 'Please stop smiling!' you feel like shouting at the people in the photograph. 'Please stop looking so goddamned happy! Can't you see what's around the corner? Can't you feel the talons of death closing around you? Can't you try and run away instead of standing there in front of the goddamned fucking camera?. . .' I know, I know: this doesn't make sense. Once upon a time I had passions and beliefs, petty obsessions and hobbies, things that I felt strongly about. I supported a team called Partizan Belgrade. I hated American capitalists because I thought they were out to dominate the world. I collected old books and butterflies in glass cases because that is what my father and grandfather had done before me. . . . Now all that is gone. I don't care about football and I don't give a damn about global imperialism and, even if I saw the world's most expensive goddamned butterfly lying there at my feet, I wouldn't bother to look twice at it because butterflies don't longer mean anything to me. . . . I know, I know: this doesn't make sense. You ask me to talk about myself and here I am spouting off all kinds of different shit. I guess you didn't really expect something like this, did you?. . . *That is what the curse does to you,* by the way: it always makes you look back, it makes you inhabit two parallel worlds. You try to explain this to those who are only living in one world, but of course they don't understand you. . . . They never learn. . . . They just don't have the capacity to feel what you're feeling. . . . Actually, can you stop this thing for a second? I didn't mean to say what I've just said and I would like it erased. . . . Anyway, what was I saying?. . . Yes, I was talking about parallel worlds, wasn't I? About how difficult it is to let go of the world that memory constantly brings up inside you. . . . Anyway, you must have heard all this before, haven't you?. . . Besides, I am only being self-indulgent when I talk about these things, aren't I? Everyone tells me that. What happened is truly terrible, they say, truly horrific and truly beyond the scope of all human understanding, but you must now move on, you must try to put the past behind you and reclaim your life again because life is a precious gift that must not be spurned. . . . Anyway, there is not much else I can say. Nothing makes sense any more. . . . Oh, yes, I will say one more thing. I will say this. I will say it because this is what I believe: the West makes me sick, it is a maggot heap of sanctimonious falseness which takes an interest in the suffering of those who are far away because it is easier and less messy than grieving and mourning for those who are dying immediately around it. Look at Princess Diana. Look at the fuss they made then. Grown men, who had not even cried at their own mother's funeral, were spotted bawling in the streets. Spotty-faced teenagers, complete with peroxide blonde hair and nose-rings, were leaving notes at the palace gates saying that their lives 'would never be the same again'. Why is it that these people whipped themselves into such a hysterical frenzy, you will ask? Why did they have to torture themselves over a woman they had never even met? I will tell you why: it is because it is easier to grieve about something that you can easily forget about than about something that will burn your insides and scar you for the rest of your life. *Grieving without comebacks*, that's what it is called. Suffering without unseemly complications. Haven't you noticed the way the West specialises in such adoptive secondhand grieving? Kidnapped babies, famine victims, chemically-poisoned war veterans, zoo animals that are kept in confined cages: doesn't our heart bleed out to each and every one of them?. . . 'Didn't you see those poor little African kids on the telly last night, all bloated and surrounded by those disgusting flies? God, how awful that must be. Pietro and me will be sending a cheque to *Médecins Sans Frontières* first thing tomorrow morning. Will you send one too?. . .' It is always like that, I'm afraid. Show the masses some little African boys being pestered by flies and they'll immediately fly into an altruistic frenzy: raising money, donating clothes, sending cheques, organising tombolas — the usual stuff. . . . But after a few days, of course, it is all gone: everyone forgets. The slate has been wiped clean and everyone is free to carry on with their perfect little bourgeois lives — shopping at *Pam* and *Lidl*, buying the latest electronic gadgets, getting pissed every Friday night, lusting after the ginger-haired secretary sitting outside the boss's office, God knows fucking what. Because that's the way human beings are, you see: *they have a tendency to discard whatever Destiny has not directly branded upon their own skins. . . .* It's like the old story of the tree that falls in the middle of the woods, don't you think? Can you really, hand on your heart, say that it happened if you are not there?. . . Take Auschwitz, Treblinka, Dachau, Hiroshima, Dresden, Nagasaki. Did the tree really fall in all these cases, or did it not happen just because you were not there?. . . Once upon a time, let us not forget, there was a little Jew boy who walked out of Auschwitz on crutches, looked around the deserted, corpse-ridden scene around him and, broken-hearted yet full of defiant spirit as he was, thought, 'Such cruelties as these will never be forgot. If only for that reason, it is good that all this has happened. Mankind will have finally learnt the lesson that evil pays no dividends. . . .' But he was wrong: the world forgets, it forgets and discards, consigning to the dustbin of oblivion anything which causes it more than the pre-allotted five seconds of bother it reserves for such calamities. That is the way that human beings are: they whip themselves into a frenzy of empathy one moment and then unburden themselves faster than if they were suffering from a bad case of diarrhoea. . . . What was it that that famous American writer used to say? Something about how you can shed tears watching dead children on the nine o'clock news and then drool over pork chops and chips twenty minutes later?. . . *Ah, that pork tastes good, don't it? Tastes real good. Fancy passing me the bottle of ketchup, honey pie*. . . . Until, of course, it happens to you. To YOU. . . . TO YOUR OWN FLESH AND BLOOD. . . .TO THE CHILDREN WHO SPRUNG FROM INSIDE YOU. . . . Do you know what it feels like then? Do you have any fucking idea? Can you imagine what it must be like to wake up dreaming about the way your little daughter laughed — so gently and so delicately, so full of childish delight — and then to remember that someone raped her and shot her in the face?. . . What more is there left for me to say after something like that? Tell me, WHAT MORE?!! . . . The worst thing, you know, was that we managed to survive everything that came before that day. The Albanian harassment in the 80s. The ultra-nationalist campaigns run by Milosevic and his henchmen. The indiscriminate NATO bombings against civilian and military targets. We survived all that only to be betrayed by a bunch of ruthless, thuggish criminals who, instead of being held accountable for their crimes, are currently extolled as freedom fighters by the so-called civilised West. . . . Anyway, there is not much else I can say. I wish I could be more articulate, that I could tell you exactly how I feel — but everything is so fuzzy inside, so difficult to bring out. . . . Yes, it is true: I wish I could tell you how it is, that I could somehow manage to bring it all up and exorcise the poison inside me. . . . But I guess that's easier said than done, isn't it?. . . Besides, you won't understand. What are words, after all? What do they really tell us about what happened and what we felt at the time?. . . It's like the story of the tree that I was telling you about. Wouldn't you say that our thoughts and experiences are like trees falling in the middle of a deserted wood? Unknown to anyone but ourselves?. . . Anyway, what am I saying? I'm talking rubbish again and I don't want to keep you here unduly, as I'm sure you have better things to do. Besides, I have talked enough already, don't you think?. . . Better to quit while you're ahead, etcetera, etcetera. . . . Actually, I will say one more thing. I will say this: once there was a little boy and a little girl. The little girl had freckles on her face and used to hide behind the washing machine whenever she wanted to be cheeky. She liked eating *pljeskavica* and watching some programme about up-and-coming young rockstars on MTV. The little boy had hair that was as black as his mother's and he liked to sit with his feet resting on

Jovana's piano stool. He used to say he wanted to be an astronaut when he grew up. He also said that he would never support Partizan Belgrade, *no matter what*. If you told him to eat his vegetables, he would turn his eyes inside out, just like his mother did when she wasn't happy about something . . . just like this. . . . Anyway, that's enough. Please stop the tape now. I do not wish to say anything else.

**

Giulietta Giordano arrived at Termini just after quarter past five in the morning. The streets were totally deserted and a crescent-shaped moon could be seen in the sky, its thin, scimitar-like form just visible beyond the mass of neon-lit signs, tourist-class hotels and dingy office blocks that surrounded the station. After driving around the building three times, Giulietta rolled down her window and, taking care to lean back so that he could not smell the alcohol on her breath, asked a policeman where she could park. 'A car park around here?' the young cop said, lazily shrugging his shoulders. 'More of a chance of finding La Ciccolina servicing the station tramps and beggars, if you ask me, signorina.' Thanking him for his time, Giulietta turned down the nearest side street and eventually found a space between a bottle bank and a green pick-up truck. As she got out of the vehicle, a black man in a trilby approached her and asked her whether she wanted to buy some drugs. He was very tall and muscular and a tricoloured feather could be seen dangling from one of his ears. He also couldn't stop accosting Giulietta with his fast-talking street-selling spiel:

'Come on, *ragazza*. Do yourself a favour, will you? Give that splendid bootylicious body of yours a treat tonight! Come on, my pretty little Roman *principessa*, don't be so boring! I'm only trying to bring a little cheer and *felicità* to those awfully sad and depressed baby-blue eyes of yours. What is it that you're looking for – speed, hash, a bit of coke, some of the old happy-happy pills? Just say what you want and *Il Big Boy Sam* will have it here before you know it!'

The black man followed the lawyer to the threshold of the station and then sauntered off back into the night. Once inside the building, Giulietta made a shocking discovery: the place was full of sleeping tramps. She could see them wherever she looked: on the floor, lying on benches, stretched out in front of shop windows, lying with their legs sticking out of telephone booths. '*Gesu*,' the criminal lawyer thought, bringing a hand to her mouth. 'I never knew that things were *this bad!*' As she began to despair of finding Zoran among such a multitude, she caught sight of someone who looked like him just ten or fifteen yards away. He was lying on a bench, his features obscured by what looked like a rag thrown over his face. Congratulating herself for being so observant, Giulietta started walking in his direction, but when she got nearer to the man her hopes were quickly dashed: it was not Zoran. He couldn't be, seeing that he had one arm missing! *Or could Zoran have lost an arm since she had last seen him?* It was a ludicrous thought, but with this sort of people one could never tell. Unnerved by the idea, Giulietta bent down and, using all the composure at her disposal, lifted the dirt-encrusted rag from the sleeping man's face. No, it wasn't Zoran. Just some dark-skinned guy with a tattoo across his face. Another refugee from the Balkans, no doubt. Another poor bastard with his own set of tragedies and half-buried recollections. Still, at least it wasn't Zoran who had lost an arm. The realisation reassured her, but it also brought home the absurdity of her predicament. 'Here I am at five o'clock in the morning,' she thought, shaking her head, 'trying to look for a tramp in a train station full of tramps. If that is not fucked-up, then what is? Besides, what if Zoran isn't here? What if my original hunch was wrong?' As she continued fretting in this manner, she spotted a young man about ten or fifteen paces away. He was sitting between a Russian-looking woman in a long fur coat and a pale-skinned octogenarian with a waist-length beard. Although Giulietta could not get a clear view of his face, she noticed that he was rocking backwards and forwards, just like Zoran had been doing the day she threw him out of the house. She decided to approach him.

'Zoran, is that you? It's me — Giulietta.'

She crouched down by his side, but the man carried on rocking slowly and staring into space, totally oblivious to her presence.

'Hello, Zoran — it's Giulietta here. I've come to see you.'

She waved a hand in front of his eyes, but once again there was no reaction — apart from the old woman by their side suddenly shifting in her sleep and muttering something about 'swimming pools' and the 'blood of Santa Catalina.'

'Zoran . . . I am here. . . . It's me, Giulietta. . . . Can you please look up at me for a second?'

Giulietta shook her head and bit her lip, unsure how to disrupt Zoran from his semi-catatonic condition. Just then a *poliziotto* who was passing by took note of her state of agitation and stopped by her side.

'*Tutto bene, signorina?*' the cop asked in the exaggeratedly masculine tone which policemen normally use to announce the arrival of the "Law." 'Is this "thing" here harassing you in any way?'

'No, no, officer — everything's fine. Thanks, anyway.'

'Are you sure? You look a bit distressed to me.'

'Yes, of course,' Giulietta said. 'Thanks.'

'Are you really sure, madam? I can't leave you here if I think you're in distress.'

'I'm all right,' Giulietta said, sticking her chin out in imitation of one of her more self-assured courtroom poses. 'Thanks for your concern, officer. I'm a criminal lawyer and Zoran here is one of my clients. He's just been telling me some details about his case. We're all right. Trust me.'

'You expect me to believe that you're conducting an interview with this "gentleman" here at quarter to six in the morning?' the policeman said.

'I'm a lawyer, officer. In my profession there are no fixed hours. You should know that being an officer of the law, shouldn't you?'

The policeman shrugged his shoulders with an expression of vague amusement and then began to walk away. Sighing with relief, Giulietta turned back to Zoran and saw that he was trembling under the pile of rags and towels and plastic bags which had been thrown around his shoulders. If that wasn't bad enough, his face had gone a pallid and sickly hue of grey, almost the same colour (it occurred to her) as some of the crumpled plastic bags themselves. Quickly dispelling the sneering cop from her thoughts, Giulietta took hold of Zoran's hands and covered them with her own.

'It's me, Zoran,' she said. 'Giulietta. Look at me. Please, look. I've come to see you. Don't you recognise me?'

'*Moj anđeo čuvar?*' Zoran said, an ember of recognition suddenly rekindling within his eyes. '*Je li ono it? Je li ono it?*'

'Yes, yes, it's me,' Giulietta continued, hardly able to contain the emotion that coursed through her. 'I've come to say that I'm sorry, Zoran. I've come to ask you to finish decorating my house. I've come to take you back with me to Veruccio.'

'Back to Veruccio?'

'Yes, yes — back to Veruccio. Back to finish the work you started.'

'Back to the work?'

'Yes, yes — back to finish the work.'

That moment the ember suddenly ignited into full consciousness within Zoran's eyes. 'You shouldn't be saying that, *moj anđeo čuvar*,' he said, staring steadily into the lawyer's eyes. 'You don't want a fuck-up like me around.'

'Don't be silly, Zoran. You're no fuck-up.'

Zoran grimaced and smiled darkly. 'How do you know, *moj anđeo čuvar*? How do you know I'm no fuck-up?'

'I saw the drawings under your mattress.'

Zoran looked down at his hands and shook his head.

'Plus I read the papers,' Giulietta added.

'What papers?'

'The ones you wrote at the clinic. They made me realise that perhaps I judged you unfairly, that perhaps I shouldn't have been so harsh on you.'

Zoran shook his head and sighed. 'Why do you want me to go back anyway, Giulietta? I will only cause you pain and more hassle. Why put yourself through all that again? Is it the old martyr syndrome once more? Do you want to sacrifice yourself once again for my sake?'

Giulietta looked down, unable to put her thoughts into words.

'Or is it because you pity me, *moj anđeo čuvar*?' Zoran continued in the same toneless voice. 'Is it because you pity the fuck-up that I have become?'

Giulietta bit her lip and carried on looking at the ground, still uncertain what to say.

'You see,' Zoran answered with a sad smile. 'You can't even find an answer. It is just pity which moves you, my *anđeo čuvar.* Spontaneous, purely emotional, spur-of-the-moment pity. That is all. But pity is no good: it has a dangerously short shelf life. You can pity me now — sitting here half-smashed and half-freezing to death. You can pity me after having read what I said to them at the clinic. But I can assure you that you won't pity me when you invite me back to your house and I start behaving like the sad, demented fuck-up that I am. . . . No, please don't say anything. I know that you have a good heart and that you think that you are doing the right thing. But you have to be pragmatic and understand that pity has a very short memory. It is fuelled by wishful thinking and never survives long. In a few weeks' time you will probably be hating my guts and wishing that you had never come here. That's the way life is, my *anđeo čuvar*.'

She raised her eyes from the ground and saw that Zoran was looking away, his features scrunched into a frown that accentuated the squareness of his jawline. She wanted to say something, to find some reassuring words, to tell him that pity was not her guiding motive and that she genuinely cared for him. But somehow the words did not come to her. Instead all she could do was sit there and carry on looking at him in silence — at his hands and at his face, at the dark purple sores around the edges of his mouth, at the pale blue vein which run down the side of his throat. Finally, after a few minutes had passed, she noticed that Zoran's expression was growing vacant again and his posture was starting to slacken. Even worse, he was beginning to murmur in Serbian again:

*'Boze pravde, ti sto spase od propasti do sadnas. Boze pravde, ti sto spase od propasti do sadnas.'*

'I don't know what to tell you, Zoran,' Giulietta finally said. 'I don't have an answer. I wish that I had, but I just don't. I could tell you *this* or I could tell you *that*, I could spin out all sorts of clever lies just like I do when I'm standing in a courtroom, but it would all be meaningless because the truth is I have no rational answer to explain why I've come here tonight. All I know — and this I can say from the bottom of my heart — is that I judged you unfairly and that I shouldn't have thrown you out like I did. That is all I can say to you.'

Zoran stopped rocking that moment and looked at her fixedly.

'Come back, Zoran,' Giulietta continued in a choking voice. 'Don't let me fall on my knees to beg you. Come back, I don't mind whatever you inject yourself with. We can work things out, I'm sure we can. Just come back with me. I don't know if I'm a martyr or what the hell I am, but I just don't want to see you do this to yourself.'

He carried on staring at her without saying a word. She looks so frail and hurt, he thought, *so full of vulnerabilities.* A strange thought came to him then. A really strange and surprising thought. He thought that Giulietta reminded him of a wooden statuette his mother had kept on her bedside table many years ago. It was a statuette of Saint Angelina of Kupinovo, the patron saint of his mother's hometown. Angelina, he remembered his mother telling him, had protected the people in Sirmie from the Turks. She had been very brave and had visited the King of Hungary to plead for her people and had never lost her faith in God when her only son died in a riding accident. Giulietta had the same expression as the statuette, Zoran realised, the same look of anxious vulnerability. He wondered why he should have remembered all this just now, but in the end decided that it didn't really matter.

'It's the cornices, isn't it?' he suddenly said, slowly propping himself against the wall behind him. 'That's what it is. You've realised that Antonio's making a complete mess so you've come down here to get me to fix them up again for you. That's what it is, isn't it?'

'What?'

'Yes, yes, I know your sort: you want perfection at any price . . . even if it means dragging yourself over to Termini at half past five in the morning. . . . Anyway,' he added with a smile, 'I guess that if you want perfection so much, I have no option but to oblige. I mean, *I can't just let those cornices remain in such a state,* can I?'

'You mean you're coming back with me?' Giulietta asked, still unsure of what was happening.

Zoran looked at her for a few seconds in silence. 'You know something, Miss Giordano?' he said at last. 'For a lawyer, you can sometimes be a bit slow on the uptake. Has anyone ever told you that?'

All of a sudden Giulietta lunged forwards and embraced Zoran in her arms. She kissed his cheeks and caressed his head, not caring about the dirt and the grease and the lice in his hair. As he clung to her body and drank in her warm scent, Zoran could hear the rumble of an approaching train, the crackle of a hidden tannoy — but it all seemed far away now, a blur of sound, almost coming from another world. Finally, he thought: 'How strange life is. How strange and wonderful and utterly incomprehensible. That when one should be down on one's knees, when one no longer sees anything but darkness and despair across the road ahead — miracles begin to happen. Twilight awakens; hope begins to sing its song. Multiple sparks start to fly through the night, splinters of invisible light that pound and shatter the already fading darkness.'

M.G.S.
2008, 2005, 2003